D0381506

"I READ *THE WEATHERMAN* WITH MOUNTING EXCITEMENT AND A SENSE OF INVOLVEMENT WHICH FEW NOVELS CAN ELICIT IN ME THESE DAYS. IT HAS ONE OF THE HIGHEST TAKE-OFF POINTS OF ANY NOVEL IN RECENT MEMORY...AND FROM THERE IT JUST KEEPS ON SHOOTING THE THRILLS AND SUSPENSE.... I RECOMMEND IT TO EVERYBODY."

—STEPHEN KING

THE
WEATHERMAN

STEVE THAYER

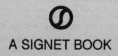

A SIGNET BOOK

SIGNET
Published by the Penguin Group
Penguin Books USA Inc., 375 Hudson Street,
New York, New York 10014, U.S.A.
Penguin Books Ltd, 27 Wrights Lane,
London W8 5TZ, England
Penguin Books Australia Ltd, Ringwood,
Victoria, Australia
Penguin Books Canada Ltd, 10 Alcorn Avenue,
Toronto, Ontario, Canada M4V 3B2
Penguin Books (N.Z.) Ltd, 182–190 Wairau Road,
Auckland 10, New Zealand

Penguin Books Ltd, Registered Offices:
Harmondsworth, Middlesex, England

Published by Signet, an imprint of Dutton Signet, a division of Penguin Books
USA Inc. Previously appeared in a Viking edition.

First Signet Printing, March, 1996
10 9 8 7 6 5 4 3 2 1

THE DEDICATION

*You can't be a really good writer unless you had crazy
parents*

*In Memory of
Pliny A. Thayer
Katherine E. Harbold
&
Leslie H. Harbold*

THE PROLOGUE

It was a cold act on a hot June day. The temperature was 98 degrees Fahrenheit—36.6 on the centigrade scale. The relative humidity was 69 percent with sticky dew points in the low 70s. The barometric pressure was holding steady at 29.71 inches. A breeze straight up from the Gulf was barely perceptible. Cumulus clouds, those little fluffy ones, dotted the sky, but they had no effect on the afternoon sun. It was broiling.

The monster in the mask stepped out of the dark shadows and into the blinding daylight. Few places are hotter on such a day than the open roof of a downtown parking ramp. The fire in the sky was a roaring furnace cooking the concrete to temperatures that made even breathing difficult. The creature began wheezing. By the calendar summer was still a week away, but already the weather was hell. A hand went over the eyes to reduce the sting of the glare. Because of the hot sun only one lonely car was parked on the roof, off in the corner.

The Sky High parking ramp sat directly beneath the tallest building in town. Towering masts off the top of the skyscraper fed the metropolitan area its electronic diet of television. These giant antennas threw a cagelike shadow across the concrete below. The monster in the mask walked into this cage made of sun rays and took refuge in the steel shadows.

The car was a red Honda Prelude, clean and shiny. The young woman who drove it parked in the same spot every day, on the roof, in the corner, in the shade of the buildings above. Next to the car was a huge transformer, army green in color. Bright yellow stickers pasted on the casing warned of danger. ELECTRICAL EQUIPMENT INSIDE.

CONTACT NORTHERN STATES POWER. The wheezing creature squeezed in behind the transformer. A high stucco wall hid the ghostly figure from view. *It* crouched and waited.

It was hot inside the mask. A black fly buzzed the leather nose. A hand waved it off. The eyes wandered to the western sky. Tiny particles floated in the dirty brown haze that floated over the city. Another year had passed. The smog was worse. The temperature rose one degree. The humidity went up one sticky percentage point. The hottest part of the day. It would stay this way for an hour; then slowly it would begin to cool.

For some reason the young woman with the red Prelude left work earlier than most. Always alone. She was stylishly thin. She carried a briefcase. She dressed the way a businesswoman should dress—not flashy, but simple and conservative. From a distance, she seemed plain-featured, short brown hair over a narrow face. This was all her attacker knew about her. But she did have one peculiar habit. She always unlocked the passenger door first, placed her briefcase on the front seat as if it were a child, then walked around to the driver's side and got into the car. It was this silly little ritual that first caught the monster's attention.

The elevator doors slid open. Right on time. A punctual woman. Her soft footsteps echoed in the lethal heat. Dizzy and nauseous; the wheezing increased. An aching stomach. A frozen heart. Suddenly, the creature was on its feet.

The woman walked through the shadows of the TV antennas and went straight to the passenger side of her car, where she unlocked and opened the door. She gently placed her briefcase on the front seat. Then she closed the door.

Viewed from a distance the assault was almost comical. Her head snapped back so fast her feet flew into the air. Then she was gone, disappearing behind a big green box. No noise. No struggle, except for one kick of her leg. All the pride she carried, all the strength, stamina, and mettle it took for a woman to make it in a man's world were left in the briefcase on the front seat of her car. In the last seconds of her life, hidden between the wall and the transformer, she was as helpless as the rag dolls of her childhood.

But in the years to come that one kick of her leg would send shock waves through a proud state. One kick of her leg would create an atmosphere of hate in a place where hate was once detested, would cost millions of dollars in police work and legal fees, and would change laws once thought unchangeable.

No, she didn't kick her attacker. With her neck locked in the crook of a strong arm she was swung around with such force that her leg hit the wall, and by reflex she kicked off the wall, knocking her attacker backwards into the transformer. The electricity bolted on line with a startling loud crunch. For a second, and it was only a second, a bare hand reached out and slapped the green metal and the arm around her neck loosened enough for her to get off one short, piercing scream.

It was the only ray of defense she was allowed. Small bones could be heard snapping in her neck. Her face glowed red to purple. Life spat out her mouth. But her perfume still gave off warm honeysuckle odors. Murder should not smell so sweet. Her head, tight against the mask, gave the wheezing creature an incredible urge to whisper something to her, to somehow explain. But then it was over. She was dead. Whoever she was.

The killer was on bended knees now, hands folded prayerwise over her body. The noisy transformer shut down. City sounds rose like heat from the streets below. A bus pulled away from the stop. A church bell tolled the hour. The offices in the skyscrapers above were insulated, sealed from the real world. The only eyewitness to this murder was a weather satellite twenty-two thousand miles above the earth.

The hidden face tilted back, gazing into the hazy sky, past the television antennas that reached for the heavens. Stared right through the four layers of the atmosphere and into dreamy blue space. With just the feel of a breeze through the eyes of the mask the creature was able to clock the wind. The sun burning the skin gave away the temperature. Moisture in the air was southern. The barometric pressure began falling, ever so slightly. The killer was proud of this knowledge. It took a special kind of an-

imal to read the weather. The monster in the mask examined the cumulus clouds as they drifted by. Breathed the
air. Perhaps it was a day away, but there was a storm
coming. A big one.

BOOK ONE

INTO THE STORM

It was getting dark so suddenly that Alice thought there must be a thunderstorm coming on. "What a thick black cloud that is!" she said. "And how fast it comes! Why, I do believe it's got wings!"

—Lewis Carroll
Through the Looking-Glass

THE TORNADO

Dixon Graham Bell back-stepped with the breeze. He paused one more time on the Nicollet Walk and looked far up Eighth Street, where cars were crawling out of a blue-black wall cloud that extended westward. Above him a dark, greenish cast was spreading over the heavens. Electricity filled the air. The humidity was suffocating. A raindrop slapped his face.

In the Great Lakes States the median time for severe weather is 5:00 P.M., after the sun's heat has done the devil's best to make the ground steamy hot and the air ripping mad. Dixon Bell checked his watch. 4:55 P.M. Five minutes to airtime. Perfect. If there is a God, he must watch TV.

He ducked into the Crystal Court Plaza, clapped his hands together, and bounded up the escalators to the skyway level. He pushed the elevator button and impatiently tapped his fingers on the mirrored wall. People were scurrying through the weatherproof skyways, heading for Dayton's department store, rushing for the bank, or just stopping at their favorite bar—heading home, their workday done. Dixon Bell glanced over his shoulder. The electronic sign on the bank entrance flashed 92°. Next it flashed 4:56. Four minutes to airtime. In a useless act he again stabbed the lighted elevator button. Then he turned his attention back to the darkening sky.

The Crystal Court is a glassy shopping plaza fastened to the base of the tallest, most elegant building in downtown Minneapolis, the IDS Tower. Its crystal cubes mirror the sun and invite warm rays year round, but they lock out the weather. Today the sun was disappearing fast and with every passing second the weather was becoming less and less inviting. Having a newsroom at the top of this skyscraper was a mixed blessing. It was great for eyeing the sky and watching the Twin Cities of Minneapolis and St. Paul unfold beneath, but it was nerve-racking when breaking stories were left standing at the elevator fifty-seven stories below.

Angry black clouds drifted toward the big blue tower. Dixon Bell turned and slammed his foot into the elevator door. The bang startled those around him. Could this be the cordial guy they watched every night on Channel 7? Then, as if on command, the elevator doors opened and the Weatherman slipped inside.

He was a big, husky man, over six feet tall. But he was well past forty now, and his husk was turning to fat. Dixon Bell was losing the battle of the bulge. He drank too much beer. He couldn't keep his shirts tucked in. His butt was getting big, his gut even bigger. It didn't help that television makes even the most slender person appear fifteen pounds heavier. His dark, curly hair was thick and salted. He had bushy eyebrows. Women thought him cute. In truth, his face would have been clownish if it weren't for a scar that cast a bitter cloud over his puffy cheeks. But his looks were deceiving. His oversized features played well on television. And when he opened his mouth to talk about the weather, people liked him. They listened. He was a meteorologist and dead serious about it. His gift for reading the weather, and it was a gift, was the envy of his peers.

As the elevator doors finally closed, the bank sign flashed 4:57. Three minutes to air time.

As Dixon Bell was stepping into the elevator at the Crystal Court Plaza, Captain Les Angelbeck was stepping out of the elevator atop the Sky High parking ramp next door. Bloodhounds were sniffing around the entrance to the stairwell. Angelbeck walked up the ramp to the roof level. The area was sealed off with bright yellow tape: POLICE LINE—DO NOT CROSS. He ducked under the tape, into the open air, and reached for his cigarettes. It was Marlboro time. In Minnesota the law was as clear as the air had once been: No smoking in public unless you can see the open sky. Today that sky had a very unfriendly look to it. The captain was wearing his raincoat. Always dressed for the weather.

He stepped over heavy cables that ran along the floor and looped over the wall to the television minivans below. A TV reporter was testing his microphone in front of a camera, preparing for a live shot. At the other end of the ramp another reporter was doing the same. The veteran cop recognized them both but couldn't recall their names or what channels they worked for. They were all stamped from the same cookie cutter—young, slender, clean-cut, and hairy, just short of nerdy, and probably from out of state.

Les Angelbeck was getting old—death-in-sight old. Retirement had come and gone a long time ago. He didn't take it. His men told him he looked like Bear Bryant, only shorter. He remembered when the great Alabama football coach retired to relax and enjoy life. He died six weeks later. Retirement kills, not work. Besides, Les Angelbeck's mind was still sharp, and his hair was still brown. But there was that smoker's cough. His men called him the Marlboro Man. Breathing was becoming more and more difficult. He knew cigarettes would one day cut off his air supply, choke him to death as sure as the young woman found atop this parking ramp had been choked.

As police work goes, in Minnesota the pay is high and the risk is low. The captain had not pointed a gun at anyone since World War II. He liked to remind young cops of that. In a career that spanned forty-plus years, he'd walked a beat in Minneapolis; he'd been an investigator across the river at the Ramsey County Sheriff's Department in St. Paul; he was once a police chief in a sleepy suburb. Now he was with the Minnesota Bureau of Criminal Apprehension, or the BCA—the state police. They coordinated metropolitan investigations and assisted small-town police and county sheriff's departments in major cases—murders, kidnappings, drug dealing. Two nights a week Angelbeck taught law enforcement at North Hennepin Community College. His position, his experience, and his contacts gave him access to every detail of every criminal case in the state.

Angelbeck found a chalk outline where the victim's body had been discovered. The transformer and the Prelude were being dusted for prints. An investigator was going over the ramp floor with a magnifying glass and tweezers. Another was doing the same inside the car.

Detective Karl Schoenberger was directing the mop-up team. He was a cold, arrogant cop. "Captain, who called you in?"

"Just in the neighborhood."

"He got her in a choke hold," Schoenberger explained. "Knew what he was doing. Made short work of her. No sex."

"It's the heat," Angelbeck told him. "A proven fact the crime rate rises with the temperature."

"Two minutes," a reporter shouted.

Schoenberger turned to the sideshow. "Those TV people love white, female victims. The killer couldn't have picked a better spot. This is where Channel 7 parks their cars. A couple of them interviewed me. I was going to call home and tell the kids to watch, but they'll only use ten seconds of me, then ten minutes of themselves. 'We know everything, blah, blah, blah.' Assholes."

Les Angelbeck bent his neck and looked up at the jungle of antennas atop the IDS Tower. Storm clouds were breaking over them. "I guess it's for the best. In some cities murder is not news anymore. Does this ramp have surveillance cameras?"

"Not on the roof. Something about the weather."

Angelbeck noted all of the windows overhead. "Anybody in these buildings see anything?"

"One lady thinks she saw a man in a mask dart out of here yesterday."

"A mask? What kind of mask?"

"Blue or black. She wasn't sure. The victim's office was right up there," Schoenberger said, pointing at a building across the street. "Apparently, she was able to watch her car from there. Somebody else must have seen something."

Angelbeck looked back at the murder scene. "Maybe not. Could be a blind spot. Rapists have a way of finding them."

"This wasn't a sexual assault," Schoenberger reminded him.

"All attacks on women are sexual assaults. What else have you got?"

"There's a good partial print on the transformer."

"There's no such thing as a good partial fingerprint."

"If he left us any other prints, we'll find them."

Les Angelbeck stared hard at the black sky to the west. He glanced over at the cop dusting the transformer. "If the weather holds." The last rays of sun were disappearing. The more ominous clouds were over the western suburbs now and moving fast. "Better get what you need, quick," he advised them. "Looks like a hell of a storm coming." A raindrop hit his wrist. Forked lightning stabbed at the city.

After years of investigative work the old cop had more than one stray thought, silent questions he directed at the chalk outline. Why here, in the middle of downtown, in the middle of the day? Why no sex, no robbery? Why no weapon? What kind of man kills with his hands? He took the last drag from his cigarette, then tossed it to the nasty wind. Raindrops began hitting like bombs. They started for shelter. The TV people stood talking in the rain.

Isn't it funny, Angelbeck thought as they ran, when a woman is murdered the pronoun used to describe the unknown assailant is always masculine. "I hope a woman did it," he mumbled to himself as he stepped in out of the weather. He was coughing. "Some big, ugly broad."

Five stories below the newsroom, less than three minutes before air time, the elevator came to a halt. The Weatherman sighed with frustration. The doors opened. Shock followed. Like a page out of a big-city nightmare Dixon Bell's eyes locked on to the eyes of a masked man—the dark, piercing eyes of a man who had been to hell and back. It was one of those frightening moments that freeze in the mind for life. A premonition of sorts. Death come calling.

He was not quite as tall as Dixon Bell, but he had the shoulders of an athlete. His manner of dress was white-collar casual—an expensive sport coat over a T-shirt and a pair of faded blue jeans. His faintly scarred hands were lazily tucked into his pockets, suggesting he was up to nothing malicious. He seemed to favor blue, for the mask he wore was blue too. Made of soft cotton, it was one of those masks that is pulled over the entire head, giving him a sky-blue dome. And in the middle of this mask, this blue cotton face, was a black leather triangle where his nose breathed the news.

Rick Beanblossom stepped into the elevator. "Hey, Weatherman, looking pretty nasty out there."

Dixon Bell shook off the fear and filed the premonition. "Hell of a storm coming. We'll lead with it." A cold pause. "If I ever get up there."

"No," Rick warned him, dampening his spirits. "We'll lead with the murder."

They rose through the air together on this hot and sticky June day, news and weather on their way to work. Two veterans of Southeast Asia: one Marine grunt with the Navy Cross but no face, and one Air Force officer with a scarred face but no medals.

Congested cumulus clouds shadowed the tower now. The sickly yellow sun was still peeking through one southwest window. The wind was spitting mad. Fat raindrops attacked the blue-tinted glass. But in the newsroom it was crunch time, and few cared about the weather. Tempers were shot—especially the temper of the five o'clock producer. Dixon Bell hustled through the newsroom and up to Chris Mack's desk. "Chris, how y'all fixed for live shots?"

Chris Mack looked up from his computer and checked the big round clock. The minute hand was inching toward the top of the hour. "We've got two today—one from the parking ramp and a traffic shot from the chopper."

"Great. I need one minute at the top. Gotta tell Bucky."

"About what? We have a murder."

"We've got weather." Dixon Bell headed for the assignment desk.

The burnout rate for news-show producers is about one every fourteen months. Studio light bulbs last longer. Part of the problem comes when they spend nine hours putting together a thirty-minute broadcast and a weatherman blows in literally at the last moment screaming he needs one minute at the top. Few stomachs can weather it. Chris Mack chased after Dixon Bell, show script in hand. "One minute? No way. You're getting worse than sports. We have a murder."

"We have a severe storm."

If times like this gave producers heartburn, they gave

Gayle Banks, the assignment editor, an adrenaline high. She was jokingly referred to as Gayle the Ghoul. Breaking news stoked her fires. The worse the news, the higher she got. "We've got severe weather? Where?"

"On top our heads in about five minutes."

Gayle poked her head into the closet space behind her, the dispatcher's shack. "Where's the storm?"

The producer was dumbfounded. "There's been no storm warning. We're under a watch." He looked out the window. "The sun is still shining. We'll go to you after the murder. We put the new reporter on it. She's nervous enough as it is."

"A third of all severe storms arrive undetected," the Weatherman informed him. "Let's not make this one of them. I'm going to issue a warning."

"You're crazy, Dixon. Only the National Weather Service can issue a severe storm warning."

"I'm not waiting for those clowns." He pointed his finger at Gayle. "Get on the radio and tell Bucky to fly south of the Minnesota River and keep his nose to the southwest."

"C'mon, he's covering the backup on 394."

"It's for his own safety, dammit."

"It's a little more than a traffic shot," Chris Mack protested. "We've got a whole piece tracked on traffic problems out there. It's great. Andrea voiced it."

The sprawling newsroom was split-level. On the larger, lower level, where they were arguing on the run, was the news-gathering operation. On the smaller, upper level were the news set and the control room. There the bright lights came up. "One minute," the floor director shouted.

"Give me thirty seconds at the top." Dixon Bell leaped up the stairs and bounded across the set. Weather Center 7 was buried behind it.

The producer shouted after him. "*No* seconds at the top!" He turned to Gayle, squeezing his brow. "This is crazy."

"He hasn't been wrong yet," she reminded him.

"Yeah, but a warning?" Chris Mack looked around. "Where's our holier-than-thou news director?"

"His asthma," Gayle said. "He went home wheezing up a storm."

"Thirty," the floor manager shouted.

Chris Mack shook his head. "Okay, let's do this. Murder at the top, then right to weather. But he'd better not issue a warning or there'll be a shitload of trouble."

"Base to *Skyhawk 7*." The producer's final orders produced lightning in one of the best news junkies in the business. For Gayle Banks, the rush to get information on the air was another kind of rush as well. As Chris Mack raced to the set to brief his anchors, Gayle began barking into the microphone, ordering pilot Bob Buckridge and *Skyhawk 7* into a new position. She shouted into the dispatcher's office, "Any storm damage, I want locations right away."

The dispatcher scanned the radio chatter. "What storm?"

Gayle whirled around and screamed as politely as she could at photographer Dave Cadieux, "You take a camera up to the roof and don't come down until you've got tape of Dorothy's house disappearing over the rainbow." Then she was back on the mike. "Okay, we've got a big change here and it's tricky—back-to-back live shots on the same horn in section one. Minivan three, we're going to open with you at the parking ramp. Then we roll tape of the dead babe, plus your beam to edit one. As soon as Beth throws it back to the studio, you power down. Bucky, as soon as that happens, you power up. We need at least fifteen seconds in between. We'll use that to intro Dixon and the weather. Then we toss it to *Skyhawk* looking for clouds—big, ugly clouds. Then, Bucky, you might have to fly your ass back to 394 for section three. All photogs on the air, stand by to chase weather."

"Ten-four," came the crackled answers.

Gayle pushed the microphone away and turned to her interns, whose mouths were open in awe. A big smile crossed her face. "God, I love this shit!"

The rain was stop-and-start now, coming in bursts. Bob Buckridge, the pilot they called Bucky, flicked his cigarette out the door over the western suburbs. He watched the white butt twirl through the dirty showers, through poisonous smog, and into the traffic jam on Interstate 394. This new billion-dollar freeway was no more efficient in rush hour than a dirt road.

Buckridge was used to being jerked around. This was television. So he wasn't surprised when they ordered him south of the river at the last minute. But he was concerned. The idea came from weather. It wouldn't be the first time Dixon Bell had outguessed the National Weather Service. "Sometimes that guy gives me the creeps."

"You don't like Weatherman Bell?" Kitt asked.

"I love the guy, but sometimes . . . He's from the South, you know."

No place is hotter on a hot day than inside an airborne helicopter. They flew with the doors off. The rain splashing in felt good. Their headsets were on so the thunder was only a rumble in their stomachs. Buckridge was undeterred by the weather. He tuned in ATIS—Airport Terminal Information Service—and listened to the latest reports. Still only a watch; no warnings. Visibility was good in three directions, and home was to the east, the small downtown airport on the Mississippi River in St. Paul. Thunderstorms were localized. He was confident he could outmaneuver any weather. Besides that, Clancy Communications was not cheap. The station had purchased a five-place-interior JetRanger III, one of the safest single-engine aircraft made. SKYHAWK 7 was painted boldly on the side in red, white, and blue. As he flew over stalled traffic on the ground, he knew he was ten times safer up in the air.

"Bell say he in Saigon when it fall."

"So he says. Air Force Intelligence. I can imagine what those creeps were up to."

Seated to Bucky's left was his friend in war and peace, Kitt Karson. Vietnamese soldiers assigned to American units were all called Kit Carson. Kitt had been Bucky's door gunner, one of the few Vietnamese trusted enough to serve on a Huey. "I follow you anywhere, Bucky. Let's fly." And fly they did, from Qui Nhon to Pleiku, from the Mekong Delta to north of Da Nang. In war Buckridge was good. Cocky good. A hot dog. "I don't go down." Through two tours of duty and two thousand missions they flew the slicks that brought the grunts to the enemy. When the call came, they returned to the landing zone, often under enemy fire, and lifted out the survivors, the wounded, and the dead. And though their ship took its share of hits, they never went down.

"Beanblossom doesn't like the Weatherman, does he?"

"Beanblossom doesn't like anybody."

"Oh no, he likes me."

"How much do you think he'd like you if you stopped feeding him stories on the Vietnamese community? Or if you lost contact with your friends in the old country? You're just another source to him."

When Saigon fell, Kitt made his way through the jungle to a Thai refugee camp. Finally safe from the Viet Cong, but not from the neighboring country that didn't want him, he wrote to his old friend Bucky, now five years back in the States, and asked for help. Bob Buckridge flew to Thailand and fought red tape with more passion than he ever had shown fighting the North Vietnamese army. Using TV news as a weapon, he threatened boneheaded bureaucrats and befriended publicity-seeking politicians. This war he won. He brought his door gunner back to Minnesota and armed him with Sony's latest Special Lens. Now it was only camera angles they shot, and their only rescue attempts were steering overheated commuters off overcrowded freeways.

Buckridge swung *Skyhawk 7* over the southern suburbs of Edina, Eden Prairie, and Bloomington, staying seven hundred feet above the ground. The beauty of the connecting lakes and the layout of sylvan parks slid by beneath him. He crossed the Minnesota River, then circled back and tipped his nose to the turbulent southwest. It had been a long time since he had seen such a haunting sky. The pilot set his microwave antenna for the live shot. Raindrops exploded on the Plexiglas skewing the freeway scars and housing tracts below. "When I was a kid," he told Kitt, "that was all woodland down there. It was beautiful then. Developers—they're worse than napalm."

"But you live down there."

"Load up."

Kitt hung up his headset and checked the cables. He tuned in the monitor in front of him. He mounted the camera on his shoulder and pointed it out the door at the ugliest cloud he could find.

The eerie green sky was narrowing—mean, swirling

cells growing thicker every second. The rain turned heavy again. Hail ticked off the Plexiglas.

The show began. Bob Buckridge could hear the schlocky music, then the chitchat of the newscast in his ears. He was hot, and wet, and bored. He lit another cigarette and glanced over at the face of Andrea Labore, now flickering on the monitor: an angel's face in a hellish sky. He blew smoke at her. "Throw it to me, you bimbo, so we can get the hell out of here."

Meteorologist Dixon Bell angrily fastened the battery pack to his belt, clipped the microphone to his lapel, and plugged in the earpiece. He threw on his coat, straightened his tie, and shot a dirty scowl over at the control room, where producer Chris Mack was sitting. He stepped up to the weather podium, a big 7 pasted to the front. It was just a few feet from the anchor desk, and precious few feet from Andrea Labore. Even a storm couldn't wash her from his mind. She was the most attractive woman he had ever known. He watched her take her place next to anchorman Ron Shea. In an awkward but necessary move she stuck her hand far down her blouse, exposing her bra strap. She pulled the little microphone through and clipped it above her breasts. She straightened her blouse and brushed back her hair. She smiled over at the Weatherman, a nervous smile. The floor director cued the talent. They were on the air.

In the beginning one man could sit at a desk and read the news, the weather, and the sports. But in today's high-tech world of rapid-fire television it takes three or four people of mixed gender just to tell one story. Video Ping-Pong.

When the music faded away and the red light came on, Ron Shea stared into the camera and read the headline. "Today the FBI released its national crime survey. It showed the number of Americans victimized by a violent crime rose last year ... up three percent from the previous year."

Next, Andrea Labore read a line. "While those statistics say the Twin Cities is still among the safest urban areas in the United States ... they also say violent crime is up here ... especially homicide."

Then Ron Shea got to the point before going to the live shot. "That dire warning came too late for a thirty-two-year-old Minneapolis woman. Her body was discovered this morning in a parking ramp just a few feet from this very newsroom. Police believe she was strangled after leaving work yesterday. The newest member of our staff, Beth Knutson, is live at the murder scene. Beth?"

They were clear. Dixon Bell noted the bad weather on the monitor. He had three minutes. He turned back to the weather center.

Throughout the remodeling that took place after Clancy Communications bought the station, the weather department had begged for a southwest window. But the promotion department wanted the weather center visible from the set, so weather ended up on the opposite side of the newsroom with a window looking northeast, worthless for spotting oncoming storms. Still, Dixon Bell made sure what viewers saw on the set was not all facade. He laid out computers, radar screens, and a digital weather station so he could work while the anchors blabbed away. Though it was highly functional, it did get encased in glossy, painted plywood and mood lighting, yellow-orange, the hue of fire.

The Weatherman checked the digital weather station. The temperature had dropped six degrees. The barometric pressure was 29.55 inches and falling. The wind was gusting up to forty miles per hour.

Dixon Bell was disgusted. With the millions of dollars TV stations spend on weather equipment, you would think they and the National Weather Service would generously share information and happily coordinate their efforts. Doesn't happen. The Weatherman picked up the phone, pushed the memory button, and the battle was on. "It is on Doppler," he scolded through clenched teeth. "It is coming off the computers. And it is on your instruments. You're just not reading them right."

"Don't pull that crap on me again, Bell," came the bitter voice on the other end. "We're in a watch, and I'm watching the same thing you're watching, and the radar doesn't indicate any kind of rotation, hook echo, or comma-shaped signal on the edge of the cloud. Nor have we had one single call about damaging winds. All we need is one spotter to call us."

"I'm calling you."

"Do you see a severe storm?"

"Yes! In my mind I see one hell of a storm!"

"In your mind? Oh, that's wonderful. Let me tell you something, Bell. We don't appreciate one bit your going on TV and contradicting our forecasts day in and day out. As for warnings, I'm going to warn you . . ."

That's when he heard it, or thought he did. It was an electronic hum coming from the monitors—a frequency so low it was barely discernible. Dixon Bell gently hung up the phone. He looked into the studio. Nobody noticed anything wrong.

The Weatherman checked his barometer. Pressure was dropping dramatically—29.51, 29.48, 29.45. The temperature was down two more degrees. He stuck his face in the radar screen. Still nothing.

The Weatherman reached behind his monitor and yanked out the cable. He punched up Channel 13 and darkened the screen till it was black. Then he punched in Channel 2. It was flashing brightly, on and off. Lightning strikes nearby. Then it happened. The screen glowed bright white and stayed that way. Dixon Bell was out of his chair in a flash.

News was rolling tape. One of the murder victim's co-workers was telling the reporter what a saint she had been. "She was the most caring person that you could imagine, always trying to make the world a better place for women. It's inhuman that she would be victimized like this."

The Weatherman ducked behind the camera operators, leaped down the stairs, and shot across the newsroom to the southwest window. The sky had blackened and a rain-free cloud base was showing its face—a scarred, tormented face with a tail cloud extending off to the north. Classic tornado storm structure. Then triple-flash lightning bolts set fire to the sky and Dixon Bell's attention was drawn to the parking ramp roof, and for a split second he saw the spot where a woman had been murdered. Then it was dark again and thundering.

Reporter Beth Knutson signed off and threw it back to Ron Shea.

Shea thanked the new reporter for having braved the

weather and welcomed her to Minnesota. He tossed it to
Andrea.

Andrea read a line about the record homicide rate and
threw it back to Shea.

"We're going to have more on this very unusual murder a bit later in the broadcast, but now I understand we
have some severe weather breaking out there. For that
we're going to turn to Weather Center 7 and meteorologist Dixon Bell. Dixon?"

The Weatherman was back on the set, thundering with
certitude. "Ron, this is tornado season, and that's what
we're talking about here—a tornado. The skies above us
right now are screaming it, and the time to seek shelter is
now, not later. Let's quick go over the rules."

"Just a minute, Dixon. I'm sorry to interrupt, but I'm
confused. Is there a tornado warning? Has one been spotted?"

"No, Ron. Officially we've been in a severe thunderstorm watch for the past hour. That watch was issued by
the Severe Storms Forecast Center in Kansas City, which
is fine if you like your weather from Kansas City. But I
was just out on the Nicollet Walk, where I saw thunderheads topping out at sixty thousand feet and the wind was
wrapping around me like a blanket."

"But the National Weather Service office at the airport
has not issued a tornado warning?"

"No, they haven't. But not to worry, I called out there
and woke the guy up. It should be coming any minute."

"So you're predicting a tornado out of this?"

"I don't predict the weather. I read the weather. This
storm has tornado written all over it, and right now it's
over the metropolitan area." Dixon Bell looked into the
camera and spoke in measured southern tones that held
viewers spellbound. "Tornadoes do not sweep you up and
drop you in the land of Oz. They kill. Split-second decisions mean life or death. Real quick, what to do. At
home, go to the basement immediately. If you can't do
that, get into a closet, or a bathroom. Get under something sturdy. If you're watching this at school, go to an
interior hallway on the lowest floor. Stay out of auditori-
ums and gymnasiums, or anything with a free-span roof.
Same in office buildings. Stand in an interior hallway on
a lower floor. Get away from windows. Remember, any

shelter is better than being outside. We don't know where this thing is going to drop. As you can see on the radar screen . . ."

As the Weatherman explained to viewers the storm cell passing over them, Chris Mack was talking in his ear. "Throw it to Andrea. Ten seconds."

The Ping-Pong continued. Dixon Bell played along. He had done all that he could. He wrapped it up with a plea to take shelter, then turned to the woman he loved. "Andrea?"

"Dixon, one man who might give us a clue about a possible tornado is *Skyhawk 7* pilot Bob Buckridge. Bucky, where are you, and what are you seeing up there?"

I'm up in the air in this real neat helicopter and I see a whole bunch of wind and rain and stuff like that. Any other questions, you ignorant . . . Bob Buckridge squeezed the microphone trigger on the control stick. "Yeah, Andrea, we're over Bloomington now and we're dogging a particularly nasty-looking cloud moving towards downtown. Dixon is right about the skies. As you can see on your monitors, this is an ugly storm approaching." Rain and hail beat down on the chopper, assaulting the cockpit. Lightning shot across the Plexiglas. Anybody watching could see his color television set turn to black and white, raindrops splattering across the screen.

Now the producer was in Andrea's ear. "Take it back, Andrea. He hasn't got anything, goddammit."

"Well, Bucky," said Andrea, "I wouldn't stay up there too much longer if I were you."

Safer here than in that ejector seat you're sitting in. Buckridge squeezed the trigger again. "Right, Andrea. It's getting pretty bad up here. We're coming home." That was his signature line. Each weekday as a kicker to the five o'clock report the anchors would turn to the studio monitor. "Now let's take one last look at traffic with Bob Buckridge. Bucky?" Buckridge would give the traffic report, then: "That's it from *Skyhawk 7*. We're coming home." The anchors would turn to the camera. Big smiles. "And that's it from Sky High News." Cue schlocky music. Pull back camera two. Countdown to network. Fade. Clear.

But this day's weather would write a script with a far different ending.

The tornado sprung from the sky over the southwest suburb of Eden Prairie, and so for the state history books the deadly twister took its name. It skipped over hilly grasslands and unfinished homes, at first doing little damage. Then it quickly found its bearings and bore down on the heavily populated suburb of Edina.

Witnesses caught in the storm's path were stunned by the speed with which it struck. Edina was hit before the National Weather Service could sound the warning sirens. It touched ground first on fashionable France Avenue, known for its shopping and entertainment. There the funnel entertained shoppers by dancing past the Edina movie theater, grabbing the tall EDINA sign over the marquee and snapping it in two, sending the first three letters crashing to the sidewalk, where they ended upside down in an explosion of sparks. The clock in the movie theater stopped at 5:08 P.M. Storefront windows exploded next, some from flying debris, others from the pressure. Mannequins dressed in the latest Paris fashions were hurled into the street. A flower shop simply disintegrated. Rose petals settled on the ruins. Edina police would report the first casualties, shocked faces staring up into the blackness, fresh flowers sprinkled over them.

"Just about fifteen seconds of turmoil ... of hell ... unreal ... I just can't believe it ... I've never seen anything like this before ... and no warning ... nothing ... no warning at all ... no sirens ... no sirens until about ten minutes after it hit ... unbelievable."

Bob Buckridge spotted the tornado right after he threw it back to Andrea. It came swirling out of the southwest, heading northeast, an awesome cone of descending smoke with a counterclockwise spin. The vortex cloud was black, but as it began to close range it quickly turned muddy brown as dirt, debris, and the theater marquee got sucked into the whirl. The crafty pilot had his headset on, tuning out the unreal world spinning around him, but Kitt Karson could hear what sounded like the roar of F-16s taking off on another mission. Thoughts of heading home, thoughts of their own safety got sucked away. Instinct and adrenaline took command. Buckridge circled clockwise and snuck up behind the monster.

The tornado hopped like a stone skipping on water, sometimes skipping entire neighborhoods, sometimes cutting a swath three blocks wide as it roared northeast from Edina through South Minneapolis toward lakes dotted with sailboats and swimmers. Homes were shredded as if by an eggbeater, torn down to their foundations.

"We were looking out the window and we saw bricks flying through the air, pieces of houses, everything . . . and a rolling kind of a cloud in the sky . . . and I said, 'Everybody down the basement, down the basement' . . . and the baby was upstairs sleeping, so I ran upstairs . . . I couldn't get the door open . . . there was such suction . . . and I was really afraid . . . and the pressure was building up in the house . . . I pulled and pulled and finally it opened . . . I pulled the baby out and I ran down the stairs . . . and I could hear crashing . . . and everybody's ears were popping . . . Then I heard this train noise, and then that woman screaming. It was terrifying."

At times dust and debris obscured the funnel. At times Buckridge flew so close they could look up and down the shaft, which extended a thousand feet from cloud to ground and swayed gently. Kitt aimed his camera right down the spout to where it narrowed at the bottom rim and the tip ripped up everything on earth. Despite all the weapons of destruction he had seen unleashed on his native country, he'd never witnessed anything like this. And when they moved in close, the roar was deafening, and when they dropped back there was a high-pitched, blood-curdling scream that made the photographer's skin crawl.

Back in the Channel 7 control room producer Chris Mack could not believe the pictures *Skyhawk 7* was beaming in. He grabbed the microphone in front of him. "Andrea, toss it to Bucky—now!" He grabbed the director next to him. "Go to it, goddammit!" He looked up at the small monitor where the Weatherman stood. " 'His own safety,' " he said mockingly. "He's got the son of a bitch chasing a tornado."

Bob Buckridge was on the air, not waiting for any cue, sounding the warning as dispassionately as he could. "We have a tornado on the ground causing extensive damage. This is a major twister doing major damage. It is moving northeast at about forty miles per hour in a line from Eden Prairie to Lake Harriet to downtown. Anybody in this path should seek shelter immediately. Again, we have a tornado on the ground in the metro area."

At the anchor desk Ron Shea got his two bits on the air. "It would be wise if everybody watching this headed for the basement. Bucky, I don't know if you can hear me, but don't you think you should back off from that thing?"

Andrea chimed in. "Yeah, we're really worried about you."

"Negative," the pilot shouted. "Stay off the radio!"

Within minutes the feed to Channel 7 was picked up and broadcast by the other TV stations. Radio stations plugged into the audio. As Buckridge described what he saw, and Kitt held his camera steady, a hundred sailboats moored at the Lake Harriet Yacht Club capsized, the masts snapping like toothpicks. The park pavilion where the summer concerts were held was destroyed. The tornado continued its dance of death and devastation for three more miles, across Lakewood Cemetery, where Minnesota's famous were buried, and through the heart of trendy Uptown. It rearranged headstones, ripped off the roofs of houses, uprooted trees, and downed power lines. Cars were all but split in two as heavy branches crashed down on them. Some drivers made it out. Others did not. A tree limb pierced a house wall like a thrown spear.

Just a big cloud swirling ... this really big cloud swirling all over ... It sounded like a locomotive, exactly like they say it does, except for that screaming woman. There was this big piece of sheet metal ... and it just flew right over me and into the tree, and I saw the tree go right into the house like a missile ... It was just unbeliev-able ... I couldn't believe I was alive."

The tornado skirted the east shore of Lake of the Isles, where stately homes stood. Then it skipped across Loring Park on the edge of downtown. A man-on-the-street theory says tornadoes do not strike at cities. That theory is all hot air and wind. Tornadoes are not impressed by tall buildings.

Bob Buckridge noted his air speed: forty-six knots. The

huge twisting cloud sometimes caused the ground to disappear. He checked his altimeter. They had climbed to eight hundred feet. With a quick glance at the monitor he made sure Kitt's pictures were being fed back to the station. Playing chicken with the twister, he could just barely hear the debris attacking his ship. He feared Kitt, hanging out the door by a seat belt, would be hit. And there were jolts. But he never stopped talking. "Anybody in a downtown building should take shelter immediately—that includes Sky High News. The tornado is on the ground, headed your way."

In a mass show of bravado, or of stupidity, all newsroom personnel held their positions.

Dave Cadieux, the photographer Gayle the Ghoul had sent to the roof, wrapped one arm around a steel pole, leveled his twenty-thousand-dollar camera on the tripod, and centered the twister in the special four-thousand-dollar lens. He was hanging on for dear life when through that lens he saw *Skyhawk 7* swing out from behind the funnel. He almost burst with pride in his attempt not to burst in the wind. If they lived, it would be promo material for years to come.

The tornado tore across the roof of the Sky High parking ramp, lifting a red Honda Prelude and slamming it into a huge green transformer. The explosion was blinding, knocking out the television equipment below the ramp. The murder scene was completely blown away, any last bit of evidence sucked up and destroyed. Pressure shattered the southwest window in the newsroom, every shard of glass sucked outward.

After deflating the roof of the Metrodome, the supposedly weatherproof home of the Twins and the Vikings, the twister jumped the Mississippi River, faked back into the clouds, then pounced on St. Paul. It tore through the drive-through of a Burger King restaurant. Destruction was instantaneous. At an Amoco station it tore the gas pumps from their moorings and sent them whirling through the car wash. It cut across the northeast corner of the capital city, dipping into quiet weekday neighborhoods sucking up trees and homes and lives. Some victims were carried by the wind two hundred yards, their bodies horribly bruised and cut. From there the twister tripped across Highway 36 and set its sights on one of the largest shopping malls in Minnesota. *Skyhawk 7* stayed with it all the way.

"The tornado is now on the ground in Roseville. If you are in the Rosedale Mall, go to the basement of Dayton's department store. If you are watching this at the Rosedale Mall, get everybody to the basement immediately. You are in the direct path of the tornado. You have only seconds."

A minute later, in one of the most sacrilegious acts in the history of Minnesota, this cyclone from hell audaciously attacked a Dayton's department store.

"It just tore the roof off Dayton's!" Buckridge barked into his mouthpiece. A thousand stones pinged off the Plexiglas. He saw Kitt's head snap back. The vibrations were worsening. "We're taking hits here! I'm coming around! I'm coming around!" He retreated in a clockwise circle, gained control, and approached again.

"I was driving to the mall when I heard the helicopter pilot on the radio talking about a tornado coming . . . I guess I should have turned around and gone home, but I drove to the mall instead. As soon as I got in the door I heard the Dayton's people announce a tornado was coming, and a man was yelling, 'Get in back! Get away from those windows!' Then the lights went out . . . and I looked out into the parking lot and saw cars spinning around, so I took cover behind a big couch . . . Then this train went overhead . . . and I heard this woman screaming for help . . . but I couldn't find her . . . It was pretty scary for a while there."

Bob Buckridge lined the tornado up with the visible horizon to the northeast and rattled off the communities he knew so well. "If you live in a line along Roseville, Vadnais Heights, White Bear Lake, Mahtomedi, Stillwater, or St. Croix County, Wisconsin, you should take shelter immediately. The tornado is on the ground and coming your way."

The tornado carved its deepest path through the St. Paul suburb of Roseville, flattening every house in its way. Yards for miles around were littered with neighbors' homes. Church bell towers were silenced. By now the tornado had been on the ground for more than ten minutes, but with Dixon Bell's early warning, and Bob Buckridge's blow by blow descriptions going out over every radio and TV station in town, half of the metropolitan area was either underground or seeking shelter.

In once romantic White Bear Lake, immortalized in the short stories of F. Scott Fitzgerald, the great tornado wrote a new chapter on urban sprawl, flattening one tacky development after another. As it steam-rollered by, no house, no boat could resist for even a fraction of a second the tragic ending.

"It was just like a jet coming over the top of our house. Then our house was gone."

Skyhawk 7 followed the tornado over the woods east of the Twin Cities. Uprooted trees were left sticking in the air. Trees left standing had the bark stripped from their trunks. It twisted across the scenic St. Croix River and into Wisconsin. Then, having spent its fury in a thirty-five-mile path through the heart of the metropolitan area, the Eden Prairie tornado disappeared into the cloud from which it had emerged a half-hour earlier.

Bob Buckridge watched the funnel slip back into the heavens. In the end there was a blinding, unnatural light with a blue tinge to it that lit up the black cloud like a fluorescent bulb. Then it was gone. He threw the broadcast back to the studio. His once smooth-running ship was bucking. His knuckles wrapped around the control stick were deathly white, scraped and bleeding. He checked his instruments. His eye caught the monitor: a close-up of Andrea. God, she's beautiful, he thought. Then, like a cruel joke, they quick-cut to Dixon Bell. The pilot chuckled. "From heaven to hell." He circled around and brought *Skyhawk 7* face to face with the back edge of the storm that had given the tornado birth. Home now lay to the west, two rivers and a mountain of violent weather away. The dark sky was tinged with red. Rainfall was heavy. Hail raked his ship like groundfire. Lightning bolts cracked around him. Below him was the St. Croix Valley, its rolling hills studded with trees and mined with lakes and streams.

Strong north winds whipped rain through the cockpit. Kitt was loading a new tape into his camera, seemingly unperturbed by events. His hair was dripping wet. His face was red. Blood trickled from his forehead. His hands were full, so he just smiled up at his pilot friend and nodded. I follow you anywhere.

Buckridge knew his ship was hurting. The vibrations would not smooth out. Perhaps his instinct told him he could make it, or maybe his foolish pride would not let him put it down, but he decided to try for Lake Elmo, a small airfield minutes away. He pulled in all the power he could and climbed to one thousand feet.

Ron Shea was trying his best to help viewers understand what they had just seen, what they all had been through together. "The special quality of life we enjoy here in Minnesota has been shattered." He assured them reporters were on their way to the worst-hit areas and advised people to stay away. Andrea Labore had not spoken a word since Buckridge told her to shut up. Shea tossed it to Dixon Bell.

"The tornado is off the ground, but the storm is not over," the Weatherman warned. The radar screen was on the air. "You can see the storm cell passing right over the metropolitan area. There are still some powerful winds in that cell, and there's a lot of debris blowing around. The all clear has not been sounded. Stay inside and away from windows."

Ron Shea interrupted. "Dixon, we're going to check back in with Bob Buckridge. He's in that storm and he may have something for us. Bucky?" There was a pause. "Bucky, are you hearing us now?" Another delay.

Then the feed from the chopper, both audio and video, was back on the air. The resonance of the pilot's voice was foreign. "This is *Skyhawk 7*. We're in trouble here. We've crossed the St. Croix heading for Elmo. My ship is out of control."

Chris Mack sensed immediately what was happening. He was on his feet screaming into the microphone so loud he could be heard on the set. "Bucky, can you put it down anywhere? Put it down!"

The silence that followed was chilling. It was the silence of a newsroom choked with fear . . . the silence of two cities bracing for even more . . . and the deadly silence of an airborne helicopter when the engine quits. Even the thunder stopped. The picture displayed on TV sets spun dizzily out of control, raindrops attacking the screen. Then the voice of Bob Buckridge came over the air one last time, hauntingly calm and clear. "This is *Skyhawk 7*. We won't be coming home."

And then they crashed.

In front of a million spellbound viewers, they crashed. With the piercing, heartbreaking sound of twisting metal and snapping trees, over the sound of a newsroom full of friends shrieking in horror, they crashed. Where the Viet Cong and the North Vietnamese army had failed, the Minnesota weather had succeeded. It brought them down.

It takes a lot to shock and silence a newsroom, they are morbid by nature. At Channel 7 the only sound was of Ron Shea feebly ad-libbing at a red light atop a camera.

Andrea Labore turned to the Weatherman. His back was to the set, his face in a radar screen. Phosphorescent green light flowed through his thick hair. The orange-fire light over the console outlined his huge shoulders. Red digits flashed around him. But the apparition didn't move. Dixon Bell seemed frozen . . . almost possessed.

No wind instrument has ever survived the full impact of a tornado, so they are measured after the fact. After this tornado the wind intensity was factored at F-5—winds topping 300 mph. The most accurate barometers fell to 26.97 inches. Canceled checks from Minneapolis floated to earth on Michigan's Upper Peninsula. In the age of satellites, radar, computers, radio, and television, the Eden Prairie tornado killed seventy-nine people and injured a thousand more. Property damage was over one billion dollars. Trees that had stood proud for a hundred years now lay on their sides, wrapped in power lines, waiting for chainsaws to come and finish what the tornado had started.

The two real heroes of the killer storm were dead in the thick woods east of town, their necks snapped in a crushed helicopter, their bodies tangled in twisted aluminum and broken tree branches, warm rain washing over them. Sirens wailed through the woods, in mourning instead of warning.

In the aftermath it was learned that most fatalities occurred in the early minutes of the storm, at the southwest end of the deadly trail, among those who weren't watching television. As it moved northeast, homes had been blown into fragments. Leveled with the dust. Gone in seconds. But as neighbors climbed out to assess the damage, there was relief and happiness that they had survived.

Thousands of sightseers poured into the hardest-hit areas, creating additional traffic problems and sparking official warnings about looting.

"Have you been able to salvage anything?"

"No . . . and we've had people who have walked through already and picked up cameras and things."

"Looters?"

"Looters . . . right . . . how they can do it, I don't know. I thought people were different here."

"What are your thoughts now?"

"I think maybe God sent that tornado to punish us. Or warn us."

Tornadoes are often accompanied by a high-pitched noise that crescendos to a scream. The spookiest part of this twisted tragedy was that as the tornado roared by, uprooted, maimed, destroyed, and killed, almost all survivors would universally describe what sounded to them like the amplified, terrified screams of a woman in an echo chamber—a horrifying, frightening cry for help they would never forget.

But not all was destruction, ruin, and death. At Channel 7 a legend was born.

THE MARINE

Marines never leave their dead or wounded behind. Or so says the legend.

He knew they had called in an air strike, could see the sliver of silver angling out of the sun, but he believed there was still time. He threw his M-16 to the ground, tore the sweat-stained flak jacket from his back, and yelled "Cover me!" the way John Wayne did in the movies. Then, with the speed of a halfback, he ran through heavy sniper fire. He reached the first bloody grunt, shot all to hell, in shock, but still alive. He hoisted him over his shoulder the way a fireman does and ran him back to the eroded ravine that served as a trench. All the time he waited for a bullet in the back. But the bullets passed him by. He dumped the wounded Marine over the dry red dirt and turned again. He checked the silver bullet in the sky. Death descending. Two more grunts lay bloody in the yellow grass just before the tree line. There was still time.

Nobody ran in Vietnam; it was just too damn hot. A dry, suffocating heat: 115° in the sun. He popped salt tablets into his mouth. He tore a blue-and-white bandanna from his head and took a swipe at the sweat stinging his eyes. The fusillade being laid down by the Marines was so intense he couldn't hear incoming, just the occasional wisp of deadly air tearing by. Again he serpentined through the firefight and grabbed another grunt. He too was alive, and the young master sergeant knew he was doing the right thing. The Marine thing. He dumped wounded grunt number two into the dusty red trench and turned for number three.

It was the dry season. The ground was rock hard. Dust hung in the air like smoke. He spit the taste of salt from his mouth. He was exhausted. The heat was killing him. Again, he pulled the bandanna from his sweltering head and wiped his red-hot face.

Seven years into the war Congress rewrote the rules for the draft. Student deferments were done away with. A lottery system was set up and President Nixon gave speeches about how much more fair it would be. A Selective Service official would draw birthdays from a fishbowl and thereby decide the fate of America's young men. He was born on the tenth of May. Growing up in the Midwest, his hero was Fran Tarkenton, number 10 of the Minnesota Vikings. At Stillwater High School his red football jersey had a big white 10 on it. During homecoming week they taped a big red 10 to his locker. He took to writing the lucky 10 on his tennis shoes. But when he turned eighteen years old his luck changed. A nameless, faceless bureaucrat in Washington cast his hand into a fish bowl and hooked May 10, on the tenth cast. His dreams of college football were deferred. He went to Vietnam.

The Marine tossed the bandanna aside. His head was bare now, a target for the blistering sun. The last of the wounded grunts lying in the scorched grass below the trees wasn't moving. But the Air Force Phantom was, screaming down from the sky. Its guns would take out everything in its sights. Its bombs would leave nothing alive. Though a thousand arguments go through a soldier's head at these moments, they pass through in a split second, and in that split second this soldier, now twenty-one years old, decided to go for that last fellow Marine lying dead still in the grass.

And dead he was. The Marine rolled him over. His neck was open, his dog tags blown away. Insects were feasting on the wounds. It was Sax, Robert J., Lance Corporal, United States Marine Corps. Twenty years old. Texarkana, Arkansas. Married his high school sweetheart. One child, another on the way. The Marine picked up his dead buddy and started for the trench. Bullets shot by him in both directions. Never in his young life had he felt so alive yet so near death. For the first time in the war the burning feeling came over him that he wasn't going to make it. He was scared. The diving Phantom grew in the corner of his eye, and the scream of the jet engines grew

in his ears, and he realized how foolish he was being, and
he dropped the lance corporal from Texarkana and ran as
fast as he'd ever run in his life.

He heard his men yelling, "Tac air! Cover! Cover!"

Again he was number 10 sprinting down the field, the
goal line in sight. But the roar in his ears was not the roar
of a crowd. His stomach was cramping. Sweat was
smothering him. He was choking on his dry tongue. It
was a sprint through hell now. He knew it was going to
be close. So he prayed: prayed he could outrun the
bombs, prayed they would miss him, as they always
missed his hero in the movies. But this was Vietnam, and
there had never been any movies like this.

The Phantom pilot flipped a switch, pulled a lever, and
dropped two hundred yards of napalm in a straight line
along the trees. Flames exploded toward the trench.

And just when the Marine thought he was so hot his
face was going to explode, it did. A fistful of the gasoline
jelly splashed squarely on top of his head, dripped over
his skull and face in an instant, then ignited. Friendly fire.
He sprinted to the trench like a human torch, toppled over
the ridge, and set the grass beneath aflame. He jerked
around on his back with violent spasms, his body out of
control. As his men tried to extinguish him, he screamed
so hard he ripped his lungs and throat and spit blood on
them between the flames.

His family was told he was in grave condition. He was
supposed to die. But the Marine hung on.

From an evac station in Khe Sanh he was flown to the
Air Force base at Yokota, Japan, then choppered to the
burn unit at the 109th United States Army hospital on
the Kanto Plains. His head swelled up until his neck disappeared. Through one eye slit the charred Marine could
see an IV bottle hung from a ceiling hook. Liquids
dripped down the tubes and ran into the back of a bloody
red hand left dangling from the whirlpool bath. They
jammed rubber plugs up his nostrils and forced a breathing tube into his mouth. Then they completely submerged
the roasted marshmallow that was his head. Bandages
that had become a part of the wound floated free in the
steaming water. Next, the dead skin began coming off, his
face floating before his eyes. When the skin wouldn't
come off, they ripped it off. Parts of his face were so

deeply burned that crisscrossing muscle fibers were exposed.

They wrapped him in a cooling blanket to bring down his temperature. Then back into the whirlpool he went, immersed in hot, bubbling water, like a never-ending baptism. It became a torture chamber, the scalding water churning and churning over his raw head, the skin being ripped from his face. One of his ears fell off. With no voice to scream, he wept in silence. Next day they pulled off his other ear.

He heard muffled voices talking over him. A sergeant trying to explain the bases for this torture. "Dead skin collects bacteria."

A woman with a funny drawl kept speaking sweet to him while holding his burnt hands. "Every day that you're free of infection, you're one day closer to living a healthy life." For days this went on. Or was it weeks? Or was it a month?

The first conscious memory of his recovery came when he awoke one morning with a feeding tube in his mouth. He was choking; choking awake. The woman wiped his blistered lips and asked him how he was today, as if there had been other days. He was spread-eagled across a steel arched frame. Strapped in. The sun was shining through the window. He couldn't move his head. Only one eye was working for now; the other was still swollen closed. But he could see her in the sun. She was young and tall. Somehow he made her understand he was awake. She put the tube back into his mouth and helped him drink his breakfast.

If the first weeks of his recovery were spent in and out of consciousness, the following weeks were spent in and out of sleep. Some nights he could hear the screams of other victims. He envied them. Crying out was still physically impossible. For him there was no relief from the searing pain of blistering wounds. Of all the wounds of war burns carry the highest casualty rate. Just too many complications.

He wore no bandages. Nurses smeared a white antibiotic ointment around his head with a butter knife. Soldiers call it napalm cream because it stings like fire. Tears got soaked up by the cream before they could leave his eyes. An increase in Demerol only added sickness to his suffering. Then one day doctors came to him with an ungodly choice. He could endure months of this torture, or they could put him on morphine, but he would probably end up addicted to the drug for the rest of his life. Think about it, they told him, let us know tomorrow.

That night the ward master, an army sergeant, whispered into the stumps that were his ears: he could administer heroin. "Send in the Marines."

Next day the Marine signaled no to the morphine.

One day during the sleepless weeks she told him her name was Angela. But because of her Texas accent, or perhaps because his mind kept thinking it over and over, her name came out Angel. She had warm brown eyes. Her army nurse's uniform showed off a shapely figure. She was attractive from the start, her black skin under the white uniform was soft and flawless. Slowly in those painful months of recovery she became to him the most beautiful, most wonderful woman on earth. The angel from Corpus Christi.

With his face buried under white cream and his vocal cords reduced to silence, his only means of communication were his arms, and there was little strength in them. If he raised his right arm off the sheet it meant yes. His left arm meant no. Even with those limits Angel had a remarkable way of knowing what he needed, and of reading his attitude. For what kind of attitude does a young man have who has been burned beyond recognition in a war he didn't understand in the first place, in a corps he was forced to join? But when his mood was darker than the darkest corners of hell and he didn't think he could go on, it wasn't pity Angel gave him. It was a scalding scolding. "Okay, just stop it, now!"

It takes a special kind of person to care for burn victims—they're horrible to look at, and most of them die. Through a slow game of yes and no Angel determined what kind of music the Marine liked and saw to it that it was played for him every day. She read to him in the beginning. She helped him drink his meals.

In his second month of recovery the swelling went down and his other eye opened up. He still couldn't move his head, so they fitted him with prismatic glasses that enabled him to see around him. He was at the end of the ward with a window to his left. A white curtain hung on his right. Angel had an army mechanic hook a book stand to the frame in front of his face. She bought him a conductor's baton and stuck a wad of chewing gum to the end of it so that he could turn the pages. Then she'd open a book or a magazine and let him read for himself. At first it was hard to concentrate through the pain, but slowly mental discipline prevailed and he came to realize that he would have been lost without his books. Angel's father taught English at East Juarez State. She knew the importance of books. As a result the Marine was given the kind of reading students hate, but the very best literature America has to offer. During his fourteen months in the hospital he read the works of Mark Twain, Joseph Conrad, and Jack London. He fell in love with the short stories of Minnesota's own F. Scott Fitzgerald. The Marine read Shakespeare.

In his third month of recovery they wrapped his face in cadaver skin. But after three days the grafts failed. Back into the whirlpool he went.

His voice returned, but he had to learn to use it over again. He took it one word at a time. Then a sentence at a time. A speech therapist came in, a Japanese woman who taught English. It would be several years before his stuttering disappeared, and even after that he had a bad habit of slipping into a Brando mumble.

With the return of his voice came the return of a personality, although one that had changed dramatically. Through the months of treatment and therapy Angel managed to retrieve his sense of humor. He made jokes about his face being blacker than hers. He asked if she wanted to see an imitation of a mummy. Then he raised both his arms and growled. It never failed to crack her up.

They grafted again, using skin from his stomach. Skin from his back. They stretched the bright pink sheets of skin over his stunted features and told him how much better he looked. He did hand exercises to prevent atrophy. He did facial exercises to keep the scar tissue loose so it wouldn't lock his jaw.

By his sixth month of recovery he could move his head about. The glasses came off. The bed straps were undone. He had miraculously escaped infection. He was feeling better. Then Angel told him her orders had come through. Any soldier knows what that means. It means good-bye.

She'd been transferred to Germany. In the days that followed she could see he was pouting. "Just stop it," she scolded. On the day of her last rounds she promised to return after dinner and bid him farewell.

No mirrors were allowed in the burn unit. Just from watching his hands heal the Marine correctly guessed his head and face were totally hairless, almost completely featureless, and probably the color of sour milk with bloody shades of pink. But he hoped.

When the sun went down he waited for her, a vigil that went on for hours. But she didn't come. At midnight the ward master drew the curtain and whispered lights out. The Marine lay in the dark, tilted his head to a position where it hurt the least, and stared out the window at the midnight sky over this land of the rising sun. The industrial lights of the Kanto Plains blotted out the stars and gave the Japanese heavens the face of a dismal abyss. So unlike home, where the North Star hung. He watched the lights of choppers as they dropped out of the sky with more charred bodies. He felt as low as he'd ever felt since his arrival. He could hear the slow hissing of a respirator: in a burn unit, the sound of death. Victims put on respirators always died. Perhaps it was time to send in the Marines.

"It's the kind of city where it should be nighttime all the time."

He turned when she said that, turned too fast, and the pain split his head. He let out a short groan. Saliva drooled out his mouth and down his crusty chin.

"Be careful now," she told him. Angel wiped his mouth and sat on the edge of the bed. "You're still a long way from well."

She was like a real angel in the dark, moving with holy grace through a battlefield of death and renewal. She took a rusty red candle from a picnic basket she had brought in and set it on the nightstand next to the bed. When she struck a match, he could see it was an industrial candle that looked more like a flare to be used in case of emergency. "Best I could do," she giggled.

The candlelight outlined her figure in halo white. It was the first time he'd seen her out of uniform. She was dressed in a Japanese kimono, shiny blue with a white flower pattern running the length. The sight of her all decked out made him jealous. "Did you . . . a date to-night?"

"No, I've been home getting ready."

"Getting ready . . . ready to . . . to leave?"

"Getting ready for you, you fool." She rolled her eyes and sighed, a deep mocking sigh. "Marines."

He was excited. He stammered as if he hadn't seen her in weeks instead of hours. "My lips . . . my lips are almost b-back to normal, and around my eyes are j-just about a hundred percent. This may sound funny, but I c-can . . . can actually feel the skin growing back on m-my nose. It itches re . . . bad."

"You've got lots of healing to go still. The major doctor told you some of the skin grafts aren't taking hold. You've got to prepare yourself. They can't just keep operating."

Weeks later, when the letters stopped, he realized what she was trying to tell him—that his nose itched because the new skin grafted on to it was dying. But he wasn't listening to it this night.

Angel slipped out of her shoes and sat on the bed. From the basket she pieced together a meal fit for the Emperor—seafood, rice, and roast duck so tender it barely had to be chewed. Deftly handling chopsticks, she carefully fed him the softest foods. It was a turning point in his recovery. His days on a liquid diet came to an end.

What he did drink that night was a bottle of wine she popped open. She said it was supposed to be good stuff. At that age he knew little about the fine taste of wine, but it was delicious, and he sipped as much as she allowed. Years after the war, after he had fallen in love with great books and plays, when he came to appreciate classical music, dead poets and dead painters and the work they left behind, when he began to respect opera and ballet and other things he didn't really care for, he took a wine-tasting class. He bought books on wine. He subscribed to a wine magazine. Over the years he became a connoisseur of sorts. He could easily have become a wino searching for the magic nectar they shared that night. But he never tasted that wine again.

When they were done eating, she took up nurse duty and cleaned the bed. She wiped his mouth, straightened the sheets, and fluffed the pillow. The saddest feeling came over him: the feeling she was leaving. But she didn't leave. She lay down next to him and rested her head on his pillow. In the hour that followed they talked in whispers, the most intimate conversation of his young life. He told her of Minnesota, of lakes and trees and the extremes of the changing seasons. She told him about the Texas heat and the beaches and storms of Corpus Christi. When the conversation graduated from weather to boys and girls, as it always does, he confessed the sins of a midwestern boy.

In high school he waited until the last minute to lose his virginity. It was graduation night in the backseat of her daddy's new Chrysler. That summer they enjoyed sex on the grass of the valley floor beneath the Soo Line Bridge. He didn't love her in the least, but the sex was good. Then he was off to boot camp on Parris Island. He had sex with one of the teenage barflies that buzzed around the base in Seattle before they shipped out. In Da Nang he paid for sex twice. But both occasions left him feeling shamed, cheated, and wanting his money back. He vowed he'd never pay for it again.

When he'd finished talking, saying much more than he should have said, there was the longest silence. He was sure what little remained of his face had turned even deeper shades of red. He could feel her near him. Her warm breath smelling of sweet wine swept over his eyes and touched his heart. Then she sat up on the edge of the bed. She had the most slender back. She stood as if to leave.

The dress had loops that looped around the buttons that ran up the side. She undid them, not the least bit self-conscious, peeled open the front, and let it drop to the floor. She was not wearing a bra, and her breasts were larger than he had fantasized. She slid off her panties. Angel pulled back the sheets and gingerly laid her beautiful black skin over the charred Marine and covered them both with the white sheets.

He was glad his hands had mostly healed. His fingers were well enough to run the length of her back and touch and caress every soft curve. He would have been content if that was all she allowed him, but she pressed her lips over his and he embarrassingly wished that they were as healed as he had claimed. She'd left the candle alive. If the scars and scales bothered her, she did not let on. When they kissed he tried to press harder, but it hurt his face. She sensed this and went on with the softest kisses a woman can give. When the kisses were done, she buried her head in his shoulder and seemed to fall asleep on top of him. So he too slept.

Sometime in the night he awoke and she was still there, lying across him, and he knew he wasn't dreaming. She was awake and her hands were inching his hospital gown over his hips. Then she had him in her hand and she was teasing him. She arched her back, putting him inside of her. They may have done it a second time that night. In his memories maybe even three times.

She dressed before the sun came up. They were both crying.

"Who'll be around to ... to ... to tell me to st-stop it?"

"You will," she answered. "Whenever you're feeling sorry for yourself, whenever your hurt and frustration start to get the best of you, you just gotta say, 'Just stop it.'" She ran her fingers over his scorched lips one last time, and, as he remembered it, she whispered that most of his healing had to take place in his mind.

His letters to Germany began the day she left. He thanked her in a thousand different words. He wrote of his feelings about their time together, avoiding the word "love" as best he could. Every day he grew stronger, and every day he wrote to her about another reflex, another muscle returned to life. He passed on to her scuttlebutt that he'd been put in for the Cross. She was military. She could appreciate that. And though he didn't know it, his letter writing was seminal—because along with the reading he was doing, he was developing into a fine writer.

Her letters back to him were sweet and funny, but they were filled with warnings he was too in love to understand. Advice about living with the scars we gather as we go through life.

In his last letter to Angel the emotions and overwrought memories of a wounded soldier overran common sense. The Marine wrote of his love for her, promised her that after his discharge he would come to Corpus Christi. The letter was written in Minnesota smug. He would rescue her from Texas. They would move to the north country, where she would fall in love with the land and the weather, and him, and they would live happily ever after in a house on a lake. All of this was written still believing his face would heal. Still denying burning realities.

Angel didn't write back. He never heard from her again. More than any letter it was this lack of a letter that finally delivered the ugly truth. Forced him to face a face-less life.

But over the years no trace of bitterness could ever be traced to his heart when it came to the angel from Corpus Christi. She came to mind whenever he saw a nurse in uniform. He dreamed of her one night after again reading Fitzgerald's "The Ice Palace." The night she laid her warm, tender body over the charred Marine and took him deep inside her remained the most beautiful and ever-lasting memory of his life.

Just stop it.

Twenty years would go by before he would have sex again.

"**H**i. My name is Stephanie. I'm a new intern."

"Hi, Stephanie. I'm Rick Beanblossom. I'm a burn vic-tim. Vietnam. That's why I wear this mask. You'll get used to it. In fact, if you hang around here long enough you'll find I'm the best-looking guy in the newsroom. Where are you from?"

"Des Moines."

"Is that in America?"

"Yes. It's the capital of Iowa."

"I see."

"They said I could work with you today."

"Sure. I'll tell you as much as I can. A lot of it is my personal opinion. Take it for what it's worth."

"All right."

"Do you know who Thomas Edison was?"

"Yes. He invented the light bulb and the phonograph."

"Who was Alexander Graham Bell?"

"He invented the telephone."

"Marconi?"

"Invented the first radio."

"And who was Vladimir Zworykin?" Rick asked her.

"Who?"

"Vladimir Zworykin. A Russian immigrant. In 1929 he invented television. Do you get the point?"

"That the invention of television is nothing to celebrate?"

"I'm a field producer, Stephanie. I research and write stories for the reporters and the anchors."

"I heard you're really good."

"I'm token quality around here. Viewers tune in to see the fluff, then I sneak up and hit them with the news. Half my stories are quasi-investigative, half are feature essays. The reporters like to work with me because I make them look good."

When Clancy Communications bought Channel 7 it was in sad shape. Though a network affiliate, it had such a poor reputation that an independent station in town was pulling in more viewers with reruns of "The Flintstones." The company decided on a quick fix. Cash. Some of that cash went into big fat contracts. They stole Pulitzer Prize-winning reporter Rick Beanblossom away from an investigative team at the *Star Tribune* with the promise of a free hand. They brought in Ron Shea from their station in Richmond and paired him with tall redhead Charleen Barington, an aging but still attractive beauty queen from Texas who'd managed to lose her accent. For reporters they recruited a corps of young, aggressive, well-educated beauties. Even the guys were pretty. Almost as an afterthought, and because he came cheap, they hired the weekend weatherman from their station in Memphis. His name was Dixon Bell. Channel 7 News became Sky High News, with Weather Center 7, Sky High Sports, and a red, white, and blue Skyhawk helicopter. As one cynical columnist wrote, "You'd have to be Sky High to take these bimbos seriously." But it worked.

"So if your kind of stories are so good, why don't they do more of them?"

"They should," Rick told her. "Now that the beauty queens and our psychic weatherman have hooked the viewers, we should be moving to harder news. We have the people to do it. But don't hold your breath. How long is your internship?"

"I don't know. How long do they give us?"

"Honey, what television news calls interns, mentors, and volunteers, others call slave labor. They use the eu-

phemisms to skirt the labor laws. Newsrooms are all take
and no give. As long as you are willing to work for free,
they'll let you work here forever. Make yourself a schedule, set some goals, and stick to them."

"My goal is to be an anchor."

"That's fine, but learn reporting. Anchor is the last job
on the way out the door. The more diverse your background, the more valuable you'll be to a newsroom."

"What do the anchors do?"

"Very little. Do you see that man over there, the one
strutting around like Supercock? That's Ron Shea, our
main anchor. They brought him in from Virginia to boost
our ratings. He's done that. But the only thing he knows
about Minnesota is how to get to work and how to get to
the airport. He's not a bad guy, but he doesn't work on a
news story unless there's a free trip involved. He does
promotion and he reads the news. His beauty-queen co-
anchor is on maternity leave. When she's here she does
even less."

"Is news a good career?"

"No, it's a good start. Don't make a career of it."

"Why are you still in it?"

"For now, money. I got lucky. There are a hundred
people who work in this newsroom. Four or five of us
make big bucks. The notion that people who work in television get paid well is one of the biggest myths in America. TV doesn't pay shit. They expect you to live on the
perks, not the paycheck. Benefits are nonexistent. There
is no security. That's why it's a young people's business.
Our news director is thirty years old. The executive producer is twenty-eight. The ten o'clock producer is twenty-
six. That's not unusual. The smart ones get their
credentials before they burn out, then move on to a real
job. If I left this newsroom today and came back in five
years, I'd be lucky to recognize ten people."

They were standing at his cluttered desk, but there was
a sloppy organization to it all. The desk was in a corner,
tucked away from other desks, and it had more work
space. Where others had only desktop computers, Rick
Beanblossom had the computer and a laser printer. His
twelve-button speakerphone looked like a mini communications center. An electronic Rolodex stored a thousand
phone numbers. Next to it was a bottle of prescription

painkillers and an open can of Pepsi. A crystal vase held a brilliant array of flowers. He had a fresh bouquet of flowers delivered to the newsroom every week. A monitor on the upper shelf was tuned to Channel 10, which was a four-way split screen displaying four different channels. The sound was mute, and he wasn't paying any attention to the pictures. "Let me give you the tour. It starts here at my desk. This is a telephone."

"I know. We have them in Iowa." Stephanie smiled at him. She was short and girlish, so young she looked more just out of high school that just out of college. On television she would come across naturally cute and perky.

"Ninety percent of the research I do, I do over the phone. Learn how to work the phones. Friendly and persistent will get you a lot more information than pushy and rude." Rick moved on. "This is a computer. It's connected to the mainframe, and its research capabilities are invaluable. If you're going to work in news, learn how to use a computer. Besides a writing tool, this gives us four wire services—AP local, AP national, UPI, and a PR wire."

"What's AP?"

"What did you major in?"

"Speech Comm."

"I see." Rick tapped at the keyboard in a slow, deliberate style. "Associated Press. United Press International. And Public Relations . . . corporate bullshit." News stories in phosphorescent orange began breaking across the screen. "The news rolls on these twenty-four hours a day," he told Stephanie. "Somebody should be checking computers every fifteen minutes. If you hear them beeping, that means urgent—a breaking story coming across for the first time. Give it to the assignment desk."

"So these stories are already written for you?"

"No, these are written too well. We have to trash them for TV."

"How so?"

"Make it simple. Write down to the viewer. Never confuse them. Don't use synonyms. Don't use quotes. Use short words whenever you can. Gasoline is gas. Automobiles are cars. Stick with one-syllable words. Use short sentences. No commas. Fewer words are less confusing. Write to the video. No pictures, no story."

"And this here is all the latest news?"

"Yes. If you're going to work in news, learn how to steal."

"From who?"

"From *whom*," he said, correcting her. "Newspapers are your best source. Then the news magazines. Watch the networks and the competition. Despite what they say, you can't copyright news. If it's an investigative piece, start with public records. Most people would have a heart attack if they knew how much of their private life was available to the general public."

"Okay."

"These computers also access our public libraries, and the libraries of some of the leading newspapers and magazines in the country. When I worked at the *Star Tribune* I could write a lengthy feature without leaving my desk. Just a telephone and a computer. But this is television and we need pretty pictures, so follow me."

Rick Beanblossom led the new intern to the front of a hustling, bustling television news-gathering operation in which Clancy Communications had recently invested a great deal of money. The silver carpeting was new and plush. The frosty paint on the walls was fresh. Big round clocks showing different time zones around the world had been fastened to an overhead beam, and nobody in the newsroom had the faintest idea if they were accurate—but boy, did they look good. New computers had been installed. Television monitors on every desk were top-of-the-line Sonys. Second-rate wages; first-rate hardware.

It was noisy. He talked into her ear. "These desks in front of the assignment desk are for the show producers. The directors work in that cube station next to them. The reporters and field producers are scattered along the walls. Management offices are back in that glassy corner that looks like a funeral parlor—and often is."

"Is that Andrea Labore over there?"

"No. That's Andrea the Bore. Every time she anchors we have to lose a story because she reads so damn slow."

An old man came their way, a sturdy old man with a proud gait and a bald head. His suit was crumpled and worn. In his arm was a file filled with papers. He had a friendly face, red and puffy. He stopped to chat, wheezing a little. "Hi, Rick—new friend?"

"Andy Mack," Rick said, "this is Stephanie. She's a new intern from some place called Des Moines."

"Oh, I've heard of that place. Welcome to America."

"Hi, Andy. Thank you."

"Andy is the Arthur Godfrey of local television," Rick told her.

"Who's Arthur Godfrey?" she asked.

"Sorry, Andy. Speech comm major."

"Say, Rick, I pulled this off the wire." The old man rifled through his papers, softly huffing and puffing, early signs of a breathing problem. "Here it is. Police in Racine, Wisconsin, arrested a man for attempted child abduction. He's heavyset and had a gun. The FBI is running a check on the gun to see if it could have fired the Wakefield bullet."

Rick examined the report. "Thanks, Andy." They moved along.

"He's a nice man."

"Yes, he is . . . until he gets a few drinks in him."

"What does he do here?"

"Everything and nothing. He used to be the weatherman."

"Are you still working on the Wakefield case?"

"Until he's found. I don't know what you read in Iowa, but in this state that boy's kidnapping is as big as the Lindbergh kidnapping." He moved her over to the wall. "This printer here is the script feed from the network. The network sends our tape room two ninety-minute feeds every day—stories from around the world complete with pictures and words. At the same time all the network affiliates are feeding stories to them in New York. That's why it's called a network. Understand?"

"I think so."

They moved in front of a long desk high on a platform. An open box of Oreos lay atop the counter. "Have a cookie." Rick handed one to Stephanie and popped another into his mouth. "Good morning, Gayle. Any white trash from overnight?"

Gayle had a telephone to her ear, a cookie to her mouth. She was on hold. "Just a fire and a stabbing."

"Did we get tape?"

"Nothing we can use. No flames, and the stabbing victim lived. You know me—no carnage, no coverage."

"This is the assignment desk. And this is Gayle, our assignment editor. In this business, she's the best. I brought her with me when I jumped ship. We call her the Ghoul. Gayle, this is Stephanie, a new intern. Do you have time for the two-minute tour?"

Gayle hung up the phone. She was a tall woman, twenty-seven years old, and not physically attractive; her beauty was her vibrant personality and her sharp wit. She balanced fashionable glasses on a beakish nose. "Hi, Stephanie. This is where stories start. That's the dispatch shack behind me. You might want to work in there when your internship is over, but if you've got a weak stomach I wouldn't suggest it. Every tragedy in the seven-county metropolitan area is beamed into your ears. The psychological damage can be irreversible, and you can make more money at Kentucky Fried Chicken. These phones ring off the hook all day long. Besides our own people calling in, people call in with news tips, most of which aren't worth a piece of typing paper. Viewers call in with complaints, and at least two or three lunatics call the station every day. Sound concerned and get rid of them." The phone on the desk rang. Gayle answered. "Assignment desk.

"We'll call them right away. Thank you." Gayle hung up. "The mail is brought here in buckets every day. That's part of your job. Every organization and corporation in the Midwest, every clown with a gripe wants us to come and do a story on them. Interns open the mail and sort it, usually by date. Then it goes into a daybook so we know what's going on every day of the week. Here's today's book." She held up a yellow folder two inches thick. "Slow news day," she said. "That's the assignment board behind me. Think of it as a company picnic and that's the list of what everybody has to bring. Stories in red ink are live shots." The phone rang again. Gayle was back at it.

Rick Beanblossom took over, pointing up at the assignments. "Reading down the board . . . Beth is doing a story on illegal contractors trying to make a quick buck off homeowners hit by the tornado . . . I see Andrea has found some puppy dogs that survived the storm . . . the

National Weather Service is holding another press conference to further explain their ineptitude ... and a photog is shooting the billboard story."

"What's the billboard story?"

"Some joker is running around town defacing billboards with a splat gun."

"Why would he do that?"

"I think it's his not-so-subtle way of protesting the uglification of Minnesota. He hit a Channel 7 billboard last week. Personally, I thought our anchors looked better with fluorescent orange hair."

"And what are you doing today?"

"Among other things, I'm writing a follow-up on the parking-ramp murder. We'll use existing tape and one of the anchors will read it."

"Do you like working on a murder story?"

"When I first started in news, murder here was a big deal. Not anymore."

"What changed things?"

"Guns and drugs, mostly. I wrote a story once about how we rented prison space to other states. We were smarter, not tougher. Now we have a homicide every other day and I'm writing stories about overcrowded jails."

"Why is this murder getting so much attention?"

"The victim was a white woman. A middle-class professional just going about her business. Murdered in the middle of the day in the middle of downtown on the way to her car. Police suspect it's a stranger-to-stranger homicide, and that's still rare here. Most people are murdered by someone they know. The old this-type-of-thing-ain't-supposed-to-happen-here story."

"Is everybody in the newsroom so cynical?"

"Stephanie, if you really want to hear criticism of television news, listen to the people who work here. Every day someone sticks their finger down their throat over something they have to write. Follow me, I'll show you the edit rooms."

Andrea Kay Labore had the prettiest face in Minnesota, long and narrow, almost skeletal, with sharp features and soft skin that tanned well. But it was her eyes that made the face. They were big, brown, and outrageously beautiful—the kind of bedroom eyes that made men fell in love, even men who only saw her on television. Her hair was bold brunette, so rich in texture she could wear it long or short, or pull it behind her ears and put a rubber band in it—didn't matter, it always fell from her head like on a television commercial.

At the same time Rick Beanblossom was showing a new intern the edit rooms, Andrea Labore found herself with her own intern to educate.

"Hi, I'm Jeff. I'm beginning my internship today and I was told I'd be going out with you—I mean, working with you—today. Sorry." He was tall, boyish-looking. He'd need another ten years of aging before viewers would accept him as a reporter. He was nervous as hell.

Andrea popped a pair of pills into her mouth and chased them with a Diet Coke. She choked on his introduction. "Oh, okay. My name is Andrea." She stood and shook his hand. "I do have a story to shoot later, but I've been filling in at anchor. Charleen just had a baby."

"I've been watching you. On TV, I mean."

"That's nice to hear. I'll show you around a little before we go out on our shoot."

Among the new hires Clancy Communications brought to Channel 7 had been Andrea Labore, a slender, athletic young woman, just a few pounds short of skinny. She escaped by an inch being tagged flat. It was the kind of figure fashion loved, and Andrea loved fashion. Every two weeks clothes ate up half her paycheck. Some weeks her wardrobe pocketed the whole thing. This was her one guilt trip. She tried to justify her spending the way other women in the business did: she had to dress for television. But she worried she was only trying to dress up a modest upbringing.

Andrea was born and raised on Minnesota's Iron Range, where ice hockey rules, where people still talk about that strange Zimmerman boy who ran off to New York City and changed his name to Bob Dylan. Life on the range is rough, the future bleak. When America's auto and steel industries went into decline, Northern Minnesota's economy collapsed. Iron ore stayed in the ground. Iron men lost their jobs. A pit of despair in an otherwise prosperous state.

Come winter on the range Andrea didn't go outdoors for the freezing sports. Swimming was her thing. Swimming was the best exercise known to woman. Gliding unimpeded through water shaped her body and mind in a way that became near-spiritual to her, as if she had been baptized in a pool of chlorine. She won a combination academic/athletic scholarship to the University of Minnesota in Minneapolis, and like many of its young people Andrea Labore left the Iron Range, never to return.

Unsure of what she wanted to do with her life, she considered majoring in journalism until a professor she trusted convinced her that journalism school was a waste of time. "Get a good liberal arts education," he told her. "You'll be much more valuable to a newsroom." She graduated with honors, earning a bachelor's degree in political science with a minor in English literature. She picked up a teaching certificate for good measure.

But it wasn't a career in news, education, or politics Andrea chose upon graduating. About the time the brown-eyed beauty from the Iron Range was being handed her diploma, the city of Minneapolis hired a new and progressive police chief to upgrade its aging and conservative police force. This new chief made the recruitment of women and minorities a high priority. Andrea joined up, winning a top spot in the chief's first graduating class. With a badge, a blue uniform, and a gun she went to work in a squad car patrolling the high-crime district of North Minneapolis.

One night in late autumn when the leaves are off the trees and the Minnesota air is bitter with frost, Andrea Labore shot and killed a man. She'd been a cop less than two years. On a routine burglary call she stepped from her squad, drew her service revolver, and ordered the suspect to freeze. He pointed a gun at her. She squeezed the trigger, just once. Once was all it took. The suspect collapsed in the sodden leaves along the gutter. He was pronounced dead on arrival at North Memorial Hospital.

Internal affairs ruled the shooting justified. The chief of police pinned a medal to her uniform. The local media made much of the beautiful and courageous policewoman. But the shooting wouldn't go away, and four months later Andrea Labore resigned. With the money she'd saved she enrolled in Northwestern University's prestigious Medill School of Journalism.

As a rule, large-market stations require small-market experience: Fargo, Duluth, Green Bay, places like that. Andrea was fortunate. She was exactly the type of reporter Clancy was looking for when they bought into the Upper Midwest market.

Andrea walked the nervous young intern up to the news set. It's what all visitors want to see when they tour the newsroom. The studio lights being off gave the set a dull, shadowy appearance, unlike the bright, glitzy set viewers saw at home. "This is where I sit when I anchor."

"It's a different view from up here."

"That's the control room over there, and the weather center is behind those computer gadgets."

As she spoke those words, the Weatherman passed in front of those gadgets. He stopped, charts in hand, and punched some pertinent numbers into a character generator. He kept his back to them. They said nothing. Then he disappeared behind the set, his head in a cloud.

"Was that him?" Jeff asked, knowing the answer.

"Yes, that was him. I'd introduce you, but he's been kind of quiet since the tornado. The pilot and photographer killed were close friends of his."

Jeff turned his attention back to the studio. "So all you have to do is look into the camera and read your script?"

"Each camera has a TelePrompTer," Andrea explained. "The script is taped together into one long sheet, and as it rolls along a belt it's projected onto a glass plate right in front of the camera lens, so you can read the script while staring right into the camera. The script is too close to the lens to come into focus, so people at home can't see the lettering. There's never more than four words per line. That's to reduce eye movement. See this pedal on the floor? You push that to control how fast you want the script to roll by."

"Is anchoring hard to do?"

"It is at first, but there are tricks you can learn. I've been told to pick up the pace a little, so I'm working with a consultant now. But my research is good."

"You research your own stories, then?"

"Oh, no. Research is the surveys they do to see how much the audience likes you. It's important because

Minneapolis–St. Paul is a major television market. Our signal goes out to more than half of Minnesota, plus western Wisconsin. Some people with cable or satellite dishes even watch us in North and South Dakota and Iowa. We do four shows, plus updates. We have a noon show, then in the evening we go on at five o'clock, six, and the most important show is at ten o'clock."

"So this is a good place to work?" Jeff asked.

"Yes, it's really good now. Our ratings are way up. We're fighting to be number one."

"Well, I'm looking forward to it."

"Later I'll show you how to do a stand-up. In this business that's the most important thing."

"I want to learn as much as I can. Is it okay if I sit in the anchor chair for a minute?"

Andrea Labore smiled that winning smile viewers always fall in love with. The young man took a seat in the anchor chair that belonged to Ron Shea. The empty chair next to him belonged to Charleen Barington. Everybody who goes into television news wants eventually to sit in the anchor chair and read the news; those who say they don't are lying through their glistening white teeth. But that electrifying chair is reserved for those special few with just the right combination of arrogance, killer communication skills, and dumb luck. Andrea was well aware of what was required, and she was up for the challenge. She knew in her heart that anchor chair would one day belong to her.

THE KIDNAPPING

The welcome warmth of June became the sweltering heat of July. The weather topped 90° every day. Rick Beanblossom stood on the high bluff of Pioneer Park overlooking his hometown of Stillwater. The vista seemed straight out of a Rockwell painting, a Tom Sawyer village on the St. Croix River. An old lift bridge was strung like an iron necklace across the heart of this scenic valley. But the view was deceptive: nineteenth-century charm with twenty-first-century problems.

There is a point where growth and development become blight and destruction. Stillwater was a village split in two. What was once a river town taken to sleep after the lumber barons packed up and left was now, a century later, waking up a tony eastern suburb where people from St. Paul and Minneapolis tried to escape the incipient descent into urban hell. The tornado had spared the town, but progress was not so generous. A heated debate developed between those who demanded growth and those who cried enough. It was one of the few stories Rick had been able to capture for television with the same impact as in print.

You can't go home again ... or so they say. Rick Beanblossom knew that all too well. He didn't live here anymore. Too many ghosts resided in Stillwater. And he was the biggest spook of them all, haunting up and down steep streets behind a mask hiding hideous burn scars unmatched in any horror movie. He was once handsome, popular, and fleet of foot. He rode in a convertible during the homecoming parade, and the town cheered for him as he ran for touchdowns that night. Because of the luck of the draw, he went over there while others stayed home enjoying the best years of their lives ... college, sex, marriage, and children with incredibly beautiful young women ... high-school sweethearts whose names he could still rattle off.

But over the years their names had changed, and now he wouldn't recognize their faces any more than they would recognize his. On storefronts below, flags still fluttered in the valley wind for the Fourth of July celebrations. "Take the American flag, old hometown, and shove it up your ass."

The year before, there was another news story in this storybook town. A nightmare. Though it never became part of the big-city-versus-small-town debate, it was always there, just beneath the surface. It was the kidnapping of Harlan Wakefield.

Twelve-year-old Harlan Wakefield and his identical twin brother, Keenan, were popular town boys with a paper route. Much of their popularity stemmed from their freakish intellect. Driven to academic perfection by forceful parents, they were already testing out of high school and preparing for college. Their remarkable talents had been displayed on local TV news and talk shows. The last leg of their paper route was on a road that took them a mile out of town, north into the country. Even in the winter, despite the weather, they rode their mountain bikes. They loved their paper route. These were the only hours of the day when they were freed from learning, freed from mother and father and allowed to be normal boys.

One morning in late spring Keenan Wakefield rode home from the paper route alone. He was scratched and filthy. He was in shock. Through fright and tears he told his mother and father a tale as frightening as any story coming out of the worst cities.

They were heading home after delivering their last paper. A big man, as Keenan described him, stepped out of the woods with a handgun. He was wearing a ski mask. He ordered Harlan off his bike and took him by the arm. He ordered Keenan to go. The boy started to ride away, but he looked back at his brother. The man saw him and fired a shot into the air. Keenan rode home for help.

The sheriff's department found Harlan's bicycle on the side of the road. They also found a spent bullet that had recently been fired. A farmer along the route reported a gun stolen from his car. Within hours a massive search was launched. The FBI was called in. Helicopters were put into the air. An all-points bulletin was issued for a "big man with a ski mask." In the days to come even the National Guard was called out to sweep miles of woodland in the St. Croix Valley. It became the largest manhunt in state history.

Dramatic headlines were splashed across the front pages of every daily newspaper in the state. Live television reports from Stillwater dominated the news at five, six, and ten p.m. Harlan Wakefield's parents were as smart as their children. They were not about to become victims of the press, so they took control. They said they wanted their son back, or at least found, and they would use the media to get it done. In the days and weeks that followed they became totally accessible. Any reporter from anywhere was given almost anything he or she wanted. They endured a total lack of privacy and tolerated the most personal questions imaginable to keep their son's name in the news. One reporter even asked them if they or any other family member had kidnapped Harlan. They kept their poise and answered no.

Rick Beanblossom was one of the people the family befriended. His initial conversations with them were done over the phone. Because he was a Stillwater boy himself, they took to him, and time after time reporters at Channel 7 News, via the new masked producer, came up with fresh angles. The Wakefields visited the station one day. He had warned them about his mask. He joked how since the kidnapping he'd been stopped and questioned four different times. He soon felt comfortable enough to visit them at their home.

One person Rick Beanblossom was never allowed to talk with was Keenan Wakefield, Harlan's twin. He too had become a victim of the crime. The morning after the abduction Keenan was missing from his bed. The nightmare seemed endless. Now Keenan's name was added to the search. But this search lasted only a couple of hours. Keenan was found crawling out of the woods down by the river, still in shock. Channel 7 news photographer Dave Cadieux was with the search party that found him. He recorded on videotape the frantic crying and stammering of a lost boy who had been wandering through the woods in the dark looking for his twin brother. It was the most gut-wrenching video shown on television during the entire ordeal. After that his parents put Keenan off limits even to police.

The FBI put together a task force of local, state, and federal officials that at one time numbered more than a hundred full-time investigators. For months bogus sightings of Harlan Wakefield were reported throughout the Midwest. But the boy genius was never found, and nobody was ever arrested.

The Wakefield family kept their boy's name in the news almost daily for six months. In manipulating the media they became as proficient as the best public relations firms. They went on talk shows. They threw benefits against scenic backdrops to attract television. It seemed they announced an anniversary of the kidnapping every thirty days. People kept sending them money, so a trust fund was established for Keenan. Thousands of dollars in donations poured in. But as the months dragged by and Harlan remained missing, the task force dwindled and the press moved on. In local newsrooms the Wakefields became a pain in the ass. Cruel jokes were made about the next Harlan Wakefield staged media event: "Will Elvis be there?"

Rick Beanblossom moved on to other stories too, but he kept his Wakefield file close at hand. He still called on the family every now and then. It had been over a year since the kidnapping. Most of his visits, like the one today, were spent listening to complaints about the media and their lack of coverage and concern. He told the family a fat man arrested in Racine, Wisconsin, was no longer a suspect in their son's disappearance. They were not surprised. Rick wrote them another check for Keenan's trust fund and then left.

A squad car pulled into the parking lot at Pioneer Park. The officer stared long and hard at the man in the mask. He shut off the engine and radioed in.

Rick Beanblossom shook his head and sighed. He hated hot weather. The sweat glands in his head were destroyed by the napalm. This made him acutely aware of changes in the weather. His long-sleeve shirt was sticking to his back. He seldom wore short sleeves.

The cop removed his sunglasses and sauntered down

the lawn, thumbs under his gun belt. Rick slowly reached for his wallet. Years of experience had established a procedure.

In the first months, following his medical release and honorable discharge, he wore a clear plastic mask, much like a hockey goalie. It was more to protect him from infection and to stem the scarring than to hide his face. He seldom ventured out then, mostly down to the burn center at Ramsey Medical Center in St. Paul. Winter wasn't bad. He read and slept. He watched a lot of television. But after a year in a hospital and another year hiding indoors a decision had to be made with the advent of spring—go out and rejoin the world or live life as a mole. The clear plastic mask was traded in for the blue cotton pullover, the most attractive, least offensive mask he could find. A comic book hero. He swore off television. Books would be his entertainment, newspapers and news magazines his diversions. His spring, summer, and fall would be spent enjoying the great outdoors he loved as a boy. But on his first day out alone he ran into the face of reality.

It was at a park in St. Paul up the bluff from the medical center. The view over the city was incredible—Stillwater times ten. On one hill stood the magnificent Cathedral of St. Paul with its huge green dome holding a cross to heaven. Another hill supported the elegant State Capital Building, resplendent in white Georgia marble. The sun was shining bright over this proud little city. First spring-day-without-a-jacket weather. The Mississippi River was raging with snow melt. The breeze was so fresh and cool it was hard for Rick to remember the hellish heat of Vietnam. He stood on a retaining wall, hands in pockets, forgetting for the moment there was anything different about him. He got as caught up in the optimism of spring as anybody that day.

There were two of them. They came up behind him. They shouted not to move and he almost fell off the wall. One big cop kept his palm on his gun. The other cop told him to put his hands in the air. His stuttering rendered him speechless. His eyes washed over with unexplained guilt. They ordered him down from the wall and up against it. "Feet spread!" He mumbled and stammered but the words would not come. Despite the uncommon valor of war he was now a cruelly deformed puppy. Their questions went unanswered. He clung, shaking, to his new mask. The park, which at first seemed deserted, now was filled with people stopping to watch. A woman's nasty little dog was barking at him. The cops handcuffed him and led him to the squad car. A man on the sidewalk remarked about the burglaries.

At the booking center they pulled the mask from his head. He avoided their eyes. They gasped in horror. He tried to bury his head between his knees. He was three hours in the county jail before the incident was resolved. An old detective with a nasty smoker's cough came into his cell, apologized profusely. Gave him a ride home. He was another year in his house before he again ventured out alone.

"What are we doing today, fella?" the Stillwater cop asked.

"My name is Rick Beanblossom, Officer. I'm a burn victim. Vietnam." He handed the young cop his calling cards, one at a time. "Here's my driver's license." After months of hassle and legal threats he'd been allowed to be photographed wearing his mask. The code number under Restrictions labeled him handicapped. "I work at Channel 7 News. Here's my press card. I'm also a volunteer at the Ramsey Burn Center. Here's my hospital pass." His speech was flawless. Plain, but firm.

"Sounds like you've been through this before."

"Often."

"Then you understand why I have to ask. We got a call."

"I understand."

"My oldest brother played football with a Beanblossom. I remember watching him when I was a kid. Was that you?"

"What's your brother's name?"

"His name was John Curran."

"Was?"

"He was killed in a car accident. It's been ten years now."

"I'm sorry to hear that. I do remember him. Nice guy."

"Yes, he was. Do you still follow Pony football?"

"I glance at the scores. I live in Minneapolis now. Don't get down here much."

The young cop returned Rick's plastic identity. "Listen,

Rick, I'm sorry about this. I'm off duty in an hour. Do you want to grab a cold one down at Cat Ballou's?"

"I'm going to start back, but thanks anyway."

"Sure. Maybe some other time." He put his sunglasses back on and looked down at the village with a pride unique to small-town policemen. Then he gazed into the blazing sky. "It's going to be another scorcher, Rick. No sleep tonight."

"No, it's going to rain tonight," Rick told him. "Don't you watch Channel 7? Heavy rains. Four inches or more. The Weatherman said so."

THE RAIN

It had just begun to rain when Sky High News signed off that night at ten-thirty. Andrea Labore threw it to the new sportscaster, who reminded viewers the Twins were in extra innings. Anchorman Ron Shea tossed it over to Dixon Bell in the weather center.

The Weatherman told viewers to be thankful for a domed stadium. He stood beside the radar screen and explained. Mild winter—wild summer. This was the most explosive type of weather situation the five-state area had faced in years. Warm air from the south was feeding these storms, and there were no cold fronts from the north to sweep them out. The front moving through tonight had stalled, setting up a barrier thunderstorms could not penetrate. "Here we go again, folks," said Dixon Bell. "Better late than never. The National Weather Service has just issued a severe thunderstorm warning that does include the Twin Cities. You should expect strong, damaging winds and even more rain than the four inches I forecast earlier. Maybe six inches or more. And that spells flash flooding."

On this particular night the Channel 7 weatherman was slightly unnerved, though viewers may not have noticed it. Just before he had gone on the air, the phone rang in the weather center. It was dateline, the number known only to family, friends, and employees. Dixon Bell picked it up.

"I'm gonna ice you, Weatherman." It was a high, raspy voice, a feminine man, or a woman impersonating a man. Also a pisspoor attempt at a southern accent.

"I'm gonna ice you, Weatherman," the voice said again. Then he hung up.

Dixon Bell had heard that voice once before, the day of the tornado. Or was it the day before the tornado? He couldn't remember. *What's he got against me? I'm just a local-yokel weatherman from the southern end of the river.*

Dixon Graham Bell was raised in a shotgun house above the railroad tracks that run above the river in Vicksburg, Mississippi. They call them shotgun houses because the rooms are built one behind the other, so a shot fired through the front door will sail straight out the back door. Vicksburg stands at the southern tip of the Delta, built on thirteen hills where the Yazoo River flows into the Mississippi. Indians called the Mississippi River "Father of Waters." They called the Yazoo "River of Death." It was in these thirteen hills above these two converging rivers that the future weatherman spent his boyhood, staring into the thunderheads, trying to imagine the fury of the tornado that had struck this town and got his life off to such a tragic start.

After the Eden Prairie tornado, the second tornado in his life, questions arose about the lack of warning from the National Weather Service. Officials confirmed that at least four sirens in storm areas didn't go off. They still hadn't located the reasons for the failures. Dixon Bell stated publicly that the National Weather Service was a technology museum, complaining that in Minnesota, as in some other states, the Weather Service does not issue a tornado warning until a person actually sights one. The first two people to sight the Eden Prairie tornado were dead. So camps seemed evenly divided between those who wanted to shake the Weatherman's hand and tell him what a wonderful thing he did and those who wanted to blame him for the tragedy.

They had buried Bob Buckridge and Kitt Karson at Fort Snelling National Cemetery. Military honors all around. But right after the funeral the Weatherman had a run-in with Rick Beanblossom. *The masked asshole,* Dixon Bell called him.

"Why did you tell him to switch positions?"

"I directed him to a safe position."

"You threw him right in the path of that tornado. Somehow you knew it was coming."

"That's ridiculous. He was out of harm's way. After that, he made the decisions."

"You knew damn well what he'd do once he saw that thing."

"Get off my back, Beanblossom, and take your grieving act somewhere else. Buckridge didn't care for you any more than I do."

The masked newsman shouted at the Weatherman as he walked away. "Why don't you go back to Mississippi, or Tennessee, or wherever the hell it is you came from."

That was the most insulting thing said, that Dixon Bell didn't belong.

Andrea Labore was another story. Too often the woman of a man's dreams turns into the nightmare that destroys his life. Dixon Bell knew in his heart that when the end came his last thought on this earth would be of a woman. If not Andrea, or Lisa, it would be of another brown-eyed beauty down the road—a woman he loved with all of his heart but who never loved him back.

It was difficult to work with Andrea. A few weeks back, before the tornado, he asked her out for the first time. She told him no. As kind as she was, and she was kind, it was humiliating. He noted this humiliation in the diary he kept. It had taken him years to get over Lisa. He swore it would never happen again. And it didn't until Andrea Labore laid those big brown eyes on him.

"As our metro area continues to grow," the Weatherman told his viewers, "and our farmlands and wetlands are paved over, these heavy rains have nowhere to go but into the street." Dixon Bell threw it back to Ron Shea.

Then came big smiles from the anchors. The schlocky music kicked in. Balloons and confetti fell from the ceiling onto the news set, just like New Year's Eve. Ron Shea hoisted a bottle of champagne onto the desk and popped the cork. The credits rolled over all of this as the anchorman from Virginia looked into the camera and told the people of Minnesota, "Good night from the number-one-rated news show in the Twin Cities."

After the broadcast Andrea Labore hung around her desk. The celebration over the ratings book quickly wound down. She finished her glass of champagne, then popped a mint into her mouth. She called up Script on her computer and tapped out a banal thank-you letter to a fan. She thought about answering another, but it was difficult to concentrate. The news director had asked to see her in his office after the show. But Jack Napoleon was still on the phone.

She opened another letter. It was from a state legislator. He wrote how much he admired her work and asked if they might get together for a drink next time he was in town. A valuable news source, he promised. Andrea crumpled up the invitation and tossed it into the wastebasket. Television 101—never answer people who want to meet you, and never date cops or politicians.

She looked over at the glassy office. The curtain was drawn. Butterflies fluttered in her stomach. What did he want at this hour? Other than that of a movie producer, perhaps, no job gives eager young men more control over the careers of ambitious and beautiful young women than that of a television news director.

Andrea Labore knew what she wanted: harder news. Since her arrival she had been assigned mostly puppy-dog stories. Good training, she was told. Every time the zoo got a new resident, Andrea got the call. She did stories about wounded eagles in a hospital for birds, and peregrine falcons living atop a Minneapolis skyscraper. She even did a piece about a pet cemetery. She swore if she had to do another animal story she'd put the beast in the ground herself.

Andrea watched co-workers turn out lamps and monitors and filter out of the newsroom. In the weather center across the way, radar screens tracked the storm clouds now stuck over the cities. The iridescent sheen they emitted cast an eerie pall over the darkening newsroom. She could make out the shadow of a large man moving across the weather center wall, and for a moment she got caught up in the spacey mood created by the high-tech gadgetry. Then news director Jack Napoleon emerged from his office in the glassy corner. He turned out lamps in the outer area and shut off the monitors. He retreated to his office without looking her way. The door was left slightly ajar. The ceiling light went out, leaving only the translucent light of a television set peeking out at her.

Up at the assignment desk the overnight dispatcher retreated to his shack to listen to scanner chatter. She heard him radio the photographers in their vans asking them to watch for flooding, shoot tape. Then the lights went out there too, leaving only a lamp to read by.

Andrea pulled tissues from her Boutique box and wiped the perspiration from her palms. She put the tissues to her mouth and spit out the mint. She shut down her computer, stood, swung her purse over her shoulder in a done-for-the-day manner, and searched the newsroom one more time. It was all but empty now. She took a deep breath, walked with purpose to the news director's office, and pushed open the door, purposely leaving it open.

"Close the door," he told her.

Andrea palmed the door closed. Outside the skyscraper's top-floor windows the two cities were being pounded with rain.

He was seated on his office couch as if he were at home, his hands clasped behind his head, his feet up on a coffee table, watching a console television set with a VCR stacked atop it. He was a handsome man. His sleeves were rolled up, exposing muscular arms thick with hair. Black slacks were stretched tight across his legs, accenting his height. At thirty years old he did not look like an ex-college athlete, but more like a former class president. Jack Napoleon enjoyed controlling people, not scoreboards.

Andrea couldn't see what he was watching, but she heard some moaning and groaning and she assumed it was a steamy love scene from a movie on videotape.

On the wall above the overstuffed couch hung a large oil painting of Jesus Christ rising through the clouds, ascending into heaven, his palms outstretched, blessing the poor souls he was leaving below. On a wall in the corner was a small crucifix. A white Bible lay on the desk beside the picture of his wife and two children. It seemed more like the office of a Baptist minister than that of a news director. Jack Napoleon was a born-again Christian.

He wasn't the first news director Clancy Communications had dropped into the Sky High newsroom, but he was the most bizarre. When he arrived at Channel 7 Napoleon shocked believers and nonbelievers alike by making his religious beliefs known at his first staff meeting. He wanted it understood the new Sky High News was to reflect Christian values, with heavy emphasis on community involvement and the family. He reminded them that if they all worked to be better Christians they would be a better newsroom. At that bit of heavenly advice, one staff member raised his hand and caustically asked if the Jews in the newsroom could be excused from becoming better Christians and just concentrate on becoming better reporters. There was little preaching after that, but his message was Christian clear.

"That was really a good stand-up you did yesterday, Andrea."

"Thank you. I'm still concerned about my anchor work."

"It's coming along well. You're getting there. And your research is good."

"I'd like to do more anchoring."

"Charleen will be back soon. Ratings always go up after an anchor comes back from maternity leave. We're going to begin promoting her return next week. Got some really cute stuff of her and the baby."

It was not the answer she had hoped for. Andrea had a gnawing feeling in the pit of her stomach that she'd be in a much stronger position if she were married and knocked up. They fell silent. He kept his eyes glued to the TV screen. She watched the cold rain on the hot earth. Their transparent images were mirrored in the storm. Great splashing drops smeared the glass.

The moaning and groaning coming from the television set was growing intense and loud. Andrea walked over to the couch and stood beside him. "My God, what are you watching?"

"Porn," he told her, matter-of-factly.

Indeed, it met all of her standards for obscene, but Andrea Labore couldn't take her eyes off the coupling. "Why?"

"Because I believe that we are living in the last days before the start of the tribulation, and the entree of the Antichrist."

Andrea didn't know what the hell that meant, but it sounded so god-awful that she almost burst out laughing.

"People are getting hurt by this," Napoleon went on. "Pornography is a multi-billion-dollar industry. Let's find out how it works. Who's behind it? Where does the money come from? An investigative piece. Maybe even roll it into a one-hour documentary after it airs on our news. Are you interested?"

The cop-turned-reporter didn't waste words. "No, not in the least."

Jack Napoleon shrugged his wide shoulders. "Maybe I'll give it to Beanblossom."

"He won't do it. He probably watches this stuff."

Then for one frightening moment Napoleon's breathing became as loud as the breathing on the videotape. He caught his breath and relaxed. "This weather plays hell with my asthma." He wiped the water from his eyes. "You don't like him, do you?"

"Rick? It's he who doesn't like me. He thinks I'm a bimbo."

The easiest way to hurt Andrea Labore was to call her a bimbo, a Barbie doll. In college a drunken frat boy once joked that if you dropped Andrea's pants you'd find a smooth plastic crotch. She thought it was the cruelest thing ever said about her. On the police force the boys often referred to her as the Barbie doll in the badge. Then with television news credentials and the most beautiful face in town came an immediate stigma. Bimbo! She fought this unfairness daily.

Thunder broke outside and startled her. City lights below were disappearing in the wind and rain.

Napoleon glanced over at the window. "Dixon Bell has been on top of this storm for twenty-four hours. At six o'clock the other stations were still predicting sprinkles. God, what a find he's turned out to be. I'm from Chicago. I know the importance of the weather."

"Yes, Dixon's good."

"I heard he asked you out."

Andrea rubbed a chill from her arms. "It was no big deal."

The news director turned his attention back to the noisy couple on the TV screen. They changed positions and went back at it like Pavlovian dogs. "I looked into the record books. In the history of television this station had never been rated number one in this market. Now it is. Do you know why we're number one, Andrea?"

"Because of the tornado."

Napoleon enjoyed her wit. "No, Andrea. Because we

stress family values. We accentuate the positive. People tune in and see good news. If we tried to do hard news every day like the other stations, they'd kill us. But do you know what the other stations have that we don't have? Awards. They promote their awards. Sky High News has no awards. That's embarrassing. I'm looking for an award-winning investigative piece."

"This stuff is legal," Andrea reminded him, as the man in the video pulled out and ejaculated over the woman's belly and breasts. Disgusted, she turned her back to the television set and raised her voice a notch. "Jack, will you shut that stuff off. I thought you were a religious man. Do you have some other story in mind for me?"

He ignored her request. "You're a poli sci major. Tell me everything you know about Per Ellefson."

At last there was a break in the action. A couple in clothes appeared on the TV screen and exchanged some lifeless banter.

Andrea rattled off everything she'd seen and read about Ellefson. "He's a successful businessman running for governor. Wants the Republican nomination. Probably won't get it. The party has been taken over by the religious right." Napoleon flinched when she said that. Andrea enjoyed the shot. She took another. "Personally, I've never met a born-again Christian who wasn't a born-again hypocrite." Napoleon's face was turning red. "Ellefson's not one of them," Andrea went on. "Too moderate. He opposes abortion but also opposes the death penalty—a cause they're zealous about. He's tall and handsome, looks good on television. Of Norwegian descent. Married. I think he has two daughters. Latest polls show him beating all Democrats. His problem is getting the nomination. I wouldn't mind covering his campaign, at least through the primary. It'll give me some badly needed credibility. I think the stories I've been doing have been too soft."

The news director was biting his lip. His breathing was growing louder, either his asthma or his anger. Jack Napoleon eyed the woman standing over him. He regained some of his composure, then returned his attention to the TV screen.

Andrea, too, turned to watch. Had she pushed too hard? The couple with their clothes on soon had their clothes off. They joined another naked couple in front of a fireplace. Andrea Labore had never seen so much sucking and fucking in her entire life. By her own admission she had poor taste in men—the ugly curse of beautiful women. Her head was swimming with confusion and anger. The intense weather didn't help. Was she being forced to watch this stuff? She thought this was a form of sexual assault. He's as good a raping me.

As the men in the video worked their magic, fast and furious, the women began to scream with pleasure—primal screams of raw sex before the flames. Lightning lit up the room. With that bolt Andrea remembered that Jesus Christ, on his way to heaven, was looking over her shoulder. Her eyes fell on the door. She couldn't shake the haunting feeling that they were being watched, that some evil force in the newsroom knew what was going on.

Andrea started for the door. She was going to fling it open when Jack Napoleon finally spoke up, stopping her dead in her tracks.

"Yes, Per Ellefson would be a good assignment for you. You can move to the political beat next week. But you watch your mouth, Andrea," he warned with a malevolent voice. "I don't like uppity women. I won't have them working for me."

Andrea opened the office door and left the news director to his dirty videos.

The newsroom was dark but for the occasional flash of lightning. Police calls echoed over the assignment desk. Andrea's police instinct still told her something was amiss. Up across the news set the weather center appeared to be bathing in the dancing brilliance of the northern lights. Again she saw a shadow breeze across the wall. It wouldn't hurt to check on the storm before she ventured home.

But Andrea Labore found Weather Center 7 abandoned. Ghostly. There was no weatherman to explain the thunderstorms moving across the bright green radar screens, no meteorologist to interpret the red fluorescent numbers emanating from the chrome instruments. The glowing computers had only each other to converse with. The overnight man wouldn't arrive until midnight—another twenty minutes. A printer sprang to life. Andrea jumped.

She grabbed her heart. Strange, she thought, that Dixon Bell would leave his station in the middle of a storm. A bathroom break, perhaps; or maybe he had gone to the roof to measure the storm in his own special way. He was like that.

The new political reporter for Channel 7 filed her suspicions in the back of her mind. She noted the time. Then she started for the Sky High parking ramp, grateful she was parked in out of the weather.

"Three-ten Able. Metrodome Municipal Ramp. On the roof. Report of one down. We'll start ambulance."

It was just past midnight and raining so hard headlights couldn't cut it. Cloud-to-cloud lightning illuminated the tempest. Thunder was a bass-drum rumble. Lieutenant Donnell Redmond brought the unmarked squad car to a halt in a bumper-to-bumper crop of downtown traffic at the foot of the IDS Tower. The Twins had beaten the White Sox in extra innings. Fans fresh from the game sprinted from bar to bar. Cars snaked slowly through the flooding streets. The lights of Minneapolis blurred in the storm. The lieutenant had his window cracked open, allowing the weather to slip in and Captain Les Angelbeck's cigarette smoke to slip out. Redmond put up with it. They inched through traffic, talked, and listened to police calls in the rain.

"Car four, make twenty-one-seventeen Lyndale on a domestic assault. Husband, wife. He's beating her with something."

Like the windshield wipers, the two cops were working overtime. "When I made lieutenant I thought I finally had a nine-to-five job."

"Sorry, Donny. I was sure our boy would be there tonight." Angelbeck brushed ashes from his raincoat.

The street corner was turning swampy. Redmond, a tall, imposing man, arrested a mosquito and smashed it against his window. "That man we're after tonight ain't nothing but a glorified bookie anyway. Don't hardly seem worth the effort."

"Gambling here used to be restricted to sleazy kitchens off back alleys," said Angelbeck, reminiscing. "Now it's a two-billion-dollar concern and a whole new criminal division. Minnesota has more casinos than Atlantic City. We've had horse racing and dog racing. We've got pull tabs and lotteries. We've got riverboat gambling paddling up the Mississippi. We lead the nation in the number of dollars spent per person on gambling. What other scheme could politicians possibly devise to take from the poor and give to the rich, and tell them they're having fun while it's being done?"

"Cock fighting and pit bulls."

The old captain laughed. "That's what it's coming to." The rain intensified, pounding the car. Straight-line winds sent waves of water racing down the busy street. "Don't you own a raincoat?"

"All squads. Report any closed streets due to flooding. City works will be notified. All squads at O-fourteen."

They were moving again, slowly parting the waters. They rolled by Solid Gold, a high-priced strip joint. The doorman, torn umbrella in hand, was opening the door to a limousine.

"Yeah, I own a raincoat."

"And how long have you been living here now?"

"Almost twenty years." Donnell Redmond had come to Minnesota from Florida to play basketball. The university boasted it didn't recruit for four years, it recruited for forty. Despite the hyperbole, it was often true. They came, played, and then they stayed.

"I'd think by now you'd have learned to dress for the weather."

"I watched the weather," Redmond told him. "The man said chance of sprinkles. He didn't say nothing about monsoon season."

"What channel did you watch?"

"Five."

"See, there you go. Watch Channel 7. That guy is right on the money. Every day."

"Channel 7 is a white-ass conspiracy. They haven't had a black face on their news in two years. Just stuck-up, uptight, funky white bitches, hairdo white guys, and that big fat white weatherman with the baby face. You don't seriously watch them, do you?"

"They're number one now."

"I'd rather drown." He clobbered another mosquito on the dashboard.

Angelbeck coughed, then cleared his throat. "I'm old, Donny. We old people have to know the weather."

"Right, yeah. You watch the weather like a goddamn weatherman so you can dress right and not get the sniffles, then you blow two packs of smokes every day. That cough of yours ain't gettin' any better, raincoat or none."

"Speaking of raincoats and cigarettes, look at that billboard."

The tall lieutenant bent his head over the steering wheel. "Looks like our boy Splat Man got another one. Your hero, too."

Under bright lights above the street the Marlboro Man was riding through the rain. But his head had been blown off and his horse was bleeding profusely. They'd taken two hits: one fluorescent orange splat to the cowboy's face and a bright yellow splat to the horse's neck. In the copious rain the dripping paint took on the hue of surreal art.

They worked their way past the stadium and started for the freeway. Angry cops in black raincoats directed traffic. It was the seedy end of town: parking lots and vacant lots, railroad tracks and decaying shacks. The nasty weather only added to the gloom. Angelbeck glanced at the rearview mirror and saw a red blur of flashing lights leave the county medical center. The siren could barely be heard above the storm.

"Three-ten Able."

"Three-ten."

"Metrodome ramp. We need a supervisor on the roof. Cancel the ambulance. Call eleven-ten. Suspect is GOA."

Donnell Redmond hit the brakes. "Man, we just passed there."

"Turn around. Let's have a look."

To most people the police chatter that night was just routine mumbo jumbo, mostly weather-related. But to cops, newsrooms, and scanner freaks the message was as clear as the night was stormy. A supervisor was needed to seal the scene. Cancel the ambulance because the victim is dead. Eleven-ten was homicide. Suspect was gone on arrival.

Redmond raced the car in circles up the parking ramp. Water was already tumbling down the levels and spilling through the walls. He drove back into the torrential rains

on the blackened roof and parked next to the one-man
squad known as three-ten Able.

Les Angelbeck buttoned up his raincoat and threw his
cigarette at the weather. Donnell Redmond grabbed a
newspaper off the seat and draped it over his head. They
walked over to the patrolman and looked down at where
his flashlight shined. They had to shout to be heard over
the storm.

"Who called it in?"

"Anonymous caller. Hung up on the dispatcher," he
told them. "I bent down to check her. I could move her
head around with my pinky."

The victim was on her back, peering up at the wind and
rain, her innocent eyes not quite closed. "This girl's not
out of her teens," Angelbeck declared. "What's that uniform she's wearing?"

"Looks like a vendor," the patrolman answered. "There
was a Twins game tonight. I think they park free if they
park on the roof."

The newspaper Lieutenant Redmond held over his head
disintegrated. He threw the wads of worthless ink to the
floor and swore. "Bitchin' rain is washing everything
away, man."

Another Minneapolis squad pulled onto the roof of the
parking ramp. A supervisor arrived. There was little talk,
though they were all thinking the same thing. Soaked
with anger and drenched with frustration, Donnell
Redmond leaned into Les Angelbeck so tight the others
couldn't hear. "That's two of them in less than a month.
This kind of thing ain't supposed to happen here."

"Let's not jump to conclusions."

"C'mon, Captain, you gonna even suggest this wasn't
the same animal that did this?"

"It's not our case."

"Yeah, well, when this sicko gets tired of parking
ramps in Minneapolis and starts St. Paul, or Bloomington,
or some place like that, it's gonna be our case. You jive?"

"I jive." Angelbeck glanced up at the dark bulbs of the
ramp lights. "Find out if the storm took these lights out."
He stared down the street at the spooky orange glow of
the inflated Metrodome. Lightning broke over it. "Damn
indoor baseball. Game would have been canceled tonight."

A Channel 7 News van pulled slowly up to the roof. A Channel 4 car came right behind. A cop rushed down to stop them.

The collection of policemen was standing in water up to their ankles now. Purple streaks of motor oil circled their pant legs. Curtains of rain blew across the ramp.

"Man, we're gonna have to call Roto-Rooter in on this one."

Then the dead girl's body began to rise, slowly lifting off the concrete floor and floating before them as if on a rolling cloud. Her broken neck flopped backwards and her young face, frozen in fright, disappeared beneath the oily water.

THE STAR

Old Jesse was a black man who pushed a broom. The job paid him little, but the work was all that he knew. The long stone hallways were his home. The boys were his family.

It was said among those boys that Old Jesse had once killed a man. Nobody was sure of the circumstances, only Jesse himself. Rumor had it was a white man he killed in a fight over a black woman—back in the days before civil rights, when murder among blacks didn't count for much. But killing a white man had cost Jesse twenty-five years.

This was the peaceful part of the night. The boys were in their bunks. He could push his broom for an hour and not talk to a soul. As he worked his way down B-East he saw the boys had forgotten to turn off the television set in the day room. Channel 7 reran the local news at 1:00 A.M. Old Jesse stopped to watch. He needed a break. The fortress was like a brick oven. He turned up the sound, just a hair.

"It's a horrible feeling ... We come to work, and we don't even know if we're going to make it home. I just kept driving around the block ... What are my options? ... Where do I park?"

The janitor shook his head, sincerely sorry for the woman.

"Police officials," said a red-haired news lady, "are holding daily briefings for the press, calling the murders two separate investigations, while at the same time acknowledging the similarities. Tonight the Minneapolis chief of police was openly musing for our cameras."

"This is a head scratcher ... what can you tell people? If you say there are no similarities between this homicide

*and the other, you can assure people there isn't a serial
killer out there ... but that means there are two killers
out there. We're trying to find out if this is a copycat or
a serial situation, or just a coincidence."*

Terrible. Just terrible. Jesse turned off the TV set and
continued down the hallway. The old man stopped in
front of an open window and leaned his long-handled
broom against the wall. He wiped the sweat from his
brow with a dirty red brakeman's bandanna. It was so
quiet he could hear the ripple of the river. He put his face
to the bars, hoping for a cool breeze off the water.

The moon high above was like a street lamp that lit up
the entire valley, and to the east of this ghostly white
moon a star was rising in the sky that shined a little
brighter than all the others. This star bothered the old
man, because it had an ugly spark to it. Jesse didn't know
much about the night sky. When he was a boy in South
Carolina his granddaddy pointed out the southern stars.
When he came to Minnesota as a young man to work for
the railroad, he learned of the North Star and the Little
Dipper. They were easy to spot. But this star shone in the
east. Every night it climbed higher and higher in the valley sky, and then every day it would get hotter and hotter.
So Old Jesse called it the Electric Star.

He pulled his railroad watch from his pants pocket.
Time was getting on. He still had B-West to sweep, and
Segregation. Come morning he would take the bus all the
way to Edina to visit his granddaughter at the police station. The boys in the prison's wood shop had carved her
a billy club with her initials engraved.

Old Jesse put away his watch and picked up his broom.
Like a shepherd watching over his flock, he leaned on the
long handle as if it were a staff and stared again at the
Electric Star in a summer sky rich with stars. Sure was
bothersome. Then he turned his back to the wicked sparkle and pushed dust down the long, empty corridor. He
did not know it then, but the old shepherd was being
called on to kill again.

Rick Beanblossom saw the star from his balcony that
night. He knew little of astronomy. Maybe it was a
planet. If he remembered, he'd ask the Weatherman.

The Channel 7 news producer was relaxing in a patio chair, gazing east over Lake Calhoun. The air was stifling. Lovers were necking on the docks. The lonely and the healthy were walking the shoreline. City lights off the still water were intoxicating. Rick stole the last sip of wine, a Cabernet Sauvignon from California. He set the empty glass on the patio table, beside the bronze shaving kit and the lit candle.

The condominium behind him was high in the sky, high in cost, and high in style. A ridiculous lifestyle for a loner. But Rick Beanblossom had money. His guaranteed contract with Clancy Communications was a four-year deal. The Veterans Administration currently valued his charred face at eight hundred dollars a month.

The steam-bath air felt terrible, but air conditioning gave him a headache. He slid his hands under his mask and wiped away skin flakes the way normal people clean off dandruff. The bartender's vest hanging from his bare shoulders was wide open. A tattered pair of gym shorts kept him comfortable. Rick still prided himself on his athletic body. His bare feet were propped up on another chair. The rerun of the ten o'clock news was playing to an empty living room, the volume just loud enough to be heard out on the balcony.

"If it can happen at a baseball game, it can happen anywhere. You have this gnawing feeling that you are not safe. Any one of us could be one of those murdered women we see on television."

Rick Beanblossom had done a story that day about the quick reverse being pulled by city council members. The press had been led to believe that all security measures in the Metrodome ramp had been in working order the night of the murder. Any problems had been caused by the rain. But the Channel 7 newsman learned through police sources that the lights on the roof of the ramp had been turned off. The teenage girl who sold hot dogs at the baseball game was murdered in the dark. The politicians now giving the pretty speeches about increased security measures were the same ones who'd ordered half of the lights turned out on municipal ramps in order to save nickels and dimes. Suddenly, all over town new lights were being discovered in previously dark parking ramps.

"Are all these extra guards and new lights still going to be there six months from now? Yeah, I doubt it."

Rick also knew that the names of those two women strangled leaving their jobs would one day get lost among a hundred other names whose murders he'd written about, murders he couldn't keep straight anymore. As the hot summer simmered to a close, the parking ramp murders would be inched out of the newspapers, fade from television screens. Fresh angles would be hard to come by. Women wouldn't be any safer, they just wouldn't be reminded of it. That's the news business. He'd seen it all before. He thought about Harlan Wakefield and of all the hours he put into that story in an attempt to prove that a good journalist could solve a major crime. Now he was convinced the boy was dead and he doubted the body would ever be found. Crime had become a major issue in the governor's race.

"It wasn't that long ago that this was just a big farm town with agrarian values where everybody thought they knew everybody else. The sun has set on that city."

Back in the summer of 1973 *Time* magazine did a cover story on "The Good Life in Minnesota." If the American good life has survived anywhere in some intelligent equilibrium, it said, it may be in Minnesota. Minnesota's citizens are well educated, the article went on to tell the world. The high-school dropout rate is the nation's lowest. The crime rate is the third-lowest in America. After that fluff piece was published, the words "quality of life" became a part of the Minnesota vocabulary—the state's clarion call.

Rick Beanblossom believed that article was the worst thing that ever happened to his state. It was all downhill after that. He could hear Andrea Labore speaking in his living room: *"With the primary only three weeks away businessman Per Ellefson is campaigning hard as the pragmatic moderate who can best maintain Minnesota's quality of life. Unlike his opponents, he has resisted calling for a new death penalty law in the wake of the recent murders."*

Rick had some reading to do, but he put it off. He had a novel to work on. He put that off as well. He remembered long talks with Kitt Karson, the only man who'd ever come to visit him.

"I think she is the most beautiful American woman I have ever seen," the young Vietnamese photographer had told Rick.

"She's everything that's wrong with television news."

"No, Rick, I think she is everything that is right. I think maybe in your heart you like her too."

Rick Beanblossom was feeling his age. He had now lived longer without a face than he had with one. But it was another face he found himself dreaming of.

"With the Ellefson campaign, this is Andrea Labore for Sky High News, in Rochester."

Too much wine and too many memories. Time to send in the Marines. The veteran of the Vietnam War lifted the bronze shaving kit from the patio table. He set it on his lap and flipped open the lid. Shiny slivers of silver twinkled in the moonlight, reminding him of that Phantom jet flashing in the sun, racing towards him. He cleaned his muscular arm with alcohol and cotton from the kit. Then he tied off the veins with a rubber hose. He scooped the white powder out of the baggie with a teaspoon. He added water from an eyedropper, then held it over the candle flame. When it liquefied, he stuck a syringe into the solution and carefully filled the vial.

Rick Beanblossom raised the hypodermic needle to the Electric Star rising in the sky, forcing out the bubbles while holding it there like an offering. Its milky purity sparkled. He looked out over the prismatic waters of Lake Calhoun and began to sing. *"From the halls of Montezuma . . ."* His soft but bitter voice melted into the city noise and the city heat of the vanishing summer.

> *Admiration of the nation,*
> *We're the finest ever seen.*
> *And we glory in the title*
> *Of United States Marines.*

The masked Marine popped the needle under his skin and shot the heroin into his arm.

THE COLORS

The heat disappeared with the Labor Day weekend. The rains of September arrived. So did the primary election. He'd made it a close race, but Per Ellefson, whose campaign Andrea Labore had been assigned to cover, lost his bid for the Republican nomination for the office of governor. The party instead nominated a relatively unknown legislator who mouthed their right-wing ideology. In an eloquent concession speech the handsome Norwegian held his Viking chin high and thanked his supporters. Then he bowed out of politics, saying he was returning to the business of business.

The Democrats nominated their relatively unknown lieutenant governor. Polls taken after the election showed that despite the unpopularity of the Democrats, who had been soiled by a Pulitzer-Prize-winning scandal, Minnesota voters were not going to have anything to do with right-wing politics. The North Star State was likely to continue its long tradition of liberal politicians. By October the only things changing in Minnesota were the leaves.

Captain Les Angelbeck left the Twin Cities behind him. He cruised east on Interstate 94, past the corn fields and the wheat fields that led to St. Paul. Then the interstate dropped into the St. Croix Valley. He changed lanes and steered for the bridge to Wisconsin.

The deep blue sky was cloudless. The afternoon sun was bright and warm. He had his window open, and the clean, refreshing breeze carried the aroma of autumn—of football, pumpkins, and McIntosh apples. Looking at the hills around him, the police captain couldn't see the forest for the leaves. Wine-colored leaves. Fire-colored leaves. The Crayola-colored north country. Spectacular. He'd heard New England was achingly beautiful like this, but he wondered if even the fabled New England autumns could match the magnificent valley God had carved with the blade of the St. Croix River. The river had a clay bottom that made the water appear brownish. On bright sunny days it appeared gold. Les Angelbeck crossed over this golden border into Wisconsin and took the Hudson exit.

With western Wisconsin slowly becoming a part of the Minneapolis–St. Paul metropolitan area, whether they liked it or not, it was a courtesy for the Minnesota BCA to lend assistance to the small towns over there. Small towns with big-city problems. A fading billboard just off the exit advertised greyhound racing, only minutes from the Twin Cities. Where was Splat Man when he was really needed?

The Minnesota cop started down Hudson's main street. At the corner Dairy Queen he hung a sharp right onto Coulee Road and climbed the steep street into Birkmose Park. The view over the river valley was breathtaking. He coughed over his coat sleeve. Police and sheriff's cars lined the parking lot. The ubiquitous yellow tape strung from tree to tree was fluttering in the breeze, blending nicely with the autumn colors. Angelbeck climbed out of the state's car. He spat out a hacking cough, then reached for his Marlboros. He showed his badge to the nearest officer. "I'm Captain Angelbeck."

"The chief is down by the body, Captain. Just follow the path into the woods. Be careful, it's pretty steep."

The park was once a graveyard. When ancient Indians died, they were buried in huge mounds of dirt along with valuable gifts, like jewelry, tools, and weapons. Then the wild grass was left to grow over their final resting place. But they didn't rest long. When the white man came to the valley, most of the mounds were destroyed for their artifacts. Years later, the few Indian mounds that had survived were made into public parks. Still the desecration continued. In the summertime people could be seen grilling their burgers and brats atop the graves. They were also ideal for sunbathing and dirt bikes. Captain

Angelbeck passed by these Indian graves and started down a steep path that melted into the fabulous colors. He pushed tree branches away from his face.

The man the captain had been asked to help was dressed in a plaid shirt tucked into blue jeans over hiking boots. He wore no gun, no badge. He looked more like a retired lumberjack than a police chief. But gray-haired Talbert Haag was the kind of cop Les Angelbeck liked—quiet, competent, and unpretentious. "It's a pretty gruesome sight, Captain. I know you've probably seen it all before, but I grew up in Hudson. It's been a long time since we've had a homicide."

"Who found her?"

"A jogger. Works at 3M." He pointed into the trees. "Looks like whoever killed her was going to hide the body, then just gave up and walked away. Or got scared away. Her jacket got tossed into the woods. We found some ID in it."

"Any witnesses?"

"We're talking to the jogger back in the parking lot. He lives up the street. Said he saw her walking this direction with a man early this morning. He says it was just after dawn."

"And a beautiful dawn it was, too. I couldn't sleep, so I got up and watched it."

"Yeah, terrible thing to happen on such a gorgeous day. Take a look."

She was lying flat on her stomach, half off the path, her hands out before her as if in worship. Her head was twisted an odd way. Her ankles were in the woods, gold and russet leaves falling over them. Besides the twisted head, the first thing the police captain noticed was her hair. Even in this hideous state of death he could see that it was long and black with a natural sheen to it. But something was wrong. The hair was bunched up around her neck. Les Angelbeck knelt down and looked into her face.

It was Police Chief Haag who gave a moral voice to her death. "It's not bad enough he murders her, for God's sake, he strangles her with her own hair."

"Is she Oriental or something?" Angelbeck asked.

"American Indian, I think. She was going to college down in Madison."

The sunshine reflecting on the girl's hair gave her tortured face a noble melancholy. Les Angelbeck stared into that face, his cigarette burning down to his fingertips. It was the same way he had stared at that girl that night in the rain, as if his staring long and hard enough would make her talk to him.

"The ME in St. Paul is sending someone over for her," the chief told him. "We don't have the forensic facilities to handle something like this. Maybe you want to talk to the jogger."

Angelbeck flicked his cigarette butt into the woods. "Is the press here yet?"

"A guy from the town paper is up there asking questions. I imagine the TV people from the Cities are on their way."

They made their way back to the parking area in somber silence, their senses torn between the smell of death over the river and the special aroma of crunching leaves under their feet. Les Angelbeck was more troubled than he could ever remember. Only this wasn't trouble with his age or his health. This was that disturbing kind of trouble that hangs overhead like a storm cloud ready to burst.

"Mr. Shelander, this is Captain Angelbeck from the state police in Minnesota. Why don't you tell him what you told me."

The jogger was a young man who was losing his hair. His expensive track suit covered a nonathletic build fighting to stay slender. "Well, Captain, it's like I said—they were walking along the path, past the mounds there, nonchalant-like. Just talking. Watching the sun come up on the water. Then I saw them disappear into the woods down there. You know, you see a lot of kids go in there, but these two weren't kids, and it was awful early in the morning. It kept bothering me, so after breakfast I came back to check."

"What did he look like?" Angelbeck asked.

"Well, I wasn't all that close really, and I was jogging, but from the back he looked heavyset, with dark, curly hair."

"Might it have been another woman?"

Shelander raised his eyebrows. "You mean a woman dressed like a man? Well, I only saw him from the back. I mean, it's possible, but it would have to be a big woman. I mean, the general look, you know, was big and husky."

"Thank you, Mr. Shelander."

The two cops, almost seventy years of experience between them, huddled over a squad car. On the St. Croix River hundreds of boat slips, abandoned for the winter, were strung out like skeletons across the water. The afternoon sun off the golden river had the bright, playful look of a watercolor. A perfect autumn day, sacrilegiously spoiled.

"This is great," the chief remarked. "I've got an unsolved homicide on my hands and the only suspect looks kind of like a husky man or a big, ugly woman."

"It's not a whole lot of help, but it's something anyway."

Les Angelbeck could see them coming across the valley. They drove down the hill to the bridge, exceeding the speed limit, then crossed the river into Wisconsin. It was a Channel 7 News van. Not a half-mile behind was a big, lumbering Channel 5 satellite truck. Barnum & Bailey.

"The first thing they're going to want to know," Angelbeck told Chief Haag, "is if this murder could possibly be related to those parking ramp murders in Minneapolis this past summer. Tell them no. You don't see any connection. This victim probably knew her killer. It's very important they don't link these murders. You know how those people get. You don't need that kind of hysteria over here."

Talbert Haag was as agreeable as the weather. "Damn right we don't. It's been the best color in years. Tourism is way up. Now this."

"Tell them she was strangled, but don't mention her hair. And whatever you do, don't talk off the record. Reporters can't be trusted."

"You know best."

The old cop who really did know best wanted to be by himself. Les Angelbeck left the convention of investigators and the arriving media circus and walked the path up past the Indian mounds, the same path the killer had walked with his victim. The insects of summer were dead. The warm breeze in his face made breathing easy. The benign sun felt good on his skin. For the first time in a long time he did not feel like a sick old man. He felt alive again. One last case. That's all he wanted out of life these days. Just one last mouth-watering case.

The captain stopped beneath the last ancient Indian grave. He cupped his hands to his face and lit another cigarette. Then the Marlboro Man gazed off toward the western sky, toward the hills of St. Paul and the blue sky-scrapers of Minneapolis. He coughed into his fist. "All right, you son of a bitch, whoever you are . . . I've been expecting you."

When Dixon Bell arrived in the Twin Cities, television weather was a pretty frivolous affair. He thought this odd in a state where weather is considered a moral issue. Minnesotans are obsessed with their changing seasons.

At one TV station in St. Paul a short, obnoxious, bald man did happy weather. Among his antics were sun stick-ons with big smiling faces, and grumpy-faced clouds. To show what was happening in Canada he'd mount a foot-stool labeled "Canadian Mountie."

Another station specialized in Weatherettes. Over the years the pretty girls giving the highs and lows just kept coming and going. Some had high tits, some had low tits; it didn't really matter so long as a big pair was giving the weather.

For a whole generation the weatherman at Channel 7 had been the avuncular Andy Mack. But Andy grew old and stale. He could sometimes be heard wheezing on the air as he stood in front of a painted map and gave the temperature readings in obscure corners of America. "And in Grangeville, Idaho, today the temperature reached eighty-eight degrees. And down in Malvern, Arkansas, it was ninety-one degrees. And up in Caribou, Maine, they made it all the way up to eighty-two degrees. Hard to believe." On Friday nights Andy went interna-tional. "And in Bangkok, Thailand, this week it got up to a hundred and three degrees. Hard to believe."

Hard for Clancy Communications to believe. They knew this dinosaur had to be replaced, even on the cheap. So they brought in the weekend weatherman from their station in Memphis.

From his stormy experience on Memphis TV, Dixon Bell had learned plenty. He knew that when the news ended, most viewers could remember nothing about the weather report they had just seen. To the average viewer phrases like "high-pressure system" and "barometric pressure" were meaningless. And viewers didn't give a Tennessee Valley damn about what was happening in Canada or over the Rocky Mountains of Colorado. They wanted to know if it was going to rain on them tomorrow. Should they wear a raincoat? Viewers wanted an accurate, or at least a fairly accurate, prediction, that's all.

After moving to Minnesota Dixon Bell decided to change things. He would teach Midwesterners about their weather. He wrote in his diary: "The trick is to do it without talking down to the viewer, without costing the station too much money, and without taking up more than my allotted time."

For starters Dixon Bell insisted on being referred to on the air as a meteorologist, not a weatherman. He didn't need to be reminded that three-fourths of the weather blabbers on local TV stations have had no training in meteorology.

Without wearing it on his sleeve, the new meteorologist let it be known that he had been trained in the military and tested in war. With new computers, new radar, and more detailed maps he transformed the weather office into Weather Center 7. Using exciting three-dimensional computer graphics, he began to explain what each element of the weather was and how they were all related. He taught viewers how to read a radar, what the different colors meant. He threw out words like "shower activity" and "zero precipitation" and used words like "rain" and "no rain." Once in a while, when there was something significant in the sky, Dixon Bell would do his Sky High forecast from the roof of the IDS Tower. When the ratings began to climb, a consultant's research showed that people weren't tuning into the new Sky High News to watch the beautiful bimbos—they were tuning in to watch the Weatherman.

But there was a disturbing element in this consultant's research that nobody could explain, though at the time of the report nobody really cared. The data showed that a small core of viewers, mostly young women, were literally turned off by Dixon Bell. They didn't like him and they wouldn't watch him.

It was children who especially loved the new weatherman. He took the weather drawings the little kids would send him and put them on the air during his five o'clock show. Working with Minnesota's College of Natural Resources, he produced a children's series called "7 Laws of the Forest." Teachers ordered worksheets from Channel 7. Then every night for a week on the six o'clock news Dixon Bell would give a three-minute lesson on the laws of nature, using sharp graphics and some excellent videotape. One night he told how two-thirds of Minnesota's trees had been chopped down by the turn of the century, and that most of the trees in the state were second growth. Students watched and filled in their worksheets. Teachers sent the completed worksheets back to Channel 7 to be used in a drawing. The grand prize for the winning classroom was a Capricorn II electronic weather station valued at more than a thousand dollars.

The forest series was so popular, he did another like it. In "7 Laws of Water" he pointed out that 60 percent of Minnesota's wetlands had been drained or filled for farming or commercial development. Another series followed, "7 Laws of the Atmosphere," in which he chronicled the state's rise in air pollution and its harmful effects on wildlife. That report was followed by "7 Laws of the Night Sky." Dixon Bell enjoyed these series for children, but there was nothing about the job he loved more than visiting their classrooms—and that's what the Weatherman was doing on that perfect autumn day that was soiled by the murder of an American Indian girl on the brilliant banks of the St. Croix River.

Dixon Bell clapped his hands together and thundered away. "What is barometric pressure?"

A boy's hand shot into the air. "It's the pressure that the atmosphere, the air above, puts on the earth."

"And how is this pressure measured?"

"With a column of mercury."

"Why do we measure things with mercury? Quick . . . someone else?"

A girl raised her hand. "Because it's the heaviest of liquids."

"And what does the average barometric pressure keep that mercury at?"

"About thirty inches," she answered.

"All together," the Weatherman said. "What happens when the barometer goes up?"

"Good weather," the class answered.

"And when the barometric pressure goes down?"

"Bad weather," they told him. The children were getting into it.

"Wonderful." He pointed out the window. "You pass with flying colors. Give yourselves a big round of applause."

The classroom broke into happy clapping. It was Sister Theresa's sixth-grade class at the Cathedral Elementary School in St. Paul. Bright sunshine was streaming through the open windows. The green domes of the Cathedral of St. Paul loomed directly overhead. The students' uniforms were clean and pressed and as blue as the sky. Their little round faces were as sunny as the day. Two weeks of planning had gone into the visit by the Channel 7 weatherman. Sketches of the changing seasons lined the room. Posters from the "7 Laws" series hung on the wall. The kids had drawn their own charts, made their own forecasts. A gifted group. Dixon Bell envied them. While he examined their work, his thoughts drifted back to some of the deprived classrooms he'd visited in the Delta region of his native Mississippi.

"Okay, now, Sister Theresa tells me that y'all have written some papers for me to hear. Who wants to go first?" Every hand in the classroom was in the air. "All right, let's start with this good-looking guy right up front. Stand up and tell me your name."

The boy had blond hair with a neat cut to it. "My name is Kerry Anderson." He was skinny and shy. His uniform hung on him.

"What would a Minnesota classroom be without an Anderson? What are you going to tell us about, Kerry?"

"My paper is called 'Extremes.'" He took a deep breath. He was extremely nervous. His voice shivered as he read. "'In Minnesota weird weather is the rule, not the exception. The Twin Cities of St. Paul and Minneapolis has more weather extremes on the average than any other city on earth, except maybe cities in Siberia and Mongolia. In the summers in Minnesota it can get up to a hundred and ten degrees, and in the winter it gets to forty below zero. The hottest day in Minnesota history was in

Moorhead on July 6, 1936, when it got all the way up to one hundred and fourteen degrees. The coldest day ever in Minnesota was on February 16, in 1903, when on Leech Lake up north it went down to fifty-nine degrees below zero.' "

"And that was without the windchill," Dixon Bell reminded him. "What is windchill, Kerry?"

The boy looked puzzled. "Ah ... that's when the wind is chilly?"

"It's a little more than that, son. Windchill is the power of the wind to cool your body. The windchill factor was developed by scientists in Antarctica doing research on the effects of cold weather on human skin. For example, if you have an actual temperature reading of twenty degrees below zero, and the wind is blowing at twenty miles per hour, then your body will be feeling a cold, a windchill, equal to sixty-seven degrees below zero. Those kind of temperatures are not uncommon during a Minnesota winter. Any time the windchill is more than fifty below zero, exposed flesh can freeze in one minute. So remember, on cold days always bundle up in layers."

More hands shot up in the air. "Let's hear from one of these pretty girls."

"My name is Marilyn Stokowski, and my paper is called 'The National Weather Service.' " She read with ease and clarity. " 'In 1844 Samuel Morse invented the telegraph. With this invention people in one town could tell people in the next town what kind of weather was coming their way. In 1849 the first official weather report was sent by telegraph in the United States. The United States started a weather service in 1870 as a part of the Army Signal Service. Then in 1890 congress organized a Weather Bureau and put it in the Department of Agriculture. President Franklin Roosevelt transferred the bureau to the Department of Commerce in 1940. It got renamed the National Weather Service in 1970. The central office is in Camp Springs, Maryland, and it has over two hundred weather stations across America, and twelve thousand volunteers throughout the country who help gather weather data.' "

Dixon Bell walked to the window as the girl continued her reading. That morning he'd watched steam rise off the river. A high pressure system had brought seventy-degree weather and lots of sunshine. The barometric pressure was near 30.70 and rising. From the slight rustle of the falling leaves he put the wind speed at five miles per hour. The vivid colors of the Midwest fascinated the Weatherman. The autumn splendor was as intoxicating as a thunderstorm. At the foot of the cathedral the garden roses were in bloom and bumblebees foraged on the fall flowers. Squirrels gathered acorns. Above the cross atop the great dome gaggles of geese were heading south. Cold weather was less than two weeks away.

"I'm gonna ice you, Weatherman." Dixon Bell shivered. He'd called again.

" 'The National Weather Service,' " the girl continued, " 'also operates the Severe Storms Forecast Center in Kansas City, Missouri, and the National Hurricane Center in Miami, Florida. They're supposed to warn us about severe weather.' " Then Marilyn lowered her paper to ask an interesting question. "Mr. Bell, how come they didn't warn us about the tornado?"

He was staring out the window, and at first the class thought he wasn't paying attention. But the Weatherman turned, his back to the church. "The tornado was an act of God. It wasn't the fault of the National Weather Service."

"But you predicted it was coming," argued the girl.

"I don't predict the weather . . . I read the weather. I read the signs, that's all."

"Shouldn't the weather service be able to read the signs?"

Dixon Bell's face turned grim. He chose his words carefully. "Our National Weather Service is in trouble," he explained. "They're supposed to be undergoing a major modernization, but it's ten years behind schedule and a billion dollars over budget. Meanwhile, their forecasters have to rely on radar and computers that are so old some of them are breaking down and falling apart. This is leaving parts of the country with no radar or satellite coverage at all. In the United States last year there were ten thousand severe thunderstorms, five thousand serious floods, and more than one thousand tornadoes—more natural disaster than in any other country on earth. Yet the Europeans are light years ahead of us when it comes to forecasting the weather."

The kids were frightened. It was perhaps too much for them to understand.

To lighten the mood Sister Theresa asked, "How did you become a weatherman?"

"I became a meteorologist in the Air Force. I received much of my training at the Air Force Geophysics Laboratory at Hanscom Air Force Base in Massachusetts. Then I was sent overseas to Vietnam, where there was a war going on and it was very important to know the weather."

"How do we become a meteorologist?" a boy wanted to know.

"Study hard, and start today," Dixon Bell said. "Math and science are the most important subjects, but don't forget English. Learn how to read well and speak well—you're going to be in the communications business. Study astronomy. Learn about the stars and the planets. When you get into high school and college, you'll have to study things like algebra, calculus, and trigonometry. Then you'll major in meteorology or physics. In fact, the University of Wisconsin right over there in Madison has one of the finest meteorology departments in the country. I lectured there yesterday."

"Can girls be meteorologists?" Marilyn asked.

"Heavens, yes. We need women badly in meteorology. Who would you rather watch give the weather on TV . . . a pretty girl—" the Weatherman raised his hands and growled—"or a big, ugly monster like me?"

Rick Beanblossom was watching an afternoon movie on the monitor. John Wayne and Maureen O'Hara were starring in *McLintock*. The Duke, his old hero, was chasing the fiery redhead, dressed only in her underwear, through a western town; the time had come to teach the bitch a lesson. The newsroom was bustling, most of the reporters having returned from the field. An unfinished story glowed on his computer. A fresh bouquet of flowers glowed next to it. Rick glanced up at the row of clocks on the overhead beam. He had a three o'clock appointment in the news director's office, God bless. Ideas for investigative stories were on the agenda.

Andy Mack stuck his wrinkled face with the cauliflower ears over the partition. In his day, back when student athletes played three sports, he had been a Big Ten wrestling champion. In the early forties he played Gold Gopher football alongside Heisman Trophy winner Bruce Smith. He could put a shot Olympic-distance. After the war Andy went into radio. One day he walked down the hall to the new TV studio and read the weather because nobody else would do it. Now, two generations later, his son, Chris Mack, was a news producer at the station and his daughter, Jill, worked down the hall in programming. But it hadn't gone well for Andy. His wife of forty years died a year back; then Dixon Bell took over his on-air job. The old man was now wallowing in alcohol and self-pity, a pioneer in television reduced to a messenger boy.

"Did you see it on the wire?" Andy asked. "A plane crashed and burned near Duluth."

"Big plane or little plane?"

Andy read the printout. "A Cessna 172."

"Single engine. Seats four. Fatals?"

"Nothing yet."

Rick thought about it a second. "Have Gayle call our station in Duluth and see if the N number on the plane is still visible. If you can get me the N number, I can find out who it belonged to and where it was going."

The small-plane crash story didn't interest him as much as the movie. John Wayne was chasing Maureen O'Hara across the street, town folks falling in line to cheer him on. The masked producer was grinning. His phone rang.

Rick Beanblossom had two telephone lines—his regular line, and the odd number the newsroom called dateline. Only a select few knew this odd number. He looked over at the phone and saw the blinking red light. It was dateline. Maureen O'Hara was screaming. Rick shut her up faster than John Wayne could and picked up the phone. "Beanblossom."

"What have you done for me lately?"

"That's my line," Rick said. He picked up a sharp pencil. "What can I do you for?"

"Well, you never did give me my Pulitzer Prize."

"Sorry, I spent it."

"How much was the actual prize?"

"Two thousand dollars. And they gave me a piece of paper that looks like a high-school diploma. Oh, yeah, and I got a free lunch."

"For all the hubbub it's rather a cheap-ass prize, isn't it?"

"There are so many journalism awards out there they've become meaningless. If you're smart like me, you cash in on it as soon as possible."

"Are you writing that novel?"

"I'm working on it. But it's not easy to write news all day and then go home and write a book."

"I'll bet. I've got something for you, but you can't use it."

"Unless?"

"Unless there's another parking ramp–like murder."

"That's a strange twist, excuse the pun."

"Is it a deal? And I won't excuse the pun."

"Okay, it's a deal. What have you got?"

"The two parking ramp murders and the Hudson murder are all relative."

"All relative?" Rick laid down his pencil. The news was a kick in the head. He lowered his voice. "What are you saying—same killer?"

"They're all relative."

"Don't play games with me. Minneapolis police are still claiming the ramp murders are separate."

"The Wisconsin girl was strangled same as the others. Her hair was tied around her neck after she died."

"Do you know what this means?"

"That's why you can't use it. But one more murder and any idiot will be able to see the connection."

"What kind of man are we looking for?"

"Right now we're looking for an it."

"A woman?" asked Rick.

"The no-rape factor bothers me. No mutilation. No calling card. That's very unmale."

"Description?"

"First ramp murder, suspect may have been wearing a mask."

"You mean like mine?"

"Relax. We checked you out. You didn't do it— goddammit."

"Sorry to disappoint you. Suspects?"

"We don't have squat. But I'm going to get the son of a bitch. This one is mine."

Dateline went dead.

Rick hung up the phone. He punched up CNN on the monitor and began thinking. Do as he did with the Wakefield kidnapping. Start a file. Gather all available info on the three murders. Collect all public documents on the victims, especially autopsies. See Freddie, the Ramsey County medical examiner. Hit the library and the bookstores for the latest books on serial killers. Do a computer search for related articles. Research the history of murder in Minnesota. Find experts, preferably some new faces who'd look good on television. Save all tapes from the killings. Do that right now. Videotape is expensive; most of it is erased and used over again.

Rick Beanblossom started down the hall to the resource center. Check all police sources. Cultivate some new ones. Be careful—cops can't be trusted, with his one exception. Feel out other reporters around town, see what they've got. Brief Jack Napoleon, God bless. He swore to himself as he jogged past the edit rooms. Only a fraction of his knowledge would make it onto the air. It was stories like this that made him wish he still worked for the newspaper. Television can tell a story first, but they can never tell it best.

At three o'clock Rick Beanblossom was dutifully seated in Jack Napoleon's office. The autumn sun was streaming through the windows. He gazed up at the painting of Jesus Christ rising through the clouds. Rick didn't have a religious bone in his body. He was a pagan, he worshipped the seasons. On the wall behind the news director's desk was a degree from the University of Chicago. Jack Napoleon was a physics major, an odd degree for television.

Napoleon began candidly. "We've had a good working relationship, Rick. I don't like you, and you don't like me. So far that's worked out fine. But how did you know I was considering you for a pornography investigation?"

"How do you know I know?"

Napoleon smiled at the little game. "It's not the first time your leather nose has sniffed confidential information out of this office. Be careful, Rick. Clancy promised you a free hand when you came over here, and I've honored that. You can moan and groan all you want about fluff news, but your stories get on the air—even the ones I don't especially care for."

It is an inexorable fact in the television business—hang around too long and you'll end up taking orders from college graduates years younger than yourself. For Rick Beanblossom this age difference wasn't easy to accept. Jack Napoleon was a member of the first generation in American history that didn't have a war to call their own. Rick's resentment of this baby-faced sycophant and his whole draft-free generation ran deep.

What happened in television news, at least at the local level, was that an entire generation of leadership was skipped. The veterans of World War II, television's pioneers, hung on until the end. But their children, the baby boomers, got their news credentials and then got out, most of them ending up in corporate America. When the old GIs retired, the newsrooms were passed on to this baby-faced generation, a generation trained in demographics, market share, and high technology. They couldn't carry on the news tradition because they didn't know what it was.

About once a month Jack Napoleon's ego would get the best of him and he'd videotape sanctimonious editorials to be aired at the end of the news show. They were usually safe subjects—drug abuse, improved education, family values. The news director called these little chats "Time to Care." The news producers called them "Time to Puke."

There were few people the man in the mask couldn't intimidate, so Jack Napoleon wisely dropped the confrontation and asked for investigative ideas. Rick Beanblossom briefed the news director on the new information his source had given him, including the fact they could not yet use it.

Jack Napoleon was ecstatic. He thought it could be the story of the year—perhaps the story of the decade. "I want you working with a reporter on this from the beginning."

"Who do you have in mind?"

"I'm thinking Andrea Labore."

"That's it—I'm out of here." Rick Beanblossom jumped from the chair and started for the door.

"Sit down, Rick!"

He turned. "She does puppy-dog stories."

"Sit down and relax."

Rick dropped back into the chair.

"The soft news was my doing," Napoleon told him. "She came here right out of grad school. No small-market experience. She had to learn the ropes. We're moving her to harder news, starting with the election. You've seen her Ellefson stuff."

"It'll never work."

"You're an investigative journalist. She was a cop. Sounds like a perfect team to me."

"She blew away a burglar one night, then quit. Hardly qualifies her as the next Sherlock Holmes."

"She's the brightest, most attractive woman in news. If we couple that face of hers with—"

Rick interrupted. "You mean a pretty face with a no face is the perfect combination."

"Don't get smart with me. I mean with her face and your research and your writing, we're going to end up with an award-winning story."

"Is that what you're after? An award? Some promotion material?"

"Oh, come on, Rick, did you have these ethical qualms when the *Star Tribune* hyped your Pulitzer Prize to high heaven?"

There was a sharp rap on the door. Gayle the Ghoul burst into the office. From the smile on her face it looked as if she'd just won the Minnesota lottery. "Get this— what a great story! That plane that crashed in Duluth, it was carrying the Republican nominee for governor, what's-his-name?"

"Is he dead?" Rick wanted to know.

"Oh, yeah," she said. "Fried to a crisp."

"Did we get tape?"

THE FREEZE

The day before Christmas was a slow news day, and at the Channel 7 assignment desk Gayle the Ghoul was desperate for stories. She tore through the daybook. "It's tough when we get all our stories from press releases. We should go back to using the newspaper. Who's on call tonight?" she shouted.

"Andrea," yelled producer Chris Mack from his desk.

Gayle stuck her head into the dispatch shack behind her and briefed the new kid. "I want you to listen extra close for house fires. Find me one of those fires where all of their Christmas presents get burned up, and the kids are standing outside crying, and they set up a special fund for them—that kind of shit. We do a story like that every year." The phone was ringing. Gayle grabbed it. "Assignment desk," she barked.

"Um, my name is Princess Afton. I'm fourteen years old and I live in Afton."

The girl sounded retarded. Gayle rolled her eyes.

"I watch Dixon Bell every night. And, um, I know that man on your TV show killed those ladies."

"We'll put a reporter on that right away. Thank you for calling." Gayle slammed down the receiver.

Across the Sky High newsroom festooned with silver garlands and candy canes sat the masked producer, gunfire erupting from his desk. CNN was reporting on riots in the Holy Land. Rick Beanblossom turned down the sound. He popped two chocolates into his mouth and licked his fingers. He pushed aside his poinsettia and picked up his file on the parking ramp murders, already an inch thick. He was sitting on the story. There had been no more killings. He looked over at Andrea's desk. Her day off. Well deserved. She was growing into a better journalist than he wanted to admit openly. On the upper level two Marine Corps Reserve officers in dress blues were stacking toys on the news set. Rick checked the overhead clocks: 4:58. Almost air time.

The lights came up on the two anchor chairs. The Marine Corps officers backed away. Ron Shea and Charleen Barington took their seats and fastened their microphones to their lapels. Christmas flowers decorated the set. Toys for Tots were stacked in front of the anchor desk.

The lights directly above the weather center remained dark. Dixon Bell stood in silhouette at the studio podium, revising his forecast. A holiday wreath hung below the big number 7.

The lights shining on Ron Shea and Charleen Barington were bright and hot. The aging beauty queen pulled a mirror from beneath the desk and quickly pushed her fading red hair into place. The clock struck five. The schlocky music kicked in.

Ron Shea gathered up his script as if he had just finished writing it and read from the TelePrompTer beneath the red light. "Good evening. Edina has long been considered one of the safest suburbs in the Twin Cities. But Sky High news has learned that Edina police are investigating a string of sexual assault cases . . . all involving single women living in first-floor apartments or town houses. Elana Martinez tells us more about these very unusual attacks."

Dixon Bell lived in an Edina town house. He didn't want to hear about sex and violence on Christmas Eve. He left the set while news rolled tape of a young woman, her face blacked out, telling through sobs of how she awoke in the middle of the night to find this big man sitting on the edge of her bed.

Two good snowfalls had ensured a white Christmas. But for days temperatures had been running above normal for December. Now Dixon Bell was calling for freezing rain. Back in Weather Center 7 he checked wind and thermometer readings one more time. This was a hard one to call; only a precious few degrees would turn that harmless rain into dangerous ice. He was trying to calculate how far the mercury would drop during the rainfall when he noticed the message light blinking on his computer. He punched the key. The following message appeared on the screen: *I'm gonna ice you, Weatherman.*

The Weatherman shook his head. He erased the message. He glanced up at the monitor. The new reporter ended her rape story with a really good stand-up, then signed off. "Elana Martinez, Sky High News, Edina."

Back to a two-shot of the anchors, Ron Shea reading: "And Charleen, we want to welcome Elana Martinez to our news staff. She joins Sky High News after a long stint at our sister station in Tucson, Arizona. She won a couple of very prestigious awards down there."

"Yes," said Charleen, right on cue, "we were really lucky to get her."

The Weatherman gathered up his script and straightened his tie.

They were ten minutes into the five o'clock newscast. Weather was coming up next. Dixon Bell was back at the studio podium readying his forecast when Charleen Barington introduced a new education feature that she'd had a hand in preparing. The Texas beauty gave the Tele-PrompTer a look of grave concern. "Are Minnesota students measuring up to the high standards set by America's top universities? That's the question we'll be putting to you all this week in a feature we call 'So You Want to Go to College.' Every night this week on our five o'clock and ten o'clock news shows we'll ask you, our viewers, questions that appear on some of the toughest college entrance exams in the nation." She turned to Ron Shea. "Ron, we'll try this one out on you."

Ron Shea turned to the camera and chuckled. "Uh-oh, I'm in trouble now."

Charleen put a finger in the air like a game show host. "Ron, what was the name of the plan to rebuild Europe after World War II?" The multiple-choice answers were spelled out on the screen, white on blue. Charleen read them off: "(A) The Geneva Convention . . . (B) The Marshall Plan . . . or (C) The Truman Doctrine?"

The answer was so obvious that Dixon Bell paid little attention.

The focus returned to Ron Shea as he studied the three choices on his monitor. "Oh, boy. I believe it was the Truman Doctrine."

Charleen smiled, a big congratulatory smile. "That's

right, Ron." The (C) answer flashed on the screen. "It was the Truman Doctrine, proposed by President Harry Truman."

Ron Shea nodded his head. "Harry Truman was a smart man."

Dixon Bell couldn't believe his ears. Yes, Harry Truman was a smart man, but Ron Shea and Charleen Barington were a pair of matched idiots, and it was about time somebody told them. The Weatherman's voice thundered out of the shadows. "The plan to rebuild Europe after World War II was called the Marshall Plan!" Camera three quickly swung to the weather center—not enough time to warm up his lights. Dixon Bell spoke in silhouette. "It was proposed by General George Marshall, who was the secretary of state during the Truman administration. At least that's what they taught us poor white trash down South." As he calmly went back to examining his forecast, the Weatherman mumbled just loud enough to be heard on the air. "Not exactly 'Jeopardy,' is it, folks?"

There hadn't been that much silence on the news set since the crash of *Skyhawk 7*. In the newsroom, telephones could be heard ringing off the hook. Ron Shea smiled sheepishly at his co-anchor. "Well, Charleen, I guess it's back to school for us."

Charleen Barington forced a smile at the TelePrompTer and read what was written. "Coming up next, meteorologist Dixon Bell will be here to tell us if we're going to have a wet Christmas."

*"**D**id he ask you out?"*

Andrea Labore kept hearing those haunting words coming from behind that spooky mask. She heard them again as the tall black gates of the governor's mansion swung open. A wreath on the front door warmly welcomed visitors. It was raining. She drove down a carpet of sloppy snow and parked in front of the carriage house. Andrea climbed out of her car, cringing at the nasty weather. The huge estate on Summit Avenue in St. Paul was being pelted. Naked branches on tall trees were bending with the weight of the icy rain. A passing wind spun the droplets in circles, threw the weather in her face. It sure didn't seem a lot like Christmas.

After the death of the Republican nominee, a battle royal broke out in the Republican Party. Backers of Per Ellefson claimed that since he'd finished second in the September primary, his name should be placed on the ballot. But the party's right wing claimed the executive committee was entitled to meet and nominate a new candidate, someone more to their liking. Minnesota's secretary of state, a no-nonsense woman, rose above partisan politics and followed a strict interpretation of the state's constitution, deciding Ellefson's name would be placed on the ballot. With only two weeks to campaign, the handsome Norwegian was elected governor in a close race that saw the lowest voter turnout in state history. To the amusement of all, the new governor told his victory gathering, "It's okay if you call me Governor Lazarus."

After he was elected, Per Ellefson kept a promise he'd made to Andrea Labore. She was granted the first interview—an exclusive. Following that interview Andrea's star rose a little higher in the Sky High newsroom.

Governor-elect Lazarus was waving to Andrea from the back terrace of the mansion, a Scandinavian sculpture in a warm wool shirt. He took her by the arm and helped her up the back steps so she wouldn't slip and fall. "He said it was going to rain."

"Who said?" Andrea asked.

"Your weatherman. He said three days ago we'd be getting rain out of this system."

"Did you watch our news tonight?"

Ellefson took her coat. "No, I'm afraid I didn't have a chance." They walked down a stone hall to the front of the mansion.

"That's why I'm late. I got called in. This family in South Minneapolis lost everything they had when their house burned down. It was really sad. The fire started with their Christmas tree, and all of their presents were burned up."

"That's a shame."

"Yes. They've set up a special fund for them."

"It seems something like that happens every year."

"Doesn't it, though?"

"What else did I miss by not watching television?"

Andrea thought the question had a cynical ring to it.

"The Toys for Tots drive failed to reach its goal. That's a first for us."

They stopped in the hallway. It was drafty, the marble cold. "That's the kind of thing we have to turn around," Ellefson said. If there had been any cynicism in his voice, it was gone. He spoke with a sincerity rare for politicians. "I believe in Minnesota, Andrea. No single issue about the state is more important to Minnesotans than our firmly held belief that life in Minnesota is infinitely superior to life in any other state. I think perhaps only two other states in this country have as much pride and love for their land as we do . . . maybe Texas and Virginia. But ours is a quiet kind of love. A cool pride. A quality of life. Whatever you want to call it, I think we're losing it. Being from Minnesota used to mean something. I want to bring that something back."

Andrea agreed. "I can see it watching the news day in and day out. There is this sinking feeling that this isn't the state I grew up in. Something went wrong." Andrea fought with herself. No question, she had been taken from the start with Per Ellefson. The first time she'd seen him in person was towards the end of the summer, at a speech he delivered at the old soldier's home in Minnehaha Park. He reminded her of a Viking warrior, what Leif Ericsson might have looked like in a coat and tie.

Strong-minded, intelligent women have a thing about seducing powerful men, as if access to power might translate into power. Andrea had always used sex more than she enjoyed it. Boyfriends inevitably disappointed her. She'd always been attracted to men of substance—the college professor with the literary awards and the sage advice, or the police chief with his heart in social justice and his hands in politics. This charismatic governor-elect was another one. Andrea Labore was tempted by the thought. She had it and she knew how to use it.

"We don't move in for two weeks," Ellefson told her. "The governor and his family moved out early so we could be in by Inauguration Day. It was very thoughtful of him. I thought you might like to see the place before my wife and kids turn it into a zoo."

They walked to the front foyer. "This place is huge," Andrea exclaimed. The halls were decked with a lot more than boughs of holly. Two thousand dollars' worth of poinsettias bought the season cheer. The first floor had been completely refurbished in the Tudor-revival style of the 1920s. A stately grand piano and a magnificent chandelier broke the coldness of the place and created an atmosphere of elegance. The art was French impressionist. Oriental rugs lay on the floor. A priceless grandfather clock reminded visitors of their own place in time.

The clock chimed the quarter-hour. Per Ellefson jumped in front of it and spread his powerful arms. "Three floors and a basement," he told Andrea, "thirty-six rooms, two cooks, a housekeeper, one manager, one assistant manager, a full-time secretary, two libraries, three offices, a solarium, a sauna, a wine cellar, a dining room that seats eighteen, and God only knows how many bathrooms."

Andrea spun slowly around, taken back in time. "It's just like the Victorian Summit Avenue F. Scott Fitzgerald wrote about in those short stories."

The governor-elect smiled. "Yes, I love reading Fitzgerald, too." Then he continued the tour. "The family quarters are on the second floor. On the average, one thousand guests pass through here every month." He pointed to a long open balcony. "To get from room to room in the family residence you have to come out into that hallway up there. Even to go to the bathroom. I'd hate to come running out of the shower in only my towel to find a tour passing through."

Andrea laughed. "It's so . . . so . . ." She was lost for words.

"It appears stately from the outside, but once you get in here and start looking around it gets pretty shabby. Some of the carpeting is thirty years old. Second and third floors are the worst. Come along, I'll show you what I mean."

He took her hand and they started up the open stairway. Andrea gazed into his snowy blue eyes. "This house must be filled with wonderful stories."

"They say the first governor to live here, Karl Rolvaag, buried his dog in the basement. There's a paw print in the concrete to mark the spot. On windy nights you can hear him howling."

"You're kidding?"

"No," he laughed. "The staff calls him the Hound of the Rolvaags."

On the second floor the elegance of the mansion disappeared. The family residence was cold, drab, and impersonal. Stuck in the fifties. The rooms were cramped and worn. The only touch of class upstairs was the white wine Ellefson poured. And the red rose he gave Andrea and the kiss on the cheek.

"Did he ask you out?"

The end of the tour took them up the stairs to the third floor of the mansion, once a ballroom. Now it was only an empty attic. The walls were peeling paint, falling plaster. Pieces of furniture were covered with black plastic.

They walked into a corner bedroom as sparse as a monk's cell. Between two windows was a daybed covered with an army surplus blanket. The roof leaked. A section of green garden hose dangled from the cracked ceiling and dripped into a silver pail. Beneath a window a rope ladder lay at the ready. Incense lingered in the air. Ellefson closed the door. "According to the fire marshal it's illegal to use this floor—no fire escape. I guess the governor's teenage son lived up here. I'm going to turn it into my hideaway."

Andrea walked to the window. Icy raindrops splattered the glass. She twirled the rose he'd given her beneath her nose. All was quiet but for the drip of the hose into the pail.

Even in the blurring rain the grandest avenue in Minnesota appeared frozen in time. Old-fashioned street lamps punctuated the beauty of it all. A horse and sleigh down the center of the street would have been appropriate. Tall evergreens on the front lawn twinkled with white lights. The same white lights were festooned on the iron fence above the snowy sidewalk. Across the way, hiding behind a row of Norwegian pines, another imposing stone residence was decorated in lights of rainbow colors. The Queen Anne house next door to the pines displayed a nativity scene below its front portico. Christmas had come to Summit Avenue.

Andrea stood mesmerized by the avenue's grace and charm. The governor-elect came up to her and put his graceful arms around her waist from behind. He leaned his chin on her shoulder. He pressed his body tight against hers. His breath was warm and sweet. His cologne smelled of the north woods. "Winter is what I love about Minnesota," he whispered. "It keeps the riff-raff out."

She turned immediately and kissed him, a deep, warm kiss. Andrea Labore had never felt so good about feeling so guilty. "Merry Christmas, Governor."

"Merry Christmas to you, Andrea."

She tuned out his wife and children. All journalistic principles came off with her blouse. Her own rules about avoiding cops and politicians fell to the floor.

On the daybed he slid off her slacks and admired her legs. Andrea worked hard to keep the weight off. Was she too skinny? She worried about this as the governor-to-be removed her bra and nibbled on her small breasts. Her nipples began to harden. He licked his way back to her face. It was her face men wanted.

Andrea's aversion to cops literally came in her face. When she was on the police force she dated a homicide detective for weeks before she decided to go to bed with him. It was a power struggle from the moment they hit the sheets. He wanted on top. He called her a bitch and pinned her hands above her head. He ejaculated in her face, then used the head of his dick to rub it in. It was her first experience with an angry cop and angry sex.

Ellefson kept rubbing his hands tenderly over her face, whispering in her ear. "You are the most beautiful woman I've ever seen. I knew from the start we'd be together someday." Then he stood to take off his clothes. She turned away from him and watched the freezing rain falling over the tree branches. When he crawled back onto the bed, she closed her eyes and waited for his caress.

But he only brushed a hand across her face. "Look at me."

Andrea opened her eyes. He was on his knees over her. His erection was long and thick. She took the Republican cannon in her hand and began stroking his ego. When he didn't move, she knew what he was waiting for. The obligatory kiss. He clasped the back of her head as she sucked him. Satisfied, he went down on her slow and easy, and Andrea began to more enjoy the experience and appreciate the man. Again she took him by the hand, this time putting it where she wanted it, helping him inside of her.

After the sex Andrea Labore buried her beautiful but guilty face into the wide, hairy chest of governor-elect Per Ellefson. Where could this possibly go? What did she have to gain? Was she really falling for this guy? But then the new governor wasn't the only man confusing her these days.

"**D**id he ask you out?"

When they first began working together on the stranglings that autumn, Andrea was as antagonistic towards Rick Beanblossom as was he towards her. She hated his attitude. She was sure he hated her face. But her work ethic and her iron will were winning him over, though the son of a bitch would be loath to admit it. Her attitude seemed to change with the seasons. Winter brought cold respect and admiration for the masked man. They were more alike than she wanted to admit. She learned he read *Time* magazine and *U.S. News & World Report* from cover to cover every week. He read the *New York Times* every morning, as well as the *Minneapolis Star Tribune* and the *St. Paul Pioneer Press*. She watched him work a computer like an electronic historian, pulling related facts and articles out of obscure periodicals. He would excuse himself, walk to a phone, and return minutes later with information reporters have no right to. In media circles it was well known that the masked newsman was "plugged in." His Pulitzer Prize-winning story on organized crime and its insidious infiltration of Minnesota's multi-billion-dollar gambling industry could only have been written with the help of the state's top cops. The outgoing governor ordered an investigation into the leaks that tarnished his image and made him unelectable, but Beanblossom's source was never found out.

Andrea tried to cultivate her own sources, but most cops never trusted her after she quit the force. Some cops thought her a traitor. She doubled her own news reading, finding *Time* and *Newsweek* easier and easier to digest. What began as a chore soon became fascinating. Not only was she retaining the news she read, she was becoming absorbed by it.

She did best the things the masked producer couldn't do, or wouldn't do, like talking off-camera with friends and families of those who had been murdered. She had a warm, caring manner. In newsrooms murders run together like Monday through Friday. As time goes by it becomes difficult to remember one grisly crime from the other. But they were women with lives before they were murder victims, and Andrea made them human again. She was convinced they had all died at the hands of a man. The same man.

Debra Ann Miller, a single woman working in health insurance. Her area of expertise: working women and their health care needs. Strangled atop a parking ramp in broad daylight on her way to her car.

Lorelei Hayne—everybody called her Sis. Seventeen years old and about to begin her senior year at Harding High. She sold hot dogs at Twins games to earn money for college. She already had her application in at St. Catherine. Strangled atop a dark parking ramp in the pouring rain on her way to her daddy's car.

Caroline Fawn. A Chippewa Indian. Majoring in music and theater at the University of Wisconsin. Engaged to be married in the spring. Strangled atop a river bluff as the sun rose on a gorgeous Indian summer day.

Andrea knew Rick Beanblossom didn't always like this humanizing effect. He fixated on things, not people. One day in the fall, as they drove back to the newsroom after an interview, he made her stop the car at a park, where he got out and admired a cluster of trees ablaze in their autumn colors. Another time it was a rose garden off Lake Harriet during the first snow. The time after that it was a 1963 red-and-white Corvette. He never said anything, just stopped and looked, and she was left to wonder what was going on inside that mask.

Women didn't seem of much interest to him, either. Through their changing relationship Rick kept his feelings towards Andrea hidden. Feigned disinterest. But every now and then came a spark of affection and what seemed a flicker of jealousy. Then he would say something that would bother her for days. Like when she mentioned her master's degree.

"I can't imagine what took you five years to learn. You must be really stupid."

And when she told him of the exclusive interview with the new governor, the masked newsman didn't want to know how the interview went. All he would say, in that smug way of his, was, "Did he ask you out?"

She cried, "Don't be ridiculous. He's married and has two daughters."

That was before Ellefson called, before he made love to her.

Andrea was happy but confused. She turned to the man elected governor. He seemed asleep. It was Christmas Eve. He would have to be going soon. She turned back to the window. The rain falling through the trees was turning to ice now, just as the Weatherman had said it would. She heard a howling noise, either the wind against the windowpane or the Hound of the Rolvaags. She crawled back into the strong arms of the most handsome man she'd ever known.

But as Andrea Labore drifted off to sleep that night, it wasn't the face of Per Ellefson she was thinking about. It was the faceless face of the man behind the mask that haunted her.

Rick Beanblossom had a corner table at the Daily News Bar & Grill, where through the window he could watch the freezing storm over the Nicollet Walk. The decor was dark; the ambiance was light: a place where print media met electronic media and they all pretended they were in the same business. Ironically, it was one of the few bars in town that didn't have a television set staring customers in the face. That was one of the things Rick liked about this hangout. Besides, he was known here. He could relax.

The bar and grill was packed, downtown workers waiting for the weather to break before they ventured home to begin the Christmas holiday. Already the streets were coated with sleet. Cars fishtailed down the block. People slid by the window or just slipped and fell. It wasn't long before photographer Dave Cadieux and television pioneer Andy Mack ducked in out of the frozen spray. They joined Rick at his table.

"How is it out there?" he asked them.

Cadieux brushed the ice from his hair. "Freezing rain.

Just like the asshole promised." He threw his coat over the chair. "They'll be chasing pile-ups all night." Cadieux was a new breed of news photographer. "Photojournalists" is what they liked to be called. The title was well deserved. They could tape together whole stories without a reporter. In television news it's not uncommon for the person behind the camera to be smarter and bolder than the person standing in front of it. It was Dave Cadieux who was rolling when the Wakefield boy climbed out of the woods searching in vain for his twin brother. And it was Dave Cadieux who stood atop the tallest building in town and shot the crew of *Skyhawk 7* as they chased the Eden Prairie tornado to their doom.

Andy Mack shook the foul weather from his coat in overdramatic fashion. Then he draped the coat over his shoulder like a cape and raised his hand in speech: "Name to thee a man most like this dreadful night; that thunders, lightens, opens graves, and roars as doth the lion in the Capitol; a man no mightier than thyself, or me, in personal action; yet prodigious grown, and fearful, as these strange eruptions are."

Rick beckoned to him. " 'Tis the Weatherman you mean, is it not, Mr. Mack?"

"Indeed, they say, the viewers tomorrow mean to establish him as king. I know where I will wear this dagger then." Andy Mack plunged his fist into his heart and dropped into the chair.

Dave Cadieux thought they sounded like a pair of fools. "What the hell are you two jabbering about?"

"Shakespeare," Rick told him.

"Yes, and very bad Shakespeare, too." Andy Mack hung his coat over the chair, sat down and caught his breath. "He's spooky, Rick. When he first came here I watched him work. I grew up here. I knew more about the weather than anybody in this town until that son of a bitch blew in and knocked me off the air. The guy knows what the weather is going to be."

Rick shrugged, didn't buy it. "It's just a gift he has, like singing, or throwing a baseball."

"No, that's talent. This guy is spooky."

They ordered their drinks. Rick stuck with red wine. The old man combed the few hairs on his head. When the drinks arrived, Andy Mack raised his glass.

"What are we drinking to?" Rick asked.

Andy gave the toast. "Back to the days when men were men, and women didn't work in the newsroom." They laughed and drank up.

"I'm sorry," said Andy Mack, shaking his head in sad resignation, "but I just don't understand these women today. Take these so-called rape cases in Edina. They say they wake up and find this big guy sitting on their bed, like he blew in with the breeze or something. How many times last year did we do a story about a woman who said she was raped, or kidnapped, only to find out a few days later that she made up the whole damn story?"

Rick raised his fingers. "Three."

"Three times last year. And they were our lead stories."

"It's a tough call," Rick reminded him. Ice pellets were pinging off the window. The masked producer glanced over his shoulder at the driving sleet. Traffic was backing up. The flashing red lights of an ambulance fought through traffic.

Andy Mack and Dave Cadieux had another round of Christmas cheer. Then another. As the night wore on, the weather wasn't getting any better, but their stories were.

"What was the most disturbing story you ever covered?" Cadieux asked the old man.

Andy Mack let his mind drift back over the years. "Long time ago, back before abortions were legal, they found a fetus on the sidewalk, like it'd been thrown from a car. And I was standing there looking at it with Catfish Bob—an old photog, he retired years ago—but we could see the little fella's arms and legs. Next day they found the woman dead in the backseat of a car. She probably got pregnant in that backseat, had an abortion in the backseat, and died in the backseat. When I see an abortion story I always think of that little fella on the sidewalk more than that woman in the backseat."

Dave Cadieux wiped his chin. "Do you remember about three years ago . . . this high-school girl had a baby in secret? Strangled it and threw it in a trash can. I was cruising around when I picked the call off my scanner. I got there before the police."

Andy Mack was incredulous. "And you shot tape of this?"

"Whether I shot tape or not, I had to look at it."

Rick Beanblossom was enjoying himself, listening to a couple of newsies with a few drinks in them trying to top each other.

Dave Cadieux leaned across the table. He was beginning to slur his words. "Did I ever tell you guys this one? Last summer, remember, a boat full of people goes over St. Anthony Falls. Capsized. Choppers are trying to pick people out of the water. Rescue boats are paddling into the falls. I'm shooting from a choice spot on the Franklin Avenue Bridge. This detective comes my way. I figure he's gonna chase me off the bridge, so I lower my camera, but I keep it rolling in case it turns into harassment. He says to me, 'Do you ever watch "Rescue 911" with William Shatner?' I say, 'Sure, what about it?' He says, 'I've got the producer on the phone. Save your tape, we might be able to work something out.' "

Rick Beanblossom and Andy Mack spat laughter across the table.

Cadieux went on. "These poor people ain't even out of the water yet and this cop is putting together a TV deal."

They shared another round of laughter. Then Rick lowered his voice to vacate the humor. "Listen, guys, I'm sitting on a story and it's driving me crazy."

"Like what?"

"I really can't say. I promised a source. But I've got a list of tapes from the resource center. If this thing breaks, Dave, I'll want you to do the editing. I'll have the scripts ready, but you'll have to edit your ass off. I've also got a ton of background material, too. We could beat the hell out of the newspapers on this one."

"How big of a story are we talking about?"

"Bigger than the tornado."

"You're joking me?"

Andy Mack cut in, excited. "I want to help."

Rick put his hand on the old man's arm. "You're in. When it breaks I'll have a list of things that have to be done fast. You'll know how to get them done."

The old man smiled, a bit tipsy. "It's those parking ramp murders, isn't it?"

It was bar talk, and Rick Beanblossom felt he'd already said too much. He turned away. Ice was coating the window now, turning headlights and taillights into iridescent streaks. Rick was watching this diffused light show when, suddenly, the Weatherman's face shone on the glass. He appeared almost as some avenging spirit as he rubbed away a spot of ice and squinted. Then he was gone. Rick leaned back in his chair and waited.

Dixon Bell entered the Daily News in his usual awkward style. He stood in the doorway, adjusting his eyes to the dark. Then he made his way to the bar and ordered a beer. Rick Beanblossom watched him the whole time. The Weatherman made heads turn. Maybe it was his newfound popularity, or his hulking physique, whatever, when he walked into a room people turned and stared. With a beer in hand he made his way over to their table, politely smiling through the crowd. "I thought that was y'all over here."

Andy Mack stood and pulled out a chair. "Sit down, Dixon."

"No, really, I can't stay. Just thought I'd grab a cold one before I head home."

"Nice weather," Cadieux remarked.

"Boy, you called this one right," Andy said, taking his seat again.

Dixon Bell remained standing as he stared out the freezing window. "The temperature is dropping fast," he advised them. "Be hell to pay come morning. A sheet of ice on everything."

Andy Mack raised his glass in salute. "Here's to the best damn weatherman in America."

"To the Weatherman."

Dixon Bell smiled, embarrassed by the toast. He sipped his beer and looked slowly around the crowded bar.

Rick Beanblossom polished off his wine. "She doesn't come in here, Weatherman."

"What does that mean?"

"It means I've never seen her in here."

"That wasn't necessary."

"I didn't mean anything by it."

"Yes, you did."

Some people call it Minnesota cool, others call it Minnesota smug, but whatever it was, Rick Beanblossom had it. He stared right through the Weatherman.

Dixon Bell turned and walked away, dropped his beer on the bar, and stormed out of the Daily News, disappearing into the demonic weather.

Andy Mack shook his head disapprovingly. "Why do you ride him like that, Rick? I've never known two men who have so much in common who can't stand each other. If anybody has reason to dislike him, it's me."

"I have nothing in common with him."

"You have everything in common with him."

Dave Cadieux yawned. "I can't imagine anything worse than being hung up on a woman that doesn't give a damn about you. Fuck them kinda bitches."

"That guy is sick," Rick declared.

"No," said Andy, correcting him. "He's spooky."

"You're drunk, old man."

Andy Mack got up to leave, his breathing heavy and strained. He wrestled into his coat. "Merry Christmas," he said, almost crying. He stumbled toward the door. "And like the Weatherman says, 'Y'all be careful out there!'"

THE ICE

By seven o'clock Christmas morning the Twin Cities were encased in ice—two cities under glass. It was still dark. Lieutenant Donnell Redmond knew the streets would be a mess. He knew this because at ten o'clock the night before he had done the unthinkable and tuned in Channel 7. He wanted to see for himself what the fat boy everybody loved had to say about the storm. After joking with the anchors about Harry Truman, the Weatherman delivered the bad news. "A warm flow of air from the southern plains overran a high-pressure system near the Twin Cities. Expect a mess come morning. Stay off the roads if possible."

Not possible if you're a cop. The BCA office was in St. Paul. Redmond lived on a hill in Minneapolis. He stepped out the front door. His feet flew out from beneath him. He went down the porch stairs on his rear end. He slid across the sidewalk on his back. Then he rolled over and went down the hill to the street on his stomach, his arms protecting his head. It was the fastest he'd ever traveled from his house to the car. He was stunned. He tried to stand, but again his feet went out from beneath him. He lay sprawled on his back across the icy boulevard, peering up at the morning stars. The sky had cleared. "Aw, man, why do I live here?"

The tall lieutenant who grew up in Florida got to his feet, very carefully this time. He looked at the police Impala in front of him. Never had it been so shiny. He skated around to the driver's side and tried the door. It was frozen. He gave it a kick. Nothing. It was a state car, so he gave it another kick. The ice fell away. The door opened. He grabbed the scraper from the backseat and spent the next twenty minutes chipping ice off the windshield. He was freezing. He didn't bother with the rear window.

Donnell Redmond threw the heater on high. The man on the radio was announcing highway closings. He adjusted the volume on his scanner so that he could monitor road conditions and steer away from accidents. The city streets were like skating rinks. Wrecked and abandoned cars blocked the intersections. Tow trucks were out in force. At one corner an NSP crew was propping up a downed power line. The lieutenant had little control over the squad car as he went slip-sliding toward the freeway, which at least would be sanded.

Already headlights were inching east and west on I-94. Top speed was thirty miles per hour as Redmond crossed the river into St. Paul. The sand, salt, and melting ice filthied his windshield. He pushed the solvent button over and over. He'd forgotten to check the blue solution. Soon it was empty. The wipers pushed aside just enough mud for him to see the road. But he was almost to work.

"Car nineteen, have you got chains on?"

"Affirmative."

"We got a strange call from a cell phone. Caller was driving around Como Lake . . . said he saw what appears to be two people down on the ice . . . might need help. But he wasn't sure in the dark . . . said it could be tree branches or shadows. Can you swing through the park before you head in?"

"We're not near there, but we'll start that way."

Donnell Redmond heard the call. He was moving slowly but steadily down the sandy freeway, approaching the Lexington exit to Como Park. At first he had no intention of exiting onto the dangerous city streets. He glanced at his rearview mirror. Through the ice he could see the blinking blue light of a sanding truck that was following him. Above him the freeway sign read LEXINGTON PARKWAY. Then his curiosity forced him to change lanes. As he started up the exit he swore at himself for being a cop.

Como Park is the largest park in St. Paul, and because of its sylvan beauty, and its zoo, it is one of the most popular parks in the Twin Cities. The decorative gates to the park's entrance are coated with ivy and flowers and could very well resemble the Pearly Gates. But in the wintertime the flowers are dead and the ivy is brown. The entrance gates stuck out of the frozen snow like a pile of rust and dirt.

The lieutenant fishtailed past the gates and steered for the lake. He applied the brakes, but they were useless. The car kept going, sideways toward the shore. "Always turn into the spin"—they told him that every year. But Donnell Redmond didn't think Minnesotan. His Florida brain spun the steering wheel in the opposite direction. The car whipped around in a complete circle and crashed into a snow bank. He threw up his hands and looked out his window at the plowed drift. "I'm cool." He kicked open the passenger door and crawled out of the car.

The park was frozen, cold and silent. The sun would start up any minute. Huge chunky snow piles blocked his view of the lake. He climbed up a pile but slipped and fell back down. Again he brushed himself off; then, gingerly, he made his way to the top of a small, icy mountain. The park pavilion was closed for the winter. Somebody had forgotten to take down the flag. Red, white, and blue icicles hung from the mast. Big ugly blackbirds picked through a garbage can out front. The white promenade on the lake's edge, where the summer concerts were held, had a ghostly appearance, its huge pillars reminding Redmond of southern plantations. White birch trees grew at oblique angles along the shoreline.

At the south end of the lake orange fencing surrounded open water. Ducks flapped about. But stalactites from the storm weighed down the fence, creating a dangerous situation. It was while he was looking toward the middle of the lake that Redmond noticed strange shadows, like the caller had reported. Almost surreal in the predawn dark of an icy world.

A triangular sign stapled to a tree warned DANGER—THIN ICE. A yellow wood rescue raft hung from another tree. Redmond slid down the bank and onto the frozen lake. He was shivering. He pounded his gloves together. At sunset the temperature had been above freezing. By morning it had plummeted to near zero. Every winter he promised himself he'd dress warmer. He never did. He moved across the lake like an Egyptian mummy, bruised and aching from his slide down his stairs. Slowly and deliberately he half walked, half slid his way across the fresh layer of ice.

The lieutenant was still a good distance away, but as he slid closer the eerie shadows began to take shape and form. It appeared to be a man on his knees praying over something. Or maybe the fool was ice fishing. Where else but in this godforsaken land would a man be stupid enough to risk his life in the middle of a lake to catch a fish on Christmas morning? "Do you need help?" Redmond shouted.

The apparition grew large and ominous, almost inflating like a balloon. The face remained dark and featureless, but its hair was icicles. Another shadow was left stretched across the ice. Redmond was startled. "Hold it there, sucker, I'm a police officer." The police officer slipped and fell.

The ghostly figure moved across the ice, away from him. The other shadow lay still on the frozen lake. Redmond's chase instincts kicked in. He clambered to his feet. "Police, stop!"

The big shadow seemed to have better footing. It ran off the lake and went north of the pavilion into the park. By the time Redmond stumbled off the frozen water the shadow was halfway up the steep hill beside a frozen waterfall.

"Now why don't he slip and fall?" The big cop started up after him. The shadow vaulted a chain link fence that protected the icy falls and disappeared over the top of the hill.

Donnell Redmond grabbed onto trees and bushes jutting out of the ice and pulled himself up the hill a foot at a time. A walk bridge ran in front of the waterfall—a white icicle twenty feet high and a foot thick. A sign on the fencing read, PERSONS FOUND IN FENCE AREA WILL BE PROSECUTED.

Redmond yelled, "You're in big trouble now, Frosty!" He jumped the fence, grabbed onto trees, and struggled up the hill beside the waterfall. By the time he reached the top he was hurting and exhausted. He thought he saw the apparition melt into shadows in the woods below. He decided to do what they do in the movies. What the hell. He drew his .357 short-barrel. "Stop or I'll shoot!" Then he fired a warning shot into the air. The gun sounded like a cannon, shattering the icy silence. The echo was crazy. But in the woods below, nothing moved.

Donnell Redmond walked to a concrete picnic table half buried in the snow and stepped to the top. Off to his right, hills of ice rolled over the golf course. Before him the woods were dark and deep. The sun was starting up, but the shadows created by the slivers of dawn only added to the hiding places. Whatever it was, it had gotten away. The frustrated lieutenant slid his gun beneath his coat. He turned and started back for the lake. He was at the top of the frozen waterfall when he heard an order that could only come from a fellow cop.

"Freeze, asshole, or you're dead!" A St. Paul patrolman standing just off the walk bridge was pointing a gun up at him.

"Don't shoot—I'm Lieutenant Redmond!" He reached for his badge, but slipped on his ass and zipped around the waterfall and down the steep hill.

The cop with his gun drawn jumped aside as what must have looked like a giant bowling ball coming at him slid by, flew over a retaining wall, and landed in a snow bank. The St. Paul patrolman lowered his gun. "Is that you, Donny?"

"No, it's Peggy Fleming, dumb fuck." Redmond got to his feet, aching and cold, checking his body for broken bones.

"I thought all you state boys had desk jobs." He holstered his gun. "We heard a shot."

"I was chasing somebody."

"Did you get a good look at him?"

"I got hardly no look at him. Just a big old shadow moving across the ice like a snowman."

"You couldn't have picked a worse morning to chase somebody. What'd he do?"

"Don't know yet. Out on the lake."

The sun was coming up on a crystalline day. The sky was ice blue, sun-splashed but frigid. The earth was iced over. Como Park was an icicle fantasy. Ice sculptures decorated the entire lakeshore. Ice angels hung from tree branches over the frozen water. Streets around the lake were mirrored and deserted.

They worked their way back to the parking lot. Another St. Paul patrolman was standing beside a squad car,

its tires wrapped in chains. He had a bag of doughnuts.
"Who've you got there?"

"It's Donny Redmond."

"Really? I thought all those state boys had desk
jobs. Do you want a doughnut, Donny?"

Donnell Redmond was physically aching and disgusted. "Do you know what those things do to our image?"

"Who cares? They're still warm."

Redmond stuck his hungry nose in the bag. "Got any
lemon?"

"What a morning, huh? Looks like Disney on Ice.
Who'd you shoot at?"

Redmond bit into a lemon doughnut and limped toward
the lake. "Frosty the Snowman," he answered with his
mouth full.

The two patrolmen followed him. They slipped and
slid across Como Lake, trying to keep their balance while
munching doughnuts.

Redmond shielded his eyes and squinted. The rising
sun off the ice made everything orange and yellow.

They were almost on top of the body before they realized what it was. And what it was was something out of
a Poe tale. The three cops stood as silent as the arctic
morning. Finally one of the patrolmen muttered, "Jesus
Christ, she has to have been dead for hours."

"Must've killed her last night in the rain."

She was a blonde, perfectly preserved in ice. Murder in
a bottle. Her twisted neck was ripped at the shoulder. Her
face was frozen in terror. Her golden hair glimmered
through the glaze, reflecting the morning sun. Her death-
bed had been a frozen lake, colder than a grave. Her coffin was an ice cube.

The two patrolmen chattered nervously in the cold.
"He about tore her head off."

"Looks to me like those parking ramp murders Minneapolis had last summer."

"The shit's gonna hit the fan now."

Lieutenant Donnell Redmond stood freezing in the sun-
light, strangely quiet. He wiped the lemon from his lips
and saw the glare of a windshield as it approached the entrance gates. A Channel 7 News van crawled slowly and
cautiously out of the park, probably monitoring police

calls. But then the vehicle turned away from the crime scene and rolled away.

"Let's keep this off the radio," Redmond finally said. "There's a phone on the promenade. Call dispatch. Tell 'em to wake up the Marlboro Man. It's our case now."

THE VICTIM

When the elevator door slid open, he saw a corpse stretched across a wheeled gurney. The penis was shriveled up like a snail. The torso and limbs were waxen white, but the dead man's head was a grotesque purple color, almost like a Vikings football fan who'd painted his face. An attendant inside the elevator pushed the gurney to the side. "Ain't you Beanblossom?"

"Yes, I am." The masked newsman stepped into the elevator. "I'm here to see Freddie. Who's your friend?"

"He hung himself. Stupid way to go, man. Use drugs, much more dignity."

"I'll try to remember that."

When the elevator door slid open again, Rick Beanblossom was in the basement of the Ramsey County Morgue in St. Paul. It was chilly. With the exception of the ice storm it had been a wimpy winter, but on this day the January temperature was hovering near zero. Rick was wearing his brown leather bomber jacket. He carried his gloves in his hand.

He found Freddie alone in a corner office, paging through the latest edition of the *National Enquirer*. "Show me the victim?" he asked.

"You just want to see a naked woman." Dr. Freda Wilhelm was a forensic pathologist and the county's chief medical examiner. She was a big, robust woman, almost six feet tall and over two hundred fifty pounds. Her dark hair was more frizz than curls, having been permed too many times. She wore a military nurse's uniform, much like the Navy vice-admiral uniform worn by the U.S. surgeon general. She had designed it herself. It was white with blue-striped shoulder boards and a gold-braided infantry rope looped ceremoniously over her right shoulder. Rick had never seen her dressed in anything else.

The pretentious uniform and her imperious demeanor made the doctor an easy target for the media. Especially the columnists. She hated the bastards. Rick Beanblossom had been the first newspaperman to write a decent article about her—told of her extensive training, that she was one of the few women in the country working in forensic science. Her overbearing personality and her risqué sense of humor helped her cope with the constant pressure she was under. Besides taking care of St. Paul and its suburbs, Ramsey County also provided forensic services to more than thirty rural counties in the Upper Midwest. When Freddie began the job she was doing three hundred autopsies a year. Guns, drugs, and AIDS had pushed that number past five hundred.

Even as Rick Beanblossom was writing her story she suspected he was only priming her as a future source. Still she loved him for it.

"Probably been a long time since you've seen a naked woman, huh, lover?"

"Are you done with her?"

"For the most part. Took damn near three days for her to thaw out. We've sliced her open, but BCA wants more toxicology exams. Meanwhile her family is screaming bloody murder for the body so they can bury her."

They walked down the white linoleum hall towards the cooler. "It's freezing down here," said Rick.

"The way I like it."

"Really? I would have thought you'd prefer the summer months."

"Are you kidding? Do you know what the heat does to a woman my size? I'd be wheezing up a storm. Say, is Andrea Labore going to get the anchor job? That Charleen is getting old—what is she, forty now? And who's that weekend anchor? Wasn't he in sports? God, he's terrible. Why take a bad sports guy and make him into a bad news guy?"

"It's a news show, Freddie, it's not a soap opera."

"It is to me."

While the police were busy tracking down the killer, the TV stations in town kept busy tracking the overnight ratings. After the Como Lake murder the public outcry and the media feeding frenzy sent newsroom decibel levels to record heights, even louder than the parking ramp murders and with more saturated coverage than the Wakefield kidnapping.

SERIAL KILLER STALKS TWIN CITIES!
Police Admit Killings Linked
Pursue Calendar Killer

With no more moral purpose at the back of it than there is in a televised football game, whatever TV station promised new information or a new angle on the serial killings won the nightly ratings war. It was that simple.

Freddie threw open the cooler door. It automatically closed behind them. The temperature was just above freezing. The dead, a dozen of them, were laid out on gurneys along the walls, covered with white sheets. The room smelled like a bait shop. Insects scurried across the floor and climbed the walls.

"Don't you people ever spray in here?"

"Doesn't do any good," Freddie told him. "They come in with the bodies. The cold gets most of them. We put plastic bags over the dead heads to keep them out. Bugs love the heads—so many points of entry, and it's warm in there." The woman knew death. She had four years of college, four years of medical school, five years of residency, and two years as a fellow in forensic pathology. Her salary was half of what most doctors earn, but she loved her job.

Freddie pulled a gurney into the center of the cooler, then grabbed a clipboard from the wall. "This is her." She read from the form. "Case number 91-1868 ... homicide ... Livingston, Tamara ... female ... twenty-three ... single ... St. Paul, Minnesota ... last seen, December twenty-four, walking south on Lexington from aunt's home ... found December twenty-five in a frozen state on Como Lake." She looked up at Rick. "Hold the door, lover, we'll push her down to the E room."

In the examination room Freddie pulled the sheet from the body. Rick Beanblossom grabbed the feet and they lifted her onto the porcelain table. The room was white and sterile with the redolence of antiseptic and formaldehyde. The lights were bright. Glass cabinets and aluminum sinks lined the walls. In neat rows on aluminum shelving above the sinks were hundreds of bottles of the formaldehyde, each clear glass jar keeping alive the tissue specimen or body part of a dead person. Freddie removed the clear plastic bag from the victim's twisted head. "If you love a good mystery, this is the place to work."

She looked a lot like the suicide he had seen in the elevator, blond hair on a purple face. But the golden hair had been matted in the freezing rain. A Y incision ran from her belly button to her shoulders. "Tell me about her," Rick said.

"Well, pretty as she was, she never won a beauty contest. Not with those tits." Freddie belted out a good laugh. "Do you have sex?"

"You're a real trip, Freddie. Excluding the killer, the only person who would know as much about this case as the police would be the person who examined two of the victims. Talk to me."

"Typical newsman—all take and no give. After all the info I've fed you over the years I think a little quid pro quo is in order."

"Such as?"

"Show me your face."

"Has the FBI examined any of the victims?"

"What's the harm? With all of the mutilated stiffs I've seen, it's no big deal. Just flip up that mask for two seconds. Show me your face, lover, and I'll let you see the brains."

"What physical evidence ties these murders together?"

"There's only one way to hurt news people—deny them access to the news." Freddie clammed up.

The attendant Rick had met in the elevator wheeled in the hanging victim with the shriveled penis and laid him out on another table. Freddie paid him no attention. "CNN is opening an office here," Rick told her, "and one of those tabloid TV shows is going do an episode on the killings."

Freddie snickered. "I could read that in the newspapers."

Rick Beanblossom circled the table, examining the woman's body. He had seen so many bodies over the years. In Vietnam. At the hospital in Japan. On the police beat. Still, he couldn't get over how fragile the naked and the dead look. Tamara Livingston was almost sticklike. Frost-white skin. There was a tear in her neck exposing muscle fibers. Rick pulled up next to Freddie, the gossip hound from hell. He put his hands on his hips and shared with her the sleaziest aspect of television news. "Our news director, Jack Napoleon . . . he bugged his own office. He has a hidden camera in there. He tapes himself seducing women."

Freddie's eyes lit up. "Really? Do you have any of the tapes?"

"I might."

"FBI doesn't want anything to do with this case. They jumped into the Wakefield kidnapping with their so-called task force and they got burned. Zilch. Squat. Nada."

"Physical evidence?"

"Oh, that's the beauty of this guy. He's in and out like the wind. Other than that fingerprint at the first murder, he's left nothing behind. It'll be hard to convict him for one murder, much less four. He uses a choke hold. Quick, clean, and decisive. Marines, cops, wrestlers, the martial arts, they all know it."

"No struggle? Scratch marks? Blood?"

"Nope. I figure he wears a nylon jacket or a raincoat, depending on the weather. They can't get a grip on his arm that way. Hasn't left any fibers or skin under their nails. Not even a hair."

"Might our killer be a woman? A big, strong woman?"

She laughed. "You mean like me?"

"Why not? You're a tough broad."

"No, this is a man's work. Serial killers are predominately white males. They prey on white females. This is a powerful man. He gets his victims in the crook of his arm, lifts them right off their feet. Three of them, like this cutie pie here, he breaks their necks. The Hudson case, he just strangled and dropped her, then did that hair thing. The MO is the same on all of them."

"No rape, no mutilation," Rick reminded her.

"He's killing for other than sexual reasons. Hate. Jealousy. Voices in his head. He's not out to commit the perfect crime. He expects to get caught. It's part of his sick plan. The crimes. The arrest. The media circus. The trial.

The sentence. Then he'll play the role of the martyr, swearing he's innocent right up to the day he dies."

"What does he look like?"

"He's over six feet tall, more than two hundred pounds. If you believe the Hudson description, he has dark, curly hair, like mine."

"I could get that from the newspapers. Keep talking."

"He knows the media. He plays you guys like a fiddle. That's part of the thrill, like the politician who runs home to watch himself on the news. How come you people named him the Calendar Killer? I'd have called him the North Star Strangler. Sounds better on television."

"He's killing one woman every season. I wanted to call him 'A Killer for All Seasons,' but it was too many words for the TelePrompTer."

"The first two victims were killed last summer," Freddie reminded him.

"Wrong," Rick told her. "They were both killed in June. One was murdered before June twenty-first, the other after the twenty-first. Spring and summer. He's killing with the calendar. He got number three over in Hudson in autumn. This is his winter kill. If they don't catch him, he'll kill again in the spring. Each murder precedes or occurs during some significant weather event. Even the Hudson murder. Dixon Bell checked with the National Weather Service. The day the Indian girl was killed on the St. Croix River, the Twin Cities airport recorded one hundred percent sunshine. It was the last day of one hundred percent sunshine before winter."

Freddie scoffed at the weather theory. "That would make sense if he had killed her in the evening, but he killed her in the morning. How did he know there was going to be one hundred percent sunshine all day? How did he know the tornado was coming? How did he know we were in for record rainfall?"

"I don't know yet, but these murders are seasonal and they're weather related. Weather buffs are a dime a dozen in this state. What do you know about that fingerprint from the first murder?"

"You mean from the parking ramp where you park your car, Masked Man?" She smiled, a wicked smile. "Relax. My police sources tell me so far it's a bust. It's only a partial print, and a lousy one. The BCA is going to feed it into their new five-million-dollar fingerprint computer if they ever get the damn thing up and running. Can't you just hear the taxpayers screaming if it spits out blanks? So who has he nailed, that news director guy?"

"So far, a couple interns who want to be on TV."

"Does Dixon Bell have a girlfriend yet?"

"None that I know of."

"I hear he's hot for Andrea Labore."

"I don't keep tabs on our weatherman's love life."

"I wanted to be a TV weather girl when I was in college. I even interned for it at Channel 9. That was years ago."

"So what happened?"

"Nobody would let me on the air because I'm fat."

"I guess you and I are just lucky that way."

"How about you, lover? Who are you hot for?"

Rick stared into the dead, purple face of Tamara Livingston. "I'm a writer. We live sad, lonely lives."

"You know there are rumors in police circles about that Andrea Labore."

Rick looked up. "What kind of rumors?"

"Show me your face?"

"I think you've done too many autopsies, Freddie."

"Yeah, five hundred a year can make you a real sicko."

"Let's have a look at those brains."

They left Tamara Livingston naked and alone on the table, only the hanging victim to keep her company. Freddie led Rick Beanblossom into the storage closet off the examination room. Round white buckets lined the floor, all labeled with names and dates. A human brain lay drying inside each bucket. They were green and white with the texture of cauliflower. "We'll pull her brain out tomorrow and let it sit in here for about three weeks, until it's dry and crunchy. Then we can cut it up for chemical analysis."

Rick pointed. "That small one there, is that a baby?"

"No, that's a TV reporter." Freddie broke up laughing. She clapped her hands together. "Boy, that Channel 7 must be a lively place to work. Kind of wish I'd stuck with television."

"It's a news show, Freddie, it's not a soap opera."

"Oh, it is to me."

THE THAW

Another page fell from the calendar. The hunt for the monster who killed with the seasons continued into February. The winter weather remained mild. Clouds over the IDS Tower were dark and gray, but they were still being perceived as nonthreatening. In the Sky High newsroom red hearts were pasted to the desks and walls. Little cupids with their bows and arrows were dangling from the ceiling. It was St. Valentine's Day. On the assignment board Gayle listed a live shot from a greeting-card store. Same story as last year—different store, different reporter. There were fresh flowers on Rick Beanblossom's desk, but then there always were.

"So what have you done for me lately?"

"That's my line. Talk to me." With the phone to his ear Rick pulled a new legal pad from his desk drawer and plopped it down in front of him. He picked up a pen.

"What do you want to hear?"

The producer reached up and killed the sound on his monitor. "Tell me you're leaving to arrest the Calendar Killer and I get to come along."

"What happened to my story on the death penalty?"

"I said I'd write it if it gets out of committee. It doesn't look like they have the votes. Any progress on that fingerprint?"

"There's a glitch in the computer. We haven't been able to run it yet."

"You spent five million dollars on a computer and it comes with glitches?"

"I do have an unrelated tidbit of news for you. You know that Andrea Labore you've been working with?"

"What about her?"

"She's the governor's girlfriend."

The news was a kick in the groin. Rick wanted to double over. He didn't want to believe it. "How could you possibly know something like that?"

"State patrol. They guard the mansion. Tell her they should be a little more discreet."

Dateline went dead.

Rick hung up the phone and grabbed his aching stomach. He was furious. How could a woman with so much brains do something so incredibly stupid? She was at her desk. He reached for his painkillers. What to do? He could wait until spring and murder the bitch. Blackmail was an erotic possibility.

Newly arrived flowers along with a small stack of valentines lay on her messy desk. She was examining notes. The beginning of a news story was glowing on her computer screen. A soap opera was showing on her monitor. She was wearing a red dress that matched the glow in her cheeks. She had no business looking so cheerful. Rick hovered over her like a lion over its prey. He waited until she glanced up from her notebook. "Hi," she said, unconcerned. She held up a videotape. "This Livingston interview is powerful stuff." She picked up another tape. "And get this, an Andrea Labore exclusive—they gave me some home video of Tamara opening presents at her aunt's house just hours before she was murdered."

Rick Beanblossom remained stone cold.

"What's wrong?"

"Let me ask you something, brown eyes. Do you want that anchor chair up there, or do you want to end up the bimbo from the Scandinavian scandal?"

"What are you talking about?"

"You know goddamn well what I'm talking about."

Andrea read the news in his eyes. She tossed the videos on the desk. "How did you find out?"

"A source. A deadly reliable source."

She turned to her computer. She could see his mask reflected in the screen. "That's what I need now, trouble from you. Just when I thought our relationship was starting to thaw."

Rick stuck his mouth almost to her ear and spoke in a whisper so intense, so wrought with anger and frustration she was visibly shaken. "We do not have a relationship.

We have a working partnership—two investigative reporters in search of a killer who preys on women. A killer some theorize may actually be a woman. Now I find out that my woman partner, a woman I was just coming to trust, is literally fucking around with the governor of the state."

She rubbed goose bumps from her arm. "Stop it, Rick. Sometimes you scare me."

He raised his voice. "Why? What do you think I'm going to do to you?"

People glanced their way. "Let's find an edit room," she said.

Andrea grabbed at her notebook and the two videotapes. They marched down a narrow hall leading out of the newsroom and entered Edit Room 3. Rick slid the glass door closed. Andrea dropped into a chair in front of the controls. She popped one of the videotapes into the edit machine. Rick stood over her shoulder.

The parents of murder victim Tamara Livingston appeared before them on three different monitors. Members of an ecumenical group of born-again Christians whose roots lay in Catholicism, they were talking to Andrea about their opposition to the death penalty, the debate now raging in the Minnesota state legislature. They asked proponents of capital punishment to please stop invoking their daughter's name.

Rick thought it was good stuff, but he didn't want to give her the satisfaction. He and Andrea argued over the sound, Andrea talking at the television monitors, refusing to turn and face him. Finally, almost in exasperation, she said, "It's not just sex. We're in love. Okay? It just happened. You can't choose who you fall in love with."

Rick felt a new kind of rage stirring inside of him. "Love? Is that your idea of love? No, what you've got going is a little romance. Do you know what romance is, Andrea? It's a suspension of reality. Because the reality is you can choose who you date. You can choose who you jump into bed with. And you can choose to end a relationship, for love or a lack of love."

Andrea turned, fury in her eyes. "And what the hell would you know about reality or love, you asshole? You use that mask to hide from both. You hide everything in there. You hide in this newsroom during the day. Then at night you run home and hide in that obscene slab of concrete over the lake. You're like those Indians who used to build those holes in the cliffs so their enemies couldn't get to them. Well, some of us have to face the real world."

On the video Mrs. Livingston broke down crying. Andrea instinctively jotted down the numbers from the time counter display. Television 101—if you can get them crying, televise it.

Rick fought to control his breathing. He still stuttered when he got upset. "And in the real world where do you think this secret relationship of yours is going to go? Is he going throw his wife and children out of the governor's mansion, marry you, and make you the first lady of Minnesota? Oh, hell, let's play it out. He's probably going to run for President just to make Andrea Labore the first lady of the United States of America. Or just maybe he's going to fuck your lights out until he gets tired of you? Or is one of you going to go public with your love and destroy the other? Or is a certain gossip columnist for the *Star Tribune* going to find out about it and destroy both of you?"

"Shut up," said Andrea. "Just shut up for two seconds." She ejected the video and popped in a second. Tamara Livingston appeared on the monitors, kneeling before a Christmas tree. Rick had seen her in death; now he was seeing what she had looked like in life. She was unwrapping a gift. It turned out to be a nightgown, a skimpy, slinky nightgown. There was no audio, but from the laughter in her face it was obvious jokes were being made about how sexy it was.

"What happened to the nightgown?"

"What?"

Rick pointed to the monitors. "The gift? She would have been walking home with it."

"They told me it hasn't been found." The tape played out. Tamara Livingston was gone. The screens turned snowy white.

Locked in a glass booth, the silence between Rick Beanblossom and Andrea Labore crackled with electricity. Rick broke the spell, speaking now with more passion than anger. "You're still fairly new to news, Andrea, so let me offer you some advice. There's only one other pro-

fession that more uses people and more hurts people than
we do. That's politicians. If it comes down to you and
him, and eventually it will, he'll hang you from a tree
limb. He'll line you up against a wall and shoot you himself. He'll do it to save his own ass, or he'll just do it out
of spite. And all of the love in the world won't stop him."

Andrea spoke with a passion all her own. "Get a life,
Rick. I mean a real life. And stay out of mine."

When the long-range forecasters at the National Weather
Service huddled in the fall to predict the winter weather,
they all came to the same general conclusion. Harsh! Temperatures below normal. Precipitation above average. But
three months later Old Man Winter limped out of town
with emphysema, destined for obscurity in the archives of
climatology. The ninety-day winter forecast was the least
accurate ever issued by the National Weather Service.
These winter forecasts are watched closely by commodities
brokers, travel agents, snow-equipment manufacturers, and
farmers. Nobody at the National Weather Service would
comment on the remarkably accurate winter forecast made
by a TV weatherman in Minneapolis. By March 21, the ice
was out on the lakes. It was raining steadily. The last stubborn patches of snow were washed away. Winter was history.

The first day of spring, Captain Les Angelbeck and
Lieutenant Donnell Redmond sat in their unmarked squad
staring at the walk path. Rain pounded the roof.
Angelbeck smoked a cigarette. The windshield was fog-
ging up. Redmond didn't give a damn. Both men were
speechless.

The trees were still bare. The grass was thick with
thatch. A pair of frightened deer peeked out of the woods
along Nine Mile Creek. The two cops watched as the big
Chevy Suburban from the county medical examiner's office backed over the curb and rolled over the grass to the
edge of the path.

The news photographers formed a semicircle in the
cold, hard rain. The ME personnel removed the plastic
tarp from the Bloomington woman's body. They lifted the
sodden sweat suit, placed it in a shiny green body bag,
and pulled the zipper tight. Then victim number five was

loaded into the back of the van. Angelbeck flinched at the muffled sound of the slamming doors.

The photographers had the shot they'd been waiting for. They ran back to their own vans.

Donnell Redmond tapped a finger on the steering wheel. "Those TV people are going to crucify us."

THE AFFAIR

Mild winter—wild summer. The heat was back, and in more ways than one. Just before midnight on May 21, the Minnesota state legislature adjourned for the year. The night air was still a sultry 78° as lawmakers left the Capitol. The paleoconservatives who now pulled the strings were awarded their cherished tax cut, but much of their right-wing social agenda went frustratingly unfulfilled—mostly because of the moderate sitting in the governor's office.

Per Ellefson rose from the stiff couch and walked to the bulletproof window. He stood buttoning his shirt before the green-tinted glass, gazing out across the Capitol approach. The Cathedral of St. Paul was dark. The stars above the dome seemed to have lost their twinkle. Other than the high ceiling his office was small and stark, a disappointment to a man accustomed to the executive suites of corporate America. The only light in the office this night was the flickering flame above an antique candle holder.

"What time is it?"

The governor looked at his Rolex. "Almost midnight. You'd better get dressed."

"Are you glad they're going home?"

Ellefson pulled on his socks and slipped into his shoes. After the March murder in Bloomington the roar to do something about the killings had grown louder than spring thunder. "I've never seen anything like this. First the state supreme court kills my idea of putting television cameras in the courtrooms, a damn good idea, and then the death penalty comes within two votes of escaping the house. You know how I feel about capital punishment,

Andrea. It's not only morally wrong, it's morally bankrupt. Yet every statewide poll shows the vast majority of Minnesotans support the death penalty—and that was before we had a serial killer on our hands."

"These murders are destroying the state's image. Now the Office of Tourism says the killings are hurting business."

Per Ellefson tucked his shirt into his pants. "Most tourist dollars are spent outside the metro area. There've been no killings up there. It's still a summer playground." He shook his head at the misperception. "These are the kind of crimes that destroy careers. The fallout from something like this is frightening. The thing of it is, this man, this monster, whatever, renders me powerless. If he were a politician or a businessman I'd know how to fight him. About all I can do is stand back and let the police do their job."

"I admire the way you've handled this. Most people do. But what if he kills again?"

The governor sighed. "The old cop in charge is in poor health. I may have to replace him. Or I could ask the FBI for a federal task force like the Wakefield kidnapping and hope for better results."

Andrea Labore finished buttoning her blouse and straightened her skirt. "God, I hate the thought of having to interview the family of another victim. It's the worst assignment in news." But she did it, actually volunteered to talk with the family. Since being assigned the stranglings there had been a marked change in her reporting. Andrea had come to realize that in TV news diplomas are worthless. She never mentioned her master's degree again. She scoured the small neighborhood newspapers for story ideas. She volunteered overtime and weekends. She did a crime story whenever she could, learning how to ask the tough questions. She began listening to her photographers more. And whether it was right or not, she hit the governor up for news tips, being careful when and how she used them. For example, it was Andrea Labore who reported that the governor's office had a lot more to do with the death of the death penalty bill than was publicly believed. Ellefson had sent his supporters in the state legislature a clear message: "See to it that bill doesn't reach my desk, or kiss your tax cut good-bye."

Andrea was proud of her professional growth, but as she stepped into her shoes and brushed the wrinkles from her skirt, she looked long and hard at her lover. In the early months of their affair Per Ellefson seemed completely obsessed with her face, with her body, physical attraction only, but slowly their passion seemed to melt into love—a dangerous kind of love.

The governor dropped a noose-knotted tie around his neck and pulled it tight. "Does that weatherman bother you anymore?"

"No, but I think he still has a schoolboy's crush on me. He's hard to read."

"He seems like such a great guy."

Andrea pulled a mirror and a hair brush from her purse. "He may be or he may not be. It's one of the problems with television. It doesn't unmask the people who work in it."

"We had him in the office here last winter to present him with a plaque for his children series. Remember that? He turned right around and gave me this electronic weather station for my desk." Ellefson picked up the weather instrument. "This thing must be worth a thousand dollars. He told me, 'No matter how wrong you are, Governor, you'll always be right about the weather.' Damned if I'm not checking this thing every day. Maybe you should have gone out with him."

She shrugged. "My problems in the newsroom aren't with our weatherman. There's a news producer who knows about us . . . Rick Beanblossom."

Ellefson set the weather station back on the desk. "That burn-victim guy who won the Pulitzer Prize?"

"Yes. He's been with us for two years now. I've been working with him on the killings. He has a lot of police sources. I think that's how he found out."

The governor stiffened. "Would he use it against us?"

"Rick's got a lot of integrity, but it's kind of a ruthless integrity. Like a million other reporters, he's writing a novel. God only knows what he'd put in that book." Andrea paused, took a deep breath, then said slowly, "Why, are you getting tired of me?"

"Why do you ask such a thing?"

She didn't look at him. "Men get tired of me. That's been my experience."

Per Ellefson returned to the couch. He took the brush from her hand. He slowly undid her blouse again, exposing a breast. The governor cupped her breast in his hand and kissed her on the lips. "I love you, Andrea, understand that. I'm trying to make the best of a difficult situation."

Andrea pressed his hand over her heart. "Sometimes I wonder if the risk is too much of the excitement."

He flopped on his back, his head in her lap. "Andrea, my love, we can't have this conversation now."

"I know, it's late."

"Yes, it's late."

Andrea Labore took her manicured fingernails and ran them up the governor's pant leg, over his zipper. There she stopped. "Since it's so late anyway . . ."

THE HEAT

The heat wave intensified in June, as did Captain Les Angelbeck's investigation into the five murders. In a larger metropolitan area, New York or Los Angeles, the killings could have been unrelated, or copycat killings. But in the quiet, quaint Twin Cities this type of crime was unheard of. For the first time in his life, and perhaps the last case of his storied career, he was hunting a serial killer.

"Isn't the fingerprint the calling card of every criminal?"

Nothing in police work had changed more dramatically over Les Angelbeck's long career than fingerprinting. It used to be a thousand cardboard boxes stuffed with fingerprint cards and a couple of folding tables in a basement storage room. The new and much-delayed BCA computer center he was now standing in had cost the state more than five million dollars. The captain twirled an unlit Marlboro between his fat yellow fingers. He cleared his throat and waited for an answer.

"Yes, but your chances of scoring a hit with this calling card are slim. It's not even a good partial print. I think the best we can hope for is a list of probables, and I can all but guarantee you they'll all be rated low probability."

Identifying criminals by their fingerprints had been routine since the turn of the century, when Scotland Yard pioneered its systematic use. When only a fingerprint led police to a suspect it was called a "cold make." On TV cop shows it happened all the time. In reality, a cold make was as rare as snow in June. Then in the 1970s the FBI assigned computers the giant task of classifying its massive fingerprint collection. By the 1980s fingerprints around the world were being converted to digital form using so-called points of minutiae, and the Automated Fingerprint Identification System was born—AFIS for short. AFIS was the most revolutionary advance in law enforcement since radios were put into patrol cars. Cold makes became as routine as spring rain. But partial prints still posed a problem.

"Looking at it, my guess is it's the left index finger. But I got nothing when I ran that. I tried the right index next. Nothing. I'm working on the left middle finger now."

His name was Glenn Arkwright. He was a fingerprint expert, or a computer expert, Angelbeck wasn't sure. His sleeves were rolled up, his tie was loose. Arkwright stuck his hands under his glasses and rubbed his weary eyes. The image of the partial fingerprint taken off the transformer atop the Sky High parking ramp was glowing on the display screen.

The computer kept asking questions. Arkwright kept punching in the answers. The cursor sped across a crazy road map of what they believed was the killer's fingerprint. To Angelbeck it seemed like a boring video game.

"A good fingerprint has a hundred digits," Arkwright told him. "This one has only seven." He hit the return button, folded his arms, and waited. The computer worked its magic, but the printer remained silent. "There is the possibility that your boy has never been fingerprinted."

"What if it's a woman?"

Arkwright laughed, a hopeless laugh. "Then you're piss out of luck. Few women get arrested, few women serve in the military, so few women ever get fingerprinted."

"And this new computer will check all ten prints on every card?"

"Yup, every one of them. It would take a man thirty years to conduct a search like this."

"How many cards are we talking about?"

"The FBI has twenty-three million fingerprint cards on file, and they receive an additional twenty-five thousand cards every day."

The technology to examine those kinds of numbers

baffled the veteran cop. "What, if any, recorded finger-prints wouldn't be in their computer files?"

"The classifieds. DEA personnel, CIA, military intelli-gence, that sort of thing."

"And how would we get those?"

Glenn Arkwright sighed at the thought. "We'd have to petition each agency and each branch of the military sep-arately. We've done it in the past. It's a bureaucratic nightmare with mixed results."

The printer jumped to life. Arkwright ripped off the pa-per as if it were routine. It was. He glanced at it, then handed the printout to the police captain.

"Kesling, Jerome John. Louisville, Kentucky. Who's this?"

"Just a man who was once fingerprinted." Arkwright pointed at the printout. "Do you see those columns of numbers? That's a very low probability rating. With a partial like this, we could get a hundred names like that."

Les Angelbeck coughed into his fist. So much for the greatest advance since police radios. He checked his watch, then looked around the sterile computer room. "Is there a television in here? My daughter is flying in from California. I want to see if this weather is going to hold."

Dixon Bell fitted his earpiece and checked his micro-phone. The burst of fire in the sky was so bright it was blinding. He slid on his sunglasses. The steamy air smelled of beer and bratwurst. The thunder was deafen-ing, the thunder of race cars.

If Minnesota is a summer playground, then the small town of Lake Country is Minnesota's summer capital. Two and a half hours northwest of the Twin Cities, Lake Country has had a reputation as Sodom and Gomorrah in the north woods since the 1930s, when Hollywood movie stars and Chicago gangsters rented cabins on the shores of the area's pristine waters. But like many a popular va-cation spot, Lake Country fell victim to the relentless ad-vance of the chainsaws. Lakes born of a glacier and surrounded by woodland were now surrounded by golf courses and condominiums. Nightlife had replaced wild-life. And at no place during the overheated summer week-ends was nightlife wilder than at Lake Country

International Raceway, a five-hundred-acre facility with a sprawling campground located smack dab in the middle of the road-race track.

The Weatherman bent over his scorching notes. A high-pressure system was entrenched over the central plains states. The National Weather Service would not confirm his numbers. He wiped sweat from his brow. The temperature was still above 100°. During a live shot too many things can go wrong, so Sky High News bought satellite time from 5:00 P.M. until 5:25, just to be safe. The engineer in the truck checked his coordinates. The photographer was having trouble with the sound. Noise from the race track was maddening.

It was the Fourth of July weekend, and record temperatures and record crowds were zeroing in on Lake Country. One hundred thousand of the rowdiest racing fans in the Midwest descended on the resort community for an all-American celebration of hot cars, cold beer, steamy sex, and the waving of the Stars and Stripes. Four hundred dragsters were competing for $500,000 in prize money. In a much lesser event, notices for a wet T-shirt contest were posted on trees, along with sign-up sheets. A thousand dollars in cash would be shared by the best-breasts winners.

"Can you hear the studio?" asked the photog.

"No," shouted Dixon Bell, adjusting his earpiece.

"They're getting you fine. You'll get it from Ron at the top of the show, then throw it to the new guy when you're done. One minute away. When I drop my arm, just start talking."

Dixon Bell shook his head in disgust. The grass was trampled to dust. He felt filthy. The echo of the PA announcer was giving him a headache. He swore into the microphone. "Whose stupid-ass idea was this? It's the hottest day in history and these motorheads have been drinking since sunrise."

At the Minneapolis Grain Exchange commodity brokers tuned their television sets to Channel 7. During the corn-and-soybean-growing season the weather forecasts of Dixon Bell had become a local market phenomenon. They could spark wild bursts of trading as brokers tried to key in on the volatile weather in the Midwest that can make or break a crop. On the exchange floor there was speculation that Dixon Bell dabbled in commodities trading, or that he was running a consulting business on the side. He vehemently denied these rumors, saying it would be unethical. He did admit to being offered high-paying jobs by private forecasters such as Cropcast, Pennsylvania-based AccuWeather, and Knight-Ridder Global Weather Services. The Weatherman turned down these offers, telling suitors he was happy at Sky High News and that he was more interested in developing new educational programs for television.

The photographer raised his fist to the sun. "Stand by!"

Dixon Bell put on his happy face. The photog dropped his arm. The Weatherman looked up at the relentless summer sun and smiled. "We did it, Ron. The hottest recorded temperature in Minnesota history. At 1:58 this afternoon the mercury up here in Lake Country topped out at one hundred and fifteen degrees, breaking the old record set in Moorhead back in 1936."

When Dixon Bell wrapped up his record-breaking forecast, he tossed it to the new guy on the other side of the race track, who reported on the record number of heat strokes brought on by too much sun and too much beer. A reporter back at the station followed with a report on global warming.

Dixon Bell went live from Lake Country at six o'clock and ten o'clock that night. When it was all over, he felt like a dirty wet T-shirt. The photographer and the engineer were heading for an air-conditioned bar in town. Dixon Bell excused himself. Much of the crowd was moving north toward the grandstands to watch the fireworks display. Others headed south for the campgrounds to watch the wet-T-shirt contest. For a minute the Weatherman stood by himself in the oppressive heat. An ambulance circled the race track, lights flashing. Then Dixon Bell bought a cold beer and set out south.

This sprawling campground in the middle of the track was known among racing fans as the Zoo, an island of lawlessness in an ocean of beer. Police were nonexistent. Security was a joke. Between the tents and the campfires super car stereo systems pulsated with hard rock—the dirtier the lyrics, the louder the music. Roadsters and motorcycles dragged up and down the dirt roads that crisscrossed the campgrounds. Dixon Bell had never seen anything like it, and he had seen a lot in his life. Everybody in sight was half-naked with a beer in their hand.

He followed the dusty crowd past hot cars and hotter women. Shirtless men sat drinking on the hoods of their sparkling machines, giving the war cry of the Zoo: "Show us your tits, bitch! Show us your tits, bitch!" Dixon Bell couldn't believe it when a young girl hiked up her T-shirt and flashed her nipples. Judging from the whistles, the incident was routine and her tits were average.

The contest stage was makeshift—scaffolding and ropes, somewhat of a cross between a boxing ring and a gallows. A sign strung across the top read, WELCOME TO THE LAND OF SKY BLUE WATERS. The crowd pushed right up against the ropes. Dixon Bell guessed there were as many as five thousand drunk and rowdy spectators. He was able to worm his way to the front, where he enjoyed a good view, but it was like standing in a steambath. He gulped his beer. Lighting over the stage was poor, creating harsh glares. The Weatherman was thankful for his sunglasses.

The master of ceremonies bounded on stage, a healthy, good-looking guy with a scratchy microphone. He was surrounded by five bouncers, large, burly men with beer froth spilling out their lips.

Next, big old Harleys roared onto the stage and unloaded six girls. Flashbulbs began popping. The judge introduced the contestants by their hometowns only. No names. Two brunettes hailed from Minneapolis and St. Paul. Lake Country was represented in blonde. Duluth was a redhead. Thief River Falls looked almost like a boy. And the oldest girl, from Crystal, looked to be a frightened twenty-one, whereas the others appeared to be nothing but slutty teenagers. They were all sipping beer, but three of the teen contestants had a spacey demeanor Dixon Bell recognized from Vietnam. They were drugged—maybe marijuana, probably cocaine.

The fun began for the crowd even before the last T-shirt was doused. St. Paul stepped out of her shorts and showed off her skimpy panties.

"Show us your tits, bitch! Show us your tits, bitch!"

Not to be outdone by St. Paul, Minneapolis peeled off her wet T-shirt and bravely displayed her bare breasts to the throng. The crowd roared its approval. The young man standing next to Dixon Bell had his girlfriend on his shoulders. She was aiming a video camera at the stage. Other video cameras were hoisted into the air. Then came an even bigger thrill. Fireworks exploded overhead. The night sky was dazzling. The crowd was ecstatic.

Within minutes the wet-T-shirt contest degenerated into a striptease show. Duluth and Thief River Falls left the stage without competing. The four girls left behind had stripped naked but for their shoes.

"How are we going to judge this?" the announcer asked his frenzied audience.

The crowd surged toward the stage, drunk and delirious with delight. Spectacular fireworks lit up the sky. Two of the girls climbed onto the ropes and made sexy gestures to the fans below. Another naked teen flirted with a bouncer. But the naked girl from Crystal stood frozen at center stage, like a deer caught in city traffic. This was the girl Dixon Bell fixed on. In the glare of the lights it was hard to see her face, but her diminutive body was starkly white for the middle of summer. A tragic figure. Soon the girls on the ropes were flirting with the bouncers on stage, and the fawn from Crystal decided it was time to leave. The Weatherman watched her gather up her clothes and clumsily step back into her panties as she quit the contest. The crowd booed Crystal's ungainly exit. Dixon Bell finished his beer and dropped the cup.

The last three contestants, naked and stoned, were now pretending to dance with the burly bouncers on the rickety stage beneath the fireworks beneath the stars. The master of ceremonies laid down his microphone, threw up his hands in mock disgust, and walked away. The contest was totally out of control. The crowd was shaking the scaffolding. "Do it! Do it! Do it! Do it!"

The girls looked like stick people in the arms of the big burly men. At stage left bouncer number one hoisted Minneapolis high into the air. She spread her legs over his face and came down on top of him.

Off to the right bouncer number three dropped to the rear of a Harley, and St. Paul dropped to her knees between his legs. The ovation was deafening.

But the main event was at center stage. The biggest and baddest of the bouncers did a slow striptease of his own, letting it all hang out, and he was hung like a stick of dynamite. He lifted Lake Country into the air. She wrapped her legs around his waist and he dropped her down over his great big firecracker and pumped her up and down as if he were pumping iron from the standing position. The sky exploded in multiple fireworks. Five thousand motorheads had a collective orgasm.

It was not a proud night for the Land of Sky Blue Waters. For a share of one thousand dollars women paid one hell of a price. Of the final four girls in the Fourth of July wet-T-shirt contest, the third-place winner had her dignity eaten in public; the second-place finisher gagged down on her knees; first place would deliver a cocaine baby nine months later—and the Crystal girl who came to her senses and left the stage, finishing out of the money, had her neck snapped in two.

THE MORGUE

When the elevator door slid open Andrea Labore found herself for the first time in a morgue. It was freezing, but it was a refreshing respite from the killer heat wave. A bubble of super-heated air was still camped over the Midwest.

"I usually don't let reporters down here. Just Rick." They were in the examination room—Andrea and the chief medical examiner, Dr. Freda Wilhelm. The doctor was wearing her snazzy uniform, a startling contrast to Andrea's expensive blue pantsuit and ivory silk blouse.

Andrea winced at the formaldehyde fumes. "I understand that, Doctor," she said, "and I appreciate your seeing me. Rick was going to come, but I thought it might be a good idea for me to see what goes on in a morgue. Besides, I've always wanted to meet you."

Freddie smiled but remained on guard. "Rick said that you could charm the socks off a serial killer." She pulled the white sheet from the body on the table. "Well, this is her, Andrea. Victim number six." She read from her clipboard. "Case number 91-1903 ... Homicide ... Petrie, Ali ... female ... twenty-one ... single ... Crystal, Minnesota ... last seen July four, Lake Country, Minnesota ... found July five, floating in a beer puddle behind a Winnebago, Lake Country Raceway."

Andrea Labore had not been on the police force long enough to see the bodies of murder victims, not even the body she had pumped a bullet into. She took a deep breath. Ali Petrie's skin was snow white. The bruising and swelling that circled her neck made it appear as if the head had been reattached to the torso. Other than to the neck, no physical harm seemed to have been done to the body—the same pattern as the other killings. "Have you ever seen anything like this before—I mean, one victim after another?"

Freddie shrugged, almost indifferent. "In every city in this country, violent women-hating is a daily truth. When a man in a rage goes hunting for a victim, nine times out of ten he hunts for a woman—any woman. The news is that terrorism against women is not news."

"I agree, but still . . ." Andrea moved closer to examine the girl's broken neck. She tried in vain to imagine the arm that could do such a thing. "What can you tell me about that fingerprint they found at the first murder scene?"

"Just what I told Rick."

"Tell me."

Freddie hesitated. Andrea waited. The county's chief gossip hound couldn't keep a secret if her life depended on it. "So far it's a bust. It's only a partial print and a lousy one. The state's new fingerprint computer spit out fifty-nine names to work with and all of them have a low probability rating. None of the names are from Minnesota or Wisconsin. The BCA is petitioning the CIA, the DEA, the FBI, and each branch of military intelligence for access to their classified prints. Good luck, huh? They're crazy if they think the name of this killer is going to pop out of a computer."

Through her reading Andrea learned that the world's first known serial killer was probably Jack the Ripper, who stalked London's East End in 1888. He killed five times—all women. The case was never solved.

The medical examiner told her even more as she meticulously arranged surgical instruments on a cart beside the corpse. "You know, Andrea, in the early sixties the Boston Strangler killed thirteen women. A suspect was arrested and confined to a state hospital, but he never stood trial for the murders. That could happen here." Freddie picked up a scalpel, so razor-sharp it glistened under the lights. "And the Green River killer in King County, Washington, has been on the prowl for more than twelve years. He's racked up forty-nine murders—all of them women. Those murders remain unsolved. That could happen here."

"So I've learned." To get at the heart of the story the

up-and-coming Channel 7 reporter had driven four hours into Wisconsin to talk to a serial killer locked up in the Columbia Correctional Institution. In her research Andrea learned serial killers often had a history of abuse or serious head injuries in childhood, or a combination of the two. They were loners with military service, or men who were denied military service for asocial reasons. They were extremely manipulative, very good at telling people what they wanted to hear. Almost charming. Serial killers often kept diaries in which it was hard to tell how much was fantasy and how much was truth. She was surprised to learn how many of them were locked up in America's prisons, how few of them had been executed. They seldom committed suicide. Even more disturbing to Andrea—law-enforcement authorities claim there are at least thirty-five serial killers roaming the country and killing at random.

Meanwhile, the man she loved, the governor of Minnesota, had just announced with much fanfare the formation of the Calendar Task Force. This task force would be spearheaded by his own Minnesota Bureau of Criminal Apprehension with assistance from the FBI. Per Ellefson, still resisting calls for a special session of the legislature to reconsider the issue of capital punishment, was putting his own office and his own reputation on the line.

"When is Charleen's contract up?" Freddie wanted to know. "You're next in line for anchor, aren't you? I can tell by the stories they give you."

"Why do you ask? Don't you like Charleen?"

"She's getting too old for television. She looks like her face is going to crack any day now. Do you like working with Rick?"

The man Andrea worked so well with, the man in the mask, remained cold and aloof on a personal level, often bitter, as much a mystery to her as the murders they were trying to solve. "Not always."

"How about Dixon Bell?"

"He's a total professional."

Freddie seemed to contemplate that answer. "I think he should lighten up. He's too tense on the air. He takes the weather far too seriously. If it's going to rain, it's going to rain."

"You seem to know an awful lot about our business."

"I'm a news junkie. You people are like family to me."

Andrea nodded to the body, guilty about discussing such trivia over the corpse of a murder victim. "You can cover her up now. I've seen what I came to see."

Freddie glanced down at the body. "No need. I'm going to slice her open. Would you like to watch?"

Andrea Labore almost smiled. "No, but I'll tell you what I would like, Doctor. I'd like to do a news story on you. Something a little more in depth, a little more personal than the usual ten-second sound bites we give people. Your expertise is going to be critical to solving these murders."

"In exchange for?"

Andrea looked puzzled. "What does that mean?"

"That means you do a fluff piece on me, and what am I supposed to do for you?"

This time Andrea smiled full out. "All right. I would appreciate it if you would return my phone calls. If you would give me your home phone number. If you would talk to me off the record when need be."

"I talk to Rick."

"Yes, that was a very flattering piece he wrote about you. I can understand why you're so enamored with him. But Rick won't put that kind of a story on television, where it can be seen by ten times as many people. I will."

A hint of admiration crept into Freddie's eyes. She was not dealing with the bimbo she'd been expecting. "I don't know, Andrea. Let me think about it."

THE FALL

The nighttime temperature was 44 degrees Fahrenheit, 7 degrees Celsius. The wind was out of the northwest at 18 mph. The news was delivered. Everybody had gone home. Dixon Bell sat alone in Weather Center 7 with his diary open and a letter before him. He'd read the letter a hundred times. The glow of radar screens and fluorescent digits were reflected in his troubled face. A killer frost had come and gone, as had the Indian summer. A low-pressure system had a stranglehold on the cities. Outside the weather-center window a cold autumn rain was falling with the slow beat of a drum.

The letter tore his heart out. He swallowed his anger. He thought of Andrea, then of Lisa. The Weatherman put his finger to his face and traced the scar down his cheek. The letter and the rain caused him to remember still another girl he'd fallen head over heels for ... how many years ago? He picked up a pen.

In April of 1975, Saigon fell. I was there—chief meteorologist for the United States Air Force assigned to the Defense Attaché's Office at the Tan Son Nhut Air Base. Because of the sensitivity of my work and my importance to the war machine I was classified "Intelligence."

In war hopes of victory rise and fall with the temperature. The general who doesn't know the weather is a fool. It was Dixon Bell who told the generals when the skies would clear so they could drop their bombs and their napalm. I guessed when the fog would lift so they could drop in their Marines. Every year I accurately predicted the start of the monsoon season. Yes, I made mistakes. And when I was wrong, people got killed. And when I was right, even more people got killed.

Saigon was hot like Mississippi in the summertime. The monsoon season came early that year, just as I said it would. I'd been forecasting from the air base for five years. On the afternoon of the 29th the city was in chaos. I was hurrying by the evacuation center when the sky opened up and dropped sheet after sheet of cooling rain. I jumped in out of the weather.

The evacuation center was nothing but a gymnasium inside a ramshackle building on stilts just off the east-west runway. It stunk inside. Vietnamese evacuees were packed in there like powder kegs. Thousands of them. All considered at high risk. Good as dead if we left them behind.

She couldn't have been more than four years old. I found her wandering around on her own, or more like she found me. She was dark-skinned, more brown than yellow, so I called her Tan Jan. She had perfectly rounded cheeks, a little chunky for a Vietnamese child. I'll bet she had some French in her. She was wearing white shorts and a red shirt, western in style, with cheap rubber thongs on her stubby brown feet.

The first time she held up the cup I thought she was just another beggar doing what she'd been taught to do. I ignored her, as I had taught myself to do. I moved along. A storm of anxiety hung over the center but there still seemed some order to the evacuation. C-130 transport planes were landing on the runways, taking on evacuees and then lifting off.

When I stopped again to watch the rain, Tan Jan was right behind me, tugging on my khakis. She held up the cup, a red liquid inside. She wasn't begging, she was offering it to me. I took the cup from her hands and took a whiff. No smell. I tried a sip. It was strawberry Kool-Aid. No sugar. It tasted terrible, but probably not to her.

Between my broken Vietnamese and some of the evacuees' pidgin English I learned Tan Jan was one of the orphans from Quang Tri. Their plane had left.

Nobody wanted anything to do with her. "No papers ... no papers," they kept telling me, and dismissed me with a wave of their hands. It was then I realized how desperate these people were to get out of Vietnam.

I used my status as a big, ugly American to push my way to the front of the exit line. Two American Marines stood behind a folding table examining papers. They appeared to be the only two Americans in the building, besides me. "This little one here missed her plane," I told them.

I must've sounded like an idiot. The Marines stared at me with their noses bent out of joint, like I was asking them to baby-sit. Marines don't baby-sit, and by the end of the war my Air Force rank didn't mean shit to them. "Where's her papers?" the corporal asked.

"How can she have papers, she's an orphan?"

"No fucking papers, no fucking exit visa."

I never liked Marines. These men were new to Vietnam. Their lily-white skin had yet to tan. "Where are those planes going?" I demanded to know.

"Those are American planes and oddly enough they're going to America."

"So y'all put her on a plane and let 'em worry about it at the other end."

"Get her some papers!"

I walked Tan Jan over to the makeshift lunch counter. We shared a bowl of bun bo soup and polished off the Kool-Aid. This chick knew a sucker when she saw one. I fell for her over lunch.

I was trying to think who on the base could get papers for the little girl when the first mortar round hit the roof. Bits of debris rained down on us. The gym was on fire. Tan Jan jumped into my arms and there she stayed. We weren't hurt, but others were badly wounded.

The incoming rounds were deadly accurate. Outside, rockets were hitting one a minute. Artillery fire began. The gymnasium was like a bird cage. The birds on the inside wanted out, and the birds on the outside wanted in. The fire squad arrived and doused the flames. Then the evacuees faced a choice—wait outside in the middle of a rocket attack, or stay inside and miss the planes. A thousand of them poured outside. I held Tan Jan tight as I could and followed.

It stopped raining. The sun came back. We stood in the welcome coolness and watched the air base shelled. A fully boarded C-130 ran down the runway and lifted into the sky. But another plane that had just landed took a hit to the wing. It spun off the runway and burst into flames. Other planes on the ground were exploding. With Tan Jan in my arms I watched all of this in the middle of a pushing, shoving mob being held back by South Vietnamese soldiers who were using their bayonetted rifles as barricades. I used my bulk and worked my way to the front.

Just when everybody thought there were no more planes we saw it drop out of the sky like a big green angel. Another C-130. But by then the runway was littered with debris and I thought it might not be able to land. But land it did. It circled over to the taxiway. The door was pushed open by a big, mean American man in a white shirt. He looked like a mechanic. He dropped the ramp. Then all hell broke loose.

The crowd surged forward. Me and Tan Jan were being shoved from behind by throngs of evacuees. The soldiers with their rifles were pushing us back from the front.

Further down the line soldiers threw their rifles aside and ran for the plane. The mob of people they'd been holding back broke rank and ran after them. Nobody needed papers anymore. Within seconds the doorway to the plane looked like a rugby scrum, only this mass of bodies was mean and ugly. I could see kicking feet and swinging fists flying out of the doorway. The man in the white shirt was hauling in children and punching back soldiers. The screaming and fighting was almost drowning out the bombs that were still incoming. The pilot must of sensed the danger of being overloaded because he began taxiing away almost immediately.

Most of the South Vietnamese soldiers hung on to their dignity and held the rest of the mob at bay, not afraid to use their bayonets. The soldiers in front of me weren't budging. Shells were exploding around us. The runway was being blown to bits. Several buildings were on fire. The stench of artillery stung my nose. I covered Tan Jan's face with my hand.

The C-130 left the taxiway and turned onto the runway, leaving behind it a mob of hangers-on tumbling along the ground. The plane came rolling our way. I saw men fighting to close the door. I knew in my heart no more planes would be taking off from Tan Son Nhut.

I'd been given my code words the day before. I was assigned my pick-up point that morning. I'd be choppered out later with the last of the Americans. Out in the Gulf the USS Midway was waiting for us. But the final evacuation would be strictly military and intelligence personnel, and when the time came who was to say it would be any more orderly than what I saw before me?

I was bigger and stronger than anybody else in that desperate mob that desperate day. As the plane lumbered our way they were still pushing and shoving each other in the doorway, trying to pull the door closed. The plane rolled by us and started down the runway. It was a long shot. An end run. But I decided to go for it. Whole hog.

I wrapped Tan Jan in my arms like she was a football and I was the tight end for the Dallas Cowboys just like I always wanted to be. I burst out of the pack and knocked down the two soldiers in front of me. Then I was off chasing the plane.

I hadn't run ten yards when I had to leap the bodies of two American Marines, the same Marines I'd argued with less than an hour before. In the few seconds I glimpsed their horribly disfigured faces I could tell they'd taken a direct hit from a rocket. I felt a shiver of shame run up my spine for the way I'd talked to those boys.

I held Tan Jan tight and ran as fast as I'd ever run in my life, ran even faster than I had when I caught that pass over the middle during the Homecoming game and made the longest run in Vicksburg history. I could hear the South Vietnamese soldiers swearing. They were chasing us, rifles in hand. Just don't shoot, I prayed. Then I heard American voices yelling, "Run, Dixon, run!" My buddies cheering me on from their bunkers. A rocket exploded at the end of the runway, the flash stinging my eyes.

If Dixon Graham Bell could outrun an airplane I'd have joined Ole Miss instead of the Air Force. But that big C-130 was so overloaded, and it lumbered down that runway so slow that I was catching up with it. This was the run of my life, a high I'd never experienced before. My sides were aching. Tan Jan was crying. She was holding on to me for dear life, didn't want to let go. But I pulled the child away and held her out to them. "Take her," I screamed. "Please, take her!"

They were still trying to close the door to the plane, but when they saw I wasn't going to try and board, that I just wanted them to take the girl, they held out their arms and waved me on. Their mouths were screaming encouragement but I couldn't hear the words. The plane was picking up speed.

Thank God it had just rained because I'd have doubled over in the heat. As it was I had just enough left in me for one last burst. I thrust Tan Jan as far forward as I could. Then the mean looking man in the white shirt snatched her from my arms and I fought to keep my balance without her. She got pulled kicking and screaming into the plane and the door swung closed.

I stumbled and fell onto the runway, still wet from the rain. The South Vietnamese soldiers arrived out of breath and put the boot to me. A bayonet slashed my face. I covered my head. They were just taking out their frustration on the only American they were free to stomp on. When their anger was spent I peeked through my bloody fingers and saw the fat plane lift slowly off the ground, barely clearing the abandoned control tower. The big green angel climbed higher and higher into the smoky sky until I lost sight of it in the Asian sun.

The Weatherman laid down his pen. It helped to record such memories. Again he picked up the letter and traced his scar. Perhaps some night he'd write about it. But not this night. He folded the letter and slipped it into his diary. Closed it. Walked to the window.

The downpour continued. Rain driven by wind had stripped the trees of their glorious colors. An occasional burst of lightning lit up the Cities, revealing naked limbs against a black sky. The ugly season. When he was a little boy back in the early fifties, his granddaddy and he got caught in a thunderstorm in Louisiana. They were driving home from Baton Rouge and his granddaddy pulled off the road because it was raining cats and dogs and he couldn't see a thing. Then lightning lit up the sky just as a truck was passing by and Dixon Bell saw that the truck had a big wooden chair strapped to its flatbed. His granddaddy told him it was the electric chair. Louisiana just had that one chair and they drove it around to the counties where a prisoner needed to be executed. To this day it remained the most frightening thing he'd ever seen.

Dixon Bell switched on a lamp over the work table and flipped through the surface maps. Three maps down somebody had scrawled in red ink, *"I'm gonna ice you, Weatherman."*

If these juvenile threats were coming every day, or every week, he might have reported them. But they came only once every three or four months. Obviously some jerk in the newsroom. No big deal.

The Weatherman checked the national database. Water temperatures were rising off the Pacific coast of South America. They already had snow in the Dakotas. He studied the computer's answers to his calculations. No doubt in his mind. Harsh winter due.

THE CHILD

"**C**aptain, I am really sorry to bother you on Christmas Eve, but we found a letter our little princess wrote. We think you should have it."

Les Angelbeck thought he could make it out to Afton and then back again. "If the weather holds." But it didn't hold. All hell broke loose, just like the Weatherman said it would. Now he was driving through an infernal snowstorm, beating a hasty retreat home. He had the letter.

Search dogs found victim number seven buried in the wet autumn leaves. She was fifteen years old, mildly retarded and strangely gifted. Her name was Karen Rochelle. An only child, her parents called her the Princess of Afton. She got off a school bus one rainy afternoon in late October and was never again seen alive.

Afton Township sat tucked into the south end of the St. Croix Valley on the Minnesota side of the river. Her rolling hills and thick woods reminded early settlers so much of the New England countryside that they drew up plans to ensure that the land would remain pristine. But now the Cities were only an on-ramp away.

The white-haired father of the murdered girl led Les Angelbeck past a lonely Christmas tree and into the girl's bedroom. A small desk stood in the corner. The bereaved father picked up a white notepad and showed it to the police captain. "I noticed the indents on the paper, so I scribbled over it with a pencil. This is what appeared."

I saw u on TV. I no u r the killer.
I saw u on TV. I no u r the killer.
I saw u on TV. I no u r the killer.

That was all it said. He handed the captain a book of first-class stamps, the Virgin Mary cradling the Christ Child. Angelbeck flipped open the book. One stamp of Mary and the baby was missing. "And you think she mailed this to somebody?"

"I don't know how else to explain it, Captain. There is no sign of the actual letter, and just that one stamp missing."

"Your daughter was mentally retarded. Did she have the capacity to write and mail letters?"

"Oh, yes. She was quite functional. She could read and write at a third-grade level. She was always sending things off—Publishers Clearing House, free samples, things like that. She loved getting mail with her name on it. But she never wrote anything like this."

"Would she have put her return address on something like this?"

"Oh, yes. Upper-left-hand corner of the envelope, just as we taught her."

Les Angelbeck examined again the small white letters in the stormy scribble.

I saw u on TV. I no u r the killer.

"What kind of shows did she watch?"

"Oh, 'Wheel of Fortune,' 'Cheers,' 'Jeopardy,' that sort of harmless fare. After dinner she watched television until she went to bed."

"Any local programming?"

"Just the news. I think she had a crush on Dixon Bell, that weatherman."

"Does anybody else know about this letter?"

"No, we called you right away."

"Let's keep this a state secret. We don't want the press getting ahold of something like this."

"I understand."

"It's snowing. I'd better start back."

But the girl's father stopped him. He and his despondent wife were the victims murderers leave behind. "Captain Angelbeck, in many ways our princess was quite blessed. She sometimes said things, saw things we couldn't explain." His last words to the old cop were "Be careful—it's easy to get lost out here."

Les Angelbeck had the car radio turned to WCCO-AM. The Good Neighbor, they called themselves. He remembered how they had sat listening to WCCO that tragic Armistice Day so many years ago.

"Your father'll be fine. If the weather holds."

For the hundredth time the Good Neighbor announced the winter storm warning. Blizzard conditions. Six to ten inches of snow. Thirty-five mph winds and a rapidly dropping windchill. Treacherous driving. Only the brave and the foolish should venture outdoors. "Welcome to winter," said the voice on the air. "We got off easy last year."

"Merry Christmas to you too," Les Angelbeck replied. He was feeling more foolish than brave. Conditions in Afton were near whiteout. The headlights were useless. He coughed his guts up, then wiped his mouth with the sleeve of his parka. He'd reluctantly made a doctor's appointment. He could breathe in okay, but exhaling was becoming increasingly difficult.

Angelbeck started the unmarked squad car down a steep road. There was no blacktop to see, only a mean ocean of white running along the tree line. No other cars kept him company. He steered a middle course. Visibility was nearing zero. So was the temperature. He knew the interstate was only a mile north, but the roads in Afton didn't run north-south. They were serpentine, rolled up and down and wound around. He was lost. No sooner had he reached that conclusion than he had another coughing attack. The big Chevy tilted right. Angelbeck violently jerked the steering wheel away from the fall. The car fishtailed off the road and stopped with the snap of a whip. He floored the gas pedal. The tires spun in circles until he could smell the burning rubber. He was stuck!

Les Angelbeck sat behind the wheel and recaptured his breath. He was not one to panic. He turned down the heater and cracked open his window, smoked a cigarette, and watched the snowstorm raging around him. He recalled what he'd heard on Channel 7 the night before.

"El Niño," Dixon Bell had told his viewers. "That's Spanish for 'the Child.' It's an unexplained buildup of warm water in the Pacific Ocean just off the coast of South America. We call it the Child because it usually occurs around Christmastime. When El Niño occurs, the effects can be dramatic. It nudges the jet streams off course and disrupts weather patterns around the world. Here in the Midwest the result is heavier than normal precipitation. Snow! And that's what we're in for tomorrow night, folks. A megastorm. A gift from El Niño. So stay home. Or wrap up your Christmas Eve early and get home!"

Good advice. Angelbeck took a deep drag on his cigarette. His mind raced over the case. His Calendar Task Force was not without leads. In fact, it had too many leads. Besides the partial fingerprint and now this strange letter, thousands of phone calls poured in from around the country. Every tip had to be written down, so many tips they could only check out the hot ones—those from other police departments or reliable sources. They had filled 150 three-ring binders with facts. They fed the facts into computers and supercomputers that spit out even more facts. They interviewed every lunatic in the five-state area. As year-end approached it was estimated the state had spent nearly two million dollars on the investigation, surpassing the amount of money spent on the Wakefield kidnapping.

An FBI agent who specialized in serial killers flew in from Quantico and joined the task force. The task force interviewed scientists at the University of Wisconsin who were studying the effects of the atmosphere on human behavior. They talked at length with a professor of climatology at the University of Minnesota. Angelbeck himself had interviewed the chief meteorologist at the National Weather Service Severe Storms Forecast Center in Kansas City. Everybody they'd spoken to was cooperative and informative. But they were of little help.

On another front, Les Angelbeck met with Glenn Arkwright that morning. "Of the fifty-nine names AFIS spit out," the fingerprint expert told him, "we've eliminated half of them. Of prints we can't be sure about, we've tracked down twenty of them. Eight of them have already died, and the other twelve have never set foot in our fair state. One guy from New York did confess to visiting Wisconsin Dells. He thought that was in Minnesota. Concerning our request for classified fingerprints ... CIA said no way. Naval intelligence said no sir. The Army sent us more forms to fill out. And much to my surprise, the Air Force okayed a limited search ... decommissioned officers of the Vietnam era only. There's just one catch—it'll take them six to eight weeks to declassify them before we can run them."

The Marlboro Man extinguished his smoke in the ashtray. He cleared his sore throat. It was time to see how bad. He breathed as deep as he could. He zipped up his heavy green parka and pulled on his gloves.

As soon as he stepped from the squad car, Old Man Winter's icy hand slapped his face. Angelbeck slammed the door closed to save the heat. He spit with the wind. He trudged to the rear of the car. The back end was hanging over a ravine. Drifting snow was up to the fender. The rear tires were buried. He had neither the strength nor the willpower to shovel his way out. He'd have to radio for help. But where exactly was he? From what he could see through the storm, a stone canyon blocked the east. A forest lay to the west. A wild river of tumbling snow wound down the hill.

The captain cleared the snow away from the tailpipe so carbon monoxide wouldn't back into the car. He hugged the snow-bound vehicle and made his way back to the front door. But the door had locked—the keys in the ignition, the engine running. A cold pang of fear shot up his back. The window wasn't cracked open enough to get even his pinky through. The back door was locked. He slogged around to the passenger's side. The gusting wind pelted his face with snow and ice. The doors were locked. Though not a man to panic, he felt foolish. The snow blitz was bone-chillingly cold and painful. He plodded back to the driver's side of the car and tried to smash a window, but he lacked the muscle and the means. Les Angelbeck clenched his teeth.

Across the road, snow-draped evergreens bowed in his direction. The howling wind was gusting up to 50 mph, churning the snow and burying the car. Ice chips battered his face. Snow tumbled into his overshoes. Rich people lived out here, but they lived a mile apart. "Stay with the car." He said it aloud so he wouldn't do anything else foolish. "Stay with the car."

The old cop took a seat in the swiftly accumulating snow. He leaned back against the front tire on the street side, where he could catch the warmth of the engine and watch the roadway. Soon another car would pass and see the headlights. He tucked his gloves into his armpits and tucked his boots under his legs. And there he sat, remembering what had happened to his father.

Les Angelbeck was still in high school during the Armistice Day Blizzard. November 11, 1940. His father had gone out hunting that morning in his shirtsleeves. Sixty-degree weather. He'd asked his son to come along, but he declined: he was at that awkward age when a boy wants to do less with his parents, not more. Two days later the awkward boy helped sheriff's deputies pull his father's frozen body out of a snow bank. The blizzard had slammed into Minnesota so fast and so furious that no warning was possible. Snowdrifts ended up twenty feet high.

In Belgium he had marched through a snowstorm like this, just another GI with a cigarette dangling from his lips. But he was young and healthy then, and there was a war to be won. Now he was old and foolish. He'd locked his keys in the car with the engine running. He could hear the anchorman on TV telling everybody about family history repeating itself, about the elderly cop who had perished in a blizzard just like his father. Only he'd been warned. He was just too damn stubborn to stay at home where he belonged on a night such as this.

On Christmas Eve, while Captain Les Angelbeck was sitting in the middle of the blizzard, Sky High News reporter Andrea Labore was sitting on the couch in her warm Golden Valley apartment, feeling as cold and lonely as the snowbound cop. The lights were out. An empty bowl of popcorn sat on the table. A snow-white TV screen was pulsating in front of her. Her blue bathrobe embraced her like an old friend.

It was this night a year ago she had toured the governor's mansion and then fell asleep in the arms of Per Ellefson. Now all she had to hold on to was a check he'd written her and a new bottle of pills.

"Take three pills a day for the first three days. Call us if there's any fever or bleeding."

Perhaps she should have waited until after the holidays, but she had wanted it over with. No pills could swallow her guilt. Andrea once thought those kinds of clinics were for naive teenagers, for the poor and the irresponsible. When the governor asked her how much it would cost, she told him. He wrote her a check for the exact amount. "Put this in your account," he instructed her, "but pay them in cash."

Andrea Labore sat in front of the blank TV screen practicing something Rick Beanblossom had taught her—for every answer you get, come up with three more questions. How could a governor so full of good be so cold? Would a good man have been seeing her at all? And what of all those speeches about the sanctity of life? He didn't seem to have any qualms about the death penalty when he wrote that check.

And what of the child? What might the child of a tall, handsome governor and a beautiful television reporter have grown up to be? She held the check in her hand. In the light of the TV screen the governor's signature stared up at her like a veto. Tears welled up in her eyes.

A polar wind slammed a horde of snow and ice into her patio window. Andrea was startled, turned to look. God was furious. She had the haunting feeling that if she threw open that window she'd be sucked into the storm—all the way to hell.

Andrea Labore got up and fixed herself a drink. She poured brandy into a Diet Coke and zapped it in the microwave. She returned to the couch. Her apartment was something of a fluffy pigpen. It was too hot. Her hands were dry. Her plants were wilting. She popped one of the pills and chased it with the brandy. She swallowed a diet pill. Vitamin pills followed. She tightened the bathrobe around her shrinking figure. The Christmas Eve blizzard raged outside her window. But Andrea ignored the sinister weather and returned to watching the snow on her television set.

The wind-driven snow was still coming down. Waves of the drifting white stuff rolled through the ravine. Across the way a tree snapped in two and toppled in slow motion. Snow blanketed his lap. His face was stone red. Glistening icicles dangled from his eyebrows. His teeth were chattering. He couldn't stop the shakes. Les Angelbeck ached for a cigarette, but they too were locked in the car. Then the car's engine died. A half-hour later the headlights died. The specter of death took flight overhead. Another victim of the Calendar Killer.

It wasn't the ghost of his father that haunted him this Christmas Eve. It was those seven women that were circling overhead. What did they feel when their time was up? Did they know they were going to die? Did they see a face? Did they cry out for their mothers? Their fathers? Did you really know the name, Princess? Only one person knew all of the answers. It was this night a year ago the killer struck on Como Lake. Might even be out there tonight in search of a winter kill. Never had the Minnesota police captain felt so helpless.

The elderly and smokers are the most susceptible to the snow and the cold. Any man who knows the weather knows that. Les Angelbeck knew the weather. He wanted to finish his career as the cop who had collared the Calendar Killer. He wanted to see capital punishment restored and justice done. But he was a detective, a man of cold reasoning and hard logic. He wasted precious little time on fantasy. There would be no cars passing by. Travel was impossible. He would finish his career a crippled old man in a crippling snowstorm. The elderly take the slow road to the grave. All things considered, hypothermia wasn't a bad way to go. It was good enough for Daddy. The family curse.

Resigned to his icy fate, the freezing policeman began to pray. The peace that passed all understanding snowed over him. The pain stopped. His hands and feet went numb. His swollen chest settled down. His face went flush, actually felt warm. Les Angelbeck felt himself dozing off, believing in his heart he would never wake up.

In the end it was just like they said it would be. The whistling wind took on a joyful harmony. He was sure he could hear children singing Christmas carols. Everything was white and beautiful. Then he saw it—a bright light at the end of a tunnel. He still couldn't move, couldn't go towards the light, but it didn't matter, the light was coming towards him. It was a shiny blue light and it descended like a savior through the swirling clouds. As it floated closer, he saw an angel below the light—a beautiful orange angel, with giant wings the color of the sunset. Closer still, he could see that the angel was carrying the blue light. This messenger from heaven was swooping down on him, as if to wrap him in its giant wings and take him away. He was ready to fly. Seemed a good day for it. But the angel suddenly stopped, the giant orange wings hovering over him. The blue light twirled in circles.

Then the strangest thing happened. The most mortal of beings stepped out of the clouds and bent over his face. He was wearing a ski mask. "Are you okay, mister?"

"I know you." Instinctively the barely alive captain tried to reach for his badge, but his brittle bones wouldn't bend. "I'm a police captain," he muttered.

The snowplow driver chuckled, a bit concerned. "I don't think Old Man Winter is impressed with your rank. I'm going to put you in the cab, it's nice and warm there."

Angelbeck's chest heaved back to life. He spat out a loud, hacking cough, only to have it thrown in his face by the unrelenting blizzard. "El Niño," he stammered. "El Niño."

The savior who descended from a snowplow—or maybe heaven *had* sent him—put his arms around the suffering policeman. "I think we'd better get you to a hospital."

THE HANGOVER

Several times during the fitful night Andrea Labore opened her eyes to total darkness. She felt sick and delirious and fell back to sleep.

When she finally woke for good she thought it was a dream. She found herself in a strange bed, a fourposter bed of cherry wood, colonial in style, spacious, warm, and male. The room was daytime dark. Thick brown curtains hung over the windows. The sheets she clung to were gold stripe, the blanket over them solid gold, the warm comforter over the blanket was warm shades of gold. A matching set. The dresser and chest of drawers matched the bed. A bouquet of real flowers sat atop the dresser, an oddity in the dead of winter. Thick autumn carpeting complemented the furniture. The bedroom must have cost a fortune. She knew now it wasn't a dream.

For Andrea this was a first. Fear and shame overcame her. She was naked but for her panties. Her clothes were nowhere in sight. Someone had stripped her and put her to bed. She buried her head in the pillow and fought the urge to cry. She tried hard to remember, but her brandy-soaked memory wouldn't take her past getting into her car.

She had spent New Year's Eve by herself. She had nothing to celebrate. Then yesterday—or was it the day before?—the governor had called and asked to see her. At first she said no, but then she gave in to temptation. They had a terrible fight in the back of the limousine. He kept telling her how much he loved her. Somebody slapped somebody. Then she started for home, alone. Then . . . ? She was in a fog.

A man's track suit, blue with red stripes, was laid out

at the foot of the bed, like a note that said, "Put it on."
Andrea crawled out of the bed and parted the curtain. The
January sun off the snow stung her eyes. She dropped the
curtain and turned away.

There was a half-bath in the bedroom. Andrea slipped
inside and locked the door. She sat on the toilet and
buried her head in her hands, but as hard as she tried her
memory would not wake up. She'd had a fight. She'd gotten drunk. She had ended up in a man's bedroom. She had
a hangover. Her hands smelled of vomit; her mouth tasted
of it. Where was her car? And where was she now?

Andrea splashed water in her face and grabbed a towel.
It was a fluffy, expensive towel with a royal design. A
clean glass was on the sink. She rinsed her mouth. The
bathroom was spotless, but something was missing. No
mirror. Just a blank wall above the sink.

Back in the bedroom Andrea Labore stepped into the
track suit pants and pulled the drawstrings tight. She
cuffed the bottoms. Then she slipped into the top, pulling
the zipper up over her bare breasts. Big letters ran across
the chest: USMC. But there was no mirror in the bedroom, either. She sat on the bed is despair and glanced
around the room for something that would identify the
man who slept here. Nothing.

At the door she paused again. She wanted to cry. Again
she swallowed the tears. She stepped into the hallway.

The noontime sun pounded home her hangover. She
could hear a television. Football. She kept one hand on
the wall and followed the autumn carpet to the living
room, her knees weak, her stomach sick from drink, her
head aching. Her eyes began to water as she stood at the
end of the hall and peeked into the room. Suddenly she
had never felt so good in her life, so relieved, so flat-out
lucky. The Lone Ranger on his best day never met a
woman happier to see a man in a mask.

"Good morning," he said without looking at her. "Or is
it afternoon?"

Andrea glanced at the big, fat hands on the grandfather
clock in front of her. A quarter past noon. "Hi," she said.
She slinked over to the couch where he was sitting and
sat at the other end, her legs tucked beneath her, her
hands between her knees.

Rick Beanblossom kept his eyes on the TV set, his

hands behind his head. He was dressed in jeans and a purple Minnesota Vikings jersey, number 10. His legs were outstretched and crossed. Thick white socks covered his feet. The king at home in his castle. They were high in the sky, and out the patio window was a breathtaking view of Lake Calhoun and the city of Minneapolis.

This room of the condominium was even better than the bedroom—not really a bachelor pad, more permanent, a man's home, a life he had built for himself inside a concrete cliff over a lake. The eloquent phantom. It was not a television set he was watching, it was an entertainment center, equal to anything at the station. The furniture was early American. But there were oddities, like a shiny new bicycle parked next to the grandfather clock. A rare collection of Shakespeare was stacked over an IBM computer. The paintings on the wall ranged from French impressionist to Minneapolis avant-garde. Stylish as it was, the place was in desperate need of a woman's touch—some lighter colors, perhaps.

Andrea waited for him to say something, but his eyes remained on the television. She wondered how often he removed his mask at home. Would he take it off for her should she ever ask? Despite the mask she could read every bitter line on his disapproving face. "Who's playing?" she asked.

He sat motionless and didn't answer.

"Is it the Vikings?" She knew nothing about football and cared even less.

"Do you see any purple?" he growled.

Andrea smiled inside and tried to figure out who was who. After a few more minutes of watching she gave it a try. "Is it the Packers and the Washington Bears?"

"No, it's the Packers and the Washington Redskins. It's the playoffs."

"And you're for the Packers?"

"Shut up."

They watched the Packers' quarterback smothered by Redskins. Rick Beanblossom threw up his hands in frustration.

She had heard jokes in the sports department about his zealous loyalty to Minnesota teams. "Why are you for the Packers? Why not the Vikings?"

"Because the Vikings are out of the playoffs. Are you

questioning my loyalty? My father was from Minnesota. My grandfather and great-grandfather were from Minnesota. There were Beanblossoms fighting in the Civil War from Minnesota. Don't ever question my loyalty. It's in my blood."

Andrea wanted to smile. He sounded like a football fool. "Is it that purple blood they joke about in sports?"

Again he fell silent. Between the Vikings being out of the playoffs, the Packers getting killed, and her behavior, she could see he was growing more agitated by the minute.

"I went out to get drunk," Andrea confessed.

"Well, you succeeded. Golden Valley police found you passed out behind the wheel of your car in the parking lot of a pancake house. They took you to the detox center. I've got a source down there. He called me at three o'clock this morning."

"Is there anywhere you don't have a source?"

"Very few, lucky for you."

"Did you put me to bed?"

"Don't flatter yourself. You were anything but sexy last night."

"Where are my clothes?"

"You threw up all over them. I was going to soak them in cold water until I remembered whose they were. So I stuffed them in a Hefty bag and hefted them down the trash chute. Give you an excuse to go shopping."

"Me go shopping?" She tossed off an ironic laugh. "This place looks like it won the Good Housekeeping Seal. What do you do, study those pictures in *Better Homes and Gardens*?"

"Having seen your newsroom desk, I can imagine what your apartment looks like. Is that where you two do it, or are you still sneaking in and out of the mansion?"

The Marine got her in that time. Andrea Labore thought the better her career got, the more screwed up her life became. That tear finally escaped her eye and ran down her cheek. She wiped it away with a loud sniff. "I'm going to stop seeing him," she said. "It's over."

The Packers' quarterback took another sacking. Rick Beanblossom shook his head in disgust. "The Central Division was once the pride of the National Football

League," he said, more to himself than Andrea. "Where have you gone, Fran Tarkenton?"

"Who's Fran Torkelson?" Andrea choked out.

The masked man finally broke away from the game. He looked over at the sad but stunning face beside him. Her plastic perfection was melting all over his expensive couch. Rick patted his lap. "Come here, puppy dog."

Andrea curled up and laid her confused and aching head in his lap. Rick Beanblossom draped an arm over her shoulder. And they spent the afternoon like that. No murders. No politics. Just watching a football game in that vast wasteland called television.

THE PENALTY

Rick Beanblossom stood alone on the top step of the State Capitol Building looking out at the ghostly white city of St. Paul. March is the snowiest month of the year, and this March was living up to its reputation. Through the tumbling snowflakes the newsman could see the magnificent cathedral on the hill across the way, a standing reminder to lawmakers of their moral obligations.

The Calendar Killer knew how to kill women, but did the state know how to kill a man—or maybe a woman? Rick Beanblossom came to the Capitol on this snowy afternoon to find out. School buses lined the avenue at the foot of the stairs. News vans, numbered like billiard balls, were parked on the sidewalk. The parkland at the foot of the Capitol was so white it stung the producer's eyes. He breathed the cold, crispy air and brushed the flakes from the top of his mask. It really was a winter wonderland. But now this wonderland was teeming with outrage and vengeance. The monster who murdered with the seasons had yet to record a winter kill. In the real world, under the blanket of white, people were scared and mad. But politicians don't live in the real world. Their world was in this building. Rick turned his back to the bright white city and walked under the marble arches and through the bronze doors.

It was a homosexual from England who put an end to capital punishment in Minnesota. His name was William Williams, a twenty-seven-year-old steamfitter who had immigrated to America. By all accounts he was a mean, ugly bastard. Williams and sixteen-year-old Johnny

Keller became lovers and traveled about the northland looking for work. But Johnny tired of the travel, and tired of Williams, and returned to his mother's home in St. Paul. Williams soon followed.

On the night of April 12, 1905, Williams went to Johnny's home. Johnny's mother angrily sent him away. Williams returned after midnight with a gun. He was drunk and enraged. First he shot Johnny Keller's mother in the back; then he shot Johnny twice in the head as he slept in bed. Williams reported the killings himself but denied he had done the shooting. The jury didn't believe him. They found him guilty of first-degree murder. The judge sentenced William Williams to hang by the neck until he was dead. At the time of sentencing the judge couldn't know how long that was going to take.

William Williams's last meal was prepared by the sheriff's wife. He was given a shave and a haircut. He prayed with his priest. He shook hands and said good-bye to all of his jailhouse friends. Then at the stroke of midnight on February 13, 1906, William Williams, his hands cuffed behind his back, was led from his cell at the Ramsey County Jail. He took the long walk.

They crept down the iron stairway to the sub-basement, where the scaffolding had been erected. The death chamber was cold and damp and smelled of mildew and fresh dirt. Thirty-two witnesses, mostly reporters, stood in a semicircle below the gallows. The deputies left Williams alone at the foot of the gallows steps. Without hesitation he climbed the thirteen stairs that led to the rope. The Ramsey County sheriff was waiting for him. The sheriff read the sentence. In a soft, almost inaudible voice Williams made a final statement, proclaiming his innocence right up to the end of his rope. "This is legal murder," he said. "I am accused of killing Johnny Keller. He was the best friend I ever had and I hope to meet him in the other world. I never had improper relations with him. I am resigned to my fate. Good-bye."

A black hood was placed over his head. The noose went around his neck. The sheriff descended the steps to the lever.

Public executions have always been an inexact science. When the sheriff sprang the trap door, the prisoner fell through it all right, but the rope stretched eight inches and his neck stretched four inches, and Williams's toes hit the floor. The knot slipped behind his neck, slowly strangling him as he tiptoed about. After a few minutes of this danse macabre the sheriff ordered deputies to mount the gallows and pull on the rope, lifting the feet off the floor. But ten minutes later Williams was still alive, still thrashing about. So the sheriff climbed back up the thirteen steps and helped pull on the rope while a deputy stood below and pulled on Williams's feet. Williams returned the indignity by emptying his bowels: the last supper. The stench was sickening. Reporters scribbled furiously. Finally, at 12:46 A.M., fifteen minutes after he had dropped through the trap door, the Ramsey County police surgeon declared William Williams was dead. And so was the death penalty in Minnesota.

Hearing Room 15 was directly beneath the Capitol's rotunda. The room was perfectly rounded. Reporters called it the Crypt. It had a low dome-shaped ceiling supported by marble columns. Committee members, all uniformly dressed in suits of blue or gray, sat at a half-circle table of varnished oak that ran around the room. Staff members sat behind them. Television cameras and klieg lights stood behind them. Press seats lined the stone wall. The hearing room was packed. But Rick Beanblossom was more comfortable in a large crowd than he was at a small gathering. People feel safe in numbers. A man in a mask with a notebook and a pen minding his own business doesn't seem threatening. He took a seat in the press section behind the committee.

As they had done the year before, the House Judiciary Committee was holding final hearings on the reinstatement of capital punishment. The bill before the committee would allow the death penalty in cases of first-degree murder, multiple murders, or the murder of a police officer. Execution would be by electrocution. Other means of execution had been methodically ruled out. Hanging—we botched it last time. Firing squad—too military. Lethal injection—doctor-assisted murder from a drug overdose, cried the state's powerful health-care industry.

Facing the committee was a long witness table with three chairs. Microphones were atop the table. The gallery bent around the room in a half-circle behind the witness table. This day it was standing room only. Whatever it was that gave Minnesota life that special quality was fast disappearing. For many in Hearing Room 15, enough was enough. The double doors were open and the crowd spilled into the echo-filled hallways. Still, for such a visceral debate the decorum within the hearing room was very mannered. The politics of life and death was a solemn and painful business. Beneath the bitterness they were still a people who believed in their government.

For Hearing Room 15 it had been a very active legislative session. Splat Man had racked up an incredible two hundred thousand dollars in damage to the state's billboard industry. Since one of the largest billboard companies in America was headquartered in the state, the legislature, in keeping with their uglification-of-Minnesota campaign, made defacing a billboard a felony with fine and imprisonment.

The state had been one of the few in the nation that still barred cameras from courtrooms. That changed. Governor Ellefson's bill to allow television cameras in Minnesota's courtrooms was passed. The state supreme court was skeptical that television would improve the quality of justice in Minnesota but agreed to a two-year experimental program in which video and audio coverage of trials would be allowed even without the approval of prosecutors and defendants.

On the issue of capital punishment there came a liberal backlash. Politically, liberals were tired of conservatives stealing the thunder on crime issues. Ideology-wise, these seasonal murders were being directed at women, the heart and soul of the liberal movement. Still, many lawmakers who supported the bill had an innate fear of perhaps one day putting to death an innocent man. Executions are final.

And so the people who still believed that government was good lined up before the twenty-three committee members to testify for and against House File 2848. And Rick Beanblossom came to listen. The witnesses were an eclectic group of liberals and conservatives, mothers and fathers, doctors and lawyers—and cops.

"And what is your name, sir?" said the bill's sponsor, committee chairman Smith Jameson.

The witness cleared his throat. "Les Angelbeck."

"Your occupation, Mr. Angelbeck?"

"It's Captain Angelbeck. I'm a police officer."

"What department are you with, Captain?"

"When I retired last month I was a chief investigator for the Minnesota Bureau of Criminal Apprehension. I was forced by ill health to step down. I have emphysema. After my retirement Governor Ellefson was kind enough to hire me as a paid consultant to the Calendar Task Force, which I had once led."

"So you are still actively involved in that investigation?"

"Yes, but in a reduced role."

"How long have you been a police officer?"

"Ever since the war."

"Which war?" Everybody in the room laughed.

Les Angelbeck smiled. "I'm sorry, Mr. Chairman, it was the Second World War."

The leading proponent of the death penalty led his star witness through well-rehearsed questions. TV cameras were rolling. "Captain, why do you think our state should reenact the death penalty?"

Rick Beanblossom thought the old cop looked more uncomfortable than ill. He heard him clear his scratchy throat and answer.

"The state has a responsibility to protect future victims. There isn't any such thing as life in prison in the United States ... everybody gets out. Executed people don't kill again. I will concede the point that execution may not deter crime, but there are some crimes so morally low and reprehensible that the only fitting punishment is death. In the past two years I have seen seven such crimes. Even if you pass this bill today, the person who committed those crimes could not be legally executed." Angelbeck stopped. His heavy breathing could be heard throughout the Crypt. The retired police captain pulled an inhalant from his coat pocket and self-consciously squirted a burst of life into his mouth. His voice sounded a little stronger. "I will also concede that people who are opposed to the death penalty have a morally superior position. But we should not put life before justice. That's moral blindness. I don't know how long I have left on this earth. But if you pass this death penalty bill, I can promise you this ... if that son of a bitch kills again, I'll catch him, and I'll outlive him, if it's only by a day."

Rick Beanblossom watched as the old cop slowly pulled himself out of the witness chair. He picked up a cane, hobbled through the parting crowd, and disappeared into the cold, hallowed halls, where his coughing echoed mockingly through the marble Capitol. Rick jotted a memo to himself.

The next witness was strong and loud. "Never in the history of the United States has a white person been executed for killing a black person. Never! The same experience blacks have had in other states will be repeated here. I'd be willing to bet that even here in the great white state of Minnesota, which has a black population of less than three percent, the first ass to be seated in your new electric chair will be a black ass!"

"Will you watch your language, Lieutenant," the chairman admonished.

In a shrewd move the leading opponent of the bill had asked the lieutenant to testify, and Donnell Redmond was hot. "I'm sorry, but all through American history the death penalty has been just an excuse to murder black men. That you want to pass this lynch-the-niggers law right after Black History Month is disgraceful."

"What if it was your daughter who was murdered?" asked Smith Jameson.

"What if it was your son who was on death row?" asked Redmond.

And so it went for three hours. One cop for the death penalty, one cop against.

One father of a murder victim for passage: "If it will save one child's life, it should be enacted."

One mother of a murder victim opposed to the bill's passage: "I can't think of anything more obscene than to have my daughter remembered for the death penalty."

Dueling victims. Sobbing could be heard throughout the gallery as parents told of the children they had lost in the most violent of crimes. A loud, obnoxious woman, who was not related to the victims, summed it all up. "The Minnesota criminal-justice system is to blame for these murders, and you state legislators must share the responsibility for the deaths of those seven innocent women. You must share the responsibility for a twelve-year-old boy who went out to deliver papers one morning and never came back. It's time for a change, and if you won't do it, then we'll elect those who will."

Rick Beanblossom's eardrums were ringing with arguments. He scribbled the pros and cons in his notebook.

Then to the witness table came a woman in an electric wheelchair, Stacy Dvorchak, a quadriplegic. She was young and attractive. Rick Beanblossom had seen her in the news before. Andrea Labore had done a story on her. She was a former Olympic swimmer who broke her neck diving into a pool. Now she was a member of a northern lawyers' group that ventured into the South to defend death row inmates. As he listened to her speak, the man without a face could think of few things more tragic than a beautiful young woman sentenced to life in a wheelchair.

"Ninety percent of the men on death row were financially unable to hire an attorney," she testified. "They were arbitrarily given a court-appointed lawyer. They weren't sentenced to death for committing the worst crimes, they were sentenced to death for having the worst lawyers. This bill is cowardly. It's a case of the shepherds following the sheep. Somebody here today said this is not a case of southern justice because Indiana has the death penalty." She paused, then hit them where it hurt. "Think of it, Minnesota—we can be just like Indiana!"

Derisive laughter circled the Crypt.

With braces on her hands Stacy Dvorchak calmly spread some papers before her and continued. "Let me tell you what the electricity bill is going to come to. Based on the experience of other states, the capital punishment bill will generate about one execution per year. At that rate, figuring the cost of a trial, court-appointed defense lawyers, state appeals, federal appeals, death house construction, and death row housing, the first ten years of the law would cost the state of Minnesota approximately thirty million dollars, or about three million dollars per condemned man."

Now groans circled the gallery.

"And how much would it cost to imprison these same men?" asked a shocked committee member

"We could presently imprison them in Stillwater at the

highest security level for forty years at a cost of approximately $750,000 per man."

Smith Jameson took over the questioning. He studied his well-prepared notes. "Isn't it true that with the recent Supreme Court rulings limiting habeas corpus appeals, the time it takes to appeal capital punishment cases has dropped from seven and a half years to less than five years, and isn't that bringing down the costs of executions?"

"Yes, sir," said the handicapped lawyer, "you could argue that."

"And couldn't I also argue that if the state court follows suit, as is expected, and also limit appeals, the time from conviction to execution will be reduced to less than three years, and won't that also bring down the costs?"

"In theory, that is correct. A rush to the gallows would lower costs, Mr. Chairman."

Jameson was locked in video combat, fighting the battle for sound bites on the evening news. "And am I not also correct in theory that the more prisoners the state executes, the more precipitous will be the drop in total costs?"

"Yes, sir, that was the experience of the Third Reich."

The chairman had just lost the sound bite battle. He angrily tapped his pen on the table. "I think you'd better go back to your calculator, young lady."

"If I could add a personal note, Mr. Chairman. I've always been proud to say I'm from Minnesota. This bill does not make me proud. Thank you."

After five hours of grueling debate they were ready to vote. Rick Beanblossom leaned forward. The roll was called. It was just as Iron Ranger Bob Dylan had written in a song: *"You don't have to be a weatherman to know which way the wind blows."* The House Judiciary Committee voted 21-2 to restore capital punishment.

The full house passed HF-2848 on March 13.

The senate voted green lights for the electric chair on March 17.

And on March 18, the death penalty bill arrived at the office of Governor Per Ellefson.

When Old Jesse was a little boy, his momma died of fever in the back of a bus. She was seventeen years old.

She was taking him up to Columbia to see Eleanor Roosevelt. The First Lady was coming to South Carolina to inspect the conditions. Little Jesse didn't know what the conditions were, but he knew who Miss Eleanor was, and he knew Momma was going to tell her all about the conditions. It was the hot and smelly season. The bus driver was a big, fat man. Jesse was too scared to go tell him his momma was dead. He thought he'd just wait until they got to Columbia and then tell Miss Eleanor But a mean old lady went and told the bus driver, and Jesse never got to see Eleanor Roosevelt. When the First Lady died, he was a full-grown man, but Jesse swore he'd cried harder for Miss Eleanor than he cried for his own momma when he was just a little boy. All of his life he believed in his heart that if they had made it to Columbia that day things would have turned out different. He never would have moved to the North. Never would have killed a white man fighting over a woman. Never would have seen the inside of the prison in Stillwater.

Old Jesse flushed the toilet. Then he flushed the toilet next to it. He walked along the wall, flushing all of the toilets. The janitor put his scrub brush and disinfectant into the bucket and walked to the door. He picked up a newspaper from the floor and read as best he could.

TO KILL OR NOT TO KILL
Minnesota Governor Per Ellefson has called a press conference Friday at noon in the Governor's Reception Room at the State Capitol to announce whether he intends to sign or veto the capital punishment bill that arrived on his desk. All four local television stations will carry the announcement live. The governor's opposition to both abortion rights and capital punishment . . .

All the boys were talking about it. "They wanna build an electric chair right out back there, in Industry. Ain't that the damnedest thing you ever heard?"

Old Jesse stuffed the newspaper into the garbage bag and dragged it into the hallway. It was nearing morning. The boys would be up at 6:15 and there was still a hallway to mop in the Segregation Unit. He moved over to the window and gazed through the bars at the St. Croix

Valley. The first ray of morning sun was peeking over the bluff. The Electric Star was gone for the season. Trees were sprinkled with white powder. The middle of March. Snowing and melting. Snowing and melting. The ice was going out on the river. Old Man Winter was losing his grip.

For twenty-five years Old Jesse dreamed of going home. Home, where it was summertime all the time. Where in the middle of winter he could throw a line into the sound and watch the warm sun come up over the ocean. He had fond memories of boyhood, playing in the marshes around Parris Island, where they turned the white boys into Marines. But when his sentence was up and they told him he could go free, Old Jesse stayed. He took a job pushing a broom. South Carolina was just a dream he once had. The Stillwater State Correctional Facility was the only home he knew anymore.

His children had been born in the North, as had his grandchildren, and now his great-grandchildren. He'd always meant to take his family down home for a visit so they could see for themselves the land that was in their blood. Southern blood. He was sure enough going to take them one day, but then he killed that white man.

Still, his family had done all right by Minnesota. One of his granddaughters was a police officer. Unheard of in his day. He was proud of that girl. Old Jess loaded the night's garbage onto his pushcart and started for the Segregation Unit. Just doing his job.

There was no way Andrea Labore could duck the assignment. Not the lead story. And when the press conference was over with, she would stand in the melting snow in front of the State Capitol Building, adjust her earpiece, stare into a camera, and feed one-minute reports to affiliated stations around the heartland: "Detroit, what is the name of your anchorman? . . . Can you hear me, St. Louis? . . . Talk to me, Omaha . . . Milwaukee, which anchor do I get it from, and which anchor do I throw it back to?" After that charade Andrea would hang around the Capitol and do live reports for Channel 7 at five, six, and ten. It was the kind of assignment no TV reporter could afford to turn down. The fact that Jack Napoleon handed her the job propelled her to the front of the pack at Sky High News—heir apparent to Charleen Barington, who was almost forty years old. Fortunately for Andrea, the governor's office said the governor would not be answering questions or granting interviews afterwards. What they didn't say was whether he was going to sign the death penalty bill or veto it.

Andrea signed in at the anteroom, then pushed her way into the crowded Governor's Reception Room, one of the most magnificent rooms in the state. The last rays of winter sunshine spilled through tall windows that framed the cathedral. Crimson draperies around the glass were faithful reproductions of the 1905 originals. The high walls of intricate woodwork were lined with great, beautiful paintings that had been commissioned by famed architect Cass Gilbert to portray Minnesota's history. Two hundred-pound chandeliers hung from the gilded ceiling.

Andrea put on a difficult smile and chatted with colleagues as she made her way to the back wall, where she hoped she could see but not be seen.

A podium stood in front of a white marble fireplace, the state seal attached. Folding chairs crowded out from there. Leather couches and matching armchairs ran along the walls. Every seat was taken. Sitting on the couch nearest the podium was an old man with a cane. He was wiping his mouth with a handkerchief. A tall black man sat next to him. The staff and the curious were standing in the aisles. Legislators led by the bill's sponsor, Smith Jameson, stood squeezed together behind the podium, along with the attorney general and other state office holders.

Andrea flipped open her notebook and dated the paper. Above her head was a painting of Father Louis Hennepin, crucifix in hand, blessing the Falls of St. Anthony. The Indians who had led him to this natural wonder looked on, their fate sealed.

The door to the governor's office opened. The bright lights of the TV cameras came up. The governor's minions preceded him. Then he appeared. Per Ellefson moved with purpose to the podium.

The line between love and hate is so fine Andrea didn't know which side of it she was standing on. They hadn't been together since the fight, though they'd talked on the phone a few times. Andrea wished her personal life were on a par with her career. But love makes weak the power of reason. She could see him through the shoulders of the men in front of her. On television Per Ellefson looked like a governor out of Central Casting. In person he was polite to a fault. He brought a lot of women into government, but they were young and attractive. Older women claimed he ignored them. Nobody blamed him for the killings. His ratings in media polls remained respectable. He kept the lunatics in the legislature in check.

The governor's voice resonated through the room. "If you're a governor, or ever dreamed to be, this will be your most difficult decision." He held up the bill. "I've always believed that meeting violence with violence solves nothing."

Directly behind the governor, above the fireplace and staring everybody in the face, was a mural depicting the signing of the Treaty of Traverse des Sioux. Standing on a platform was Territorial Governor Alexander Ramsey. Seated to his right was General, and future governor, Henry Sibley. Seated in between the two was Sioux Chief Little Crow. In 1851 the Dakota Indians were starving. The government threatened to hold back promised food and horses unless they signed two treaties: the politics of life and death. Little Crow signed. The Dakota Sioux sold southern Minnesota for twelve and a half cents an acre and were given a small reservation along the Minnesota River. After the Sioux uprising of 1863, Congress abrogated both treaties and the Sioux were driven out of Minnesota. Little Crow was shot by settlers, scalped, beheaded, and his remains put on display. For a hundred years his skull lay in the basement of the historical society across the street.

"As the courts and Congress narrow the grounds to block executions," Per Ellefson went on, "the twin burdens of justice and mercy fall more and more on the nation's governors. The judge and the jury can say they were just doing their part. The man who throws the switch can say he was just doing his job. But governors have no such refuge. In this bill before me today the governor retains the power of clemency ... the power of justice and mercy."

Watching the tall Norwegian speak made her uncomfortable. Andrea swallowed hard and looked away. On the wall to the governor's right was a Civil War painting of the Fourth Minnesota Regiment entering Vicksburg, Mississippi. They were the first regiment to march into the city after its surrender. The Old Warren County Courthouse could be seen on the hill in the background. War was something Andrea Labore had never understood. She thought of what Vietnam had done to Rick Beanblossom. He was still haunting her, but in a different way. What kind of a relationship can a woman have with a man without a face? In the newsroom her newfound friend was betting the governor of Viking descent would sign the bill into law. "It's in his blood," he was telling people. Before Christmas Andrea would have taken that bet.

"I have never been one to follow the polls," the governor said, announcing his decision, "but this is something the people of Minnesota want. To veto this bill would be the height of arrogance."

The politics of life and death. Per Ellefson signed. And on March 19, capital punishment in Minnesota was law once again.

And with the height of arrogance, on March 20, the last day of winter, the Calendar Killer struck once again.

THE FOG

Fog the color of skim milk shrouded the suburban hills of Edina. Warm temperatures, snowy ground, and cloudy skies were pouring moisture into the air. The rising sun was of little help. Even the poles supporting street lamps disappeared into the soup.

In squad car nine Officer Shelly Sumter cruised slowly through the spooky hills, her fog lights on, her shift near its end. Shelly's father worked for the railroad. Her grandfather was a janitor at the state prison in Stillwater. He had the wood shop there make her a billy club with her initials carved into it; she carried it with pride. She was in high school before she learned her granddaddy had done time in Stillwater. A long time. The family secret. Never discussed. Shelly always meant to research the crime through court records. Then she'd put it off.

"Car nine. Mud Lake Town Homes. Sandpiper Court and Oriole. Possible prowler."

Edina police still gave priority to prowler calls. The rapist who appeared in bedrooms out of thin air had never been caught. Shelly radioed her affirmative. She almost had to drive by memory up to the town homes. Where the fog met the snow it was blinding white.

She turned her spotlight on the row of attached houses and cruised by slowly. The young police officer at first saw nothing. Then suddenly she spotted a shadow on a snow-covered hill across the street. The large, ghostlike figure ducked out of one cloud patch and disappeared into another. She radioed for backup. She flipped on the cherry-red roof lights and got out of the car. She drew her gun—a first for her. In her other hand was a heavy flashlight.

Shelly Sumter made her way up the bank through the soft, sloppy snow, but in the fog her memory was playing tricks on her. Were there more town homes on this side of the street, or was this the bank into the park? She kept the flashing red lights of her squad car over her shoulder.

A pair of headlights came, parting the suburban fog. Her backup? She turned to signal. But the headlights kept on going, a Cadillac that couldn't care less.

Then *it* had her by the throat. Her flashlight went cutting through the milky morning air like a crazed beacon. She dropped it and grabbed at the arm, a big, powerful arm. Only her toes were scraping the snow. The gun was taken from her hand like it was candy and tossed into the slush. She clawed at the arm with her fingernails but couldn't get a grip on the jacket, a slippery nylon, so she clawed at a hand, drawing blood.

Shelly Sumter had done everything right. Given her exact location. Called for backup. Turned on the squad lights. Drawn her gun. Proceeded with caution. But now the suspect had her in the crook of the arm and was choking the life out of her. The only sound she was aware of was her own desperate gasps for air. For every move there's a countermove, she thought. What was it? Starved of oxygen, her brain couldn't come up with the answer. The last thing she saw was another pair of headlights penetrating the deadly fog.

Shelly was alive and breathing, but she didn't feel her assailant drop her and run. She was still alive and breathing when her backup arrived and found her lying facedown in the muddy snow. She was gasping for life inside the oxygen mask when they loaded her into the ambulance. Officer Shelly Sumter kept on breathing all the way to the Hennepin County Medical Center, where they hooked her up to life-support systems and plugged her in.

THE DIARY

In the spring of my senior year I dropped out of Vicksburg High School and joined the Air Force. All because of a girl. A real Southern belle. I was a teenager in love. Worse yet, I was a Southern teenager in love. Had my honor to think about. But she wasn't in love with me. Far from it.

I sat behind her in homeroom class for three years. We sat in alphabetical order, and her name being Lisa Beauregard, I sat by her in other classes too. It took me two years to build up enough stature and nerve to ask her out on a date. In the South we live for football and beauty pageants so finally my senior year I asked her to the Homecoming Dance. Lisa was nominated for queen and I got nominated for king. I was feeling pretty good about myself when I asked her.

Well, she didn't really say no. She said she planned on going with a bunch of girlfriends and that we should all meet at the dance and all have a good time. She promised me a real date in the future. So despite the fact that the night before I had won the Homecoming game with a legendary run, I went to the dance by myself and kind of pretended I was with Lisa. As it turned out she got elected Homecoming Queen that night, but I lost out to my good friend Bobby Conn in my bid for Homecoming King. So I waited a few humble weeks and then asked her to honor me with that promised date.

She wrote me a letter, a note really, folded here on this page.

My Dear Dixon

About the date I owe you ... isn't there some

other way I could repay you for the wonderful friend you've been? I didn't mean for you to misunderstand my feelings for you. One of the reasons why I won't go out with you's because, I've been going out steady with this older boy I met during this summer in Jackson and I'am awful fond of him still. I guess things never happen that please everyone envolved, but I didn't mean to hurt you . . . honest.

Your Dear friend
Lisa Beauregard

I was shocked! This is America and I was nominated for Homecoming King and I was the starting end for the Vicksburg Greenies and she's telling me about some slick from Jackson.

So this goes on my whole senior year . . . I ask her out . . . she says no. Vicksburg is just a small town. The end of high school is in sight and I've got no wife in sight. The prom is coming up . . . in high school, the ultimate beauty pageant. I decided to shoot the works. Go whole hog. I would write her a love letter. Spill my guts. Lay it all on the line. What the hell, my honor was already in the toilet. I stopped in at the Rexall Drug Store downtown and bought a new ink pen and some real nice paper. I cleaned my sloppy room. I dusted the old desk my granddaddy had given me. Then I took a shower. I dressed up in good clean clothes and then sat down at my granddaddy's desk to write the most important letter of my life.

I began, *My Dear Lisa* . . .

I told Lisa the whole sad story, how I didn't *like* her . . . *love* was the word I was looking for. I underlined *love* three times. I told her how I had been loyal to her for three years. That all my heroics under the bright lights of Vicksburg Memorial Stadium were just for her . . . two hundred thirty-eight yards receiving and two touchdowns my senior year. Okay, it wasn't a great year, but it wasn't bad. One of those touchdowns came against Yazoo City, and with the other touchdown, the long run, we won the Homecoming game. And they were both for her. I told her how much I wanted to take her to the prom. I pointed out what I thought my attributes to be and what she'd be losing out on. I begged her, and yes siree it was begging,

I begged her to please, please go out with me. Give this boy half a chance.

The next week Lisa was so kind to me, so sweet, I swear it was the happiest week of my life. She didn't talk about it, but it was there. I could feel it. It worked. Move over William Shakespeare, my pen breaks hearts. Then she wrote back.

I took the letter into study hall and read it . . . every ungrateful, selfish, cruel, heartless, wanton, merciless, savage, inhumane, malicious, malevolent, fucking word of it!

Letter folded here on this page.

My Dear Dixon

I read your letter and have thought about it ever since. I wish you wouldn't refer to it as your "sad story", because it is only "you" who has made it sad. You have asked me out so many times and each time I have tried to say no as sweetly as I can. I was nice to you because I liked you as a friend. So you see you have made it a "sad story" by not being able to face up to the fact that I will *never* go out with you. For going out with someone is about a girls only choice in this world. And I choose not to go out with you.

You say that you think you love me, how can you love someone you've never even been out with? So you think, why don't I go out with you and give you a chance? Because if it really is love you feel, and maybe it is, then it is one sided love.

You talk about how for the past three years you felt first as if you didn't amount to anything, and now finally you think you are, something. Well, Dixon to me your being on the foot-ball etc. and being put up for "King" isn't worth too much. Well Dixon, I like a person for what they are more than what they do. I've gone out with all types of boys, just because I like them for themselves. Now I suppose you ask, why don't I like you for yourself? I do, Dixon. But in a different way, not the way you like someone to go out with.

So Dixon, I'am not the loser, you are. You've lost out on alot of fun in High School. You tell me you've been "loyal" to me and have never gone out with anyone else. That's not loyalty, that's being rediculous. There are many girls I know here in Vicksburg who have said they would like to go out with you. Why have you been so foolish as to pass up such chances? I don't really think its because you love me, for you can learn to love many people in this world. I believe it must be because your afraid to. You've waited so long and if you wait much longer, it will almost be impossible for you.

Dixon, get a girl and have some fun. If you'd do that I know in just a short while you'd have to think twice to remember me as anything but a friend. Please take my advice and don't think I don't understand how you feel, but I'am sorry you don't understand how I feel, that makes the answer NO!

Love
Lisa Beauregard

So you think, what a dumb bitch! Okay, she was no literary genius, neither was I when I was eighteen. Now I suppose you ask, what did you do then?

Christ almighty, I was destroyed. I wasn't sure I could make it out of the building. You know the part where I underlined *love* three times? Lisa underlined *never* three times. I went to my locker in a daze. I grabbed my letter jacket. I walked out of Vicksburg High School. I ran down the hill and across the football field, I leaped the stadium fences and I never went back.

I walked home trying my best not to cry. She was a Southern belle and I was white trash. Like a lot of boys down home I was foolish enough to believe those days were gone with the wind. It was a long walk where we lived down by the railroad tracks above the river. That walk home with that letter in my pocket was the first time I really put my finger on it.

When I was growing up in Mississippi I only wanted to be two things. I wanted to be a Dallas Cowboy and I wanted to be a weatherman. When I get mad, when I'm hurt, when my blood reaches the boiling point I am like the idiot savant. My mind locks onto the weather and only the weather. I gather in all relevant data and spit out a forecast faster than a computer. It is a gift, like the autistic who knows only math tables. When I was a boy it was this gift that let me win the Delta Science Fair every year with my weather projects. As I walked home that day with that letter in my pocket I took off my jacket because it was hot . . . 81°. The air was saturated . . . 69 percent humidity. A warm breeze was straight up from the Gulf . . . 12 mph. I smelled heavy rain coming . . . maybe ten, maybe twelve hours away. But, you see, nobody had to tell me these things. I knew them to be the facts. I was in love, I was hurting, and my mind was reading the weather.

I went straight to my neat little room in our unpainted house. I sat on the edge of my bed and I read that letter again. When I was done with it, I just sat there crying my eyes out like a little baby. I was going to walk back up to the Rexall Drug Store and buy some sleeping pills this time. Then I saw it flopped over the chest of drawers next to my bed. FLY ABOVE THE CLOUDS. JOIN THE AIR FORCE. It was a poster I'd ripped off the wall when the recruiters were at our school. Had these jet fighters whipping through the clouds. We were in the middle of the Vietnam war then and they'd set up a recruiting office at the Old Warren County Court House up on the highest hill in town. It's the same courthouse where some Yankee boys from Minnesota lowered the Confederate flag and raised the Union flag after the fall of Vicksburg. It was about two miles from our house and I think I ran the whole way. My legs were rubber as I climbed those long, steep stairs only to find a scribbled sign on the office door. SORRY. CLOSED EARLY. BACK AT 8 A.M. I'm pounding on the window . . . what do you mean closed early . . . there's a war on! I held up my letter. But there was no one to see it.

I wasn't quite fast enough for football scholarships, but the University of Mississippi offered me a scholastic scholarship in their physics department. And a professor from LSU came up to talk to me about my weather projects. He wanted me to go there. Before Lisa wrote that letter I'd pretty much decided I'd be going to Ole Miss and study science. Of course my secret goal was to be the star tight end on the football team and play in the Sugar Bowl and then get drafted by the Dallas Cowboys and win at last the love of Lisa Beauregard.

Next morning after the letter I'm sitting on the steps of

the Old County Court House in the pouring rain looking out over the valley where the River of Death flows into the Father of Waters. I knew I was going away and never coming back. I was sitting there in the rain when the recruitment officer arrived.

It's late now. The newsroom is dark and deserted. All quiet on the weather front. Time to lay down this pen and go home. There's a blue moon out there tonight. A rare occurrence. It happens when two full moons occur in the same calendar month. The second of those moons is called a blue moon. No one really knows why. Some believe it's the moon of love. Others believe it to be the moon of impending doom.

THE FINGERPRINT

The snow was gone. Rain was breaking up the last sheets of ice on area lakes. Captain Les Angelbeck sat on the edge of the hospital bed, buttoning his shirt. The morning paper was on the pillow beside him. Through the spring drizzle he could see the white bubble roof of the Metrodome. The electronic billboard in front of the stadium kept flashing the date of the Twins' home opener.

His fifth-floor room at the Hennepin County Medical Center was as bright and cheerful as the weather was gloomy. He suspected it was a room for women having babies. A green oxygen tank stood next to the bed. His walking cane was next to the door. The television hanging from the ceiling was going, but the sound was dead. Andrea Labore was mouthing the noon news. The front page of the *Star Tribune* flashed on the screen. Les Angelbeck ignored the TV and continued dressing until the Weatherman appeared. Then he picked up the remote and pushed the mute button.

"Dixon, I know this is Tornado Awareness Week, but what exactly is a mock tornado drill?"

"Well, Andrea, according to the National Weather Service that's when a mock has actually been sighted."

Les Angelbeck broke up laughing, but it was a laugh choked with phlegm. He grabbed hold of his aching side. He muted the sound again after Dixon Bell had given the forecast. He was slipping into his shoes when Donnell Redmond walked into the room, carrying a brown envelope.

"So how did your biopsy go?" asked the lieutenant.

"It was benign."

"So you're only dying of one thing instead of two?"

"At this point, yes." Les Angelbeck swallowed the choke in his throat and smiled. "Donny, it was the damnedest thing I've ever heard of. They call it videoscope surgery. The doctor cut this small incision in my side and then he pushed in this long probe with a tele-scopic lens attached to this tiny video camera. Then my insides showed up on a television the doctor was watching. The whole operation was done on a television screen. Doctor never took his eyes off it. I had the procedure done yesterday and I'm going home today."

Redmond looked up at Andrea Labore, her lips moving but no sound coming out. "Maybe they should put your insides on regular TV."

"Maybe." Les Angelbeck slipped gingerly into his suit coat. He draped a tie around his neck. "Did you check on her?"

"No change," Redmond reported. "Her granddaddy is sitting down there beside her. They got her head locked into this big metal halo so she looks ike a dead angel. There's tubes shoved up her nose and more tubes stuffed down her throat. Her jaw just hangs open, like those re-tards you see in those nuthouse movies. She has one eye open real spooky-like and she's strapped into this electric bed that rolls back and forth so she don't get bedsores. And that one eye just stays put as she rolls from side to side."

"Everybody in the hospital refers to Officer Sumter in the past tense," Angelbeck sadly noted.

"I pray she dies. Lord Jesus, forgive me for what I say, but I pray she dies. She'll be at peace, and we can fry that sucker for what he did to her."

"We have to catch the sucker first," Angelbeck re-minded him, tactfully forgetting the lieutenant's testi-mony before the judiciary committee.

Donnell Redmond noticed the newspaper lying on the pillow. "Did you read it?"

"Yes, I read it."

"Did our boy write it?"

"Oh, yes," said Angelbeck. "There's a few non sequi-turs, but the killer wrote it." He picked up the morning copy of the *Star Tribune*. "What did you find out about it?"

"There were some lawyer hassles," said Redmond, filling him in. "They finally handed it over late last night. At first look, it was written on paper from a reporter's notebook. The editor told us newsrooms order them in bulk through a mail-order house. Used a Bic pen. Black. Medium point. Killer is probably right-handed and printed the letter using the left hand."

Les Angelbeck unfolded the newspaper and once again read the letter on the front page.

I WILL STOP NOW

FOR EVERY SEASON THERE IS A WOMAN. A WOMAN TO BE BORN AND A WOMAN TO DIE. AND FOR EVERY MAN A SEASON TO KILL AND A SEASON TO STOP KILL-ING. I WILL STOP NOW.

YOU HAVE NO EVIDENCE. NO WITNESSES. I APPEAR OUT OF THIN AIR. IF YOU WAIT MUCH LONGER IT WILL ALMOST BE IMPOSSIBLE FOR YOU. I WILL BE ONE OF YOU. I WILL PASS YOU ON THE STREET. SIT NEXT TO YOU AT THE BASEBALL GAME.

MINNESOTA YOU THOUGHT YOU WERE SO MUCH BETTER THAN US. NOW YOU ARE JUST LIKE THE REST OF US. DON'T THINK I DON'T UNDERSTAND HOW YOU FEEL, BUT I'AM SORRY YOU DON'T UNDERSTAND HOW I FEEL. I GUESS THINGS NEVER HAPPEN THAT PLEASE EVERYONE ENVOLVED, BUT I DIDN'T MEAN TO HURT YOU . . . HONEST.

The hard-to-retire captain tossed the paper onto the bed. "The poetry isn't much better than the spelling. But in a way, maybe our killer is right. We finally got around to lowering our standards to the national level. What else did you find out?"

"We know it's not a ghost. It bleeds and it has big feet." Donnell Redmond rattled off the latest clues. "The blood we scraped from Sumter's fingernails is O positive. It's one of the most common blood types in America, but it's something. The tracks found in the snow were made by a size-fourteen athletic shoe with 'Alacrity' carved in the heel. It was a cheap shoe made in Korea. The company went out of business years ago and the shoe was never on sale in the Midwest. It's sticking to its ways. At-tacked her the same time of the morning that I chased it through Como Park. It was the last day of winter. It was foggy."

The noon news was over. Andrea Labore smiled goody-bye. Les Angelbeck picked up the remote control and killed the television. Andrea faded away. The old cop's fat, shaky fingers worked a knot into his tie. "And what is that you've got there?"

Donnell Redmond had forgotten about the brown envelope in his hand. He shrugged his big shoulders. "Ain't looked at it yet. Glenn Arkwright tossed it to me on his way out the door. Had to pick up his kids at day care or something." Redmond pulled a computer printout from the envelope and examined it. "It's more of that fingerprint mumbo jumbo," he told Angelbeck. "Looks like AFIS spit out two more names. One is a new print from FBI files and the other one is from those declassifieds the Air Force sent to us."

"Tell me one of them is from Minnesota," begged the captain.

"Dream on, Marlboro Man. West Covina, California, and Vicksburg, Mississippi."

The Marlboro Man had a coughing spasm, his death rattle. He wiped his watery eyes. "Well, add them to the list, anyway."

"Ain't that funny," said Redmond, studying the printout. "Unless I'm reading these numbers wrong, and I might well be, this man from Mississippi is rated higher than all the others."

Angelbeck tightened the noose in his tie. "Really? What's his name?"

The lieutenant unfolded the printout. "Bell, Dixon Graham."

Les Angelbeck went cold. "Dixon Bell?"

Donnell Redmond read the AFIS printout again. "Yeah, that's what it says here. Dixon Graham Bell. Vicksburg, Mississippi." The lieutenant looked into the horrified eyes of Captain Les Angelbeck. "Ain't he that TV weatherman?"

BOOK TWO

TWO YEARS INTO THE STORM

BOOK TWO

TWO YEARS
INTO THE
STORM

"I'll be judge, I'll be jury," said cunning old Fury;
"I'll try the whole cause and condemn you to death."
—Lewis Carroll
Alice's Adventures in Wonderland

THE ARREST

*"**A**nd then the policeman comes and they done take the Weatherman away."*

Les Angelbeck was furious. The arrest was a media circus. They hadn't even begun to make their case when events spun out of control. At the booking center he pushed and cajoled his way to the front of the pack—a pack of his own kind. His leathery face was almost up against the glass that viewed the garage. The big metal doors at the top of the ramp rolled open. A squad car pulled in, followed by a blue van, then two more squads. The motorcade rolled down the ramp and into the sally port. When the two metal doors dropped closed behind the prisoner's parade, on popped a red light. A platoon of cops piled out of the vehicles.

"Um, he was at our school talking to us about things we could do to help keep the air clean, ya know, when a bunch of policemen showed up in the doorway ... and they wanted to talk to him. Then he never came back."

More than forty thousand tips. Three hundred investigators. A thousand interviews. Eight thousand written pages of reports. Whole computer programs. And some damn good gumshoeing. No, police didn't get lucky. They did it the old-fashioned way: they earned it. They were almost sure they had their man.

The infighting began almost immediately. The BCA literally had ahold of him. They made the arrest. The governor's office had a man at the scene. Hennepin County had the most rights to him—four murders. But the Hennepin County jail in Minneapolis was medieval and hopelessly overcrowded. So the decision was made to house him at the Ramsey County jail in downtown St.

Paul. The facility was modern, below capacity, and not far from BCA offices. Meanwhile, the task force was blaming the governor's office for alerting the media. And this was no tip; this was an air raid.

"We ran to the windows 'cause we could see all of your television trucks and stuff outside ... and we saw them bring the Weatherman out of the school in handcuffs and put him in the police car. He had his head bent down really far ... but you could tell he was crying."

The detention center fell ghostly quiet as they led the Weatherman through the electronically controlled doors and into the brick booking area. Dixon Bell's puffy face was ash white. His eyes were bloodshot. His suit coat was off. The tie around his neck was askew. His shirt was coming untucked. The shiny steel handcuffs on his wrists looked like obscene jewelry. Lieutenant Donnell Redmond had him by the arm.

The lieutenant walked Dixon Bell over to a small table. He unlocked the cuffs and turned the prisoner over to the booking officer, a bear of a man in a brown-and-tan deputy sheriff's uniform. The Weatherman was asked to empty his pockets into a metal box. Each valuable was recorded on paper. Then the deputy led him over to a machine with two video monitors for eyes. It resembled an instant cash machine. The army of cops followed.

"What is this thing?" Dixon Bell asked in a soft, shaky voice everybody could hear.

"It's a fingerprinter," the deputy told him. "It'll record your fingerprints."

"How does it work?"

"I'll just roll your fingers across the glass plate one at a time, and you can see your print on the TV screen there."

"You mean there's no ink?"

"No ink. I'll show you. Give me your hand."

Dixon Bell reluctantly held out his big left hand. The deputy took hold of it, and as the fingers rolled across the lighted glass the black lines of his fingerprints appeared on the monitors, where they were recorded for computer analysis. The Weatherman forced an ironic smile. "I'm glad television is finally being put to some good use."

The deputy smiled too. His gruff looks were deceiving. "This contraption has made my job a hell of a lot easier."

Fingerprint expert Glenn Arkwright brushed by Les Angelbeck. He stepped forward and leaned into the deputy. "Do the left index finger again."

The deputy was mad. "I know my job, thank you!"

Dixon Bell was perplexed by the outburst. For the first time since being dragged through the electronic doors he took a slow look around the room at the convention of law-enforcement officials. The place was wall-to-wall cops. "Sure are a lot of people interested in these fingerprints," he said. Looking up, he found himself staring at Les Angelbeck, who was standing in the front, leaning on his cane, forever clearing his throat. A veil of betrayal fell over the Weatherman's face, and he turned his back on the old cop.

Captain Les Angelbeck had first met meteorologist Dixon Bell in Peavey Plaza, a sunken gathering place of concrete steps and water fountains alongside Orchestra Hall on the Nicollet Walk. It was where the old cop requested they get together and talk. Only two days had passed since his biopsy and he still felt weak, but the cool fragrance of a spring breeze worked wonders on his emphysema. The morning chill had yet to lift. The skies were overcast. Man-eating puddles left over from the snowy winter stretched across the plaza. Along one of the concrete steps someone had spray-painted, WHY IS IT OPEN SEASON ON WOMEN? The semiretired cop gazed up at the sturdy blue IDS Tower and wondered which one of the windows below the bramble of TV antennas belonged to the Weatherman.

It was the second time in the investigation that Dixon Bell's name had come up. Angelbeck remembered victim number seven, the little retarded girl from Afton who had a crush on the Weatherman, and that letter she wrote. *I saw u on TV. I no u r the killer.* Did she mail him that letter? Then came the fingerprint. The Weatherman also fit the description given by the jogger in Hudson, Wisconsin, on the morning of that murder. But the Hudson description was of a person's back from a distance. Also, they'd have to conduct a search of Bell's office and home in hopes of finding the girl's letter. And that fingerprint was only a controversial partial. FBI experts in Washington were saying the print belonged to Dixon Bell. Minnesota's own expert, Glenn Arkwright, wouldn't go along with them. He wanted more time. So did Les Angelbeck. But circumstantial evidence was mounting, and the governor's office wanted an arrest.

Angelbeck saw the tall, husky weatherman loping across the street towards Peavey Plaza. He'd been watching him on television since his arrival at Channel 7. Before that he used to watch the avuncular, and somewhat reliable, Andy Mack. Like most loyal viewers, he was upset about the switch. But also like other viewers, he was won over by Dixon Bell—won over by his knowledge, his accuracy, and good old-fashioned southern charm.

He stood to greet him. "Dixon Bell, I'm Captain Les Angelbeck. I'm with the Calendar Task Force."

They shook hands. "Hello, Captain. Why did you want to meet down here?"

"Cops and newsrooms don't go together." He lifted the pack of Marlboros from his coat pocket. "Mind if I smoke? Nasty habit of mine."

"Do it while it's still legal."

Donnell Redmond had seen a Channel 7 News van leaving Como Park minutes after he'd lost the frosty monster in a foot chase. At the time the lieutenant figured they'd heard the strange call on their police band. Now he was asking Angelbeck why a news crew couldn't see three cops standing over a body in the middle of a frozen lake on a sunny morning. A source in the Channel 7 newsroom told Angelbeck the take-home policy on news vans was very loose. They needed permission from the assignment desk, but the written records of who took what van when were sloppy at best.

They took seats on the concrete steps. The air grew cool. "You're a veteran, aren't you, Dixon?"

"Yes. Air Force. Twenty years and out. And you?"

As they spoke the BCA was busy perusing the Weatherman's military records. Dixon Bell's blood type was the common O positive, the same blood type Officer Shelly Sumter had drawn from the killer's hands.

"Army," Angelbeck told him. "World War II. Not many of us left." He lit his cigarette and pointed at the Weatherman's face. "I noticed the scar. Wounded?"

Dixon Bell passed a finger down his cheek. "Saigon. Took a beating over a girl."

"Vietnam, the television war."

"Yes, the television war. But I don't think you called me down here to swap war stories, Captain. What can I do for you?"

Angelbeck turned away and coughed. He wiped his mouth and caught his breath. "I'm sure you've heard something about it, media has been drumming it up, about these murders being seasonal and weather-related. Maybe it's silly, but we check out every angle."

"Not so silly. We know human behavior is affected by the weather. They've been doing some interesting studies on it at the University of Wisconsin."

Angelbeck nodded. "That's in Madison, right? Didn't I read you lectured there a couple of autumns ago?"

"I've lectured there several times."

"The thing of it is," Angelbeck went on, "some of these murders are happening before these big storms. Now is that possible?"

"Sure. There are dramatic changes in the atmosphere ahead of a storm."

"How much ahead?"

"Usually hours, but in some cases days."

"If I remember right, you predicted every one of those storms."

"I don't predict the weather, Captain. I *read* the weather."

The police captain pointed his cane at the low gray ceiling of clouds drifting over the TV antennas atop the IDS Tower. "What kind of clouds are those?"

Dixon Bell bent his head skyward. "Those are from the cumulus family. They're flat, so they'd be stratocumulus. Elevation . . . about six-thousand feet. Lead gray in color. Unsettled. If they fuse, they'll bring us some more drizzle tonight."

"And this wonderful breeze in my face?"

Dixon Bell grinned at the test. "Since it's in your face, it has to be southeasterly, doesn't it? And since it's only rustling that flag in front of Orchestra Hall, you can put the wind speed at four to seven miles per hour."

Angelbeck blew smoke into the slight wind. "That's amazing."

"The weather is so complex and so poorly understood," Dixon Bell explained. "Most people lack even a basic understanding of how the weather works. It's a failure of our educational system. We'll force algebra and book reports down their little throats, but we can't begin to explain to children where the tornado came from that turned their lives upside down."

Les Angelbeck shook his head in sad agreement. Then he sighed in frustration. "What kind of man do you think is behind these murders, Dixon?"

"I can't answer that, Captain. You're into another science now."

"But you must have some opinions, with the weather angle and all?"

"No, not really. I'm a meteorologist, not a newsman. We're a pretty benign group."

How true, Angelbeck thought, but how cold. And when he reminded the Weatherman that he had boldly predicted the storms preceding the killings, which damn near implicated him in the murders, Bell's reactions were cool as ice. After years of interviewing murder suspects the cagey cop had his own built-in lie-detector test—a spark of guilt in their eyes, of mendacity in their voice, the nervousness in their hands. But the Weatherman's hands were as a calm as a summer day. They were also free of scratch marks. From Dixon Bell that day he got nothing—nothing but a meteorologist proud to share his knowledge of the heavens.

Les Angelbeck watched intently as the Weatherman's big fat fingerprints rolled across the blue TV screen one at a time. The deputy was talking to him. Angelbeck moved a step closer so that he could hear.

"I live in Roseville." The deputy spoke softly as he rolled the right thumb. "I wasn't home when the tornado struck, but my wife and kids were. They were watching you and they ran to the basement. We were lucky, I guess. It just blew out the windows, glass everywhere." The deputy was choking up, trying to say thank you—not easy for a cop booking a murder suspect.

Dixon Bell understood. "This is quite a gadget y'all have here," he said, changing the subject.

As fantastic as it was to believe, Les Angelbeck felt in his heart that they had the right man. Right under their nose the whole time. Hiding in plain sight. Brilliant. But just because they had the right man didn't mean they had a good case. Was the FBI correct about the fingerprint, or was Glenn Arkwright justified about his doubts? In a jury pool how many, like the teary-eyed deputy, lived in the path of the Eden Prairie tornado? Or like Les Angelbeck, watched Sky High News religiously?

Two days after the Peavey Plaza meeting the police captain paid another visit to Dixon Bell, this time at his town house in Edina. He brought Donnell Redmond with him. Per Ellefson had again been briefed by the two cops. The governor's office was pressuring them for the arrest.

The Weatherman's town house was contemporary and suburban. Sparsely furnished. A glorified apartment. The dwelling of a man who cared more for his work than his home. "Am I a suspect?"

"Yes, technically you are a suspect," Angelbeck informed him.

"Are you crazy? Do you have any idea what this would do to my career? I'm on television!"

Lieutenant Redmond remained sullen as he browsed around the place.

Dixon Bell raged on. "When I took over the weather it was just two minutes of highs and lows and a chance of rain they stuck in between news and sports. They had old men and bimbos with big tits reading it off a TelePromp-Ter. I made it something. I used it to teach children. I'm negotiating a documentary contract with the station right now. Documentaries are dead. They don't do them anymore. But they're going to do them for me."

Angelbeck tried to explain the situation. "We have a witness who saw somebody who looks something like you with one of the victims before she died."

"Saw somebody who looks something like me? Is that the best you can do?"

"There's also a fingerprint," Angelbeck told him.

"Whose fingerprint?"

Redmond exploded. "Your fingerprint, sucker! We

got this computer that turns fingerprints into numbers. And this computer says those numbers belong to you."

"It's inconclusive," said Angelbeck. "It's just a partial print from the scene of the first murder. The one at your parking ramp. But this computer spit your name out on a list of probables."

Dixon Bell was cool. "Maybe it is mine. I park in that parking ramp five days a week."

"Do you park behind the transformer?" Redmond wanted to know.

"Would you submit to a polygraph—a lie-detector test?" Angelbeck asked him.

"Absolutely not. Those things are bogus. Don't you guys watch '60 Minutes'?"

Donnell Redmond was an inch taller than Dixon Bell. He folded his arms and stepped into the Weatherman's face. "Don't you remember me? Como Park? A cold Christmas morning? I chased your frosty ass over the waterfall. You left that girl in an ice cube out on the lake."

"That's sick."

"Y'all listen to me, cracker. You're lying right through those TV teeth of yours. Now we're gonna fry your ass."

"I've never had any trouble with you people."

"Oooh, is that right? I ain't never met a white boy from Mississippi who didn't have trouble with us people."

Les Angelbeck stuck his cane between them. "Lieutenant, why don't you wait in the car."

Dixon Bell walked to his patio window and studied the sky. He heard the front door slam. "It's going to rain," he muttered. He saw Donnell Redmond march to his car, climb in, and slam that door too. He eyed the Weatherman from the front seat as he talked on his two-way. "He's not from Minnesota, is he?"

"I'm sorry about that, Dixon. No, he's from Florida. It's the Edina officer. Has a lot of cops smelling blood."

Dixon Bell turned. "You mean the electric chair?"

"If she dies, maybe."

The Weatherman tried to wrestle his heavy breathing under control, as if he were the one suffering from emphysema. "If I came in tomorrow and answered all of your questions, and submitted to your stupid polygraph machine, could you keep this out of the news?"

"Yes, I could," Angelbeck assured him. "If anybody

were to ask, we're just getting some advice on the weather factor?"

So Dixon Bell agreed. "I'm visiting a classroom tomorrow morning. I'll be in after lunch."

But the governor's office forced them to break the promise they had made to the Channel 7 weatherman. They marched into an elementary school, put handcuffs on him, and took him away as news cameras rolled—and children watched.

After the suspect had been booked and jailed, Les Angelbeck and Donnell Redmond sat under a bright fluorescent table lamp at the Bureau of Criminal Apprehension, paging through the Weatherman's diary, found in a search of his weather office, reading his most intimate thoughts. Angelbeck wiped his weary eyes, then put a hand to his aching chest. There was no such thing as growing old with dignity. It was humiliating. His doctor wrote a letter making him eligible for a handicap sticker. He'd die before he'd stick that thing on his dashboard. It had been a long frustrating day.

The chilly spring days were getting longer, but they were still too short for all of the work that had to be done on this case. Dixon Bell wore a size-fourteen shoe all right, but a search of his home and office turned up no cheap athletic shoe called Alacrity. The best they could find was a brand-new pair of Nikes.

"Look at here, March thirty-first," said Redmond, pointing at a page in the diary. "It says, 'a note really, folded here on this page.' And here, two pages later, 'Letter folded here on this page.'" He flipped through the diary. "There ain't no note and there ain't no letter."

Angelbeck tore through the pages. "Dammit. Get back up there and search that office again. Take a team and search that entire newsroom."

"We can't do that. Judge says weather office only."

Then the police captain thought about his wily source in the Channel 7 newsroom. "How long after the arrest before you got up to that office?"

Rick Beanblossom reached up and turned off the news. He popped open a Pepsi and swallowed two painkillers.

He stared at the big fat file on his desk. If Captain Les Angelbeck felt in his heart they had the right man, Rick's heart was telling him quite the opposite.

The other stations in town were clobbering them, as were the networks. The newspapers were having a field day. There were rumors about a diary. Rumors about a love triangle at Channel 7. Overnight the Calendar Killer was renamed the Weatherman. For the first time since the Gulf War, no viewer phone calls were being allowed through to the newsroom.

The tornado that tore by Sky High News and blew out a window, the tornado that caused *Skyhawk 7* to crash to the ground, was nature's most violent act; the deaths of their colleagues a shock. But it was a shock they could deal with. After the tornado took the lives of two of their best, Sky High News went on to become the most-watched news station in Minnesota. Critics stopped calling what they did fluff news and more respectfully referred to it as soft news. Other stations in town tried to copy their formula. The bimbos and the bozos kept coming and going, but with less frequency. Those who stayed with Channel 7 grew in their roles. All of this had spiraled out of a tornado. But none of these hearty souls knew how to deal with the storm of trouble now raining down on them. This was no violent act of nature but the most violent acts of man. Their man, police were saying. Their weatherman.

Andrea Labore strolled over to Rick's desk. She put her nose to his flowers and smiled, a sweet, sad smile. "Grab some dinner? We should talk."

Her face was sweeter than the flowers, the scent of her perfume more calming than the pills. She set his heart on fire. Her strengths were his weaknesses. But what did she feel for him? Love? Pity? Dateline was ringing. Rick looked up at the row of clocks. "Ten minutes," he said in a reassuring voice.

"Ten minutes," said Andrea. Then she was gone.

Already he felt better. Rick picked up the phone. "Beanblossom."

"Read any good letters lately?"

"Can't say as I have. How long have you suspected our weatherman?"

"The arrest got all screwed up. Almost two hours

passed before we got somebody up there to search his weather office. There are some letters missing from there."

"What kind of letters?"

"Besides the letters from the Afton girl, two letters that were folded inside the diary. My guess is someone from the newsroom walked over there and searched that office before our people got up there. Someone with a leather nose for news."

"If that someone took the letters, why wouldn't that someone have taken the whole diary?"

"Why take the diary when he can photocopy the entire thing in a matter of minutes?"

"Then why didn't he just photocopy the letters?"

"Because he didn't want us to have them."

"And why is that?"

"I suspect they seal the Weatherman's fate. I want those letters, Masked Man."

"I'll ask around."

"I spoon-fed you your first news story before you even knew you wanted to be a newsman."

"Was that out of respect, or pity?" There was no answer, but he was still on the line. "A lot of people think you've got the wrong man."

"Murder number one. Your own Sky High ramp. His fingerprint was found at the scene. Two feet from the body."

"That fingerprint only has seven points of ID. Worthless in a court of law."

"Shame on you, Mr. Beanblossom—you have other sources. The fingerprint is hardly worthless. FBI says it's his."

"And what does your man say? Arkwright's his name, isn't it?"

"Your weatherman was in Lake Country on the Fourth of July. We have reason to believe he was at that wet-T-shirt contest."

"There's videotape of that contest. Can you find him in the crowd? Can any of the five thousand drunken motorheads put him at the scene?"

"This case is like a chain. It's made up of links. There may be a few missing links now, but in the end we'll link

*him to all eight murders ... then we'll chain his ass to
the chair."*

"Excuse me, but last time I checked Officer Sumter
was still alive."

*"Check again. She died fifteen minutes ago. I want
those letters, Masked Man."*

Rick Beanblossom punched up Script on his computer.
He began typing up the obituary of Shelly Sumter, to go
on the air immediately. He mumbled into the phone.
"Like I said, I'll ask around."

*"Don't you dare let me see that diary showing up on
your news show."*

Dateline went dead.

THE VISIT

Ramsey County Adult Detention Center—2 West, D Pod, Cell 340. Dixon Bell sat alone on his bunk, staring out the window at the sunny weather above the muddy river. But this window was seven layers thick, with a motion alarm. It was as if he had stepped through the looking glass. His face was all over television, for all the wrong reasons. The district attorney called him a serial killer. The judge denied him bail, and he was locked up like a zoo animal in this high-tech podular jail that hung over the white sandstone cliffs of St. Paul.

Railroad tracks ran directly beneath his cell, so close he could see wisps of engine smoke as the trains chugged by. They chugged by often, and then the whole building shook. If he could somehow smash through that window, it was only a three-story drop to the tracks. He thought about busting out. These days he thought a lot about escape.

It was summertime. Eighty- and ninety-degree temperatures. His window faced south. People were boating right in front of him. Off to his right he could see the High Bridge arched from cliff to cliff. To his left was the Wabasha Street Bridge, and further downriver were the dramatic arches of the Robert Street Bridge. From there the mighty Mississippi wound around Pig's Eye Bend and started for Vicksburg. If he could bust out he'd just follow the river home.

The brick cell was triangular. Two bunks were attached to the wall. Dixon Bell had the cell to himself, but every once in a while when the jail was full they'd toss a harmless bum in there with him. He had an aluminum toilet that made a lot of noise when flushed; that way the deputies could hear it. If a prisoner flushed his toilet too often the deputies would come up and shake him down. They were sheriff's deputies and they despised being called guards. He had an aluminum wash basin and a mirror. On the wall was an intercom button. Each prisoner was allowed two sheets, a towel and a wash cloth, a few bathroom items, toothpaste and brush, and a couple of books, paperbacks only.

Cotton cumulus clouds floated across a clear blue sky. High pressure was in control on this day. He could see a refreshing breeze off the water, but he couldn't feel it. That was the most punishing aspect of all, being removed from the natural elements and locked in climate control. The Weatherman was made to wear jail greens and sandal slippers. He was locked in his cell from ten o'clock at night until five o'clock in the morning. If he was a good boy he'd be promoted to "trustee" and allowed to stay up until 1:00 A.M. and watch television. To date, he hadn't been very good.

There were ten cells in his pod: five upstairs, five down. They opened up into a day room with a winding staircase, where the prisoners spent most of their time. Meals were served in the day room. There were telephones on the wall, some broken exercise equipment, and a new television set. Dixon Bell had destroyed the old set.

Within minutes of his arrest the media had turned on him. A feeding frenzy. They chased him with cameras, microphones, and satellite trucks. In and out of court, in and out of jail; whenever he caught a glimpse of the dazzling summer sun, they stepped in front it.

The television set in the day room was bolted to an iron sling that hung from the ceiling. Channel selection and volume were controlled by the deputies inside the control room, to keep prisoners' hands off the set and to prevent fights. During his first week of imprisonment Dixon Bell was watching the news on CNN when they ran another story on his arrest. The Weatherman was livid. The story was so distorted, so slanted against him—"Just skip the fucking trial and fry me, why don't you?" He filled a paper cup with water and tossed it into the back of the set. Boy, did that sucker blow! The Weatherman was locked in Isolation TFN—Till Further Notice. Now he was out.

It was in Isolation that he began thinking about escape—if not for the freedom it might bring, at least for the challenge. He was a scientist. He had to set aside his emotions and frustrations and approach escape in a cool, calculating manner. If there was a simple way in, logic dictates, there was a simple way out. As one prisoner suggested, "Use the door."

The big steel door to his cell slid open and closed along a thick metal rail that was bolted to the floor. Only one deputy manned the control room, and he had to keep an eye on two different pods. That meant he was watching the Weatherman's pod only half the time. One day when the deputy was out of sight Dixon Bell, big and heavy, stepped up on this rail and bounced up and down a few times. Sure enough, after a week or two of bouncing he felt the rail give a little. So the Weatherman did some calculating about pressure points and weight distribution, and he figured with enough time he might be able to snap that rail right off. Of course it had to be snapped at just the right point, so that he could slip it back down there and the door could slide open. He'd keep working on it.

"Dixon Bell."

The echo sounded like a wake-up call from the deep blue sky.

"Dixon Bell."

The Weatherman pulled his head out of the clouds. He was being summoned over the PA system. He got off his bunk and walked out of his cell to the railing.

The deputy down in the control room was leaning over the microphone. "That reporter with the mask is here to see you."

Rick Beanblossom slipped his driver's license under the bullet-proof glass and signed his name. The deputy ordered him to wait while he fetched his supervisor. The masked newsman admired the view of the river. The hot summer sun was noon high and sparkled on the water. He was on the sixth floor of the jail. Visitors Center. He showed the supervisor his press credentials and his hospital card. They recognized the name. After satisfying their curiosity, electronic bolts slipped, metal doors opened, and he was escorted down a concrete hallway to a sound booth with no door.

"Just pick up the phone and look right into the television," he was told. "He'll be up in a minute."

Rick placed his notebook and pen in front of him. He held the receiver in his hand and stared into the monitor. It was black-and-white. An empty chair and a bare desk. A brick wall. Five minutes passed. He saw dark shadows behind the chair. Then the Weatherman came into view. He took his seat and picked up the phone. "It's nice to see you on television again," Rick joked.

"Yeah, and commercial-free." For Dixon Bell jail had to be the ultimate humiliation.

Rick glanced over his shoulder, very uncomfortable. Then the Marine noticed the pajama top the former Air Force officer was wearing. "You look like Viet Cong."

"My first thought, too. How y'all doing at the station?"

"Don't you watch?"

He shook his head, a tormented man. "I can't."

The news producer nodded in sympathy. "Andy Mack is back doing the weather. Charleen's contract is up soon. They slip Andrea into the anchor chair every chance they get. The only reason you're not on the air is because you weren't granted bail. Napoleon was really upset about that. Ratings would have gone through the roof."

The Weatherman turned a smile at the thought.

They sat staring at each other on television screens. An awkward silence ensued, the silence of two proud and stubborn men. Rick finally broke the spell. "You haven't given an interview since your arrest. Why me?"

Dixon Bell ran his fingers through his graying hair in the sad realization that he needed all the help he could get. "There's an old cop who put their whole case together. Les Angelbeck. Do you know him?"

"I've talked to him on the phone a few times."

"That old boy is dead wrong. This is a setup. I've been framed."

"No, Angelbeck was never that kind of cop."

"I'm not saying he framed me. I'm saying he fell for it, and he's too old and sick to see that." His southern accent sounded thicker. He was no longer the poised person who delivered the accurate forecasts.

"What do you want from me?" Rick asked him.

"Clarence Darrow once said criminals shun reporters more than they do cops, because reporters are smarter and less merciful. I want you on my story. You're better than any detective. I know how bad you wanted to solve the Wakefield kidnapping. This is even bigger than that, and I'll give you everything. Full access. Those women were murdered to set me up, and if anybody can prove that, you can."

Rick Beanblossom picked up his pen and doodled in his reporter's notebook. "Tell me about your diary."

"The police have it."

"I know that. Tell me what they have."

"My thoughts, my memories. Some of it is very intimate. I used the diary to keep from slipping away."

"Slipping away from what?"

The Weatherman turned away from the monitor. Then he bowed his head, almost in shame. "Reality."

"Are you insane?"

"No, I am not insane."

"But you do admit to a degree of mental illness?" Dixon Bell didn't answer. "Would you consider using insanity as a defense?"

"Never. I'm innocent."

"Tell me about the letters in your diary."

"How did you know about those? There's been nothing in the news."

"I *am* the news. Tell me about them."

"What's to tell? Cops keep asking me about them, but my lawyer says not to comment until she's read them. Cops say the FBI has them in Washington doing tests."

"They're bluffing," Rick told him. "The letters are missing. They've turned your office upside down trying to find them. They've even tried to get a search warrant on the newsroom."

The Weatherman was stunned. "Missing?"

"Tell me about the letters."

"There are times we'll have to talk off the record."

"Off the record, then, tell me about the letters."

"Don't it seem funny to you that something so personal that happened down home so many years ago would interest so many folks up in this neck of the woods?" Dixon Bell wiped his mouth before speaking again. He stared straight forward into the monitor. "That letter from the killer that appeared in the *Star Tribune* ... some of the lines in it were taken directly from those letters."

"How is that possible?"

"Simple. The killer walked into my office, lifted the letters from my diary, and copied them. The perfect frame-up."

"Then why didn't the killer put the letters back so they'd be found?"

"I don't know. I thought he did—I thought Angelbeck had them. If they find those letters, my ass is cooked."

"Have you told Stacy Dvorchak about the letters?"

A guilty look spread over his face. "No. I figured she'd see it for herself as soon as she got her hands on them."

"What else haven't you told us about?"

"I also got threats."

"What kind of threats?"

Dixon Bell rubbed his temples trying to remember. "Some lunatic would call me on the phone, or write me notes saying he was going to ice me. He had a really faggy voice, kind of mocking a southern accent. Once the message was on my computer. Another time I found it written on a surface map."

"Did you report them to anybody?"

"No. They didn't happen that often. I shrugged them off. It's television."

"How often? About once every season?"

Dixon Bell was looking sick. "About the time of the tornado. The ice storm. A couple of rainy nights."

"Did you save any of the written threats?"

"No. The computer message I erased. The surface maps are thrown away."

"You may have erased it from the screen, but it could still be in the computer. I'll see if I can retrieve it."

"I know computers. That's not possible."

Rick Beanblossom flipped a page in his notebook. He stared at Dixon Bell's weatherbeaten face on the black-and-white monitor. They'd been talking almost an hour, the newsman often playing the devil's advocate. Their visiting time was almost up. The Weatherman was growing hostile. Bitter. Rick kept at him. "Tell me about Andrea."

Dixon Bell shrugged his big shoulders. "I guess I was in love with her. What else can I say?"

"That her beauty drove you mad. That your unrequited love drove you to murder."

"That's bullshit. My problems started long before I ever laid eyes on Andrea Labore."

"Yes. Your problems started in high school with Lisa Beauregard."

Dixon Bell was startled. "You've read my diary."

"I've obtained a copy. You just said I could have everything."

"Then you've got the letters."

"No, I don't have the letters, nor have I seen them. Tell me about Andrea."

Dixon Bell leaned into the television screen, his voice changing tone, growing louder and more intense—angry. "Yes, what about Andrea, Beanblossom? How long have you been in love with her?"

He sounded like the old weatherman now, the arrogant TV star Rick Beanblossom always despised. Rick thought hard before commenting. "Good God, what makes you ask something like that?"

Dixon Bell snickered at the question. "You think you can hide everything behind that mask, don't you?" He laughed, a small mocking laugh. "When I first met you I felt sorry for you. The poor burn victim. Man without a face. But where others came to admire you, even if they didn't like you, I came to loathe you. You wear that mask like the Lone Ranger. I sometimes wonder how bad your face really is."

"Get to the point."

The Weatherman laughed again, louder and more erratic than before. "I see right through you, Beanblossom. That's why you've never cared for me."

Suddenly, Rick was feeling very uncomfortable. "Cut to the chase."

"Andrea?" The Weatherman took a deep breath, shaking with fear at his own insights, but seemingly enjoying himself. "Since the day you slipped on that mask you've felt the need—no, almost a compulsion—to surround yourself with physical beauty. I've heard about your beautiful condo, and the beautiful furniture, and the beautiful art on the walls. You go out and buy a beautiful new car every year. The fresh flowers on your desk. Boy oh boy, when you saw that face of hers, I'll bet it was love at first sight. And because those big brown eyes were something you couldn't possess, beauty you couldn't go out and buy, you openly despised her, ignored her, made sure everybody in the newsroom knew that she was the worst thing to happen to television news in the history of television news. I saw it from the start. It was in your eyes, in your voice—it was written all over your blue cotton face. I'll bet there were even times when you wanted to strangle her."

Rick watched the Weatherman laughing crazylike on the television set. "You seem to think you can read people the same way you read the weather."

"So are you going to tell her? Make your move?"

"I have no moves to make, Weatherman. I accepted that a long time ago. Perhaps that was your mistake."

"You underestimate yourself, Kemo Sabay. I'm just a fat, middle-aged TV weatherman whose goose is probably cooked. But you ... you'll never grow old. You'll just go out and buy a new mask every year. Go for her."

"Why? So you can see me fail, like you?"

"Yes. Fall flat on your face."

THE DEFENSE

One day after Rick Beanblossom's visit to the Ramsey County jail defense attorney Anastasia Dvorchak, the quadriplegic everybody knew as Stacy, sat at a table face-to-face with the Weatherman. Interview Room 2 West was a plain brick room. Lawyers and cops only. Total privacy. There was a distress alarm on the wall, just in case. Stacy had been working on his defense for a month. She began with the good news. "Edina police held a press conference. They say you're no longer a suspect in the string of rape cases out there."

Dixon Bell yawned. "Well, hell, they tried their best."

"What does that mean?"

The Weatherman remembered seeing her on television during the death penalty hearings, swimming against the tide of popular opinion. Andrea Labore had done a story on her, about how Stacy Dvorchak boldly ventured into the South, driving herself thousands of miles in a specially equipped Ford van she called St. Jude, patron saint of lost causes—all to save death row inmates from the electric chair, or the gas chamber, or lethal injection. Though appeals were her area of expertise, she welcomed the opportunity to defend a man she felt she knew through television.

"Remember I told you every once in a while they toss a bum into my cell? Well, a couple of weeks after I'm in here they assign this hustler to my cell. He was a real New York street type ... tells you his whole life story and everything that's wrong with the world at machine-gun pace, and you nod your head a lot. He was a healthy, good-looking guy, and one night he starts talking to me about women."

"If ya see a woman ya want, Dixon, ya just take her."

"What do you mean, take her?"

"Take her."

"You're talking about rape, aren't you?"

"I ain't whistlin' Dixie."

"He starts laughing. Then he jumps down from his bunk and sits next to me, all buddy-like."

"Dixon, I'm what cops call a tree jumper. Let me explain. The average shmuck on the street sees a beautiful woman he's never laid eyes on before and says to himself, 'I could never have one that pretty.' I see a beautiful woman on the street, I say to myself, 'That's the one I'm having tonight.' You know all that crapola the shrinks put out, that rape is an act of violence, not sex. It's friggin' bullshit. Forced sex is the best sex. You don't hurt 'em, ya fuck 'em! Never carry a weapon. If you get caught, it hurts your case. A big guy like you could take any woman he wanted."

"How many women have you taken?"

"Fuck, who counts? I've been at it since junior high school. Nine out of ten of them don't even report it, and the ones that do usually can't prove jack shit. I've had some beautiful women, Dixon."

"So how did you get caught?"

"I didn't. I'm not in here for tree jumpin'. I sold some crack to a narc. I'll get a year in the workhouse. With overcrowding, I'll be out in ninety days."

"He waited for me to say something, but I had nothing to say. Finally he pats me on the leg before he climbs back into his bunk."

"Dixon, after you beat this rap, look me up. We'll get together for some drinks."

"And did you report him?" Stacy asked.

Dixon Bell shook his head, amused. "Wake up, Dvorchak—he was a cop. A plant. I'd been expecting him."

Stacy Dvorchak was momentarily stunned by her own naiveté. This would be her first jury trial. To what lengths would the state go to convict this man? She adjusted the pen holder on her hand brace and checked off the points as she talked. "You've been indicted on seven counts of first-degree intentional homicide. Counts one through six, the maximum penalty: 'Upon conviction of this charge, a

Class A Felony, the penalty shall be life imprisonment.' The maximum penalty for count seven: 'Upon conviction of this charge, a Class A Felony, the penalty shall be death by electrocution.' They're really only after count seven—the murder of Officer Sumter. The capital offense. In order to prove you killed her, they're going to try to prove you killed six women before her. It's a bold but risky strategy. And if we beat those seven counts . . . Wisconsin will be waiting in the wings to try you for the Hudson murder."

"I'm up the Yazoo," muttered Dixon Bell.

"What's that?"

"The River of Death," he told her. "I believe the term used in this neck of the woods is Shit Creek. It means they're all determined they're going to sit my ass in the electric chair."

"I'm forced to sit in an electric chair every day."

The Weatherman apologized. "I'm sorry. I wasn't thinking."

Stacy Dvorchak dived into a swimming pool one night and broke her sixth cervical disk, the bone that sticks out at the base of the neck. She lost all bodily functions below that point. After five months at a rehabilitation center she was left with control of her arms and some wrist movement. That she broke her neck doing what she did best, what she enjoyed most, haunted her still. But her spirit couldn't be broken. She had family, friends, and her work. She was a patron of the arts, a regular theatergoer. She held season tickets to Viking football. Thank God for the dome. The weather was her adversary. Minnesota is for the healthy. In the snow and cold she was like a caged animal. She sometimes ventured south as much to escape the arctic winters as to fight for the right.

"You may be looking at two trials: The criminal trial, and then, if you're found guilty, the sentence trial. The second trial is called the penalty phase. This is a separate hearing. The jury will be asked to choose between a prison sentence and the death penalty. Now you can waive your right to a jury trial and face a judge. I believe in the first phase of the trial you'd be better off with a jury. I can sway a jury, but it's hard to move a judge when the circumstantial evidence is stacked against you. However, and you hear me good, if you're found guilty and we go into the penalty phase, we'd be much better off facing a judge than a jury. It's a hell of a lot easier to say 'Off with his head' when responsibility is divided by twelve. Since the death penalty defies all logic, I can argue common sense to a judge."

"I'm innocent. I want the jury."

The building shook like a minor earthquake as a train passed below. Stacy Dvorchak wrote notes on her legal pad in the slow, deliberate way she'd mastered. She didn't talk for five minutes. On television she often came across as loud and bitchy. In reality, she was a quiet, intense woman. Dixon Bell watched her work. "I have two assistants now working full time on your defense," she told him, "but the jury will see only you and me at the defense table. It'll give us that underdog look. Minnesotans have a natural resentment toward the rich and the powerful. Where else can you see millionaires out mowing their lawns? You'll stand trial at the Hennepin County Government Center in Minneapolis. Do you know the building?"

"I did a live shot from the garden in the lobby once. They keep bugging me about a lie-detector test. I think I should take it."

"Absolutely not."

"Why? If I pass, their case is shot. If I fail, it can't be admitted in a court of law."

"If you pass, it's irrelevant to their case. If you fail, how are you going to keep it out of the news?" She scrawled some notes. Then the attorney for the defense awkwardly reached into a bag that hung from her electric wheelchair and pulled out a bottle of raspberry mineral water. "Can you open this for me?"

Dixon Bell screwed off the top, then set the bottle on the table in front of her. He sat back and watched as she picked up the bottle with both hands to quench her thirst.

Stacy spread papers before her until she found the sheet she was searching for. "I've already obtained a list of some of the people they're talking to, potential witnesses. You're going to have to fill in the blanks. General R. L. Patterson?"

"Commanding officer. Vietnam. He ran the air base."

"John Dupre, Memphis, Tennessee?"

"He was the news director at the Memphis station. I was the weekend weatherman."

"Lisa Gilbert, Dallas, Texas?"

"Never heard of her ... How long?" the Weatherman wanted to know.

"Another hour."

"No, I mean how long before we go to trial?"

She unfastened her pen holder. Not a good sign. "I don't see this coming to trial before the end of the year. This list is just the beginning. They're going to have us running all over the country, and we still won't be able to check out everybody."

"I can't wait that long," he confessed. "I'll go crazy in here."

"I'll take another stab at bail."

The Weatherman watched in self-conscious awe as his attorney, unjustly sentenced to life in an electric chair, drank her raspberry water, strapped on her pen holder, then went back to scribbling notes on her legal pad like a child. He knew he had a damn good lawyer, but it was like having a sunny day in subzero weather.

THE EPIPHANY

When the news show was over, when the weather had been guessed at and the Twins' score given, they walked around the lake beneath Rick Beanblossom's home in the sky. It was a hot, humid night. Tropical air was up from the Gulf, the kind of weather meant for outdoor baseball. Heavy traffic circled Calhoun Boulevard. On the glassy water that mirrored the lights of Minneapolis, sailboats were moored for the evening while ducks frolicked just offshore. A slight south breeze kept mosquitoes at bay.

"Children and dogs are the worst. I avoid them like the hot sun. Especially children. They don't understand. They're afraid of me. Some run from me. Others taunt me to mask their fear."

It was near midnight when he realized he'd been talking all night. But Andrea Labore was a good listener. Joggers swept past them. They stepped down to a fishing dock and walked out over the water. The new moon of the midsummer was bright overhead. The water was so clear they could read the beer cans on the bottom. An old man was fishing in a rowboat toward the middle of the lake.

Rick talked on. "The doctors would push my face around with a pencil and talk about me like I was a steak. They kept telling me about the wonders of plastic surgery. About what great surgeons they had at the burn unit in Fort Sam Houston. At first I believed them. I believed my hair would grow back. That plastic surgery would restore the skin to my face. But the plastic surgery was only to cover the muscle and bone and stave off infection. The only hair that ever grew was beneath my chin."

Andrea held his hand and rested her chin on his shoulder. "If I ever asked, would you show me your face?"

The question didn't surprise him. He calmly shook his head no. "The day I bought this mask was the last day I looked in a mirror without it on. I swore I'd never look again. And I never have."

From the fishing dock out over the water they had a panoramic view of Minneapolis. The skyscrapers the city was so proud of were ablaze in light, and foremost among them was the venerable IDS Tower. The red warning light atop the transmitting antenna shone just below the Little Dipper. "My God," said Andrea, "we can see the newsroom from here!"

Rick looked up at the top row of lights. "Sky High News, where we accurately report all rumors."

"Why did you do it—jump to television?"

"Besides the money? I thought I could bring newspaper quality to television news. Give it some literary content. But it can't be done. No matter how much sweat you pour into it, it all comes out tits and glitz. Nothing personal. And you?"

"I don't know," she said. "Ever since I was a little girl I wanted to be on television. Even before the shooting I didn't like being a cop. It's a man's world. Women can't compete. In television, I can compete. I want that anchor job because it's like swimming—it's the gold medal at the end of the race. I know it's not noble and worthy of the news business, but it's something I want. Can you understand that?"

"I understand, Andrea. I won a few sprints in my day. But what these clowns running news stations today don't understand is that there's a whole generation out there who grew up watching Edward R. Murrow, and Huntley and Brinkley, and Walter Cronkite. We watched President Kennedy die, we watched the war in Vietnam from the very beginning to the very end. We know how good television news can be." He pointed to the skyscraper across the lake. "And we know that *that* isn't it."

"Are you going to stay with us?"

"Never be loyal to a company," he reminded her. "In the end, they're not going to be loyal to you. I figure I can wring one more contract out of them before the well runs dry."

"And then?"

"I've got some dreams in the mail."

"Your novel?"

The warm breeze was dying. Humidity was on the rise. Mosquitoes began the hunt. Andrea slapped at one of the tiny bandits, but it stole away with her blood. "Have you had a girlfriend ... since ... you know?"

The masked Marine shrugged. "I know what you're asking," he said to her, matter-of-factly. "The only way I can have sex is to pay for it, and I swore I'd never do that. So I make love with my VCR. I can walk into a video store and rent any fantasy I want."

"That's kind of two-dimensional sex, isn't it?"

"Yes, but it's safe sex. I'll probably outlive all of you."

"I suppose. If you call that living." The lights of his high-rise condominium were reflected on the water. Andrea turned and gazed up at the expensive boxes, one atop the other. "All those bedrooms stacked to the stars." She brushed her fingers up his arm. "Which one is ours?"

Rick Beanblossom lost himself in the lights off the water. He shook his head. Didn't know what to say. The moon floated over the east end of the lake. "It's been a long time, Andrea. Don't joke about something like that."

Andrea smiled at him, a warm smile free of guile. "I'm not joking. I've given it a lot of thought." She took his hand. "Come along, Mr. Beanblossom."

Old Jesse strolled across the roadway and grabbed hold of the chain link fence that separated Industry from the rest of the prison. He needed a break. The hot summer nights were hard on his aging bones. Each night seemed more hellish than the night before, and sure enough, almost directly over his head was that Electric Star illuminating the sky like a sparkler in the grass.

The janitor could see the construction through the fence. Beneath the red brick wall that ran along Stagecoach Trail were bulldozers, piles of dirt, and pallets of bricks. The state was actually building the damn thing. Yes, right below Guard Tower 4 and behind the electric shop they were constructing a Death House.

On television they said the Weatherman's blood type was the same blood type as the man who had killed his granddaughter. That his shoe size was the same size they found in the slushy snow. They said the Weatherman lived in Edina, only blocks from the murder. That he killed because it was the last day of winter. That he killed because the weather drove him to kill. That he killed a police officer to defy the new law. That's what they were saying on television.

Jesse had been watching the news on television since television news was invented. He often met the criminals as they went from a black-and-white image on a television screen to flesh and blood in Stillwater. But never before had he known the victims of their crimes. They were strangers sobbing on a TV set. Then one day on the noon report the news lady with the big brown eyes came on the air and said Officer Shelly Sumter was in the hospital. They showed her graduation picture from the police academy. They ran videotape of her being wheeled into the emergency room. He was shocked. He rushed to her bedside. The day she died was even more shocking. Another TV reporter talked into the camera as if he had known her for years, and at the same time he reduced Shelly's life to one minute and thirty seconds. And now the state was building a Death House.

If Old Jesse had killed that man down home in South Carolina, he'd have been dead now more than a quarter of a century. But he killed the man in Minnesota, and instead of sending him to his death they sent him to Stillwater. Sometimes it seemed as if Minnesota was changing faster than the weather.

Andrea Labore lit a candle and ignited a golden glow in a bedroom that was shades of gold. The curtains were left open, but they were so high in the sky only the man in the moon could peek in on them. They lay side by side on the gilded sheets.

The unflappable, unshakable Marine was nervous as hell. In the months since her world-championship hangover they had talked often, had shared story ideas, traded gossip, confessed their wants and fears, but they'd never been intimate. Rick Beanblossom had come to accept the fact that he could only be a friend to this beautiful woman.

But now his lips were over her lips, and her mouth was warm and open and inviting him in, pulling him in, and, he thought, another one of the Weatherman's improbable forecasts was coming true. Rick wrapped his arms around her as they kissed, and marveled at how light and slender she was. When their lips finally parted, he kissed his way down her neck to her breasts, and there he rested his head as she stroked the back of his mask.

He had worried about Andrea's reactions, but she didn't seem the least bit nervous. Her patience and her gentle hands put him at ease, the way a nurse in Japan had eased his suffering a score of years ago. He unbuttoned her blouse without fumbling and slipped her bra strap from her shoulder. The lace brassiere dropped with ease below her breast and he took the nipple into his mouth. Her breasts were small but firm and round, and he tried to suck down to the bone. The harder he sucked, the tighter she held him.

The hot summer breeze through the window was seductive, her perfume intoxicating. Rick had forgotten how the warm, soft flesh of another pressed against his own charred skin could lift his spirit and send it soaring to dizzying heights, higher than any narcotic. He slid her cotton slacks from her sleek legs. She rolled over on top of him and he slid his hands down the back of her panties and pulled her into him.

Andrea was a surprisingly bold lover. She removed her panties herself and straddled him on her knees, her bold brunette hair tumbling forward, accenting her sharp-featured countenance. Rick outlined this celestial face with his fingers, then traced her neckline until he was cupping the pair of breasts dangling over him. She kept her eyes on his eyes the whole time. He let his hands trace her tummy and around her hips, then up her thighs between her legs. He pressed two fingers inside of her and she drew a sharp, erotic breath. Rick reached behind her and pulled her knees toward his head. She straightened up, sensing exactly what he wanted. He slipped his head down the pillow until all of the woman that was Andrea Labore was directly above him and he covered her with his mouth as she repeated his name over and over again.

On her back she was as sensuous, almost greedy, as she

was lovely. She helped him off with his clothes. By the time the only piece of cloth he was wearing was over his head they had become inseparable—more than sex, a uniting of spirits the burn victim had known only once in his life. An eternity later he collapsed on top of her and the love he had bundled up inside of him for so many years spilled down her creamy soft legs and onto the golden sheets.

There seemed nothing to prove to Andrea, nothing to hide. So comfortable was he with this woman that it was she who held him in her arms as they listened to night sounds filter up from the lake below, ducks and geese and waves lapping at the shore.

They had barely recovered from the first union when they made love a second time. They were both perspiring, her sweat as intoxicating as her perfume.

In the wee hours of the morning, when they were too tired to make love, but too excited to sleep, they talked. Talked shop. Talked about the Weatherman. He shared with her more of what he knew.

"It's so hard to believe," said Andrea. "Can it be true?"

"All I know is that I interviewed two different men. Schizophrenic, perhaps. Multiple personalities, I don't know. Maybe he's just a freak of nature. But a murderer? I still don't buy it."

"Because?"

"I showed you the diary. The murders aren't mentioned even in passing."

"Rick, that diary was very disturbing. He may have been substituting those women for me and that Lisa girl. That's what the state is going to try to prove."

"Even in a television newsroom I don't think we could have been that blind. They have a lot of circumstantial evidence, the diary of a very disturbed man, and a partial fingerprint they're not sure about. I don't think that's enough for a conviction, much less seven convictions and a death sentence. I say we continue this investigation with the assumption they've got the wrong man. Let's find out who had access to his office, to his computer, to his private phone numbers. Who has been in the newsroom that doesn't belong there?"

"It's a newsroom, it's not a fort. Strangers run in and out of there every day."

"Are you afraid the killer might be somebody at the station?"

Andrea crawled into his arms and rested her face on his chest. "No, I'm afraid the killer might be Dixon Bell."

Rick Beanblossom ran his fingers through her wet hair and kissed the top of her head. "The murder of Mary Rogers," he suggested.

"I don't remember a Mary Rogers. Which one was she?"

"Different city, different time."

Andrea was feeling sleepy. "Tell me about her."

"Well, it was in the summer of 1841, and the body of young and beautiful Mary Rogers was found floating in the Hudson River off the shores of New York City. She'd been strangled by a piece of lace tied so tightly around her neck it was hidden from sight."

"New York hasn't changed much, has it?"

"Just like television news of today, the city's newspapers back then were recklessly sensational with their reporting. Not only did they detail and print every piece of evidence, but the newspapers drew their own conclusions about that evidence, going so far as to name their own suspects. But for more than a year the mystery remained unsolved."

"And then what happened?"

"Then in November 1842 a brilliant young writer gathered together every published inch of newsprint on the murder of Mary Rogers. Get this ... he never visited the scene of the crime. He didn't interview any police officials or suspects, nor did he examine any of the physical evidence. All he worked with was the published stories before him. He picked up his quill pen, he dipped it into a bottle of ink, and he methodically tore into shreds each newspaper's theory about the murder. He concluded by naming two new suspects who had been ignored by the police and the press."

"Let me guess," said Andrea. "The writer was Great-Grandpa Beanblossom?"

"No," Rick told her, laughing, "but you're close. The writer then penned his theories and conclusion about the murder into a thinly disguised detective story and had the story published in a New York magazine. At the time of publication he said if he had misinterpreted just one of the many details about the crime, then his conclusion would be equally suspect. And guess what happened?"

"Tell me," said Andrea, fascinated by the story.

"Police went out and made two arrests, and their confessions confirmed in full not only the conclusion of Edgar Allan Poe, but of each detail that led him to that conclusion. The first great detective's mind did not belong to a cop. It belonged to a writer."

"And that's what we're going to do?"

"The same thing I've been doing with the Wakefield kidnapping. We go back over every story of every killing, each piece of evidence. The answer may be in there somewhere. Did we misinterpret something? Did we overlook something? Did somebody lie to us, including Dixon Bell?"

"And what do we tell Jack Napoleon?"

"We cut him out. We're on our own. Stay out of his office," Rick told her. "Don't discuss anything of importance in there."

"Why, he's our news director, for God's sake."

"He wired his own office. Audio and video."

"You have to be joking! How long have you known about this?"

He evaded the question. "Don't worry about it. I'm working with Dave Cadieux. When the time comes, we'll fix his ass."

Andrea Labore flopped back on the pillow and shook her head in disbelief. She looked out the window and saw the moon sailing slowly out of sight like a ship off the horizon. "Do you think it was fate that threw us all together in that newsroom?"

"I never liked him," Rick confessed. "Not from the start."

"Napoleon?" she asked.

"Yeah, him too, but I meant the Weatherman. I've never been able to put my finger on it, but the first time I saw him do the weather I was here at home watching television. I sensed something wrong with him. When we met, he knew I saw it. He's still scared of me. He's like those little kids who taunt me to hide their fear."

"Then why go out on a limb for him?"

"Because he's not a murderer. He's something I haven't quite figured out yet, but he's not a murderer."

Andrea laid a bare leg over his legs and leaned into his shoulder. She yawned, then nibbled at his muscular arm. "I'm tired," she said.

"Tired?" Rick laughed. "You should be half dead." But he was tired too. He threw an arm around her. "You know, Puppy Dog, as exhausted as I am, I still want more."

"Me too," she whispered. Andrea Labore positioned herself on top and they made love for the third time that night.

She fell asleep in his arms as he lay staring out the window at the predawn sky. There was that star again. He thought of Dixon Bell on the jail monitor with that crazed laugh, as if he were starring in some late-night horror flick. Then his thoughts returned to Andrea, to their night together. Was this just a one-night thing to her? Did she love the man, or did she just like the mask? He wanted her for the rest of his life, but what did she feel? She was hard to read. Rick Beanblossom was still awake and holding Andrea tight when the summer sun began to rise and the sky turned as gold as the gilded room.

THE SOURCE

The green months of summer surrendered to the orange months of autumn. Leaves exploded in fiery colors, then zigzagged to the ground. The skies outside the windows at Channel 7 were more often gray than blue.

Jack Napoleon was standing over Rick Beanblossom's desk with a tip sheet. "Do you know they now make X-rated videos right here in Minneapolis?"

Rick choked on the soda he was using to wash down two aspirins. He swallowed hard and wiped his mouth. "I'd heard there was a production studio up in the warehouse district."

"Are we efforting to get this?" The news director dropped the tip sheet on the producer's desk and stomped off.

Rick picked up the sheet. It listed the studio's address and phone number. Maybe he'd drop in one afternoon and watch them efforting. He slammed the information atop his Wakefield file and sent a sheet of paper from the file to the floor. Rick bent down and retrieved it. It was the stolen-gun report from the farmer along the paper route. He read over it quickly, then shoved it back into the file.

The white-hot lights came up on the news set, spilling over Rick Beanblossom, causing him to squint. Andy Mack was at the weather podium, preparing his forecast. Ron Shea and Charleen Barington were strapping on their microphones. And there was Andrea, under the lights.

Across from the anchor desk sat a smaller desk in front of a blank blue screen, onto which the control room could project just about anything they pleased. When a local story broke, they would sit a reporter over there and project on the screen a row of computers and desks and call it the News Center. When an international story broke, they would project a display of clocks and monitors in the background and call it the Satellite Center. It was also the Sports Center, Election Center, and whatever other center they wanted to trick viewers into believing, because management was convinced their viewers were too damn stupid to figure out it was all one desk in front of a blank screen and the reporters were just sliding their asses in and out of the same chair.

Tonight Andrea was doing a story from the News Center—or maybe it was the Satellite Center, Rick wasn't paying that much attention. They were carrying on as secret lovers, never dating. She confessed she wasn't totally comfortable with him yet, and, besides, the secrecy made the relationship more exciting. He couldn't complain. It had been a long time since he'd been happy. Her face was recognized on the street. He was a man in a mask. Could she be blamed? Perhaps he was being foolish, but he was shopping around for a ring. He'd do anything to get her that anchor job.

Dateline was ringing. Rick picked up the phone. "Beanblossom."

"What have you done for me lately?"

"That's my line." Rick grabbed a pen. "What have you got?"

"Against the advice of his attorney Dixon Bell took a polygraph test. He beat the damn thing."

"You mean he passed?"

"No. You're going to say he passed. I'm saying he beat it."

"You believe in the lie-detector test," Rick reminded him. "I did a story on it for you."

"A man without a conscience could very easily beat a polygraph test. I'm not fooling around anymore, I need those letters."

"What letters?"

"Don't give me that shit. The letters from his high-school sweetheart you pulled out of his diary. The letter from the little Afton girl."

The newsman swore, "I don't know anything about those letters."

"You listen to me, Jarhead. I want those letters, and I'll

bring you and that entire newsroom down along with the Weatherman if need be."

"What does that mean?"

"That means I know where you get your heroin."

Rick Beanblossom froze. His stomach cramped. His head was thundering. He shielded his eyes from lights bright as the sun over the news set. Few men could intimidate him, but this man could. His knowledge of people's weaknesses and his wealth of secrets was frightening. "All right, listen, I've never lied to you. After I heard of the arrest I went over and searched his office. I found the diary. I photocopied it. But the letters were already gone. It was the first thing I noticed."

"Where did they go?"

"If he's innocent, he never got a letter from the Afton girl. As for the diary letters, guilty or innocent, if he thought you were closing in on him he'd hide them, or destroy them."

"No, he wouldn't destroy them. He'd take them to his grave with him. This is a man who never lets go." The conversation was interrupted by a wheezing cough attack. Rick waited, surprised the old bastard was still alive. *"Tell you what I'll do, Masked Man. I'll make you a trade. You find those letters and hand them over to me and I'll hand you the governor's head on a silver platter. How many reporters have brought down two governors?"*

Rick laid down his pen and rubbed his temple. Per Ellefson, the epitome of Mr. Clean. Andrea's ex-lover. "What about him?"

"I want those letters."

Dateline went dead. Rick hung up the phone. His aching head was doing cartwheels. It was bullshit. He was no more addicted to heroin than he was to television. Weeks would go by without even a thought of the junk, even months, then the needs would overtake him. His wounds had made him the strongest person he knew, but not even *semper fi* could stave off the darkness when it fell. Then he'd send in the Marines. At times he couldn't help wondering if these were the same ugly needs, perhaps gone mad, that drove another man to murder with every change of the seasons.

He watched Andrea at the desk in front of the phony

blue screen rehearsing her lines. What did his source have on this governor? Would it hurt Andrea? He picked up the aspirin bottle again. It was empty. He threw it into the wastebasket and dug out his prescription pills.

THE TRIAL

Delayed another week because of a snowstorm, the fourth such storm of the winter season, the trial of Dixon Graham Bell got under way in Minneapolis during the first week of February, Hennepin County Government Center, Courtroom 659, District Court Judge Stephen Z. Lutoslawski presiding.

The meteorologist on trial could have warned them of the coming snow, but nobody in meteorology would touch his forecasts. The storms were Texas hookers. They wound up in the Panhandle gathering Gulf moisture, then hooked north, following the Mississippi River until they met up with the arctic cold around Minnesota and Wisconsin. The Weatherman could see the storms coming from his jail cell over the river. They were not blizzards; there wasn't a whole lot of wind with them—they just dumped tons of snow. Minnesota typically averages fifty inches of snow a season. By Dixon Bell's reading, that amount would double during the winter of his trial.

Courtroom 659 was sterile, suburban in design. It had no character. No windows. Low ceiling. Dark paneling with fake marble trim. Tan carpeting. The prosecutor's table was to the left facing the bench. The defense table was off to the right, but it didn't face the bench; it had been turned to face the jury box and the lone television camera. The witness stand was to the right of the judge. An American flag stood behind the bench. Above the judge's head was the state seal.

Even before jury selection got under way courtroom seating became an issue. The ghouls start lining up in the hallway hours before court. The entire right side of the spectators' area was reserved for the media, one person

from each news organization. Rick Beanblossom was
back there on most days.

The first two rows on the left side were reserved for
family members of the victims. The only regular was an
old black man, usually dressed in janitor garb. Rick
learned that he was Officer Sumter's grandfather. Behind
the family members sat the ghouls, people who liked to
watch. The courtroom next door had also been reserved
for the trial, but people there had to sit and watch the proceedings on television like everybody else.

The trial was being broadcast on national cable television, a station called Court TV. Dixon Bell had never
heard of the show, but he correctly guessed they broadcast sensational trials from around the country.

The local stations tried live coverage, but they soon
learned what any criminal lawyer could have told them
from the start: real trials are long and tedious and often
boring. In this trial the prosecutor was going through
seven murders, one at a time. Jurors were told they could
expect to be sequestered three to four months. The local
stations, including Channel 7, killed their live coverage
fast and only summarized the juicy stuff on the evening
news. They promised to cover the Weatherman's testimony live should he decide to take the stand.

Stacy Dvorchak was unhappy about the draw that
turned the trial over to Judge Lutoslawski, a silver-haired
hangman's judge whom defense attorneys out of court often referred to as Judge Polack.

The prosecutor was Jim Fury, a man cunning and
scholarly in appearance but cheap in dress. The trial was
a career opportunity for him. He had two assistants, both
women, but they never questioned the witnesses.

The jury was young. Dixon Bell liked that. With the
three alternates there were eight women and seven men.
Each of them was made to swear he or she had never
watched the news show on Channel 7. Half of them
swore they didn't watch television at all. The TV camera
next to the jury box was small and unobtrusive. Although
Stacy tried her best to kill the television coverage, everybody but Dixon Bell forgot about the camera after the
first day.

Police Captain Les Angelbeck was one of the early witnesses. For somebody who was supposed to be retired

and dying of emphysema, he was moving around pretty damn good. He kept telling reporters he'd live to see the Weatherman fry. Dixon Bell thought the captain had a remarkable gift for manipulating the media—just the right sound bite at just the right time. In the good-cop-bad-cop bit, he always played the good cop, and he was very good at it, but Dixon Bell knew from experience Angelbeck could be one mean and devious son of a bitch. Answering the state's questions, the captain was fluent, almost mellifluous. But during questioning by the defense he had a hundred coughing spells and even more apologies.

Angelbeck was followed by Lieutenant Donnell Redmond, who was even more polished and articulate than the captain. Although the diary letters remained missing, nobody could argue the fact that the task force had put together a compelling case.

The fight over the fingerprint broke out during testimony about the first murder. Prosecutor Jim Fury made a major point of it during his opening statement. "Beyond the overwhelming weight of circumstantial evidence," he told the jury, "we have physical evidence that puts Dixon Bell at the scene of murder number one. We have his fingerprint."

An FBI expert flew in from Washington and explained to the jury the history of fingerprinting and how Dixon Bell's name came out of the AFIS computer. He testified that of all the names on the list of probables the computer put the Weatherman's name at the top, and that the AFIS computer was 98 to 100 percent accurate in its ability to search and match a print. The partial fingerprint found on the transformer atop the Sky High parking ramp was blown up to poster size along with the print taken at the detention center after Dixon Bell's arrest. The FBI agent stood with a pointer, talking about similarities. Anybody watching the jury's reaction could see they were impressed.

The first break for the defense came when the state made the mistake of putting Minnesota's own fingerprint expert on the witness stand to bolster their argument. Stacy Dvorchak cross-examined Glenn Arkwright from her electric wheelchair at the defense table. "This AFIS computer reads digits assigned to so-called points of minutiae, correct?"

"Yes, that's correct."

"How many points of minutiae are in a good fingerprint, Mr. Arkwright?"

"A good one has a hundred."

"One hundred." Stacy held up the fingerprint card. "And how many points of minutiae—that is, digits—did this fingerprint found on the transformer atop the Sky High parking ramp have?"

"Seven."

"What is the least number of points that a man has been arrested and convicted on based on a partial fingerprint found at a crime scene?"

"To the best of my knowledge, one jurisdiction, I don't remember where it was, reported a hit made on only eight points of minutiae."

"So to convict Dixon Bell on the basis of this fingerprint, the jury would be asked to set a new low record for this AFIS computer?"

"To the best of my knowledge, that would be the case."

"Mr. Arkwright, how many names did this computer give the Calendar Task Force to work with?"

"I believe when the suspect was arrested there was a total of sixty-two names."

"And the computer eliminated sixty-one of those names and said Dixon Bell is the man you want?"

"No, that's not the case." Arkwright explained. "An AFIS system makes no decisions on identity. It only lists suspects. Its function is to reduce the number of comparisons a fingerprint expert has to make. The final conclusion still rests with the experts."

"So you had to examine sixty-two sets of fingerprints, just like our FBI friend?"

"Yes, I did."

"And did you find a match to the parking ramp print?"

Arkwright paused before answering. "The final conclusion of the Calendar Task Force was made by the FBI."

"That doesn't answer my question. Did Glenn Arkwright in examining those sixty-two fingerprints find a match?"

"My finding was inconclusive."

Stacy Dvorchak wheeled over to the posters of the two fingerprints and picked up the pointer. "Mr. Arkwright, you're the state's leading fingerprint expert. You were assigned to the Calendar Task Force. Can you tell the jury, is this partial fingerprint on the right the same as this complete fingerprint on the left?"

Arkwright paused again and adjusted his glasses. "In my opinion there's not enough of the partial print to reach a conclusion."

Rick Beanblossom marched up slippery sidewalks and trudged over snowbanks to the warehouse district. The renovated brick building he entered was warm and clean inside. He stomped the snow from his shoes and unzipped his jacket. The video company was listed as being on the fifth floor. He took the stairs.

At the end of a long hallway was a pair of double doors that read, HY PETER PRODUCTIONS. A security guard with piss-yellow hair and bloodshot eyes stood watch. "You got a part?"

"No, I'm a news producer. Mr. Peters said he'd talk to me today."

"What's with the mask?"

"I'm a burn victim. Vietnam. How do you explain your face?"

The surly guard was lost for words. He mumbled, "Go on in."

Half of the studio was lights, cameras, and cables running along the floor. Black plastic hung over the warehouse windows. Fat beams supported a high ceiling. A dozen people roamed about. Everybody seemed preoccupied with nothing. Nobody was nude. Nobody paid much attention to the man in the mask.

It was the set itself that surprised Rick. Peters told him this would be a good day to stop by. It was a television news set. The anchor desk read, CHANNEL 8, I WITNESS NEWS. The logo behind the two anchor chairs was a big eightball. Behind the weather chair was a map of the United States with a smiling Mr. Sunshine over the heartland. It was obvious they had studied the local news shows. Many a small-market station would be proud to broadcast from the set.

Standing at a desk at the rear of the studio was producer and director J. C. Peters. He was on the phone. Rick worked his way to him. He overheard a conversation about money. "How'm I supposed to find that kind of cash in this town? I can't even find a good deli." J. C. Peters slammed down the receiver. "Investors! What's with the mask? We don't have a mask in this shoot."

The news producer extended his hand to the porn producer. "My name is Rick Beanblossom. I'm with Channel 7. I'm doing research on adult videos. You said we could talk today."

Peters offered a weak handshake. "Channel 7, huh? Tell your news director I said fuck you. What's with the mask?"

"I'm a burn victim. Vietnam."

"No shit? You mean that's real? You gotta wear that all the time? I love it." Peters began shouting. "Mortie? Mortie, where da fuck are ya? Mortie, can we get a mask like this here? I love this."

Mortie, who looked like a maintenance man, shuffled over. "I'd have to rewrite the script."

"So take ten minutes and rewrite the fuckin' script. Got his face burned off in Vietnam. You didn't get anything else burned off, did ya?"

Rick Beanblossom grinned. "No, just the face."

"Thank God. What didya say your name was?"

"Rick."

"Yeah, Rick, you wanna be in my movie? Mortie here will write ya a good part."

"No, actually I wanted to ask you about amateur videos."

"Aw, Christ, I hate those two words. Get back to me in ten minutes." The director stormed through a jungle of video technology to the set, shouting orders. "Everybody on the set! In your places!"

Rick Beanblossom moved behind the cameras as they began lighting the set. Add a couple of computers and an assignment board and the place would look just like a television newsroom. He was struck by this amazing resemblance when she came and stood next to him.

She had a gorgeous figure and a provocative smile. Heavy on the perfume. Her hair was rustic red. Tight skirt. Bloused top. The kind of woman men would describe as a real cutie pie. "J.C. said you have to wear that mask all the time because you have no face."

"Yes," Rick said to her, "that's true."

"I think I know how you feel. My brother had real bad acne."

Rick tried not to laugh. "What's your name?"

"My name is Carolyn, but everyone calls me the Little Bimbo."

"I like Carolyn. Are you in this movie?"

"I'm just a fluffer with a bit part." She had a little girl's voice.

"What's a fluffer?"

"A fluffer's job is to keep the guys hard between takes. It's important because it saves a lot of time. I'm hoping to get bigger parts, but it's not easy. In this business a girl is washed up by the age of thirty. I'm almost twenty-six now and I still haven't had a leading role. Maybe later would you like to come over to my place and watch TV. I live right downtown."

The invitation took him by surprise. "That's very sweet of you, Carolyn, but I have to say no. Thank you, anyway."

"Is it because you don't like me, or any of us who make these?"

"No, that's not it at all."

"You're not married, are you?" She was like the child that will not stop asking questions no matter what the answers.

"No, of course not."

"Are you in love?"

Rick looked up at the empty anchor chair and thought about that one. "Yes, I believe I am."

"Does she love you?"

He let a sad laugh escape. "I'm not sure. I'm not sure she's sure."

"Because of your face?"

"I suppose."

The Little Bimbo shook her head. "How sad. You shouldn't judge people by their face."

The lights faded up and down on the news set. The actors took their places. There was a sexy female anchor and a young stud of an anchor, both in blue blazers with an eight ball on the coat pocket. There was a busty, slutty-looking weather girl. The sports chair was still empty. The mouth of J. C. Peters seemed always on fast forward. "Hey, Rick, ain't there a good restaurant in this

town? I been eatin' Chuck Wagon for six weeks. Ain't
you fuckin' Lutherans ever heard of spices?"

Rick walked up to the director. A stagehand courte-
ously brought a stool over for him to sit on. "Your set
looks as good as ours."

"Channel 7, huh? You think your weatherman done
them women, Rick?"

"No, I don't think so."

"Me neither. Makes no sense."

"So how do you make these kinds of movies?" Rick
wanted to know.

Peters leaned over to him and talked with his hands.
"Lay out a script. Plan on at least ten come shots. Keep
it straight. No faggot shit. You need at least three scenes
of straight fucks. Those are your meat shots. Get some
good close-ups. Remember, people are watching these at
home on their TV sets. They can run 'em in slow motion,
they can play 'em over and over again. You can't fool
people anymore." He was back to shouting directions.
"Okay, lemme see my lights, c'mon!"

The studio went dark. White lights came up on the I
Witness News team. "Why don't you just tape an orgy?"
Rick asked.

"Stay away from orgies. Orgies are expensive. Two
faggots always end up fucking each other, then ya got a
nightmare in editing."

"What else?"

"Get yourself some good screamers. Men love to hear
women scream."

"Do these women's groups bother you with their protesting?"

"Yeah, yeah—every time there's a woman raped or
murdered they come after us. You got more violence on
your news show every night than I got in my movies. Sex
don't cause violence. Violence causes violence. I don't
like violent movies. I like 'em sweet and simple—boy
meets girl, they fuck."

Rick tried to get to the point. "I want you to tell me
about amateur videos."

The master of porn was livid. "I hate those two
words."

"Why?"

"Because they're killing us, that's why. They're the hottest thing on the video market."

"What exactly are they?"

"Just what they say ... amateur videos." Peters explained the problem. "These people get a video camera for Christmas and they turn around and start shooting each other fucking. Then they go and sell the tapes to a distributor. It's usually some guy banging his wife, or the neighbors come over and hump one another. They got no quality. No story. But they're real, ya know what I mean? What other business could amateurs walk into and take over?"

"Television news," Rick said. Peters laughed. "Do you ever get your hands on any of these amateur videos?"

"Yeah, people bring 'em to me all the time. Once in a while when I get a good one I'll distribute it, but most of 'em are shit."

"So the more real they are, the better they sell?"

"Exactly, Rick. Your hidden camera is your best bet. Don't let the bitch know she's being taped."

THE SEX

March came in like a lion. Blowing snow, falling temperatures. There were few signs of spring. City workers were hauling truckloads of snow down to the river and dumping it. Harriet Island across from the Ramsey County jail was growing into a small white mountain.

Most of his days were spent in court, but in the evening Dixon Bell would be transported back to St. Paul and returned to D Pod, Cell 340. He watched some television, mostly mindless game shows and old movies. No more news—not even Andrea. His evenings were spent sitting on his bunk staring out the window. Staring south.

The Mississippi River was frozen, a pristine highway of unbroken snow flowing beneath the bridges and around the bend. Street lamps up and down the bluffs were yellow, like fireflies, and their reflection off the white earth created a candlelight glow. The only bright lights were at the foot of the Wabasha Street Bridge above a billboard advertising Sky High News. Splat Man, where are you? Trains passed beneath him, and almost every hour of every night a siren would wail in the distance and the Weatherman would watch the flashing red lights of an ambulance as it dropped down a steep street and raced across the bridge on its way to the emergency room at the Ramsey Medical Center. These were the sights and sounds of a jail cell in St. Paul, Minnesota, on cold winter evenings. Dixon Bell had been locked up for ten months. If the jury found him not guilty, where might he go to get his ten months back?

During those ten months the meteorologist had been bouncing up and down on a rail bolted to the floor. This was the rail the steel cell door slid over to open and close.

One night while he was tiptoeing up and down on this rail it finally snapped, just where he wanted it to snap. Now he was scared he'd be caught. But he had the deputy's movements down to a science. The rail was better than a crowbar. He hurried it into his cell and chipped a few tiny pieces of mortar from around the brick in the wall over the river. Then he stepped outside his cell and placed the rail back on the floor. The deputy in the control room walked over and looked up at Cell 340 and saw Dixon Bell sitting on his bunk.

The first night and the next morning he was the most worried. But when the deputy came upstairs to slide the door closed, it worked like a charm. Slid right open the next morning too. From then on it was cat and mouse. The deputy in the control room would disappear from sight for two minutes and Dixon Bell would run out of his cell, pick up the rail, chip some mortar from around the bricks, then run out and place the rail back on the floor. The deputy returned and looked up, saw the Weatherman sitting on his bunk, staring out the window. He taped letters of support on the wall to hide the gashes. He kept the chips of concrete in his pocket until he had to use the toilet; then he'd flush them. By his calculations, with his size and weight, he'd have to get six big bricks out of that wall before he could squeeze through and lower himself down to the tracks with bed sheets. It would take weeks, maybe months. But he was on trial for his life. It wouldn't hurt to keep chipping away.

Even by Minnesota standards it was a hard winter. Every morning they had to leave St. Paul before dawn in teeth-chattering temperatures just to get to court on time because of poor road conditions. The trial was wearing everybody down. Lines outside the courtroom grew shorter and shorter. Court TV said ratings were falling off. If it had been a network series, it would have been canceled. Everybody was waiting to see if the Weatherman would testify in his own defense.

The state had left no legal path unplowed. Prosecutor Jim Fury turned out to be even more cunning and shrewd than he appeared. Stacy Dvorchak was doing a hell of a job, but after six weeks of negative testimony Dixon Bell couldn't see a whole lot of sympathy over there in the jury box. Some jurors were avoiding his eyes.

The parade of quacks had begun. Much to his credit Judge Lutoslawski limited the state and the defense to two psychiatrists apiece. They pretty much said what they were paid to say. Like the state's shrink from New York, a self-proclaimed expert on serial killers. Dr. Harcourt Joffre was a clinical professor of psychiatry at New York University Medical Center, which was affiliated with Bellevue Hospital. He had built a career studying the darker side of human behavior. He interviewed a very uncooperative Dixon Bell for all of two hours. He examined the diary. Then he raised his hand in a court of law and swore to tell the truth. He was a young, slender man, late thirties, with one of those finely trimmed beards popular in the psychiatric community. Slight New York accent. Answering Prosecutor Fury's questions: "There's no way these women can live up to what he's made them out to be in his mind. He fell in love with women that don't exist."

"You mean Lisa and Andrea?"

"Yes."

"And if one of these women had given herself to him?"

"They would have shattered the illusion. He would then go off and find another woman to say no to him. A woman he knows in his heart he can never have."

"So by saying no to him, these obsessive loves of his only increased his obsession with them?"

"Precisely."

"To the point of murder?"

Stacy objected to the question.

The judge agreed with her. "Sustained."

"Let me rephrase that, Doctor. Can obsessive love lead a man to murder?"

"Yes. All too often in our society. There have been several cases in the past few years of men murdering women they fell in love with on television or in the movies. Until they killed them, they had never even met them."

Jim Fury glanced over at Dixon Bell, then turned his attention toward the jury. "But could it drive them to kill someone other than their obsessive love?"

"Sure," said the doctor. "The most famous case being

that of John Hinckley, who tried to assassinate President Reagan back in 1981 to impress a movie star."

To Dixon Bell this line of reasoning was bullshit, pure and simple—that he fell in love with Andrea Labore and then went out murdering women because of her. Yes, he fell in love with Andrea Labore, but he worked with her. He didn't fall in love with a two-dimensional image on his TV screen like those couch potatoes who go to bed at night and jack off after watching their favorite anchorwoman read them the news. And what about Lisa? If he killed out of obsessive love, why didn't he wipe out half of Vicksburg, Mississippi? Answer that, you quack!

Fortunately Stacy Dvorchak had a more intelligent and professional approach. She picked up a psychology book so that the jury could read the big fat words SERIAL KILLER. She wheeled over to the good doctor and held the book up to his face. It was like threatening a Southern Baptist with a Bible. "Who wrote this book, Dr. Joffre?"

"I did."

Stacy fumbled through the book until she found the page she'd marked. "Clinical portrait of a serial killer," she read. "Abused as a child. Broken home. History of petty crimes and bizarre behavior. Is that correct, Doctor?"

"That is the clinical portrait, yes."

"In your clinical portrait of Dixon Bell, did you find any evidence that he was sexually or physically abused as a child?"

"No, that was not the case."

"Were his parents divorced?"

"No. I believe his mother was widowed."

"Does Dixon Bell have a criminal record of any kind?"

"None that I'm aware of."

"Any history of bizarre behavior?"

"Other than a lifelong obsession with the weather, none that I could find."

Stacy was amazed. "Doctor, if obsession with the weather were considered bizarre behavior, nine out of ten Minnesotans would be put into straitjackets." The courtroom burst into laughter. Even the judge smiled at that one. Stacy continued. "Doctor, have you ever heard of a serial killer who killed out of this obsessive love?"

"I'm not familiar with any particular case."

"Isn't it an accepted fact in your profession that the average American male will fall in love three times during his lifetime?"

"Yes, I accept that."

Stacy shrugged her shoulders. "So what's so unusual about Dixon Bell having been in love twice—my God, once in high school?"

"But he had no relationship with these women."

"No relationship? He talked with them, worked with them, laughed with them, shared sorrow and pain with them day in and day out for years at a time. How else do you fall in love?"

"But he had no intimate relationship."

"Oh, you have to sleep with a woman to fall in love with her?" Stacy went on with her questioning, clutching the doctor's book to her heart the whole time. "Isn't it a fact, Doctor, that in our society men and women are breaking each other's hearts every day? That every hour of every day someone is saying, 'No, I don't want to date you,' 'No, I don't love you,' or 'No, I can't marry you'?"

"Yes, but you're missing—"

"And isn't it possible, Doctor—indeed, probable—that Dixon Bell just isn't lucky? That two out of the three times he was supposed to fall in love he just plain struck out?"

"I'm not sure that's the case here."

"But isn't it possible?"

"Well, yes, it's possible."

"Thank you, Doctor. No more questions." Stacy started back to the the defense table; then suddenly she stopped and wheeled. "Oh, one more thing, my good doctor. In your reading of the diary, did you happen to come across a murder?"

"No, I didn't."

So the state went through seven murders in six weeks, one piece of circumstantial evidence piled atop another, a partial fingerprint that may or may not have belonged to the Weatherman, and two shrinks who said exactly what they were paid to say.

As he neared the end of his case, Prosecutor Fury introduced a surprise witness—too much of a surprise for the defense. He called to the witness stand a young woman named Davi Iverson. She was blond, a bit chunky, a nice complexion with too much eye makeup, heavy on the purple. She was no beauty, nor was she unattractive.

Meanwhile Stacy Dvorchak was searching the witness list for her name. No Davi Iverson was listed. Stacy loudly objected, halting the proceedings. Judge Lutoslawski called the attorneys to the bench, or in this case to the side of the bench opposite the witness stand, where he could walk down and converse with the woman in the wheelchair. Dixon Bell could see them mumbling so nobody could overhear what they were saying. Jim Fury spelled out what he was up to. It almost brought Stacy Dvorchak back to her feet. She could be heard loud and clear. "Outrageous. Mistrial. Miscarriage of justice if this is allowed to continue."

Dixon Bell along with the jurors sat staring at the young woman on the witness stand, wondering more than ever who she was and what she had to do with the case. The judge got Stacy settled down and they went back to arguing points of law, with Prosecutor Fury shaking his head in disappointment. Finally the attorneys returned to their tables and Judge Lutoslawski instructed a deputy to excuse the jury.

Stacy informed her client that the witness must testify in front of the judge first; then he would decide if the testimony could be heard by the jury. She assured him that would never happen.

Prosecutor Fury: "State your full name."

"Davi Faye Iverson." She had a soft voice, very nervous.

"Where do you live, Miss Iverson?"

"I rent a town house in Edina."

"Do you live alone?"

"Yes. I'm single."

"And what do you do for a living?"

"I'm a bank teller at First Edina Savings on France Avenue."

"Miss Iverson, have you ever been raped?"

Oh, God! Dixon Bell thought he was going to be sick. If this didn't beat all. He couldn't hide his disgust. The deputies were glaring down at him. Stacy told him to relax; the jury was out of earshot. The red light atop the TV camera looked like a blazing fire. Everybody in the media section, including the masked asshole, were stretching their necks like giraffes. Nothing like an alleged rape victim to spice up a slow news day.

"Yes, I have," she told Jim Fury.

"Tell me about it."

Davi Iverson poured herself a cup of water, stalling for time. She stared at the floor out in front of her. She spoke in a slow, halting voice that was so soft she could barely be heard. Fury pushed the microphone closer to her mouth. "It was really hot that night and I left the patio window open. I must have forgot to lock the screen door because that's how he got in. He just walked in. I thought I heard something, but I was too scared to get up and look. Then I saw this big shadow come through the bedroom door, and I was going to scream but he got to the bed really quick and put his hand over my mouth."

"Go on."

"Well, he talked in a real soft whisper and told me if I didn't scream I wouldn't be hurt, and if I did scream, he said he would snap my neck."

"Those were the words he used, 'snap your neck'?"

"Yes, the first night. He let go of my mouth and I didn't scream, but I was still scared."

"Go ahead."

She cleared her throat and drank some more water. "This is hard to explain. He kept petting my hair and talking in a really sweet whisper. He told me we were going to make love and how beautiful it was going to be. He didn't make it sound dirty or anything. He said I was his fantasy and that in the dark I could be anything he wanted me to be. He said I should do the same . . . let him be the man I always dreamed of."

"What happened then?"

"Well, he started kissing me and stuff, and he put his hands on me and he told me how beautiful I was, and . . ."

"Was he hurting you?"

"No."

"Was he seducing you?"

"Yes, kind of. He was very gentle, and he was saying sweet things to me that no man ever said before, and he said it in a really sweet way."

"What happened then?"

She didn't answer.

"Tell us what happened next."

"He, um, he pulled off my nightgown and my panties."

"Did you let him?"

"Kind of."

"And?"

"And then he got undressed and we had sex—he had sex."

"Did he force you to have sex with him that night?"

"Kind of, because I thought he might kill me if I didn't."

"And what did he physically feel like?"

"He was a big man. Tall and kind of husky. Not fat, more like a football player. He had this thick curly hair and a round face. And he always smelled nice, kind of minty, like cologne."

"Would you know that smell again?"

Stacy Dvorchak interrupted. "Your Honor, if she comes over here and begins sniffing my client you're going to get laughed off the bench."

"Thank you, Counselor." The judge glared at the prosecutor. "Don't even ask."

Prosecutor Fury went back to his questioning. "And after the sex, what happened?"

"He was really sweet. He held me tight and whispered more nice things to me."

"Did you have sexual intercourse with him a second time that night?"

"Yes."

"And when did he leave your apartment?"

"It's a town house. After the second time."

"What did he say before he left?"

"That we could do it again. That we could be secret lovers."

"And were you?"

She didn't answer for the longest time. Finally she muttered, "Yes."

"How did this work?"

"Before he left the first night I gave him my telephone number. He would call me up after I was in bed. It was usually late. Then I would go unlock the patio window and screen and I would get into bed and wait for him to come, just like the first night."

"And would he show up?"

"Yes."

"How often?"

"Sometimes once every two or three weeks. Sometimes months would go by."

"How long did this dangerous affair go on?"

"Almost two years."

"Why? Why did you let it go on? Why didn't you call the police?"

She choked on her shame and stared up at the ceiling lights, fighting back the tears. "I mean, everything I wanted, he did for me. And I would do everything for him. Some of us don't get asked out, you know. In the light of day I'm not a pretty woman. I've never had anybody love me like that before. He would always ask what I wanted, what made me feel good, and he always did it. It was exciting. It made me feel good."

"When did it end?"

She nodded at Dixon Bell. "After he was arrested."

"Objection, Your Honor."

"Overruled, Counselor. There's no jury here."

Prosecutor Fury continued. "When did you realize your lover was the weatherman on Channel 7?"

"After about a year. I was watching the news on 7 and they were joking around before he walked over to do the weather, and he leaned over the desk and whispered something to the lady anchor. They all laughed, but I froze. I found out he lived in Edina. I thought then that it was him."

"Did you ever confront him with this knowledge?"

"No. I kept planning to, but I always chickened out."

"Is the man who prowled your neighborhood looking for unlocked windows, the man who would become your secret lover, is he in this courtroom today?"

She looked surprised at the stupid question. "Yes, he is."

"Will you point him out, please."

"That's him over there. Dixon Bell. The Weatherman."

The prosecutor walked up to the witness stand and patted her hand. "It took a lot of courage for you to come here today. Thank you."

The prosecutor returned to his table. Davi Iverson got up to leave.

"Sit down!" It was Stacy Dvorchak. "I want to remind

you, young lady, that you're under oath, that there's a
man on trial for his life here, and that if you don't answer
my questions truthfully, you'll roast in hell!"

Even Dixon Bell was intimidated. Anger was a side of
his attorney he had not seen. Davi Iverson took her seat
again, looking like a frozen field mouse watching the descent of a hawk.

Stacy wheeled her electric chair over to the witness
stand faster than anybody had ever seen it move before.
She lined herself up face-to-face with her client's accuser,
one woman to another. "Did you ever perform oral sex on
this man who came in the night?"

"Yes," she muttered.

"Did you allow him to have anal intercourse with
you?"

"Yes."

"Did you allow him to tie you up?"

"Yes."

"In the two years you prostituted yourself, did you
ever—"

"Objection, Your Honor."

"Counselor," said Judge Lutoslawski, "behave yourself."

"In the two years you let this rapist into your bedroom
and spread your legs for him—"

"Counselor!" admonished the judge.

Stacy rephrased the question. "In those two years, were
the lights ever on?"

"No."

"In those two years, were the shades ever up, allowing
moonlight in?"

"No."

"In those two years did he ever talk above a whisper?"

"No."

"In those two years did he ever hint at who he was?"

"No."

"Did he ever whisper a forecast into your ears?" The
courtroom burst into nervous laughter. "And this perverted affair happened in the two years before my client
was arrested?"

Tears were falling from Davi Iverson's eyes now. Even
Dixon Bell was feeling somewhat sorry for her. "Yes,"
she answered.

"In other words," Stacy explained, "you repeatedly allowed this strange man into your apartment in the middle of the night knowing full well a serial killer was stalking the Cities, and at the same time Edina police were warning the public about a rapist stalking that community, the very community you live in?"

"Yes."

"For the record, Your Honor, Edina police investigated my client after his arrest and concluded in their written reports, quote, 'Dixon Bell is no longer a suspect in the Edina rape cases.' Unquote. Your Honor, I move this witness be dismissed and not allowed to testify before the jury."

The judge leaned over the witness. "Miss Iverson, the deputy will show you to the witness room. You're to wait there."

The deputy took her arm and escorted the surprise witness from the courtroom. She appeared ready to faint.

Prosecutor Fury addressed the bench. "Your Honor, there are a thousand unsolved rapes out there every year, and probably three times that many that go unreported. Dixon Bell didn't just wake up one day and begin killing women. I'm establishing a pattern here. He probably began window peeping, moved on to rape, and then graduated to murder."

Stacy cut in. "Your Honor, I remind you that none of the victims my client is charged with killing was sexually assaulted. He has never been charged with any crime, much less a sex crime, and none of this woman's incredible story is the least bit mentioned in his diary, which contains his innermost thoughts."

The prosecutor was having none of that. "As we've established, Your Honor, this is not a normal diary. It's the sentimental ramblings of a psychopath. It's not unusual that he would omit his crimes."

Stacy shot back, "Your Honor, in this state alone I can cite three news stories from the past two years where a woman claimed to have been kidnapped, only to find out it was a hoax. Nobody knows why some women make these things up, but they do. Trials like this bring out the wackos."

Judge Lutoslawski pressed his fingers to his temples, then ordered a recess while he considered his ruling.

During this welcome break in the trial Dixon Bell was paging through the newspaper when he stumbled across two articles of interest on the penultimate page.

NORTH SIDE RAPIST STRIKES AGAIN

For the fourth time in as many months a man broke into a woman's home in North Minneapolis and raped the woman living there at gunpoint, Minneapolis police reported today. The suspect in all four rapes has been described as a dark-skinned black man, medium build, wearing new athletic shoes. The latest assault occurred . . .

When it was rapes in white-ass Edina it was front-page news and TV coverage galore. When it was black women in the projects of North Minneapolis, it was two paragraphs in the back of the paper.

The second article appeared in the gossip column.

BARINGTON GETS NEW CONTRACT

Sky High News Channel 7 anchorwoman Charleen Barington will be making her home in the Twin Cities for at least three more years. The fortysomething redhead was given a new three-year contact to continue her anchor duties on the six and ten o'clock news shows, news director Jack Napoleon said in a statement. Rumors of Barington's demise in the wake of falling ratings, plus her age . . .

Dixon Bell folded the paper. Andrea Labore had to be depressed beyond words. Rick Beanblossom said she'd been offered an anchor job at the Clancy station in Indianapolis. That had to have the masked asshole sweating bullets, if he could sweat. He couldn't live without her enchanting looks any more than he could live outside of Minnesota. To what ends would Beanblossom go to hang on to that bewitching face?

When court resumed, Judge Lutoslawski handed down his decision. In light of the fact that no crime was ever reported, Davi Iverson's story lacked credibility and would shed unfair light on the defendant. Her testimony would not be allowed.

Dixon Bell sighed in relief.

It was snowing that night as they drove I-94 back to St. Paul. A nuisance storm. One to two inches. Spring would be late. The heater went out in the van. Still, the Weatherman was feeling warmer about the day's events. Soon he could tell the jury his side of the story, how he was threatened, followed, robbed, framed.

But before that happened, cunning Jim Fury had one more witness up his sleeve.

Jesus Christ ascending into heaven through fluffy cumulus clouds can be seen on the office wall behind her. A physics degree from the University of Chicago hangs behind the desk. It is dark outside, probably after the ten o'clock news. Charleen Barington takes a seat on the couch in front of the console television set. The set is on but can't be seen. Only the flickering white light spills over her. The sound is down. News director Jack Napoleon comes into view. He pulls up a chair and sits in front of her, pats her knee in a fatherly way.

When it came to gathering the news, Charleen Barington was invisible. She was an anchor. She returned to work after six weeks of maternity leave with the birth of her second child, the tot shamelessly promoted for the evening news. Her beauty-queen looks and hourglass figure returned to work with her, but her red hair seemed a shade duller, her makeup a bit heavier. For weeks upon her return she would come into the newsroom at 9:35 P.M., go straight into makeup, be on the set at 9:55, read the ten o'clock news, and be out the door by 10:35. One hour of work on a six-figure contract. But that contract was up. Where Ron Shea was just coming into his silver-haired fifties, ideal for television news, and paid twice what his female co-anchor was being paid for doing the same job, Charleen Barington was now forty years old—the twilight of her career. She desperately wanted one more contract.

Jack Napoleon begins, his hands folded prayerwise in

his lap. "We've really never had a chance to get to know each other. Clancy signed you before I got here. This time it's strictly my decision. I think we should start, Charleen, by laying our cards on the table." He taps her knee with his finger. "Tell me what you want."

Charleen nervously slips her hands under her long, gorgeous legs. Sits on them. She is hesitant. "I want another three-year contract. A signing bonus. And I think I'm entitled to more pay to bring me closer in line with Ron. That's what I want."

They weren't news people anymore, if ever they were. Ron Shea and Charleen Barington had been elevated to anchors but reduced to a pair of PR flacks. Their job was to sell Sky High News.

Napoleon rubs his hands together in deep thought. "Charleen, you're forty years old now. You have a small child and a baby at home. Have you given some thought to part-time reporting with us, and maybe more time at home with your family?"

Charleen clears her throat, obviously disappointed. "I don't think I'm ready to step down from the anchor desk. Besides, who would replace me? Andrea?"

Napoleon sighs. Troubled. "Andrea wants it, perhaps deserves it. But I don't think she's ready yet. Andrea doesn't put viewers to sleep, but they do slip into a dreamlike trance. And it wouldn't be a wise move in the middle of the trial."

Charleen perks up. "Then I'm needed at the anchor desk."

Napoleon sighs, deeply troubled. "The thing of it is, Charleen, I don't see a three-year contract. This is a young people's business. I'd be sticking my neck out with Clancy." He has his finger on her knee, drawing cute little circles.

Charleen Barington has a pretty face. She won a Texas beauty pageant and she went into television. She was no different than a thousand other pretty people who every year choose a career in broadcasting. She runs a finger over the back of his hairy hand and slips into her most seductive Texas accent. Charleen didn't get where she is without charm. "I think I've earned a new three-year contract and I came to your office tonight to get it. Let me know what I have to do. There, my cards are on the table."

The news director now has both his hands on her knees. He is leaning into her. "Your work habits are becoming the butt of newsroom jokes—jokes that are spilling into the gossip columns. It would be hard to justify a three-year contract. I'm reluctant to give it to you. My cards are on the table."

The aging beauty queen watches as his hands caress her legs. She is firm and direct, but still polite. "My work habits in the newsroom are hampered by the schedule you expect me to keep outside the newsroom. I have spoken before every insipid civic group I can imagine, and I have joined enough moronic family groups to raise an army of toddlers. All of this for Clancy Communications and Sky High News. Am I expected to break news stories, too?"

He pats her leg, further up the thigh, very understanding. "I know, I know, we ask a lot of our people. But it's important our anchors be seen out there in the community. That's why I'm thinking about this part-time reporter position for you." His hands are approaching her hips now.

Charleen leans into him. Kisses him, just a sweet touch of the lips, then runs her long fingers through his hair. "What do I have to do to get the first year of that contract?"

Napoleon drops to his knees. He caresses her thighs, slowly inching up her dress. "I have needs, Charleen. Lord Jesus help me, I have needs."

"Tell me about them, honey."

The news director reaches up and grabs hold of her throat with his big right hand. He squeezes gently. "Did you ever have sex while being choked?"

She smiles, a nervous laugh. "No, I never have."

Napoleon, also nervous, laughs along with her. Then he reaches behind her neck and violently jerks her head into his. They are nose to nose. The news director talks in a nasty whisper, difficult to hear. He traces her mouth with his finger. "First year, three percent raise. You get down on your knees and you pray to me, worship every inch of my manhood." He passes his hand down her neck and unbuttons her blouse, exposes her black lace brassiere, rubs his hand over her bare belly. She is breathing hard.

There is a pair of scissors on the end table beside the couch. Napoleon reaches for them. He passes the sharp chromium blades up her bare belly to her bra. A frightened look appears in her eyes. He snips the bra in two and her white and freckled breasts spill out. He sucks on them like a man dying of thirst. Then he breaks away and begins slowly snipping her dress between her legs. "Ten thousand is as high as I'll go on the bonus," he tells her. But he is already as high as her crotch with the scissors. Her skirt splits in two. "Second year," he explains, as he pulls her skirt from beneath her, "two percent raise. You spread your legs wider than they've ever been spread before and you take in every last inch of me." He lays the scissors down and jams both his hands beneath her and grabs her ass. She drops her head back. "Then, to get the elusive third year on that contract," he instructs her, "you get on your knees, put your face in a pillow, and put this beautiful ass of yours in the air, and pray. I mean it—pray so I can hear you."

Charleen is nodding, excited, frightened. She understands what has to be done. She strokes the back of his head. "I won't sign a no compete clause," she moans.

Napoleon is tearing away her blouse. "If you can suck it out of me, I'll waive the no compete clause."

From here the negotiations get better than anything in any video store. Jack Napoleon pushes his female anchor to the couch and literally rips her clothes from her. When he has her down to only her panties he again picks up the shiny scissors. He is on his knees over her shapely body, ghostly white. He slides the scissor blades up the side of her leg, scratching her, drawing blood, up under her black bikini panties. He snips. Snips again. Napoleon leans back and pulls the panties free.

Forty minutes later the tape plays out. Sky High News anchor Charleen Barington, in living color, earns everything but the no compete clause.

The rewind button is beeping.

Rick Beanblossom got up off his couch. He rewound the contract talks, then pushed the eject button. The amateur video popped into his hands. He stuffed the video into a padded mailer. Then he peeled off the address label he'd typed up and attached it to the envelope.

J. C. Peters
HY PETER PRODUCTIONS
466 First Avenue North
Minneapolis, MN 55403

THE SUSPECTS

The trial was delayed another five days due to the annual tournament blizzard. This late winter storm strikes every year during the state high-school hockey tournament, or so says the local weather myth. The storm gave Minnesota over one hundred inches of snow for the season. A flood advisory was issued for parts of the state, a mighty tepid warning for record snowfalls. Dixon Bell, sitting at the defense table reading the morning newspaper while waiting for the jury to be brought in, thought flooding was more a probability than a possibility and should be taken more seriously at this point in the season. He wasn't buying the ninety-day forecast of below-normal temperatures and a dry spring. Strange winds were blowing. When he'd finished studying the weather page he turned to the metro section. Once again his friends at the newsroom in the sky were making more news than they were reporting.

NEWS DIRECTOR RESIGNS

Channel 7 news director Jack Napoleon submitted his resignation to the station's owners, Clancy Communications, in the wake of a Sky High News sex scandal. Anchorwoman Charleen Barington has taken a paid leave, the station said. Reporter and part-time anchor Andrea Labore will take over the anchor duties in the interim.

The scandal broke last week after a local tabloid reported brisk sales of an underground videotape that shows Jack Napoleon engaged in sexual activity while discussing a new contract with an on-air personality. In the video the news director can be seen choking the woman.

Stacy Dvorchak, attorney for former Channel 7 weatherman Dixon Bell, now on trial in Minneapolis charged in the serial killings of seven Minnesota women, says she will try and have the tape shown at the trial. Dvorchak told reporters yesterday, "Police got the right newsroom, but they arrested the wrong man."

Prosecutor Jim Fury called that accusation "ridiculous" and said the tape was totally irrelevant to the trial. He was confident the judge would not allow it to be admitted.

Jack Napoleon's reign in the popular newsroom atop the IDS Tower was plagued by a series of bizarre incidents that began almost as soon as he arrived in the Twin Cities. He was only on the job a month when the Sky High News helicopter crashed after . . .

Dixon Bell put down the paper and looked around. The man in the mask was standing in the back, chatting with colleagues, the newspaper in his hands rolled tight as a club. What did he know? If police weren't investigating Jack Napoleon, then surely Rick Beanblossom would be.

Before this welcome bit of news a black cloud of depression had been stalled over the Weatherman's jail cell. If worse came to worst he had three square bricks in the wall chipped loose, would slide right out of there. The Order of Masons would be proud of him. Now, as the jury was ushered in and the court was called to order, the meteorologist from Vicksburg, Mississippi, felt a warm ray of hope. But like the winter sunshine, it didn't last.

"Your Honor, the state calls Lisa Gilbert."

She was a frumpy woman, fat, unattractive. She was fiftyish-looking, maybe younger. Her dull brown hair, probably dyed, was tied back in a bun. She wore a frilly black dress skirted over granny shoes.

Stacy Dvorchak muttered a question to Dixon Bell. "Didn't I once ask you about her?"

"I've never seen the woman before."

The Gilbert woman was sworn in, then took the witness stand. She kept her eyes forward, avoiding the defense table. There was an aristocratic arrogance in her demeanor that Dixon Bell found disturbingly familiar. After the Davi Iverson secret-lover testimony he didn't know what to expect. But nothing could have prepared him for the lightning bolt the prosecutor had aimed at his heart.

Jim Fury doing the questioning. "Where are you from, Mrs. Gilbert?"

"Dallas, Texas."

"And before that?"

"I was born in Natchez, Mississippi. Daddy moved us up to Vicksburg when I was a little girl. There I was raised."

"Did you know Dixon Bell when you lived in Vicksburg?"

"Yes, sir, I did."

"How did you know him?"

"We went to high school together. He said he was in love with me."

Dixon Bell froze like an icicle. God almighty, it was Lisa Beauregard! He knew in his heart right then and there that it was her, but his mind and his mouth were rejecting it. He was on his feet, talking down to Stacy. "I've never seen this woman before in my life." Three deputies were coming at him. "Is nothing sacred to these sons of bitches?"

With the braces on her hands Stacy was clawing at his arm, trying to pull him back into his chair. "Sit down, Dixon. Sit down."

Judge Lutoslawski was pounding his gavel. Two deputies dropped their big paws onto the shoulders of Dixon Bell and pushed him back into the chair.

Stacy Dvorchak was furious. "Your Honor, this is the second time in this trial that Mr. Fury has pulled this stunt."

Prosecutor Fury responded with lawyerly glee. "Your Honor, Mrs. Gilbert's name has been on the witness list for six months. The attorney for the defense had plenty of time to interview her. She'll have the chance to cross-examine her today."

Again the attorneys were called to the bench, where they argued in loud, intense whispers while the Weatherman, hotter than the Delta sun, sat glaring at this obese woman who claimed to be Lisa Beauregard. After the war he had had fantasies about killing the bitch. He'd do it with his bare hands. He'd take that letter she wrote him and literally stuff it down her throat and up her nose. Then he'd cover her face with his hands so she couldn't spit it out. Make her eat her own words. Choke her to death on her lousy prose. Three deputies were standing over him. Two more deputies, big suckers, came in from the hallway. The women in the jury box were staring at him, and Dixon Bell could sense their fear.

Stacy Dvorchak lost this round. As she so eloquently informed her client, "Judge Polack ruled the fat lady of the circus could testify before the jury."

Prosecutor Fury continued with his questions. "Do you remember a love letter Dixon Bell wrote you in the spring of your senior year?"

"Yes, I do. He said that he loved me and that he wanted to take me to the prom."

"Do you still have that letter?"

"No. I don't remember what became of it."

"Do you remember the letter you wrote back to him?"

"Vaguely. I told him I didn't ever want to date him and I wouldn't go to the prom with him."

"Could you be more specific about what you wrote?"

"No, sir, I'm sorry, I can't. I keep telling your police, I just never thought about it that much. I have children older than I was back then."

Dixon Bell could see Jim Fury was eating this shit up, as were the smug little lawyerettes he had on his team. "Please tell the court everything you've heard about Dixon Bell since high school."

Lisa Gilbert never looked at the man she was testifying against, the man who worshiped her in her youth. "That he was in the Air Force. Then somebody at a reunion said he was a television weatherman in Memphis, and then he moved to Milwaukee. I guess they meant here. Then my momma called me last year to say that he was arrested for these murders. It was in the Vicksburg paper."

"Is it fair to say, Mrs. Gilbert, that you didn't give Dixon Bell much thought after you graduated from high school?"

"I didn't think about him hardly at all. Back in those

days I was pretty popular and I got asked out by many admirable young men."

"Were you surprised when the officers from the task force showed you the passages from his diary, the passages that spoke of his never-ending love for you?"

"I was shocked."

That did it. Dixon Bell was out of his chair. He was standing and screaming until his lungs hurt. "You're not Lisa! Lisa was beautiful! You're just some ugly fat lady trying to hurt me!"

Two deputies had ahold of him. Stacy was reaching for his arm. "Dixon, sit down. This is what they want."

Judge Lutoslawski was pounding on the bench with his hammer. Everybody in the media and ghoul sections was on their feet. Even in his anger Dixon Bell could see the glowing red light atop the television camera. If they wanted good television, by God he was going to give them good television.

"Don't tell me I ran off to war and risked my life for some fat lady! I loved that girl! You're just trying to humiliate me like you always did. You tell lies—you pervert my diary! I did nothing to deserve this! I'll kill you, bitch!"

"Mistrial," Stacy was screaming. "The prosecution planned this provocation. I move for a mistrial."

"I'll kill all you bitches! I did nothing to deserve this!"

The judge ordered the jury to leave the courtroom, and the women jurors gladly complied, but some of the men lingered in the doorway to watch. The deputies, five strong now, were tripping over Stacy's wheelchair as they tried to wrestle her client under control. They spun him around toward the media section—and there he could see Rick Beanblossom standing against the back wall with a stare colder than ice. He knew. Somehow the bastard knew. The deputies finally handcuffed Dixon Bell and wrestled him from the courtroom. The Weatherman stumbled by the witness stand. He could smell her. She still wore the same enchanting perfume. Ain't that funny, he thought.

Rick Beanblossom didn't believe Jack Napoleon had murdered those women any more than had Dixon Bell.

Napoleon's blood type didn't match the blood under Officer Sumter's fingernails. His shoe size didn't fit the prints found in the snow. A source told Rick the fingerprint found on the transformer did not belong to the news director. All of that evidence pointed to the Weatherman. Only the time frame fit Jack Napoleon—fit him like a glove.

Meanwhile the Channel 7 news staff was functioning as normal. Television newsrooms change news directors almost as often as Minnesota changes seasons. They were used to waiting for the new boss to arrive. At the assignment desk Gayle the Ghoul was directing a team of reporters and photographers about the Cities, pacing the floor in front of the assignment board like a panther, trying to talk into a phone and a two-way radio at the same time. She popped a cookie into her mouth.

Dave Cadieux stole a cookie from the desk, pulled videotapes from a metal rack, and disappeared into an edit room. The photojournalist hadn't spoken to Rick Beanblossom since the Napoleon-Barington affair.

Up on the news set the aging but reliable Andy Mack was taping new promotional pieces with Andrea Labore, he at the weather podium, she at the anchor desk. Andy revised his forecast for the bit. Some flooding had begun on the Red River along the North Dakota border. Nothing unusual with heavy snowfall. Andrea turned on cue and asked about it. The weatherman circled the area on a monitor with an electronic pen and explained the minor flooding to the camera.

The floor director shouted, "Clear! Let's try it again, Andy."

Andy Mack had gone from off-camera announcer in the days of live television commercials, to children's show host, to newsman, to weatherman, to whatever they asked him to do until the day he retired, or the day he died. A life in television. A local sports hero whose exploits on the gridiron and the wrestling mats only senior citizens could remember. Now he was back in his element, talking weather and memories to a new generation. The gleam had returned to his eyes. His cheeks glowed. The drinking had stopped.

Rick Beanblossom was proud of the old man, though he knew it was only an interlude. The station was already interviewing meteorologists around the country in hopes of replacing Dixon Bell. As he watched Andy Mack and Andrea Labore saying their lines, Rick marveled at the seductive power of television on both sides of the camera.

The news producer pulled open his desk drawer and took out the ring. Held it in his hand. The diamond sparkled in the television lights the way he saw the stars sparkle over Lake Calhoun. When to pop the big question? Perhaps in the spring, the air fresh with romance and new beginnings. Easter Sunday would be a good day. Would she say yes? Probably not. But then again, when they were alone at night it was hard to imagine her saying no. She had his mind swimming in doubt. Again he glanced up at the anchor desk. The glow about her face was straight out of heaven. He admired the diamond ring one more time before slipping it back into the desk drawer.

The trial was at a halt again while the judge considered the mistrial motion. Most legal experts didn't give the motion a prayer in hell, but thought that Judge Lutoslawski was generously giving the defendant time to cool off and compose himself after the morning's outburst. Rick picked up the thick trial file and walked to the edit rooms.

Two monitors sat beside the edit equipment: one for viewing, one for editing. A tape popped into the edit machine would appear simultaneously on both screens. So what Rick Beanblossom saw when he walked into Edit Room 1 was the Eden Prairie tornado coming at him, times two. The soundtrack was the high-pitched howling of the ghostlike winds. Then *Skyhawk 7* swung out from behind the tornado and he could almost see the faces of Bob Buckridge and Kitt Karson. Out of respect for the dead men the video was rarely shown. Rick swallowed a lump in his throat. "What are you doing?"

"Putting together a tape of my best work," Dave Cadieux coldly told him.

"For what?"

On a shelf above the edit monitors was a single large monitor where Andrea Labore and Andy Mack could be seen taping their promo. The sound was down to the faint level. The photographer lifted his head to this upper monitor. "I'm getting out before I end up like Andy Mack there and television is all that I know. I'll shoot commercials, or tape weddings, or make dirty movies for J. C. Peters, but I'll make a living."

"Something we did?"

"I'm glad we nailed Napoleon. He was scum. But I think what we did to Charleen sucks. No, Charleen wasn't a news person, but she wasn't a bad person, either. I'm not going to spend the rest of my life trying to catch people screwing in closets."

Rick watched as the tornado jumped the river and bore down on St. Paul, *Skyhawk 7* in pursuit. "Manipulating the media is like predicting the weather—it's an inexact science. Would the results somehow have been different had I written the story for a newspaper?"

"You said together we could change things. We could bring newspaper quality to television news. That's what you told me when you came here." Dave Cadieux killed the tornado. He ejected the tape and slipped in another. "Maybe television is where you belong, Rick. Other than a mask, you're not that much different."

The prize-winning newsman said nothing.

On the two monitors before them appeared the tormented visage of Keenan Wakefield. He was emerging from dense woods, scratched and filthy. Freezing. A search crew surrounded him, trying their best to comfort him, afraid the boy was going into shock after a cold and fruitless overnight search for Harlan, his missing twin brother.

Dave Cadieux rewound the tape and played it again. "The day I shot this tape I went home and cried. Best work I ever did. But there are so many people blubbering on the news these days it doesn't affect me anymore."

Nor did the sight of the crying boy genius have much of an emotional affect on Rick Beanblossom. The four-year-old tape aroused his curiosity more than his sympathy. "I know that spot—it's down by the river. Run it again," he told Cadieux.

As the tape was being rewound, screams came from the newsroom. Rick looked up at the large monitor to see Andy Mack clutching his chest and stumbling to his knees in front of the sky-blue weather wall. Andrea rushed to help him. Rick burst out of the edit room, ran through the newsroom, and bound up the steps to the news set.

Andrea was stretching the old weatherman out on his back. She jammed her thumb into his mouth so he wouldn't swallow his tongue; then she dropped her mouth over his.

Rick slipped the thick trial file under his head as a rest. "C'mon, everybody get back, let him breathe."

The news people formed a semicircle in front of the cameras.

"There's an ambulance on the way."

"Is Chris Mack working?"

"No, he's off today."

"Run down the hall and get Jill."

A photog ran for Andy's daughter in the programming department.

Andrea brought Andy Mack back to life. He was conscious, but pale white with fright, the bright lights illuminating his chalky face. Rick bent over him. "Just relax, Andy. We'll get you to the hospital."

"I always wanted to go like this, in front of the weather wall, doing what I do best."

Andrea was pumping his chest. "Stop talking like that. You're going to outlive us all."

"But I wasn't the best. He was." Tears came to the old man's eyes as he clutched Andrea's hands. "I was warned. It was on my computer this morning."

"You were warned about what?" Rick asked.

The old weatherman was wheezing hard now. "He got back at me, Rick. Even from a jail cell the bastard reached out and got me. I told you he was spooky."

"Andy, you're not making any sense. Lie still."

He reached out and grabbed Rick's shirt and pulled him close. Andy Mack choked out his last words. "Tell Dixon I'm sorry about those women." His face turned purple. Saliva drooled out the corner of his mouth. Then he was gone.

Rick looked up at Andrea. He looked over his shoulder, but nobody else was within earshot. He bent over the body beneath the weather wall. "Andy? Andy, what are you saying?" He plunged his hands into the weatherman's chest, trying to pump some life back into him. What had he said? "Andy? Andy, talk to us." Rick leaned over the dead purple face and breathed into the mouth.

The news people that had gathered around took another

step back, now faced with death they could see and feel for themselves. Rick Beanblossom was kneeling over the body Andrea knew to be dead. What was it he had said about those women? About Dixon Bell? The mouth-to-mouth resuscitation was futile. Rick raised his fist to the television lights, then slammed it into the lifeless chest of Andy Mack. "You come back here and talk to us, you son of a bitch!"

THE ESCAPE

It was the night after Lisa testified. Up to then, up to the time the trial got under way, Dixon Bell had earned most of the privileges available in the jail. The deputies paid him scant attention, since all he seemed to do was sit on his bunk and stare out the window. That night freezing rain was falling over the river. The lights up and down the bluffs were mesmerizing, the yellow-orange radiance evaporating in the dark, inclement weather. He was still upset, still wondering what the jury was thinking after the way he'd acted in the courtroom, still trying to accept this fat middle-aged woman as the Lisa Beauregard he remembered. He was cursed with an excellent memory in a world where so many things are best forgotten.

The deputy came up the winding staircase in the day room to lock him in for the night. As the deputy slid the cell door closed, the rail on the floor flew into the air and the steel door crashed off the track. "What the . . .?" he swore.

Dixon Bell was out of his bunk in a flash, pulling bricks out of the wall as fast as he could.

The deputy could see him in there trying to escape, but he couldn't gain entry because the heavy door was stuck. He sounded the alarm.

If Dixon Bell had been a skinny man, he could have squeezed his way out and jumped for his life. One arm was through the wall, his head and his neck were through, and he was wiggling for all he was worth when four deputies broke into the cell and got hold of his legs and his buttocks. They were beating on him while at the same time trying to drag him back into the cell. His head was outside in the rain. It was cold, and wet, and as refreshing as freedom. Again they'd fucked up the forecast. Snow was melting over the railroad tracks. Patches of black water were showing up in the Mississippi. People were driving by on River Road, and there was this TV weatherman with his head stuck right out of the jailhouse wall, screaming like a banshee.

"Say, didn't he used to be on Channel 7?"

The deputies finally got him pulled inside and stomped the living hell out of him. They threw him into the empty cell next door and shot the bolt. The detention center was lit up like a Christmas tree. Alarms were ringing. Dixon Bell ran to the window crying like the madman everybody believed him to be. He was bleeding through his nose. He was trying to pound through seven layers of glass when the first thunder of spring exploded over the bluffs. Icy raindrops streaked the window. Cars were stopping along the road and people were staring up at him. Then the flashing red lights of an ambulance appeared on the Wabasha Street Bridge and started across the water.

Dixon Bell was locked in an Isolation cell—TFN. There was no window to the outside world. Solid brick. A bunk. A seatless toilet. A stainless steel sink and one roll of toilet paper. In the steel door was a small observation window. His spirit was broken, his body bruised and aching. His case may have been lost. Still, his perceptions of the weather had never been sharper. Even totally removed from the elements, he knew that the temperature out there was falling. More snow was on the way. He knew the wind direction and the barometric pressure. Most important, he knew the thirty-day forecast.

The trial was delayed yet again because of the defendant's mental state. Judge Lutoslawski had yet to rule on the mistrial motion. The deputies at the jail were in hot water over the escape attempt. As a result they tried to make life in Isolation even harder for Dixon Bell. They took out his sixty-watt light bulb and screwed in a forty-watt bulb. The dim light was on only during the daylight hours. No reading material. He was allowed no visitors—or so he had been led to believe.

He was sitting on the floor in the corner, his knees

tucked into his chest. It was past dark. The light was out. The only ray of illumination came from the hallway lights spilling through the observation window. Looking through the dim light, he saw an apparition approaching his cell. It was wearing a blue mask. The Phantom of the News. A deputy let him in, then locked the door to the Isolation cell and left them alone.

"How'd you get in here?"

"A source."

The Weatherman laughed, his first real laugh in months. "I swear, I'll arrive in hell someday only to find Rick Beanblossom has a source there."

The masked newsman didn't say anything at first, just stood there leaning against the door with his arms folded, blocking the light. Dixon Bell could feel his cold stare in the dark. Finally Rick spoke up, in that halting, haunting voice of his. "The deputies told me off the record it was the best escape attempt they'd ever seen."

"Thank you." His curiosity got the best of him. "I still haven't figured out how you did in Jack Napoleon like that."

"What makes you think I was behind that?"

The Weatherman enjoyed another good laugh. "The Bible-thumping news director is gone. A worthless pornography investigation is killed. The aging-beauty-queen anchor is forced to flee the state in disgrace, promising a multi-million-dollar lawsuit against a giant media corporation you despise. And the love of your life, Andrea Labore, ascends through the storm clouds to the coveted anchor desk. How'd y'all do it?"

"Videotapes," Rick told him. "Tapes of Napoleon forcing Andrea to watch porn. Tapes of him forcing reporters to have sex with him in exchange for contracts. Tapes with interns. Tapes with a woman who wanted to be the new weather girl."

"You bugged the news director's office?"

"No," Rick said, "Napoleon bugged his own office. We bugged his bugging operation. One of the photogs rigged it so that whenever the video camera was turned on in his office, it would also record in Edit Room 4. We'd just pop in a blank tape every night and then check it in the morning. The stuff was a pornographer's dream."

Dixon Bell shook his head in amazement. "There's

only one way to get news people—turn them on each other. Though I kind of liked Charleen. I guess she did what she thought a woman has to do."

They were both silent for a moment; then Rick Beanblossom said, "Andy Mack had a heart attack. He's dead."

If Dixon Bell was surprised, he didn't show it. "I'm really sorry to hear that now. He had wonderful weather instincts."

"Did you get along with him?"

"As well as could be given the circumstances. I took his job."

"Did you ever feel threatened by him in any way?"

"No, he wasn't that kind of man."

"Did he ever visit your house? Know where you lived?"

"No. Why do you ask?"

"I found a message left on his computer. It said, 'I'm gonna ice you, Weatherman.' Did you put it there?"

"How could I do that?"

"Do you have telephone privileges?"

"Yes."

"Digital phone, laptop computer—if anybody could find a way to do it, you could."

"Maybe he left it there himself."

"You mean the same way you left that message for yourself?"

"That's ridiculous. Did I give him the heart attack, too?"

"No, God did that."

"Why all of the questions about Andy?"

Rick Beanblossom began to pace the small cell like a caged tiger while the Weatherman remained seated on the floor. "I've run it through my mind a hundred different ways and it frustrates me to no end. Andy had access to everything in the weather center, including your schedule, your diary, your computer, and your home address. Even your fingerprints."

Dixon Bell couldn't believe what he was hearing. "My God," he muttered. "Can you plant a fingerprint?"

"I don't know. I got a source to check Andy's fingerprints against the transformer print. It's no match. Andy's blood type was O positive. That matches the blood found beneath the fingernails of Officer Sumter, but it's a common blood type of millions. His shoe size was thirteen, close to the size of the prints found in the snow, but a clandestine search of his Edina home turned up no athletic shoe called Alacrity."

" 'Clandestine search'?"

"Andrea and I broke into his house last night. Well, Andrea broke in. I followed. Ex-cops make great burglars. Anyway, we found love letters written half a century ago, but no letter from that murdered retarded girl in Afton. You know, victim number seven, I think she was. The one that watched you every night."

"Karen Rochelle," the Weatherman reminded him.

"Yes, Karen Rochelle. We found no letters that belonged to you. No newspaper clippings of the murders. No threats. No clues. Nothing more than the dusty house of an old man, filled with memorabilia. A proud man who starred in college, who went to war, who married a local girl and raised a family while building a career in television . . . then bitterly watched it all slip away, one precious memory at a time."

"You don't think he did it, do you?"

"I don't want to hurt his son and daughter with potshot allegations. My police sources think the theory is bunk. Andrea is skeptical, to say the least."

"Andrea thinks I murdered those women, doesn't she?"

Rick stopped his pacing and peered through the little window. "Are you going to take the witness stand?"

"You saw me in court the other day. Stacy says it was bad. How bad?"

Rick Beanblossom moved away from the window, allowing the light from the hallway to spill across the bitter face of Dixon Bell. "You looked like a madman. You looked like the kind of man who would strangle seven women. Or maybe eight."

"Did you see her?" he asked Rick in a plaintive voice. "I believe in God now, because when I left high school I prayed he'd get her. I mean, in my most malicious dreams Lisa was never fat."

"Tell me about her."

The cell was damp and chilly, but the Weatherman's hands were sweating. He tried to rub them dry. "You read my diary, or, as Mr. Fury would say, 'the sentimental ramblings of a psychopath.' For near thirty years that girl haunted me. I was in Nam when my friend Bobby Conn wrote me that she'd gotten married. As the years rolled by I was able to go for months at a time without thinking about her. Once a whole year passed—I swear, not a thought of the bitch. But then it would happen. She would come to me in a dream. These dreams hurt like hell and I would wake up in tears. Then the dream would bother me for days on end. Drive me out of my skull. Sometimes the dream was about her wedding. I lost count of how many times I attended that fucking wedding. I skipped my ten-year reunion 'cause of her. I wanted to go home for my twenty-five-year reunion, but I still couldn't bring myself to deal with the specter of the lost cause. You see, in my mind—and that was the only place I ever saw her—Lisa Beauregard never aged. All those years she remained the epitome of the eighteen-year-old southern belle. Even after I fell in love with your precious Andrea, the Mississippi Queen would show up in a dream to remind me that I'd been down this road once before."

"So what should have been written off as a high-school crush instead became a lifelong obsession."

"You are so insightful, Mr. Beanblossom."

"Oh, my insights go much deeper than that, Mr. Bell." He let that hang in the air a moment. "Davi Iverson," Rick said to him, "the bank teller with the secret lover. The witness nobody believed. She quit her job and moved away. Ridiculed right out of town. But to me she's been the most credible witness in the whole trial. I still can't bring myself to believe you murdered those women . . . but you were the stranger in the night who came for sex with that girl. How many others were there, Weatherman?"

"The masked asshole strikes again. Say what you want about him, the boy has a leather nose for news. I never hurt any of them women. And I sure as hell didn't kill anyone."

A train passed below, and both men were shaking with the walls. The light in the hallway was flickering, blackening off and on the face of Dixon Bell. "Now y'all want a story you can use?"

"It would help."

"Even as my sanity continued to deteriorate, my knowledge of meteorology and the earth sciences continued to grow, to the point where Dixon Graham Bell became one of the most admired and most controversial men in his field."

"And the most popular man on local TV," Rick added.

"That's right. It's warming much too fast out there."

"You've been locked up too long, Weatherman. It's freezing outside."

"That's part of the problem." Dixon Bell tried to explain the inexplicable. "When I'm upset like this, my mind locks onto the weather. I'm like the idiot savant. It's warming too fast in the West. The jet stream is retreating north in a straight westerly flow. Way-above-normal temperatures are headed this way. Record snowfall melting. Heavy rains. You can expect major flooding along the St. Croix River, the Minnesota River, and the Mississippi. St. Paul right below us here and your old hometown of Stillwater should bear the brunt of it. Should crest around Easter. Nobody will believe me anymore. But they'll believe you. Y'all been warned now."

THE FLOOD

On Easter Sunday the St. Croix River in Stillwater, Minnesota, crested at 695 feet above sea level, 20 feet above normal. To save Main Street the decision was made to build an emergency dike of sand and sandbags along the east side of the town, from Elm Street on the north to the south end of Lowell Park. On Good Friday the downtown business district had been sealed off from Second Street to the river, and one thousand volunteer workers labored day and night to lay down five thousand feet of sand to stop a raging river that was rising one foot every twelve hours.

National Guard troops were called in. High school was canceled and students rushed to help out on the dike. The warden at Stillwater prison offered several dozen trustees. Two generator units were set up which provided six thousand watts of power to maintain a lighting system. Volunteers worked under floodlights during the night hours. Women and children walked along the makeshift dam providing refreshments and food. Helicopters and minicams beamed the rising disaster back to their newsrooms.

At the interstate lift bridge, the iron necklace across the valley, water surged over the roadway and up to the railings. With giant ice chunks ramming its tower legs at high speeds there were doubts the landmark could be saved. River blasting was undertaken to break up the ice jams and relieve pressure on the old expanse.

"I've lived here all my life. I never thought I'd see anything like this again. This is worse than '65. We didn't get much warning, did we?"

It was like that up and down the state. The Mississippi River and its tributaries were gobbling up valuable land from near the headwaters in Itasca State Park to Hannibal, Missouri. People became riverfront property owners overnight. A month earlier the region had battled snowdrifts twenty-five feet high. Torrential rains in early April were the crowning blow. According to the Red Cross, more than twenty thousand people from Minnesota and Wisconsin had been driven from their homes. Fifteen people had died in the flood waters, half of them children playing. The preliminary damage estimate topped one hundred million dollars. The city of St. Paul was in a state of emergency as the Mississippi River crested at twenty-seven feet above normal. The detention center was flooded. After viewing the angry rivers from an Army helicopter the President of the United States declared forty-eight counties disaster areas.

By the time the daylight hours had slipped away on Easter Sunday, Stillwater's Main Street looked like a flooded battlefield. Soldiers patroled the streets. Ice literally exploded upriver. Flashes of lightning in a steady drizzle added to the warlike scene. Strong southeast winds were making the situation critical.

The first leaks appeared on the northeast end of the city, then spread to the middle section of the dike back of Hooley's Supermarket. Water was seeping through the soaked earth to the railroad tracks. An antique locomotive parked in Lowell Park was surrounded by several feet of river. Underground water pressure broke up Chestnut Street in front of the interstate bridge and sent manhole covers rolling down the sidewalks. Pumps were put into action to stem the flow. Truck drivers were finding it increasingly difficult getting loads of sand into critical areas. The rampaging St. Croix banged against the dam, already halfway up the sandbags.

Rick Beanblossom was up to his knees in the brown water on the north end of the dike near Hooley's. He and a group of prison workers were throwing sandbags on top of sandbags as fast as they could, piling the eight-foot dike even higher. Rick's frayed and fading fatigue jacket was sodden with mud. But the stenciled USMC could still be seen on one side of his chest, BEANBLOSSOM on the other side. His leather gloves were soaked to his skin. His waterproof boots didn't work as advertised. His mask was a darker shade of blue, almost black in the rain. He was exhausted. He'd been working at the dike day and night since Good Friday.

This night an old man in a life jacket and yellow slicker was working feverishly alongside him. Rick thought he recognized him from the Weatherman's trial. "If it holds tonight, I think we've got it licked," Rick said, worried about the man's health.

"Been watching this ole river flow for more'n thirty years."

"What's your name?"

"Jesse. The boys just call me Old Jesse."

A woman passing out sandwiches was staring at them.

"Well, Jesse, I think we could all use a break."

Another dynamite bomb exploded upriver. Rick instinctively covered his head. His heart skipped a beat or two. He turned to watch. Chips of ice fell slowly to the river through the wide beams of the floodlights. The lift bridge held its ground.

The woman who had been staring at them handed the old man a sandwich and poured him a cup of coffee. Rick was too tired, too jumpy to eat. He turned his back to them and waded up the tracks to the locomotive.

"Excuse me, are you Rick Beanblossom?"

Rick turned. It was the sandwich lady. He wiped sand from his jacket and pulled off his gloves. "Yes, I am."

She was a fortyish woman with a round, smiling face and a healthy figure under her rain gear. She self-consciously tried fixing her dark hair in the filthy weather. "I don't expect you to remember me, Rick." She extended her hand. "Leanne Sutter. Leanne Olsen when we went to high school."

In his mind he said, "You're not Leanne Olsen. She was young and beautiful. I dated her in the tenth grade, used to ride my bicycle over to her house. Her mother fixed us tacos." But it was Leanne all right. He could still see the teenage girl in the warm eyes and the welcoming smile. Sentimental memories came back in a flood. He had seldom seen high-school friends after the war. A few, Leanne among them, had come to see him upon his return home. But nobody ever came back. He avoided reunions. "Hello, Leanne." Rick Beanblossom embraced his old friend, kissed her cheek. He thought he saw a tear in the corner of her eye. Maybe it was the rain.

"We used to read you in the *Star Tribune,* then you won that Pulitzer Prize, and now we watch Channel 7 all the time." She was trying to talk too fast. "I thought it was you over here. Well, of course it's Rick, I said to myself. He's like the rest of us, he's not going to let the old hometown go under. My two boys are sandbagging down the line. They're in high school now—the new one, of course."

"You look wonderful," he told her. And he meant it.

Again she brushed back her hair. "Oh, God, Rick, I look like a sandbag."

"And your husband?"

"He's an engineer. He's parading up and down the dike with a walkie-talkie. His back is bad and he can't do any heavy lifting. Did you ever marry, Rick?"

It was the first time he wasn't bothered by the question. He stuck his hand in his jacket pocket and squeezed the small velvet case that housed the diamond ring. He seldom went anywhere without it. "No," he told her, "but maybe soon. Nothing's official yet. In fact, she should be coming down here tonight."

"Oh, I hope it works out for you, Rick." She rattled off names he hadn't heard in years. Rick asked about classmates he was genuinely curious about; but like the antique locomotive, she couldn't say what had become of the rest of the class, what track their lives had taken. Leanne kissed him good-bye. Made him promise a dinner visit. "Bring your friend." Then she returned to the line and disappeared into a thousand bodies that swarmed over the dike.

Only when he had these few moments to pause and reflect did Rick Beanblossom marvel at how accurate had been the Weatherman's forecast. With him in jail, and Jack Napoleon resigned, and Andy Mack dead, Sky High News had warned of the flooding threat in the most cautious of terms—looking back, too cautious. Even so, Channel 7 had been sounding the alarm days ahead of the competition, and river miles ahead of the National Weather Service.

The Minnesota weather had passed into the realm of mysticism. It was almost as if an incensed Mother Nature were conspiring to stop the trial of Dixon Bell. The Ramsey County jail was inundated with water, the prisoners moved to the upper floors, forced to double and triple up in cells. The sheriff asked the judge for time to make new security arrangements. When court finally resumed, Judge Lutoslawski denied the mistrial motion and the state rested its case. Then Stacy Dvorchak began her defense, one murder charge at a time. The passages she chose to read from the Weatherman's diary were markedly different from those of the prosecution. The psychiatrists she called to the witness stand concluded Dixon Bell was nothing more than an angry but harmless, sentimental fool who found it a lot easier to deal with science than with society.

It was an hour after her last live broadcast and nearing midnight when Andrea found him along the dike. She waded through the water in her jeans. Her stylish blue vinyl raincoat wasn't up to the windy weather. The hood kept blowing off her head. Still, she was the warmest thing Rick had seen in days. She came close but they didn't embrace. "We miss you in the newsroom," she said.

"This is one story I couldn't stand by and watch." He led her away from the dike, away from the wrathful river. They were standing in two feet of water in the falling rain. His mask was flecked with mud. Maybe it was exhaustion, maybe it was seeing Leanne again, but Rick decided the time was right. It was Easter Sunday. "I was hoping for some place a bit more romantic, but what the hell." The man without a face pulled the velvet case with the diamond ring from his jacket pocket and gave it to her to open. "I wanted to hate you, but you turned out to be such a gutsy girl. I mean, gutsy woman. I mean, what we have, I never thought we'd have, or I'd ever have. And it was you who made it happen. That took a lot of courage, Andrea, because, well, I'm not exactly the guy next door. Anyway, I'm very proud of you."

She stared at the small case in her hand. "Rick, what is this?"

"Open it," he said breathlessly.

Andrea opened the case, turning white with surprise.

Drizzle splashed over the diamond, but still it sparkled in the floodlights.

"It's an engagement ring," he said, as if it could be something else. "I never thought I'd be buying one. I love you, Andrea, and I want you to marry me." He smiled with sincere joy, quite proud of himself, then added: "Please."

She was shaking; shaking her head. Tears were falling from her beautiful brown eyes and mixing with the raindrops. In his innocence and his love he at first believed she was shaking her head out of disbelief. Crying with joy. But when she finally pulled her watery eyes from the ring and lifted her flawless face to his faceless mask he knew the answer.

"I never expected this, Rick," she said slowly, almost pleading to be understood. "It's a shock to me. I'd never dreamed of marriage. The way we have it now is . . . is so great. You turned out to be such a wonderful man. Rick, you know I'm so fond of you, so admiring of your talents and how you've ordered your life. But . . ." She sobbed again, put her arms around his neck and hugged him. "Rick, listen to me. I may be in love with you. I'm still not sure." Andrea released him from her grasp and stole another peek at the diamond. "And part of it may be that I don't think I have the courage to live my life with a man who . . . well, who's not exactly the guy next door. I'm so very sorry." She handed back the ring, still apologizing. "I thought our deep friendship with each other would somehow always be just that. Now I don't know what to think. At least give me time to figure out my heart. I'm just not ready for this now. I'm sorry, Rick."

Rick Beanblossom took the ring back and stared over her shoulder at the flooding river, wide and mean and filthy brown. He searched the small town where he was born and raised, as if the answers to all of life's riddles could still be found there. Water blurred his vision. All of his adult life he had moved through society with a mask to hide his face and his feelings, and as humiliating as that had often been, no incident could compare to the rejection of his marriage proposal. Never in his life had he felt so foolish, so weak, so goddamn small. "It's . . . ah

. . . o-okay." He was stuttering. "Was . . . a-a long shot."
He pocketed the ring. "Re—refundable," he tried to joke.

Andrea wiped the drizzle from her face and gazed
across the water. "You are in my heart, I can tell you that
now. Maybe we can talk some more after the river goes
down. I'm so sorry, Rick. This is all my fault."

She left it at that and he watched her go, watched her
wade through the water beneath the yellow floodlights
and up the hill to the news van with the big 7 pasted on
the door. He watched them drive away. The taillights disappeared in the rain, just the blinking orange lights of
detour signs scattered beneath the bluffs.

The Marine again pulled the velvet case from his fatigue jacket and removed the ring. Every day since Vietnam had been a struggle for survival. His creed was to
live one more day and make it a good one. Now he
wanted to die. Rick Beanblossom pulled his hand back
and flung the diamond engagement ring into the angry
waters of the St. Croix River. And the largest flood in
Minnesota history began losing its punch.

The flood is the river's way of cleansing itself. Every two
decades or so the river regurgitates and throws back
ashore everything man has dumped into it over the years.
In Stillwater, no sooner had the flood waters receded to a
safe level than the sandbags came down and the cleanup
began. Volunteer workers along the banks of the St. Croix
River discovered tons of garbage among the stinking mud
and goo. They found motor parts, sunken boats, and
splintered canoes. They found the rusted body of a
Volkswagen Beetle. They came upon a diamond ring.
And twenty miles downriver, on a rocky shore just above
Prescott, Wisconsin, they found the almost totally decom-
posed body of Harlan Wakefield.

THE CROSS

Rick Beanblossom steered his new Corvette up the cloverleaf and headed north on Interstate 694. His bronze shaving kit was on the seat beside him. Bright arc lights stretched through eastern suburbs that were overdevelopment nightmares—little boxes made out of ticky-tacky with names like Woodbury and Oakdale and Maplewood. Traffic was light but potholes were many. Winter had taken its toll on the roads. He turned up the heater a notch, searching right up to the end for the perfect temperature.

To the masked newsman it was no longer a question of why; it was a question of why not. He looked down the road and all he saw was more of the same. Faceless grief. Another murder, another kidnapping, another crooked politician. A life alone chasing the miseries and the venalities of others. It was the emptiest of feelings. All bitterness was gone, as was anger, and revenge—the human emotions worth living for. Now he was left truly a shell. Hollow inside. Everybody who talked to him sounded like a distant echo. He heard the words but couldn't make out the meaning. A cowardly feeling hung over him. Nothing seemed of interest. Not even news. His heart was reading empty.

As he drove the freeway he tried to concentrate on the story that had occupied his mind and his time for so many months. Dixon Bell was the Edina rapist, had to be, but he was not the serial killer. But did Dixon Bell really confess to the Edina rapes? *"I never hurt any of them women. And I sure as hell didn't kill anyone."* Dixon Bell was the Edina rapist and unexpectedly ran into Officer Sumter. Killed her.

Beanblossom theory number two: Andy Mack was the serial killer, killing to set up Dixon Bell. He was the one who before each murder threatened the man who took his job, the threats Bell told him about. *"I'm gonna ice you, Weatherman."* The same damn threat was found on Andy's computer after he died. A form of confession? He knew Minnesota's weather. In the end he was a bitter old drunk.

Theory number three: Jack Napoleon was the serial killer. The murders had begun shortly after he arrived in the Twin Cities. He was from Chicago, had a feel for midwestern weather. He majored in physics, knew meteorology. He knew the weather center operation. He thought women were the ultimate sin. He may have thought Dixon Bell was the devil on earth.

And theory number four: none of them was the serial killer. The killer was still out there. Or the murders were unrelated. Copycat crimes. The killers were running free. Except that the killings had stopped. And what of that fingerprint? No matter how Rick added and subtracted, it kept coming back to the Weatherman. Dixon Bell was the Edina rapist and the serial killer. Dixon Bell did everything but kidnap the Wakefield boy. Hell, maybe he did that too.

The autopsy results on Harlan Wakefield were inconclusive due to the decomposition of the body. Medical examiner's best guess—the boy genius had died of a gunshot wound to the throat area. In his prime Rick would have been down at the morgue pumping Freddie for every last detail, examining the body himself. As it was, he just made one last phone call to a police source.

"Were there any tire tracks found at the kidnap scene?"

"Just the bicycles—no sign of a car was ever found."

"Who questioned his twin, Keenan? He never talked to the press?"

"The sheriff took a statement. The FBI interviewed him the next day. His parents took over the show after that. Wouldn't let anybody near him. He was put under the care of a child psychologist."

His source got Rick the transcripts of the two interviews. But Rick found nothing. The same source refused to part with the dirt he had on the governor. Not without the missing letters.

"Give it up, Masked Man. You've spent your whole life fighting lost causes."

As he sped down the freeway that looped the east metro, his blue cotton face kept dropping down over the steering wheel as he tried to shake all the demons out of his head. News, alcohol, drugs, J. C. Peters and his I Witness News team fornicating right before his eyes—none of them worked for him anymore. Highs were a thing of the past. That morning another manuscript had come back in the mail. Another rejection slip. Rick Beanblossom would never be the novelist he dreamed of being, would never solve the Wakefield kidnapping or clear the Weatherman, would never get the girl. He was past forty now. His face was the scum on the rim of a whirlpool bath. His youth was spent. On what he had picked as the last night of his life he accepted all of this. He stepped on the gas.

It was unexpectedly cold. There hadn't been an accurate forecast broadcast in Minnesota since Dixon Bell went off to jail. Rick turned up the heater another notch. Headlights sped by in the opposite direction. Red taillights disappeared in his rearview mirror. A firefight where nobody gets hit. Up ahead was a billboard, its blinding lights shining down on him. Ron Shea and Andrea Labore stood ten feet tall, their Chiclet teeth smiling over commuters, their names boldly printed beneath a giant 7. THE NEW SKY HIGH NEWS. The Marine shook his head. If only Splat Man were for hire.

What a fool he had been. What a big, fucking fool! To believe that a woman of her beauty and charm would marry a hideous beast like him, as if there were some magic rose that could break the evil curse and return to him his princely looks. Every woman fantasizes about sex with a stranger in a mask. Perhaps that's all he was to Andrea Labore. The anonymous fuck. Some sick fantasy come to fruition. When all was dead and done, the Weatherman would have the last laugh.

As Rick passed beneath the bright lights of the billboard, he reached over and flipped open the bronze shaving kit and checked his stash one more time.

Just stop it.

After all those years he could still hear the angel from Corpus Christi trying to pull him through. *"Whenever your hurt and frustration start to get the best of you, you just gotta say, 'Just stop it.' "*

Rick Beanblossom left the Channel 7 billboard behind him and caught Highway 36 east out of the Cities, through the woods of Lake Elmo, where Bob Buckridge and Kitt Karson had crashed and died. East towards Stillwater. Towards the river that cut through the valley where his life had begun.

On the night Rick Beanblossom drove past her face on the interstate, Andrea Labore was having the fight of her life in the governor's office in St. Paul. She stood in front of the bullet-proof window, rubbing her arms before the green-tinted glass. Crimson and gold curtains hung to the sides. "It's freezing in here. I thought winter was over with."

"Why are women always complaining?" The Viking governor plopped behind his desk between the American flag and the navy blue state of Minnesota. He buried his head in his hands in frustration. "They know!"

The holler startled her. "They know what?"

"You were followed or something."

"What are you talking about?"

Per Ellefson leaned back in his chair and shook his head in resignation. A burden shared. "Smith Jameson and his right-wing gang in the party . . . they know about the abortion. They've got a copy of that check I wrote you, and they've got records from the clinic. I told you to go out of state."

Andrea walked from the window and took a seat in an antique chair, as uncomfortable as a rock. "How long have you known this?"

"From the start." He choked on his guilt. "Why do you think I signed their precious death penalty bill? They promised me you'd be kept out of it."

"What if the Democrats find out about it?"

The governor tossed off a cold laugh. "Democrats are wimps. They're the least of my worries. This is a party fight."

Andrea wasn't listening. The fatal possibilities were running through her mind. Her career? His career? "And if Dixon Bell is found guilty and sentenced to death?" she asked.

Per Ellefson stared at the electronic weather station on his desk. The temperature was nearing the freezing mark. "That's not going to happen. Every criminal lawyer I've spoken with tells me the same thing . . . They may have enough for a conviction, but there's two parts to that trial. They don't have enough for a death sentence. Not with a Minnesota jury they don't."

Andrea laughed bitterly. "I think you're living in a dream world. The sun set on that state years ago."

The governor got up from his chair and walked around the desk to Andrea's side. The abortion revelation had blown the steam out of their fight. "Even if they vote the chair, it's a couple of years down the road with the appeals. We're in this together, Andrea. My re-election chances are good, and you're sitting in the anchor chair."

"So what are you saying?"

He stroked her hair. "That we stick together. I want to start seeing you again."

She bolted from the chair, back to the safety of the window and the flags. "No, absolutely not."

"Are you dating someone? There are rumors."

"No, I'm not dating someone." Andrea looked out at the Capitol mall, dark and deserted. Barren sidewalks rolled over lifeless grass thick with thatch. Winter weather. Only the snow was missing.

The governor came up behind her and took hold of her shoulders. "I may be turning into the very politician I came here to replace, but this politician is still in love with you. And you're in love with me. Tell me you're not."

Andrea Labore remained silent.

He smiled a cocky smile at her lack of response. "You're like a lot of women—the worse we get, the more you love us." The governor grabbed the embroidered gold trim of the state flag and wrapped it around them both. "Let's do it in the flag. I'll be the Star of the North."

Andrea struggled free of the flag, free of his arms. She walked over to a big brown sofa, equally uncomfortable. She rested on it, her face buried in her hands.

He was coming her way. "I just want to hold you," he

said, taking a seat beside her. Playing with her hair. Rubbing her leg. Kissing her cheek and neck.

Per Ellefson was good, and Andrea hated herself for enjoying it. But she'd come too far to slip back into the arms of the biggest mistake of her life. Another man was on her mind. She put a hand over his mouth. "Please stop it."

Per Ellefson kissed her hand and slipped into his most seductive voice, his smooth I-get-what-I-want voice. He stroked her hair so hard it was almost an embrace. He placed his other hand over her breast. "I've always wanted to do it to you in your wedding dress. Will you call me on the day you get married?" The governor kissed her ear. "Remember the Christmas Eve we did it in the mansion? Santa Claus was never so good to me."

Andrea stood to leave, but he forced her back to the sofa and laid his strong Nordic body across her slender figure. "You've been getting it somewhere, haven't you? Who is he?"

"Are you going to rape me now?" she mockingly asked him.

"You'd like that, wouldn't you? You fuckin' women are all the same." He threw her to the floor and stormed back to his desk, his seat of power.

She got to her knees, realizing at last what a cheap relationship it had been. "How many of us fuckin' women have you had since you married?"

The governor laughed, a mean laugh. "Marriage makes women look so plain." His back was to her as he got up and moved to the wall. "I know what turns you on." He opened an oaken armoire. Inside was a television set. He turned it on, found CNN. "Go ahead, masturbate. I'll watch during the commercials."

Andrea got up off the floor. She brushed the wrinkles from her clothes, her back to him and the television set. "You're sick," she told him, walking out of the governor's office for the last time. "I can't believe the people of Minnesota would elect you to anything."

"There was a day they wouldn't have," Per Ellefson yelled after her. "But like you said, the sun has set on that state."

On what he took to be the last night of his life Rick Beanblossom drove Highway 95 north out of Stillwater. He followed the pines that followed the river, over the sheer cliffs and into the woods. At Arcola Trail he cut off the highway and drove down the blacktop until it came to an end. An old logging road parted the hills. The sky was black and filled with stars, but there appeared to be lightning in the north. Years had passed since he'd been down this dirt road. A few executive homes had been wedged into the hillsides, but the sylvan terrain remained largely unspoiled. A trio of deer leaped through the light beams. He kept an eye out for Chief Fallen Rock. Then the road dropped under the railroad tracks. Rick pulled over, parking the dusty Corvette among the trees.

Up the footpath and onto the tracks. Shale rock crunched under his feet. Empty beer cans lined the rails. The night was desolate and spooky. The temperature continued to fall. Pines and firs waited impatiently for the aspen, the birch, and the elms to spring their leaves. Every now and then a strange sound broke through the stillness, creating an eerie feeling in his bones, that feeling that follows everybody in a walk through the dark woods, the feeling he was being watched. Rick buttoned his Marine fatigue jacket up to his neck and continued walking the deserted railroad tracks. Then, upon seeing what he came for, those eerie feelings vanished. It was still there. The old Soo Line Bridge stretched across the valley.

In its day the trains barreled out of the Minnesota pines, roared across the half-mile of single track two hundred feet above the St. Croix River, and then disappeared into the rolling hills of Wisconsin. That's what the Soo Line had built the bridge for, but over the years the five-span steel marvel got used for so much more. It was photographed and painted. It was ogled by boaters below and tramped across by adventurers above. All of the threatening signs in two states couldn't keep people off the bridge. No cliff or ridge in the valley possessed its mystique, or its view.

The high-school kid with the low draft number had a going-away party on this rickety bridge. The trains were running then. The boys would stand between the rails atop the center span, beer in hand, and wait for the blinding light of the locomotive to pop out of the woods and

bear down on them. Then they were off and running, trying to beat the train across the wide expanse, the engineer
cursing them from his cab as they jumped to safety one
railroad tie ahead of death. What fools! What fun! He
made love to a girl that night on the forest floor. Then
back up to the bridge he came to be with his buddies,
their butts on the wooden planks, their arms draped pre-
cariously across the pipe railing, their feet dangling over
the water. Just the guys. Drinking and talking into the
night; talking of college and war, of girls, cars, and football. Drunkenly discussing the existence of God.

Kids still had parties here, but the trains didn't run anymore. Rick Beanblossom stepped out onto the abandoned
bridge and followed the rusted rails to the center span. He
was as high as a man could get in the St. Croix Valley. No
railing bordered the north side of the tracks. The railing
along the narrow walkway on the south side was danger-
ously loose. It was not a bridge for the faint of heart. On
a Wisconsin hilltop above him the blinking white lights of
a transmitting antenna picked up news, weather, and
sports from the Cities and relayed them to the farmland
beyond. Beneath him the silhouette of an owl soared over
the pernicious river and rested on a treetop. But for a stiff
breeze down from the north, it was a silent night. Clear
and cold. As quiet as quiet gets in the out-of-doors.

It wasn't until he reached the heart of the bridge between the cliffs and turned his attention northward that
Rick realized that it wasn't lightning he had seen in the
sky on his drive up. It was the aurora borealis. The northern lights. A sight rarely witnessed in the Cities. A forest
fire in the sky. Flaming auroras arced the northern sky
from horizon to zenith, luminous streamers of greens and
blues and whites dancing over the polar ice caps. A rainbow ballet. Silent artillery. A prismatic firefight. Every
now and then a dramatic burst of crimson or pink would
send shivers up his spine. Brilliant beyond belief. The
Weatherman had explained this awesome phenomenon
one night on the news, something about solar flares on
the sun and the magnetic poles of the earth. But faced
with such spectacular fireworks, who needed an explanation?

The Marine sat down on the oily planks of the
walkway and leaned his back against a railing pipe, his

tortured face to the towering light show in the north, his back to the south. There may have been better places to end his life, but few more poignant or spectacular.

Just stop it.

He heard Angel's voice again. And this time he smiled to himself. But the man in the mask couldn't stop it. He couldn't make the hurt go away. His teeth were chattering so loud they seemed to echo through the valley's stillness.

When he was a little boy he'd ride along with his father in the old Nash Rambler as they traversed the roads and highways of the valley. Signs along the way read: WATCH OUT FOR FALLEN ROCK. Fallen Rock was an Indian Chief, his father had told him. He went into the woods one day to find food for his cold and hungry people and never came back. The tribe was lost without their bold and noble leader, so they posted those signs along the road. The little boy kept his sweet face pressed to the glass, believing every word of it. On the last night of his life it was these precious childhood memories that came floating down the river and back into his mind.

Rick Beanblossom pulled the Navy Cross from his jacket pocket and held it before him. *"Tac air! Cover! Cover!"* Shaking, he draped the honor around his neck. A hypodermic needle came out of his pocket. He removed a chunk of styrofoam from the tip and held the milky poison up to the northern lights shimmering in the sky. Enough pure heroin to kill a platoon—but what a way to go. So what's the last thought a man has before he leaves this world? He thinks of a woman he loved a long time ago. "I'm sorry, Angel."

The master sergeant hummed the Marine Corps Hymn as he rolled his sleeves over his elbow, choking his veins. During the last stanza he stuck the needle into his arm and sent the boys into battle. It was the last needle Rick Beanblossom would ever pop into his skin. When the job was done, he tossed the needle over the edge and imagined it spinning through the frosty air before hitting the receding river below and sinking point-first into the clay bottom.

Suddenly he was freezing. This dying business was cold. The veteran of Vietnam, the veteran of a hundred battles fought in city newsrooms, curled into the fetal position and laid his masked head down on the cold, oily planks that ran along the rails. The cross around his neck slipped over the side. Dangled from the bridge. Swayed in the north wind. Reflected the crazy dance of the northern lights. He closed his eyes to the powwow in the sky. It got so quiet the only sound he could hear was the lullaby of the golden river on its way to Stillwater. Then the Marine dropped into a deep, deep sleep. And the valley temperature dropped right along with him.

"All squads, effective immediately we'll be going to a two-channel dispatch for the remainder of dog watch. All squads at two-fifteen."

Captain Les Angelbeck sat behind the wheel of a state squad car and watched in tears as the last photographs were snapped and the dead body was placed on a stretcher and loaded into the back of the ME van. The overnight photographers from the TV stations flooded the vehicle with klieg lights as it pulled away with a full police escort, red lights flashing in the crispy night air. The old cop tried to remember the last time he had talked with him. It was on the phone. What was said? Who was telling his family? He blew cigarette smoke at the frost on the windshield and choked on a cough. This was difficult. The killing of a police officer in Minnesota was rare.

It was unseasonably cold. The sky was cloudless, but there appeared to be lightning off to the north. The wind down from Alberta was sharp and icy. The mercury dipped below the freezing point, chilling his heart. That the dying police captain had outlived the young and lively lieutenant from Florida who loved the state but hated the weather sent pangs of guilt rippling up his crumbling spine. He stared through the smoky windshield at the horde of angry black faces gathered at the intersection of Plymouth and James Avenue North.

"Squads, do we have an Able car for the Hennepin Bridge? Eastbound, above the island, report of a DK pedestrian in traffic."

Lieutenant Donnell Redmond had just left the Fourth Precinct in North Minneapolis when he spotted him. He was wearing high-top athletic shoes so new and so white it looked like a pair of feet trotting down Plymouth Avenue. The North Side rapist? Redmond had a hunch. He pulled the unmarked squad to the curb. He was feeling good about himself. His testimony at the Weatherman's trial was considered exemplary. There was talk of promotion.

This inner-city rapist never garnered the media coverage the white-ass rapist in Edina was able to generate, but he had police puzzled for a year. A young black man was preying on black women in their homes in the neighborhood around North High School. He came through open bedroom windows, unlocked back doors, and twice he barreled right through the front door. He was described as being of medium height and build with very dark skin. His trademark—he always wore new athletic shoes so white that's all some of his victims could see while being assaulted. Cops called it the case of the horny sneakers.

Redmond was out of the car. "Yo, bro, hold up there."

The suspect stopped and turned, both hands stuffed into a black baseball jacket that said sox, only the sox had been inked over. "Watcha want, man?"

Redmond flashed his badge. The suspect had dark skin and he was the right size. "Awful cold night for a stroll, ain't it?"

"Just got offa work. Goin' home. Why you harassin' me?" The jive talk sounded scripted, probably learned by rote at gang meetings.

"What work you coming from and what home you going to?" Redmond was in his face now, his hands on his hips. The big lieutenant wanted nothing more than to get into his warm squad car, go home to his warm wife, and crawl into their warm bed. Past midnight now, it had been a long day. But at the very least he was going to get a positive ID out of this man with the costly new shoes.

"Squad ten-fifteen is requesting more help at Plymouth and Emerson. Who's there now? Ten-four. We'll call State Patrol."

It was the difference between Minneapolis and St. Paul. In St. Paul blacks cheered and generally cooperated when police arrived on the scene. In Minneapolis blacks grew to riot proportions at the sight of flashing red lights. Les Angelbeck could never figure out how a river could put so much distance between two cities. The old police captain watched as the Minneapolis officers tried to get

statements. Nobody was talking. Everybody was yelling.
A large white-and-orange ambulance was parked outside
the perimeter. Prostitutes worked the busy corner like
flies, uninhibited by the weather or the law. It was that
kind of neighborhood.

By New York or Los Angeles standards the area was
probably respectable. But by Minneapolis standards
North Minneapolis was as bad as it gets, a predomi-
nantly black, low-income, no-income, high-crime, drug-
trafficking area squeezed between freeways leading out of
town. Urban renewal had been there and gone, along with
every other social experiment the government had to offer. It was once the proud domain of the postwar working
stiff. Now whole blocks of new housing had been built in
North Minneapolis to look like town homes, with colonial
and Victorian facades and splashes of the popular midwestern Queen Anne style. Architecture comes to the
poor. But in reality it was nothing but a plywood slum.
The projects. Fresh paint on old problems.

Squads from the housing patrol tried to keep the angry
crowd on the curbs and off the streets. Les Angelbeck
sucked cigarette smoke into his rotting lungs. The river
between blacks and whites was so wide maybe it could
never be bridged—not even in Minnesota.

*"Squad four-ten, make twenty-three-seventeen Fremont
on a domestic dispute. She's got a restraining order . . .
he's there."*

The inner cities had become a darker version of the Old
West. Instead of white, the gunfighters were usually
black. Instead of facing each other in the middle of the
street, they faced each other toe to toe on cracked sidewalks. The guns, smaller and deadlier, didn't hang from
the hip; they were hidden in jacket pockets, tucked into a
holster, slid beneath a belt. Donnell Redmond waited for
answers to his questions. "Where you from? You from
Gary? Chicago? East St. Louie? You ain't from around
here."

The White Sox fan, probably a gang member, maybe a
rapist, looked about to run. He was shivering up a storm.
Redmond's police instincts told him to go for his gun before the suspect went for his. But it was too late. The
magnum force came out of the Sox jacket so fast he saw
only the exploding flashes, heard the roaring thunder,

then felt the body blows to his midsection. In the end there were four shots fired. Lieutenant Donnell Redmond only got off one of them. The last thing the tall cop saw as he fell that cold night was the pair of horny sneakers stumbling down Plymouth Avenue. Somebody was crying, "I been shot," but he couldn't tell who. It may have been himself.

"Three-ten Able. Twelfth and Queen. See the yellow cab there on a no pay."

The shooter was found dead on North Emerson, four blocks away. There was a big handprint on his shiny white sneakers where his last gesture on this earth was a feeble attempt to wipe away the specks of blood.

The mob in the street didn't know exactly who was dead or why, but their inner-city instincts told them a cop had shot a black man. Black leaders were already shouting warnings into the TV cameras. They could sort out the details in the morning. Tonight they were promising the revolution.

Les Angelbeck rolled his window down and flicked the cigarette butt into the street. The biting north wind blew the last sparks into the crowd. They were beginning to disperse, retreating to their subsidized housing. It was too cold to protest. The revolution would have to wait until summer.

One by one the muddy white squad cars of the Minneapolis Police Department began to pull away. So did the State Patrol and the housing authority. When the news photographers saw that the cops were leaving, they too packed up their vans and got the hell out of there. Yellow tape was left strung from tree to tree, as was the chalk outline of a tall man curled up on frozen grass beneath bare trees. Tomorrow the TV reporters would stand in front of the spot and reduce the man's life to one minute and thirty seconds. The old cop turned up the heater to fend off the cold. He dropped the squad into drive, wiped an angry tear from the corner of his good eye, and rolled away.

"All squads, Lieutenant Donnell Redmond of the Minneapolis Bureau of Criminal Apprehension was killed in the line of duty tonight in our city. Lieutenant Redmond leaves behind a wife and three children. Funeral arrange-

*ments will be announced. See your supervisor for burial
duties. All squads at two-fifty-eight."*

Anatomy of a television news story:

Begin with a brown-haired, brown-eyed beauty in her
mid-twenties. Her name is Melissa. Or Alyssa. Or let's
call her Tricia. She earns nineteen thousand dollars a year
on a two-year contract. When her contract is up and she
asks for a raise she'll be television history. She begins her
story with a live shot, standing in front of a hospital
emergency entrance talking at the camera. It is nighttime.
An ambulance can be seen behind her. "Well, Brad, it
seems our friends up at Channel 7 make as much news
these days as they report. This is the remarkable story of
an award-winning reporter and Vietnam veteran apparently determined to commit suicide. But fate intervened."
Tricia the TV reporter glances down at her portable monitor.

Flash to a grainy black-and-white photograph of Rick
Beanblossom at work in the *Star Tribune* newsroom on
the day he was awarded the Pulitzer Prize for investigative reporting. The photo was snapped from a distance
because he refused to have his picture taken. Tricia's
voice was recorded over a slow zoom of the photograph.
"Rick Beanblossom is a burn victim who can often be
seen around town in his trademark blue pullover mask.
Four years ago he left his job at the *Star Tribune* and took
a news producer's job at Channel 7. Newsroom co-
workers say he wrestled with bouts of depression, and
severe headaches for which he took prescription painkillers."

Go to tape of the St. Croix Valley. Camera pans the
width of the Soo Line Bridge. Tricia is still blabbing
away. "Last night the news producer, a highly decorated
veteran of the Vietnam War, came to this abandoned railroad bridge over the St. Croix River, apparently determined to take his own life."

Throw in a sound bite from a sheriff's deputy, not to
exceed ten seconds.

*"From the needle kit found in his car, it appears he
shot a large amount of heroin into his arm and laid down
to die. He had no other reason to be up there."*

Back to scenic shots of the St. Croix River. Tricia talking. "But what the ex-marine didn't know was that last night we were headed for record low temperatures for this time of the year. He also couldn't know two canoeists would be paddling beneath the bridge at the crack of dawn."

Cut to sound bite of canoeist pointing up at the bridge. This bite most important; it can run fifteen seconds.

"We were on the river watching the sun coming up . . . It was really bright and it felt good because it was so cold. Anyway, I saw this reflection off the bridge up there, like somebody signaling us with a mirror or something . . . so I climbed up there . . . and this guy with the mask was lying there . . . and I thought he was dead . . . and this cross around his neck was hanging over the bridge reflecting the sun. We never would have seen him up there if it hadn't been for that cross."

Go to tape of the cross displayed at the hospital. Tricia speaking over it. "That cross was the Navy Cross that Rick Beanblossom was awarded for saving the lives of his men during a napalm attack in Vietnam. An attack that cost him his face, and like last night, almost cost him his life."

Cut to a sound bite from the doctor at the hospital. Be sure to flash his name and title on the screen as he speaks. Give him five seconds.

"If it hadn't been for the cold, and being found so early this morning, he'd have died last night. Somebody up there is watching over him."

Next, Tricia the TV reporter does a fifteen-second stand-up atop the Soo Line Bridge, taped earlier in the day, talking into the camera as she walks with trepidation along the railroad tracks on the rickety span two hundred feet above the river, about the height of an eighteen-story building. It's scenic as a postcard, but she looks scared to death. The photographer made her do it. "Doctors say the record low temperatures last night slowed Beanblossom's heartbeat, thickened his blood, and prevented the overdose from killing him. But the Pulitzer Prize-winning newsman isn't out of the woods yet. He was rushed from this bridge near death to Lakeview Hospital in Stillwater—ironically, his hometown."

Master shot of the hospital, then a quick cut to a second sound bite from the doctor.

"Basically he's in a light coma ... but comas are still a medical mystery. He could be in it for days, or weeks. That much poison is a tremendous shock ... But his vital signs are strong."

Return to a live shot of Tricia standing in front of the emergency entrance at the hospital. "And Brad, the latest word from Lakeview here is more of the same. News producer Rick Beanblossom is still in a coma. Serious but stable condition. Back to you."

"Thank you, Tricia." At the studio the anchor turns to the anchorette. "Our prayers are with him tonight."

Anchorette nods her head in sympathy. "I'll say, he's a good one."

Anchor turns to camera two. "By the way, we want to welcome Tricia to our news team. She's an award-winning reporter from station WTOL in Toledo, Ohio."

Anchorette nods her head in agreement. "We were really lucky to get her. We'll take a stab at tomorrow's weather next. Stay tuned."

"**M**aster Sergeant Beanblossom, I'm Lieutenant Russell. I know this is a torturous time for you, but the colored nurse, Angela, said you might be able to talk now."

"Yes. I c-can talk."

"What you did is a credit to the Marine Corps, son. Esprit de corps at its best. We're very proud of you. And don't you worry about your face. The burn unit at Fort Sam Houston is the best in the world. When you get back to the States they'll fix you up like new."

"Sem ... sem ... semper some shit."

"Semper fi. Always faithful. I understand. Part of my job, Master Sergeant, and it's not an easy job, is to log and classify casualties and MIAs. On the day you were wounded another Marine, who we know to have been Lance Corporal Robert Joseph Sax from Texarkana, Arkansas, was killed in action. He was the third Marine you tried to rescue that day. Do you remember?"

"Hard day to for ... forget."

"We don't want you to forget just yet. You see, after the napalm attack we were unable to retrieve the lance corporal's body. The truth of the matter is when we withdrew from that position there was really nothing left of him to retrieve. Do you understand? The thing of it is, Lance Corporal Sax for the past several months has been listed as missing in action, even though we know that he was killed. What we need from you is confirmation of his death. We'd like to give his family the peace of mind they deserve. For the record, Master Sergeant Beanblossom, was it Lance Corporal Sax you tried to rescue that day? And was he dead?"

"Nnnn . . . no. Was not him."

"But it had to be him. He was the only Marine unaccounted for."

"Ef . . . FNG."

"Excuse me, Master Sergeant, but there were no Fucking New Guys in your platoon that day."

"Was not Sax."

"I know what you're trying to do here. On the one hand, it's admirable. On the other hand, it's illegal as hell. You could be court-martialed."

"Nnnn . . . not Sax."

"You men have to stop doing this. These families have a right to know the fate of their men. Sax left a wife and two children. Don't do this to them."

"Was . . . not Sax. Ef . . . FNG."

"All right for now, Master Sergeant Beanblossom. I'll give you to the end of the week to change your mind and tell me the truth. You'll have to sign some papers one way or the other. Yes, you're right. As long as he's classified missing in action the checks keep coming to his wife and children. Once he's declared dead, the checks stop. But I don't think that's worth a lifetime of anguish—the anguish of not knowing if and when he died. You think about that."

"As long as he's missing, the checks keep coming."

"As long as he's missing, the checks keep coming."

"As long as he's missing, the checks keep coming."

Rick Beanblossom came out of his coma with a scream, sweat dripping down his chest. The sheets were soaked. He tripped getting out of bed and fell to the floor heaving from the gut. The IV needles were ripped from his arm.

A nurse was over him shouting, "Get the doctor! He's back!"

The Marine came to his knees, covered his bare head as if in an air raid, and tried to bury his face in the linoleum. "You lying little son of a bitch!" he cried out. "You lying little son of a bitch!"

THE TWINS

It was a wonderful spring day. The rains had stopped. The sun fired the sky. Minnesota's rivers had receded to livable levels. Lilacs and apple blossoms were in bloom. Trees were outlined in soft spring green. The fresh air smelled of new beginnings. It was the kind of day where a boy rides his bicycle through the gathering sun after school without a worry in the world. Such was the feeling Keenan Wakefield enjoyed as he rode his mountain bike over the ridge and followed his favorite paved path into the woods north of Stillwater.

He was sixteen now and completing his second year of college. Already his parents were talking about Oxford and Harvard Law. Four years had passed since his brother's disappearance. At that age four years is an eternity. By the time they laid Harlan's remains to rest it was hard for Keenan to remember he even had a brother, much less a twin. The publicity briefly flared up again, but soon died out as the case of Harlan Wakefield went from unsolved mystery to just another unresolved death. But still Keenan's trust fund grew. The checks kept coming. As he pedaled swiftly through the trees he knew the finest education money could buy was within his grasp.

For four years, since the widely reported kidnapping of Harlan Wakefield, it had been the worst nightmare of every child in the Upper Midwest. While the child is out playing, a man in a mask emerges from the woods with a gun in his hand. On this sunny day, as he steered his bicycle through the darkest acres of woodland, that nightmare became instant reality for Keenan Wakefield. A man in a blue pullover mask stepped out of the woods with a large pistol in his hand and pointed it into the air. Keenan, scared out of his wits, swerved to miss the man in the mask. He lost control of his bike and tumbled into the woods. He rolled over on his back. The man in the mask was coming at him, gun in hand. It was a big, ugly hand-gun, black and green and caked with dry mud. Keenan froze, at first too frightened to cry out for help. The masked gunman grabbed him by the shirt and stuck his black leather nose up against his face. "Hi, kid. Remember me?"

Keenan gulped until he choked. His face broke out in a sweat.

The man's eyes were on fire. "Me and you are going to go into the woods and I'm going to do to you want I did to your brother, Harlan."

Keenan squirmed and kicked in a half-assed attempt to get free. He finally got up the courage to speak. "I know who you are. You're that burned guy from Channel 7."

Keenan Wakefield again tried to squirm away. Again the man with the gun pulled the kid's face into his mask. "I've got a friend who is a policeman and he says the FBI wants to talk to you, but Mommy won't let them. Why is that?"

"You people are supposed to leave me alone."

The masked gunman picked the boy up by the shirt and dragged him into the woods. He threw him down on the forest floor. "Do you know how reporters used to get sto-ries in the old days? When somebody wouldn't talk they'd send some boys from the dock over to slap him around. My kind of journalism." He wound up and kicked the boy in the ass. "Where did you go that morning?"

Keenan began crying. "We were delivering papers."

"No—the morning after that."

"I went to look for Harlan."

"Why didn't you go look where he was taken? You were a mile away, down by the river. Why?"

"I thought the kidnapper might have driven him to the river." The boy kept trying to get to his feet, but the man in the mask kept kicking him down.

"I looked at the tape of you coming out of the woods that morning. There's no road to the river anyway near that spot."

"Yes there is."

"I grew up here, kid. I had a bicycle too. I know every

street, every path, and where every dirt road goes. So don't bullshit me, you lying little son of a bitch! Where did you get the gun?"

Keenan wrapped his arms around a tree trunk for protection. "What gun?"

The madman in the mask was kicking at the tree, as if he could fell it with his feet. He shoved the rusty pistol into the boy's face. "This gun! The gun a scuba diver my station hired pulled out of the river yesterday. The gun you and your brother were playing with that morning. The gun that went off and killed Harlan. The gun you threw into the river along with your twin brother."

The boy stopped his struggling and collapsed on the ground. He covered his face with his hands and cried like a baby. "We stole it from a car on a farm."

Rick Beanblossom stood over the broken boy with the freakish intellect. The Marine was physically and mentally exhausted, still weak from the overdose. But, boy, did he feel alive. Sunshine filtered through the trees and the golden light fell across his wide shoulders. He wrestled his temper under control, now sure of the truth that eluded him for four years. "So you carried your brother's body halfway to the river and hid him in the woods, and the next morning you got up early and dragged him the rest of the way before search teams could find him?"

Keenan Wakefield was blubbering between the sobs. "Are you going to put this on television and tell everybody?"

"If it was an accident, why didn't you just tell? Or did you really think you were that smart?"

"It was your fault. You guys wouldn't let me. You made such a big deal out of it, I couldn't tell."

The last angry journalist remembered all of the hype, the endless media coverage, the countless Harlan Wakefield publicity spectacles, stories he himself had written and produced. A file three inches thick. On a slow news day they could always revisit the Wakefield case. A body would be mourned. Buried and forgotten. But as long as he was missing, it was news. And the checks and the sympathy kept on coming.

"Tell me this, college boy—did Mommy and Daddy know?"

THE TESTIMONY

Andrea Labore moved with grace briskly through the crowded atrium of the Hennepin County Government Center, thick with media people. The bright morning sun was streaming through the tall, glassy design. News photographers were not allowed up into the courts, so they had to stake out the lobby area, watch the elevators, the entrance, and the exits. One of the photogs shouted after her, "Good story, Andrea. Way to go."

The two banks of elevators were jammed with a waiting throng of county workers, lawyers, cops, and reporters. Just when Andrea thought she'd have to wait for the next lift to the sixth floor she was recognized. A couple of male lawyers gladly held the elevator door for her, and nobody objected to riding up to court with the newly crowned queen of the evening news.

The hallways on the sixth floor were as overloaded as the elevators. Even those who knew that the chances of getting a seat were hopeless wanted to be there. Andrea pushed through the rabble, and those big brown recognizable eyes did as much to clear the way as did her press pass.

"You did a wonderful job on that Wakefield piece, Andrea."

"Don't be ridiculous. I just voiced it."

At the door to Courtroom 659 a male deputy, who of course knew that face, still checked her pass. A female deputy searched her purse. Then she passed through a metal detector and into the courtroom.

Folding chairs had been added along with extra deputies. A cameraman and sound man were double-checking the television equipment. Reporters were leaning over the front railing as eager as children at a circus. But Andrea knew the man she was searching for wouldn't be up front, he'd be in the back. And that's where she found him—in the corner chair leaning against the wall. The seat next to him was one of the few still unoccupied. Her colleagues stood and smiled as she apologetically slid past each one of them.

"Andrea, you did a really good stand-up on that Wakefield story."

"No, it was Rick's story all the way."

Andrea Labore slipped into the open seat next to Rick Beanblossom.

His arms were folded. He stared straight ahead, wearing the mask of his usual expression. Then a large woman in a military uniform passed through the metal detector and hunted for a seat. Rick turned and watched her squeeze her fat butt into a chair on the other side of the aisle. It was Dr. Freda Wilhelm, the Ramsey County medical examiner. Andrea remembered her well from her trip to the morgue, had wanted to do a story on her, but Freddie the gossip hound had backed out at the last minute.

The courtroom was packed. The doors were closed. Disappointed moans could be heard from the hallway. Anxiety was high. Andrea leaned just far enough to her right so that her shoulder rubbed up against Rick's shoulder. She thought he leaned an inch her way. Warring feelings passed through her body, through her mind—warmth, shame, pride, love. In the midst of these feelings she wanted desperately to hold his hand. Then she relaxed a bit, seated beside the familiar and the comfortable. Despite the crowd Andrea Labore had a clear view of the witness stand. She watched with more interest than most when Dixon Bell raised his hand and swore to tell the truth, the whole truth, and nothing but the truth.

It was so quiet in the courtroom Dixon Bell could hear people breathing. The ceiling lights seemed brighter from the witness stand. The lone television camera was aimed at his head with the accuracy of a high-powered rifle. The multitude of faces in the gallery seemed a blur, their collective gaze more curious than hostile. He could barely make out the man in the mask in the back of the room, but he couldn't see who was sitting beside him.

Stacy Dvorchak was dressed in a black suit and a bright pink blouse. She looked as pert as she did professional. She would begin her questioning low-keyed from the defense table. "No theatrics," she had warned him. "This isn't television. This is law."

Prosecutor Jim Fury and his two assistants armed themselves with pens and white legal pads. Judge Lutoslawski folded his hands as if beginning a prayer. The faces in the jury box seemed open and concerned. Whatever he may have said and done earlier, whatever they may have heard, they now seemed genuinely willing to give him his day in court.

Dixon Bell stared at the silver microphone in front of his face. The tired cliché "electricity in the air" never seemed more apt. When he finally opened his mouth to testify, he tried to speak as intimately as was humanly possible. His rich southern tones wafted through the courtroom. The Weatherman spoke for three days.

Day one. Monday, the first day of May. The morning temperature was nearing 70 degrees. Barometric pressure was 30.01 inches and on the rise. The sun was in full force. A soft southerly breeze was up from Missouri—all and all, a great spring day. But Dixon Bell couldn't see or feel the encouraging weather. Courtroom 659 had no windows. His strength came from the sky. He felt naked and weak without windows.

"What's it like to work in television news?" Stacy asked him.

"We would go on the air at five o'clock with the evening news and by seven minutes after five the newsroom telephones were ringing with people calling in who didn't like a story they had just seen. And the phones would go on ringing for an hour. We called it the stupid hour. Seven days a week, three hundred and sixty-five days a year, viewers called us to complain about what they just saw on the news. No matter what story we did, no matter how we did it. What other business has to put up with that? And on a bad weather day, who do you think took the brunt of the calls? Every year during the first snowfall, whether it was in October or December, five hundred people would call me on the phone to tell me that it was snowing."

Jim Fury stood to object. "Your Honor, I fail to see the relevance of this diatribe on television news."

"I will allow it, Counsel. Overruled."

Stacy continued from the defense table. "So you often received angry calls?"

"Yes, daily."

"Threatening calls?"

"Often."

"Do you remember any threatening calls in particular?"

"Yes, I do. One caller kept at it for nearly two years. He sounded strange, like maybe a feminine man, maybe even a woman, and he kind of tried to make it sound like a southern accent."

"How often would this person call you?"

"With every change of the seasons."

Prosecutor Jim Fury was on his feet again. "Your Honor, the state has to object here. The witness is framing his answers in almost poetic fashion."

Judge Lutoslawski came as close as he would come to losing his temper during the trial. "Mr. Fury, it is my job to see that this man is given a fair trial. It is not fair if you are constantly interrupting his testimony. I will not allow it. Take it up on cross-examine. Getting me good and mad is not going to help the state's case. Overruled." He nodded to Stacy. "I'm sorry, Counselor. Please continue."

"You said this person called you with every change of the seasons. And what would this person say to you?"

Dixon Bell could see that the long trial was wearing down even Judge Polack. The Weatherman seemed barely to hear Stacy's question. "Um, he always said, 'I'm gonna ice you, Weatherman.' "

"That's what he said to you?"

"Yes."

"And you got one of these warnings about the time of each of the seven murders you are charged with?"

"Yes. Yes, I did."

Jim Fury was ready to again leap from his chair, but thought better of it. He remained quiet throughout the rest of the morning testimony.

"Dixon, can you tell the jury how being on television affected your personal life?"

The Weatherman shook his head in resignation. He sighed. "Oh, boy, how do I relate it to y'all? You almost have to be in the public eye to know. I've been followed down the sidewalk. Chased down the freeway. Jumped in supermarkets. Cornered at ball games. They all want to talk about the weather, like that's all I think about twenty-four hours a day. Almost like they expect me to do something about it. Even with all that, the good far outweighed the bad, until I was arrested, of course. Then . . ."

After lunch Dixon Bell changed into a clean shirt. He had sweated through the morning shirt. By noontime he could smell his own perspiration. He was thankful for the dark blue suitcoat that had hidden the nervous stains from the jury. He pulled the tie up around his neck. It was a red tie—bright, confident red. He almost felt as if he were dressing for airtime. The only thing missing was his battery pack and a clip-on mike.

When court resumed the afternoon temperature outside was 74°. The wind had increased slightly with the heat. Inside climate-controlled Courtroom 659 Dixon Bell again took the witness stand and was reminded by the judge that he was still under oath. The courtroom seemed much clearer than in the morning, or maybe he was just a little more relaxed. He could make out faces in the crowd. There was that old black man in a seat reserved for family. News anchors from other stations in town were there—unusual for them to actually be working on a news story. Rick Beanblossom was in the back, his stone face intact, his ass having been saved by an unexpected night of cold weather—unexpected to everybody but Dixon Bell. Just think, if the forecast had been even half-assed accurate, the Marine would have dressed warmer and the son of a bitch would be dead now. As it was, he was alive and well, breaking news stories and once again wooing Andrea Labore. He could see her seated next to him, her doubting brown eyes locked on his face, her skeptical ears tuned to every word he spoke.

"Dixon, how do you explain what Mr. Fury calls this 'mountain of circumstantial evidence' against you? Circumstances the state claims places you at or near every murder scene?"

The Weatherman thought long and hard before answering Stacy's question. He measured his response carefully. "I'm not a detective. I can only offer my theory. I think I was followed. I was followed and set up by one of those obsessive fans, a person like Mr. Fury claims I have become. That's what I think. Whoever killed those women is someone who wanted to be me. For every person on television, there's a hundred people who tried to get on television and failed. It wouldn't have been that difficult to find out my schedule, especially if they worked in the newsroom at one time or another."

"Dixon, let's go back . . . back to the beginning and tell the jury how you came to meteorology, how a man from Vicksburg, Mississippi, ended up a TV weatherman in Minnesota."

And that's how the afternoon session was spent, with Dixon Bell talking about the less-traveled roads his life had taken, about his natural curiosity, even as a boy, with the weather that gathered over the swamps of Louisiana and then blew across the river into Mississippi. If there was anybody in the court that day who was bored by the strange life of this strange man, they did a good job of masking it. The same in television land. Court TV said the ratings were phenomenal.

Day two. Tuesday, the second of May. A cool front had moved through overnight, dramatically dropping temperatures. Skies were overcast. The barometer was falling. The morning sun was nowhere to be found. Dixon Bell was back on the stand.

Stacy Dvorchak was zeroing in on key pieces of evidence, having waited until her client was more relaxed. "Then, Dixon, how do you explain your fingerprint being found at the first murder scene?"

"Simple. It's not my fingerprint."

Stacy let it go at that. She flipped a page in her legal pad.

Jim Fury raised an eyebrow of admiration. The woman knew how to score points. He could see how impressed the jurors were with the way this quadriplegic lawyer handled herself.

Stacy adjusted the braces on her hands. "Somebody once said that only in our old age can we look back and say who we loved and who we didn't. The Lisa Beauregard we've all come to know through your diary testified before this court. You hadn't seen her in more than twenty-five years. Looking back now, can you say whether or not you were really in love with her?"

"I've thought about that a lot since my outburst in this court, for which I am truly sorry. I know now in my heart of hearts that if I live to be a hundred years old I will look back and say that I was in love with Lisa Beauregard, and that her rejection of my love set the course for the rest of my life. I have nobody to blame for that but myself."

"In your diary you also wrote of your love for Andrea Labore, a newswoman many of us have come to know through television. Are you really in love with her?"

"Sometimes I would think Lisa was just a high-school infatuation . . . that my love for Andrea was real love. But now I know there's no difference in the way I feel. Yes, I love Andrea Labore. I fell in love with her the moment I saw her. I'm sorry that love has caused her so much trouble."

"Dixon, you never dated either one of these women. Never kissed them, slept with them, fought the fights people falling in love fight. How can you say you loved them?"

"It was a higher love. Almost spiritual. I didn't fall in love with their bodies, I fell in love with the woman."

"No, you just fell in love with a pretty face, and it didn't matter what was behind that face."

"That's not true."

"Then why did you twice fall madly in love with women you simply could not have?"

"Just bum luck, I guess. Or maybe I watched too much television when I was a kid, I don't know. We can control who we date, who we sleep with, but I'm not sure we can control who we fall in love with."

"Did you love these two women enough to kill for them?"

"No."

"To kill to spite them?"

"No."

"To kill others to hurt them?"

"No."

"Did you love Lisa enough to kill her if you couldn't have her?"

"No."

"To kill Andrea if you couldn't have her?"

"No."

"But you wrote in your diary, 'Now I'd like to strangle her. Put my hands around her pretty little neck and choke the life out of her. No more Andrea.' "

"I was writing figuratively. I was frustrated. Humiliated."

"And was it this frustration and humiliation that led you to kill seven women?"

"I can't believe you asked me that, Stacy. I've never killed anybody. I've never killed anybody."

Day three. Wednesday, May third. An upper-air disturbance sent clouds back-pedaling out of Wisconsin and into Minnesota, bringing off-and-on showers. A dreary start to a dreary day. The day before, Judge Lutoslawski had dismissed court early instead of letting the state start in on a weary and agitated Dixon Bell. But now the Weatherman was back on the stand, and it was Prosecutor Jim Fury's turn to ask the questions. "I hold in my hands your diary. In it you write, 'I am going insane. I'm hanging from the cliff of reality by a rope and the strands are breaking one by one. You see, we mentally ill know we are ill. We do not act crazy, we go out of our way to act normal. At times it's a hell of an act.' So are you insane, Mr. Bell?"

"Those words were written in the late hours of the night after an exhausting day. That diary was the last thing I did before I went home at night. Don't tell me that a person's attitude at the end of the day is the same as at the beginning of the day. It's not."

"So this diary simply reflects a bad attitude, is that it? A man who has had a bad day?"

"Those words were never meant to be read by anybody but me. They are my most precious memories. They are my most intimate thoughts, my fears and fantasies. Things I would never even mumble aloud to myself. Why don't you read the part about the people I helped in Vietnam, the lives I saved? The good I did in Memphis, and all of the lives I saved right here in the Twin Cities? Why don't you read those parts?"

"I ask you again, Mr. Bell, are you mad? Insane?"

"No, I am not."

"When you worked at Channel 7, where did you park your car?"

"I had contract parking at the Sky High parking ramp."

"That's directly below the newsroom, isn't it?"

"Yes."

"Could you see the roof of the ramp from the newsroom?"

"I don't know. I never went looking for it."

Jim Fury laid the diary back on the evidence table. "Three years back. A stormy July evening. Record rainfall. Do you remember it?"

"Yes. A perfect deluge. Eight inches of rain. I issued a flash flood warning."

"What time did you leave the newsroom that night?"

"I don't remember."

The prosecutor picked up a printout from the table. "According to the security computer you slid your ID card into the exit door at 11:33 P.M. What time that night was teenager Sis Hayne reported dead atop the Metrodome parking ramp?"

Dixon Bell could see Andrea Labore flipping frantically through her notebook at the back of the courtroom. She had been in the newsroom late that night, in the office of Jack Napoleon. "I don't know."

"Eleven-fifty-eight p.m.," Jim Fury told him. "How far is Channel 7 from the Metrodome ramp?"

"I don't know, I've never parked there."

"It's about ten minutes." The prosecutor moved on to the state's third murder charge. "Christmas Eve, three years back. A freezing ice storm. Do you remember it?"

"Yes, I accurately forecast the storm."

"Did you take a station vehicle home that night?"

"I don't remember."

"Did you sometimes take a station vehicle home when you worked at Channel 7?"

"A couple of times, maybe."

"Did you ever drive a station vehicle through Como Park in St. Paul?"

"I've done some weather broadcasts from the park. I don't remember doing the driving."

"Do you remember Lieutenant Donnell Redmond, who testified at the opening of this trial?"

"He questioned me on several occasions. I was sorry to read of his death."

"And did you see the lieutenant that icy morning in Como Park?"

"I wasn't in Como Park that morning."

Jim Fury's voice was rising in intensity with every question. "Tell me, Weatherman . . . Tamara Livingston, your victim Christmas Eve, your winter kill . . . ?"

Stacy was livid. "I object, Your Honor."

"Did you sneak up on her that night, or did you drive right up to her in that Channel 7 News van, introduce yourself as the famous TV weatherman, and ask her if she needed a ride?"

"Your Honor, I object, this is outrageous."

"I can just hear how you did it," Jim Fury went on over the objection. "In that smooth southern accent of yours you said, 'Get in out of the freezing rain, girl, you'll catch your death.' "

"The objection is sustained. The jury will disregard Mr. Fury's speculation, and in the future Mr. Fury will wait until I rule on an objection before he continues his questioning."

Jim Fury arrogantly ignored the judge. "Mr. Bell, where were you on the Fourth of July?"

"What year?"

"You know damn well what year."

"I was doing a live broadcast from the raceway in Lake Country."

"Did you attend a wet-T-shirt contest?"

"I don't remember."

"You don't remember a wet-T-shirt contest?"

There were too many bodies in the courtroom. The temperature was reaching the uncomfortable level. Dixon Bell wanted to loosen the knot in his tie, but he knew that would look bad. "There was record-breaking heat and humidity that day. After my last broadcast all I remember is downing beers and watching fireworks."

"Did you ever get a letter from a young girl who lived in Afton?"

"I receive too much mail to remember every letter."

"Oh, you would have remembered this letter, Weatherman. She wrote, 'I saw you on TV. I know you are the killer.' Does that lift the fog from your memory?"

"I never got such a letter."

"Have you ever been to Afton?"

"Yes. There's an elementary school out there I've visited. And there's a good restaurant on the river."

"What size tennis shoes do you wear?"

"Fourteen."

"Those are big feet."

"I'm a big man."

"Where did you live before your arrest?"

"I have a town house in Edina."

"And how far is that town house from the spot where Officer Shelly Sumter was strangled to death by a large man with size fourteen tennis shoes?"

"I don't know."

"Two and a half blocks."

"I can't possibly be the only person with big feet who lives in Edina."

Jim Fury stormed back to the evidence table and grabbed the diary. He waved it in the air. "This book I hold in my hands is not a diary. This is a road map to the murders of seven women, maybe more. A map drawn in code by the mind of a psychopath and then followed to the last inch. The sick, demented mind of Dixon Graham Bell. A schizophrenic, clairvoyant weatherman."

Dixon Bell made no attempt to match Jim Fury in volume, but he more than made up for it in raw intensity. "Go ahead and start a diary, Mr. Fury. Write down what you truly think of your wife, or your neighbors, or your boss. Put into words your real politics, believing in your heart that nobody will ever see these words. Then I'll take your words and I'll leak them to the newspapers one page at a time. I'll read your words with a sarcastic voice on national television and we'll see if you don't sound like a madman. Let's see how long you keep your job. You've perverted my diary. You've used my words in a way that should be illegal. People don't read books any-more. They watch television." He pointed at the camera, the red light glowing like a warning. "The words you read from my diary are probably the only reading most of these couch potatoes will get all year." He turned his at-tention to the jury box. "If you jurors are going to judge me by what I wrote in my diary, for God's sake read the whole book. Read it yourself. Crawl into bed with it at night and turn the pages. That's how books are meant to be read. That's the spirit I wrote it in."

A cloudy day later, in his closing argument, Prosecutor Jim Fury told the jury, "Dixon Graham Bell came north to our state and used his knowledge of meteorology and his hatred of women to turn our theater of changing sea-sons into theater of the macabre."

In her defense of the Weatherman Stacy Dvorchak told the jury the state's case was like bad journalism. "First you reach a conclusion. Then you go out and find the facts to support that conclusion. The facts that don't fit, you simply ignore."

Judge Stephen Z. Lutoslawski then gave the jury their final instructions. The alternate jurors were excused and seven men and five women were ushered out of the court-room to begin their deliberations.

They stayed out longer than any jury in the state's his-tory.

Rick Beanblossom sat alone in the seductive spring sun on the north portico steps of the oldest county courthouse in Minnesota. Constructed shortly after the Civil War in the popular Italianate style of the day, the proud building of red brick and graceful arches stood amid the Victorian homes on Stillwater's South Hill overlooking the pictur-esque St. Croix River. In the old days a weather flag was flown just beneath the American flag from the pole atop the dome. A red flag meant thunderstorms likely. A black flag meant a tornado had been spotted. But flags no longer flew over the South Hill. Justice was administered at the modern suburban courthouse up the highway, and the Old County Courthouse had come within one commissioner's vote of the wrecking ball.

If it had been the old days a fair-weather white flag would be flapping in the breeze on this day. The sky was perfect. The oaks and ashes were springing to life before the man in the mask. Thick, weedless grass rolled down the hill to Pine Street. The mid-May temperature was 75°. It had been ten days now. The jury was still out. As the weather turned toward summer, Dixon Bell was returned to the Ramsey County jail in St. Paul to await his fate. A thousand trial watchers were running around town with beepers fastened to their belts. Rick again checked the battery, seeing no good coming out of any verdict, as if somehow the Weatherman were his own evil twin.

The parents of Harlan Wakefield vehemently denied that they had known all along how their son had died. The state attorney general promised an investigation into the investigation. Keenan Wakefield was once again in therapy. Rick Beanblossom shuddered at the thought of a twelve-year-old boy dumping his twin brother into the river and then watching his own face disappear beneath the water. His parents had developed in him an intellect no boy should possess at that age, an intellect that left him void of love and emotion. Rick wrote and produced the story of the boy genius gone mad, including the media's own dubious role. Andrea Labore gave his words voice and a face.

Rick brought her down to Stillwater, to the banks of the river where the body had been dumped. She did a stand-up in Pioneer Park overlooking the town. She did live reports from the river's edge with the still-intact iron lift bridge serving as a dramatic backdrop. They worked well together, and Andrea ended up getting a lot more credit for the Wakefield story than she thought she deserved. But her anchor job was secured.

Although he was happy for Andrea, the masked producer no longer cared about news credits. A week out of the coma he cracked the Wakefield case. The next week he got the publisher's letter from New York. This week Andrea invited him to dinner. It was like being born again. So when he was done typing up the sorry truth about Harlan Wakefield, Rick Beanblossom typed up his resignation to Clancy Communications.

The river had reminded everybody of its awesome power. But something powerful had happened to Rick Beanblossom while building that dike. He was accepted among his own people without question, without stares or whispers. They smiled at him where they once had grimaced. Andrea told him people had been smiling at him for years, he was just too blind and bitter to notice.

Rick junked his needle kit. He threw out a damn good X-rated video collection. He thought of buying a house. He remembered the fun he had showing Andrea this small town where he had grown up. Today it was a fast-growing suburb. Back then it was just a blue-collar river town people drove through to get to the bridge to Wisconsin. They played baseball in an alleyway between old houses that had been built for lumbermen. The garages kept the ball in play. Mrs. Miller's yard was a home run. In later years they looked back and counted the casualties. Of the score of kids that played ball in that alley, seven went off to Vietnam. Only four came back, one without a leg, another without a face. A mighty high price for one sandlot baseball team.

The church he attended as a boy stood on a hill up the street, its steeple blessing the canonized valley below. It wouldn't hurt him to drop in there some Sunday morning. And his junior high school was right across the street. They were getting ready to close it now, and another fight was brewing over whether to convert it to condominiums or to bulldoze the memories to the ground. Rick could still rattle off the school motto: *Non Scholae Sed Vitae Discimus*—We Learn Not for School but for Life.

Some of the stately homes on the South Hill had been restored and converted to bed-and-breakfast inns. Wouldn't it be fun to buy a grand Victorian and fix it up? The Cities were but a ghost of what they could have been. Perhaps it was time to come home. He had spent years clawing his way out of this town; now he was going to claw his way back in. Like the august courthouse behind him, the old hometown still seemed a place worth fighting for.

On the courthouse lawn beneath a pair of tall evergreens stood a monument to the county soldiers who enlisted and fought in the Civil War. Rick Beanblossom walked down to the memorial and read the inscriptions.

Atop a slab of granite an infantryman of that day marched south in righteous glory, a bayonetted rifle in one hand, a fistful of determination in the other. Six score and ten years later stood the wounded veteran of another civil war. He reached into his coat pocket and once again pulled out the letter from New York. Again he unfolded it and read. It was every writer's dream.

E. P. Dutton
2 Park Avenue, New York, N.Y. 10016

Dear Rick:

For a first novel this is a fine start. You write well and powerfully. This was a tragic period in our history. Your vivid descriptions of the horrors of war and of the soldiers who must live with the mental and physical wounds was very moving. In reading it, it was obvious to me you are a veteran and this book is very personal to you. You've written a novel with a lot of heart and guts. I think it could do quite well.

Are you represented? I would like to hear from you in any case.

Hilary Avery
Associate Editor

His historical novel about the year 1968. Five years of work. A dozen rejection slips. A book about four small-town boys in the Midwest who graduate from high school together and then go their separate ways. Four different directions. West to Haight-Ashbury. East to the bloody streets of Chicago during the Democratic National Convention. North to Canada to avoid the draft. And south by southeast—Vietnam.

Rick Beanblossom refolded the letter and tucked it neatly into its envelope. The proud Marine would read the letter a hundred more times before his novel was published. Dream achieved.

THE AUTOPSY

They had to wait for the body to cool. Already there was talk of an investigation. The corpse was photographed while still strapped to the chair. The electrician unplugged the electrodes and then staggered from the room. The smell of burned flesh and bone was too putrid to work in. The Weatherman was left sitting in the death chamber all by himself.

By the time the ME assistants got to him he'd been left sitting for an hour. The grim, excruciating task of removing the corpse from the chair was left to them. They were shocked by what they saw, what they smelled. He was coated with white foam. His swollen face was half black leather, half blackened flesh. His clothes were nothing but charred and tattered remains. Rigor mortis had set in. They had to pry the electric crown from his head. Then they unstrapped him from the chair and carefully lowered him to the stretcher, still in a grotesque sitting position. From there the scene got almost comical. Four of them worked to straighten his limbs, slimy from the foam. Whenever they got an arm to lie down, a leg would pop up. Even with their face masks on, the stench of burned flesh nauseated them. It took them forty minutes to get him strapped to the stretcher. Finally they wheeled him from the prison, through the cold November rain. They loaded him into the back of the big Chevy Suburban and drove him one last time around the two cities he had grown to love—down to the Ramsey County Morgue in St. Paul.

The Weatherman was placed on a gurney, then stripped and peeled of his charred rags. The burned leather was removed from his face with a razor and a tweezers. His toe was tagged. They tied a plastic bag over his swollen head and covered him with a white sheet. He was pushed into the cooler alongside ten other stiffs. The temperature was 38°. Bugs crawled up the walls. They closed the cooler door and left him there.

The next day he was wheeled into a sterile examination room, as white and cold as snow. The medical examiner was a huge, frizzy-haired woman in a military uniform; she was named Freddie. She began the autopsy with a joke. "Let's turn out the lights and see if he glows in the dark." Her assistants guffawed loud and hard. Freddie slapped her knee, then pulled the sheet from the body.

A long blister of fried pus ran from his right leg to up over his chest. His shaved head was fried bloody raw above the eyes. His eyebrows were gone. His face was black as coal, a frozen grimace of excruciating pain. Torture. One eye was wide open and bulging. The other eye had been burned closed. His jaw was locked, his cheeks and nose clenched in violent contortions. Maggots had replaced tears vaporized in the fire.

"Oh, Dixon, look what they did to your lovely face. I hate to say it," Freddie told her assistants, "but the state really screwed this up. It was that fucking sponge."

"Yes, it was the sponge," said an assistant named Cynthia.

The assistant named Carl agreed. "We better enjoy this while we can. I don't think there are going to be any more executions in this state for a long, long time."

Freddie looked at Cynthia and grinned. "Cynthia, why don't you inspect the groin area for us."

Cynthia giggled, turned red, then went ahead and spread his fat thighs. "Oooh, it's not as bad as I thought."

"What did you expect to find, excrement? That's one of those myths about executions," Freddie told her, "that they shit their last supper. That doesn't happen."

"But it looks like he did wet his pants," Cynthia said, pointing to a yellow stain on his inner thigh.

"No he didn't. That's a semen stain. What a way to go, huh? Death is the ultimate orgasm."

Cynthia giggled again and turned away.

Freddie bent over and kissed his raw head. "I loved you, Dixon Bell. I'm sorry it had to end like this." She held up her hands as if conducting an orchestra. "All right, kids, plug in the shears. Let's cut this son of a bitch open and see if that cheeseburger is well done yet."

They cut him open with a Y incision, from his belly button to both shoulders. "I'll be damned, he does have a heart."

"What did you expect, a barometer?" Again they broke into belly laughs.

"If we don't finish this soon it's going to cloud up and rain on us."

Freddie could hardly control herself. Cynthia and Carl were in hysterics. When the laughter died, Freddie leaned over the charred stiff and shook her head in pity. "What was it Judge Polack said when he sentenced this sorry bastard?"

"Until you came along the people of Minnesota held dearly human life. No more. You have been convicted of the most serious offenses against peace and dignity, against the state and humanity. The jury has concluded the only fair penalty is taking your life. Let the ritual begin. Dixon Graham Bell, on the last stroke of the clock on the last day of October, it is the sentence of the court that a current of electricity be passed through your body until you are dead. May God have mercy on your soul. May God have mercy on us all."

Freddie shrugged her big shoulders. "Well, let's cut off the top of his head and see if God had any more mercy on his soul than he had on his face."

"Why do we have to cut off the top of his head?"

"Because we have to take out his brain," Freddie explained. "Then we suspend the brain in a bucket for about three weeks until it gets hard. When it's nice and crunchy we slice it open and try to find out what the hell was wrong with this guy."

They fired up the Stryker saw, and with the chilling whine of the circular blade they went about cutting off the top of the Weatherman's skull. Then they opened up his head like it was a cookie jar. "Look at that—baked hard. What is this?" asked Carl, picking at the black soot. "Charcoal?"

"That was the blood," Freddie told him. "Now let me in there."

Freddie slipped on a fresh pair of rubber gloves. She slowly slid her hands into the skull and wrapped her fingertips around the fried brain. Then she gently pulled the Weatherman's mind from its burned casing and held it in her hand. "Do you think if we squeeze it, it'll spit out a forecast?"

They were having a last laugh when the Weatherman bolted upright on the table and grabbed Freddie by her throat. "Put it back!"

The medical examiner tore away and went screaming from the room, brain in hand. The two assistants went screaming after her. The Weatherman sat on the table shouting, "You bring that back here! Bring it back!"

The electronic bolt shot open. The deputy slid aside the steel door. Dixon Bell was sitting on the edge of his bunk, his head buried in his hands. He was crying. "Give me back my mind. I want it back."

"Are you all right, Dixon?"

The Weatherman wiped the tears from his eyes. He looked out his window at the night sky. It was raining. A steady downpour. The only thing visible was the translucent lights of the High Bridge festooned between the cliffs. He put the temperature at 55°. The barometer was below 30 inches and falling. He sensed a north wind. "I had a nightmare," he told the deputy. "A terrible nightmare. I'm okay now."

"You sure? Can I get you something?"

"I'm fine. Thank you for your concern."

"Actually, I was just coming to wake you up. The jury is in, Dixon. They've reached a verdict."

BOOK THREE

FIVE YEARS INTO THE STORM

The queen had only one way of settling all difficulties, great or small. "Off with his head!" she said, without even looking round.

—Lewis Carroll
Alice's Adventures in Wonderland

THE TOUR

From literature to Hollywood, from the morning headlines to the evening news, the convict on death row has
always been portrayed as one of the great martyrs in the
American drama. As the years go by, the crime does a
slow fade into the past and the punishment becomes the
story. The murderer becomes the victim. And so it was
with Dixon Graham Bell, convicted on seven counts of
first-degree intentional homicide and then sentenced to
death, a verdict that sent a wave of shock through the
courtroom.

Appeals were filed, but the Weatherman's conviction
and sentence were upheld by the Minnesota Supreme
Court. Congress put more limits on habeas corpus appeals. The Federal District Court in Minneapolis refused
to review the case, as did the 8th U.S. Circuit Court of
Appeals in St. Louis. Stacy Dvorchak's final appeal was
before the United States Supreme Court. The nine justices
were expected to consider it in the fall. If they refused to
hear the case, the governor of Minnesota would sign his
death warrant and convicted serial killer Dixon Graham
Bell would be rescheduled for execution.

And now, as Dixon Bell's appeals were exhausted and
his date with death neared, his punishment became the
news event of the year. So much so that Clancy Communications through Sky High News filed a federal civil
lawsuit in Minneapolis to be permitted to do a live broadcast of the execution, or at the very least videotape the
execution to be broadcast on the evening news. They employed the same argument they had used to gain access to
the state's courts: television reporters with cameras, the
station contended, have just as much right to cover the

ritual as newspaper reporters with notebooks. Channel 7 wanted their weatherman back on the air any way possible.

Rick Beanblossom followed Warden Oliver J. Johnson through the Stillwater State Correctional Facility. The warden was giving the media a tour of the new Death House facilities. No cameras were allowed. Rick no longer worked for the television station, but he wanted to stay with the story, so he promised a lengthy feature to a Minnesota monthly magazine.

Before pushing on, the warden addressed the entire group. "I just want to give you a little background about this solemn business. The concept of the electric chair came from Thomas Alva Edison. In the 1880s he sent an electric chair around the country to demonstrate the power of electricity. Stray dogs, cats, even an orangutan were strapped into the chair and electrocuted. In fact, the only electrical appliance older than the chair is the light bulb. The first man electrocuted," Warden Johnson went on, "got it in Auburn Prison in New York State in 1890. The first woman to be electrocuted died in the electric chair at Sing Sing in 1899. The youngest person sentenced to die in the electric chair was a fourteen-year-old boy convicted of killing an eleven-year-old girl. That was in South Carolina in 1944. Witnesses say the boy was so small his arms kept slipping out of the straps."

Rick sensed a few watts of cynicism. "Warden Johnson, do you really believe in the death penalty?"

Oliver J. Johnson was every bit the image of Joe DiMaggio, tall and slender with thick silver hair. He had a soft demeanor and a kind face. His silver suit, European-cut, tailor-made, matched his hair. He spoke with professorial rectitude. "When I accepted this position I swore an oath to carry out the duties. I'll do so without hesitation."

That didn't answer Rick's question. They continued moving through Cell Hall A-West, Receiving and Orientation. It was noisy, the hallways crowded with inmates, like a school during the hour break. Suddenly they stopped dead in their tracks, their eyes drawn to an ominous black sign above a tall steel door. DEATH ROW. All conversation ceased. Warden Johnson held up his hands and issued a fair warning. "To date only one man in Minnesota has been sentenced to death. In the meantime we've decided to use this special block of cells to house the worst of the worst . . . the serial killer, the sexual psychopath, the slayers of women and children. Anybody who does not wish to enter this area can wait out here. We'll only be a few minutes. Absolutely no talking to the inmates. Once inside I'll answer no questions."

A guard checked every badge as the group marched through the steel door to a double-barred entrance. One set of steel bars slid open and the warden and a dozen reporters squeezed into a small holding area. The bars behind them slammed closed. They were locked in. Everyone was straining to see down the block. Then the bars in front of them slid open with a spooky clang and they shuffled into death row.

Warden Johnson again raised his hands. "For your own safety as well as the security of the inmates, this is as far as I can let you go."

They were about a quarter of the way down the row. Rick Beanblossom stepped to the front. The cell block was stone quiet, the hallway clean and spotless. It smelled of Spic 'n Span. The cells were locked tight. Tall windows had so many bars across them they kept the sun at bay. A big television set fastened to the wall was dark. Unsmiling guards, uniformly neat, stood back against the yellow brick wall, a safe distance from the inmates. Down the row a few murderous hands could be seen dangling out of the cell doors. Now and then a stream of cigarette smoke would flow like dragon's breath between the bars. The eerie silence that pervaded the block was in stark contrast to the noisy prison outside. A cigarette butt shot across the hall and landed at the foot of Warden Johnson. Rick saw no sign of Dixon Bell.

"This," said the warden, "is where we coddle the prisoners. If any of you care to spend the weekend, we have a couple of empty cells."

There was some nervous laughter. Then from way down at the end of the row came the most horrifying sound imaginable. It was human for sure, but with the ring of a hyena—a crazy yelp between ecstasy and torture that bounced floor to ceiling, then echoed off high walls.

The reporters stepped back. Rick thought he saw the warden roll his eyes.

"I think we'd better leave now." With that Warden Johnson ushered them out of death row.

Safely outside the block there was a collective sigh of relief. As many times as he had come to visit him, it was still hard for Rick Beanblossom to believe the Weatherman was locked up inside there.

Warden Johnson continued his spiel as they left the cell hall and marched down the main hallway. "We are adopting the basic method of execution that has been used in the states of Florida and Louisiana for years, though we think we've improved on it to make it less routine and more humane. A lot of thought has gone into this. No detail has been overlooked. Several officials from Florida and Louisiana have been hired as consultants."

Redd Battlemore, a veteran reporter from the *Pioneer Press,* muttered to Rick, "Think of it, Minnesota, we're going to be just like Florida and Louisiana."

They stopped at an exit door. "We'll be going across the prison yard now to Industry. That's where the actual Death House is being built. It's ninety percent complete," he said, almost apologetically. "I'll remind you again that prison construction is the most expensive construction there is. If taxpayers want to lock up criminals and throw away the key . . . please let them know the dollar cost. It's billions."

Stillwater was an old-style fortress prison built circa 1910. It housed one thousand four hundred prisoners. Seven guard towers surrounded the high brick walls. As they walked out of the drab building and into the welcome April sunshine, Rick Beanblossom peeled through his reporter's notebook, jotting notes. The prison yard had a blacktop running track and a baseball diamond with a weed-littered outfield. Inmates were taking advantage of the spring weather. Ten days earlier it had snowed. Today the temperature was nearing 80°. The inmates jogged around the track, oblivious to the visitors. Several of them stopped to shake hands with Warden Johnson in genuine respect. Rick watched as one inmate after another handed the warden a letter or a legal form, or asked him to look into something for them. He seemed to say yes to every request. The tour group worked their way across the yard to the Industry buildings.

The warden leaned into the masked newsman and pointed. "Do you see that little fat guy waddling around the track? He's been here since 1967." Rick watched the balding old man in the dirty T-shirt and sweat pants work his way around the blacktop.

"He's a drifter," the warden said. "They don't even know how many women he killed around the country. At the last parole hearing we just said, 'We'll talk to you again in ten years.'"

"What prisoner has been locked up at Stillwater the longest?"

"We have one who came here in 1952. He's been here ever since. And we've got an old janitor who did twenty-five years before joining the custodial staff. Say, before I forget, I have a copy of your book in my office. I'd appreciate it if you'd sign it before you leave."

"I'd be happy to."

"How's it selling?"

"Well, it didn't make the *New York Times* best-seller list. But the reviews were good, and my publisher wants a second book."

It stood unmarked, like something out of a Nazi death camp. This Death House had been constructed beneath the prison's west wall, which ran along Stagecoach Trail. It was right behind the electric shop and next door to the wood shop. The new red brick exterior and the spotless white trim seemed oddly out of place beneath the rustic bricks of the fortress wall. Rick remembered riding his bicycle up Stagecoach Trail when he was a boy. He'd always had a strange feeling about this place, always stopping his bike to stare at the long, imposing walls with the barbed wire and the guard towers.

The press left the sunshine behind and crowded into the Death House. They stood before a prison cell that was smaller than anything they'd seen in the main complex.

Warden Johnson continued. "When, and if, the governor signs the prisoner's death warrant, the commissioner of corrections will then set an execution date in consultation with the trial judge. Approximately three weeks before that date the condemned man will be brought here to the Death House and housed in this isolation cell. He will not be allowed out of this cell until he walks to the chair. This is to prepare him mentally and physically for execution. It is in this cell the prisoner will be served his last meal, three hours before the execution. We're told most condemned men request a favorite meal from their childhood. Something Mom used to make. This one particular prisoner may be fond of southern cuisine, so the cook is studying southern recipes."

Rick Beanblossom stepped into the tiny cell, bone bare. He'd seen better cages at the zoo. He carefully studied the bare necessities as the warden talked on.

"After the meal, about two hours before the execution, the prisoner's head will be shaved and a conducting gel will be rubbed into his skull. His eyebrows will also be shaved. Hair is a poor conductor of electricity and it burns. The last thing anybody wants in the death chamber is a fire. He will then be dressed in all-cotton clothes."

A guard joined them from the death chamber and handed the warden what appeared to be a medieval torture device. Warden Johnson held the metal and chains up for display. "When the prisoner walks to the chair he will be wearing these special four-point handcuff restraints. They are specifically made for escorting death row prisoners on their last walk. As you can see, they have large screws on top. If a struggle were to ensue, the guards could simply turn these screws, instantly breaking the prisoner's wrists." The handcuffs were passed among the group.

Then they proceeded down a short corridor. The warden stopped in front of a small room. The door was open. It resembled a sound booth from the Sky High newsroom. "This," said Warden Johnson, "is the executioner's room. The steel door is locked and secured from the inside. Only the executioner can open it. He will be wearing a hood during the execution. All of this is for his security. In here are the voltmeter, the ammeter, and the switchboard. As you can see, there are actually two switches, a red one and a green one. When the yellow light above the switch goes out and the green light comes on, the executioner throws the green switch. This throws power into the circuit breaker box. Then when the other yellow light goes off and the red light comes on, the executioner throws the red switch. The red switch is the power out of the circuit breaker box. Out of the box and into the condemned man."

"Who's the executioner?" asked a field producer from CNN.

"We hope we can get a volunteer from the prison staff. If not, we'll go outside the prison system. If necessary we'll recruit from outside of the state. Nobody outside my office will ever know the identity of the executioner."

The gathered press looked skeptical. Rick brushed by the warden and into the executioner's booth. He scribbled more notes. "Warden, how much of NSP's electricity will you actually use to kill the man?"

"As a matter of fact, Mr. Beanblossom, the prison's own generator will take over from Northern States Power just prior to the execution, causing all of the lights in the prison to dim. When it is over the lights will dim again, as power is returned to the utility."

"That doesn't answer my question."

"We will use a fluctuating cycle two minutes in length. The initial jolt of electricity will be two thousand volts. Brain death will be instantaneous. The voltage is then dropped to one thousand volts, then to five hundred volts, this to prevent the burning of the body. Then back to a thousand volts, and ending with another two thousand volts to complete a one-minute cycle. Then the procedure is repeated. It's all over in two minutes and all of this is done automatically. The executioner only needs to throw the two switches. The executioner can override the automatic cycle on a simple hand signal from me, should anything go wrong."

After everybody had peeked into the executioner's booth, Warden Johnson led them through another steel door and into the death chamber. What they had all come to see: the chair.

Big and fat and made of oak, it had a glossy finish and sat on a black rubber mat. The dark grains running through the chair were buffed to a shine. On the top of the back brace was a wood headrest. Adjustable. A leather strap dangled from the headrest like a noose. Holes were drilled into the heavy arms and legs. Other straps had yet to be attached. The chamber the chair sat in was unfinished, cluttered, and dusty. Workers, none of them inmates, flitted about.

"As you people reported with your usual overkill, the inmates in our furniture-manufacturing building did refuse to build the chair. In retrospect, I regret giving the order. It was a mistake. The chair was constructed by an out-of-state private contractor after several other prisons refused to build it. Now, the chair itself is not electrified." Warden Johnson stepped up to the chair and explained. "The electrical current will run into the prisoner's head and out his right leg. Let me show you." He lifted a metal helmet that looked like it matched the handcuffs. "This is the headset that will be strapped onto the prisoner and connected to the executioner's booth. As you can see, this 'death cap,' as it is sometimes called, is lined with copper. The wire mesh inside will be covered with a natural ocean sponge that has been soaked in a saline solution. This damp sponge under the headset will sit directly on top the prisoner's head. It is used to convey the two thousand volts of electricity into his skull. Everything is designed to conduct electricity quickly and smoothly. Anything that is not a good conductor of electricity or is highly flammable, such as hair and synthetic fibers, is removed beforehand."

Someone asked, "Who hooks him up?"

"A special squad of guards will strap him into the chair. A certified electrician will connect the electrodes to his right leg and to the headset. On a signal from me the electrician will then throw that switch behind the chair. That's the switch for our generator. It also triggers the lights inside the executioner's booth."

While Warden Johnson stepped forward to explain coming features, Rick Beanblossom walked up and plopped himself in the electric chair.

The warden didn't see him and continued. "A telephone connected directly to Governor Ellefson's office will be installed on that wall. And that, ladies and gentlemen, pretty much concludes today's tour." Warden Johnson turned back to the chair, now occupied. "Mr. Beanblossom, what the hell are you doing?"

The man in the mask ignored him, lifted the death cap from the floor, and placed it atop his head. He sat dead still in the electric chair in a Lincolnesque pose. Then Rick Beanblossom began singing a jingle he remembered from a television commercial when he was a boy: *"Electricity is penny cheap from NSP to you."*

Nobody laughed.

If it was the most bizarre sight Warden Oliver J. Johnson had ever seen in his years at Stillwater, he wasn't admitting it. "By the way," he told the reporters, savoring the thought of it, "all of you must undergo a full rectal exam before you will be allowed to leave."

THE ROW

When the tours passed through, Dixon Bell, inmate number 137389, crawled into his cell—out of sight, but never out of mind. For the past two years, as his appeals dragged on, he had been incarcerated at the Minnesota Correctional Facility in Stillwater. Rick Beanblossom's hometown. A mirror image of Vicksburg. Through the looking glass. The town was set on the west side of the river instead of the east. High bluffs. Rolling hills. Thick woods. Even an old restored courthouse high on a hill. The prison was just off Highway 95 heading south out of town, with a terrific view of the St. Croix Valley.

But life behind those high walls was monotonous. Dixon Bell found it difficult to keep his mind occupied. Sleep was his only lover now, and he crawled into bed and eagerly waited for her sweet embrace. His thick hair had thinned and gone mostly gray. He had dropped thirty pounds. Again he took to watching television. He learned through TV news that the Death House was nearing completion. It was almost six months behind schedule and a million dollars over budget. Death penalty opponents were still trying to have the funds cut off.

Once in a while he would put pen to paper and answer some of the letters that were delivered to his cell every day during the 3:30 lockup. All of his letters, both incoming and outgoing, were photocopied and reviewed by authorities. The letters were from all over the world, letters of support and letters of hate. Some of the letters enraged him so much he felt like strangling the writer. Others moved him to tears.

Stillwater shattered almost every myth Dixon Bell held about prison life. Inmates didn't have to put on uniforms.

They were allowed to wear their own clothes at all times. A simple V was cut into the heels of their shoes so they could be tracked if they escaped.

The uniformed guards were totally unarmed. In his past two years at Stillwater he had yet to see a weapon. Most of the guards were young and relatively friendly. They could retire at age fifty-five, and most of them did. The guards that didn't like being among the inmates bid for the tower jobs. There were even women guards—women guards at a men-only prison. One of Dixon Bell's favorites was a young woman named Carol. When she first began her duties at Stillwater, she wouldn't tell him her last name, so he just called her Carol Theguard. Like others in the prison, she slowly warmed up to him.

The prison's educational system was equivalent to that of a community college. Literacy programs were given top priority. A four-year degree program was offered through the University of Minnesota. Inmates went to school or went to work. The Industry Division turned out a line of farm equipment tops in the Midwest. Stillwater's rate of recidivism was one of the lowest in the country. Most inmates got a decent education and never came back. When Per Ellefson became governor, he was so impressed with the prison's overall record he reappointed Oliver Johnson warden despite loud complaints from the right wing of his party. In political circles Johnson was known as a bleeding-heart liberal. They would have had him canned a long time ago for coddling prisoners except that his programs worked. The inmates loved their warden. Dixon Bell respected him. The warden, however, intensely disliked the Weatherman. Dixon Bell once asked him about it.

"I began here as a guard in the laundry room when I was twenty-one years old," Johnson said. "Just me and thirty-eight inmates. I earned my college degree in this prison, the same degree program offered to the inmates. I helped make Stillwater a model for the country. My greatest fear has always been that a man like you would come along . . . a criminal so beguiling he could convince an entire community he was good, whereas he was evil . . . a monster so vile the laws would have to be changed to deal with him. You shined a spotlight on us. Prisons don't operate well under the spotlight."

"Did it ever occur to you that I might be an innocent man?"

"No. You killed every one of those women, Dixon. If I didn't believe that with all of my heart, I'd tell the governor to take his electric chair and shove it up his ass. But I'll walk you to the chair. Just so that we can be done with you, and I can get back to running a correctional facility. As far as I'm concerned you're just a cold wind blowing through the system."

Since there had been no death penalty in Minnesota, there had been no death row, so when Dixon Bell first arrived at Stillwater he was locked in the Segregation Unit. After several months Warden Johnson allowed him to join the general prison population. He was even assigned a teaching position and moved to the educational wing, Cell Hall A-East. When the media reported this move, there was a general brouhaha because the Weatherman wasn't rotting away on death row. Once again accused of coddling prisoners, Warden Johnson had no choice but to return his most notorious inmate to the Segregation Unit. That's what the warden meant about the spotlight.

The Weatherman's cell was six feet by ten feet. It was eight feet high. The bunk was attached to the wall. There was an aluminum toilet. He had a foot locker. He was allowed a small metal desk with a metal chair. In the corner was a portable Sony TV. The walls were painted light blue. The bars on the door were brown and yellow. The whole prison was done in the depressing shades of autumn: brown and gold.

Much like at the county jail, they were locked in their cells only from 10:00 P.M. until 6:15 A.M. Then three times a day they were locked up for about twenty minutes while the guards counted bodies. If nobody was missing, the doors were unlocked and they were again free to roam.

In the day room outside the cells, metal tables and chairs were bolted to the floor. An RCA with a twenty-six-inch screen was bolted to the wall. Every time some law-and-order bozo toured the prison he left screaming to the media, "They got color television sets!"

Tall windows climbed three stories to the ceiling. But these windows were screened and barred, and the Weatherman could not always see the sun and the moon. The

Seg Unit had its own exercise yard. Dixon Bell was allowed outside two hours a day. Right now tulips were in bloom around the foundation. The birds were up from the South. Ice was out on the St. Croix River. In Minnesota the rainy season was under way. He took in every last minute of fresh air, no matter how threatening the sky. Even so, he felt he was losing his sense of the weather. He had been too long removed from the elements.

After the brouhaha over the Weatherman's not being locked up on death row, and to show they weren't being coddled, whenever the media or the politicians came to inspect the progress of Death House facilities, the guards would hang an ominous black sign over the Seg Unit that read, DEATH ROW. The inmates would scurry back into their cells and the guards would bolt the doors. All television sets would be turned off. The guards would stand at attention and put on their mean and ugly faces. Inmates would wear their most hardened scowls. A couple of them would grunt and groan; a few had developed comically horrifying screams. The tour group would then peek in, looking either very pleased or very scared. As soon as they departed, the cell doors were unlocked, and with a hearty laugh the inmates would go back to doing whatever it was they were doing before being so rudely interrupted.

Most of the men in the Seg Unit went to class or to their prison jobs during the day, but since Dixon Bell was supposed to be rotting away on death row he stayed behind. He read books. He wrote a weather feature for the prison paper. He answered letters. And for two years he watched television. The routine pushed his frustration level to the boiling point.

"Do you have any final words before the will of the people is carried out?"

"Yeah, shit-for-brains, I got some final words. You got the wrong man! It's not my fucking fingerprint. I was in all those places because the real killer was following me. Following me because I'm on television. I was set up. Can't you see that? Beanblossom knows. Angelbeck knows, the old bastard just won't admit it. You dumb assholes got the wrong man. The day after I fry he's gonna go out there and kill again. Every season another

dead body on your hands. What are you gonna do then? Who y'all gonna kill next?"

Few of the inmates believed Dixon Bell would be executed—or so they kept telling him. But the state had spent millions. Sooner or later Minnesota would have to execute somebody. He may not have been sitting on a real death row these past two years, but that Death House they were building out in Industry was as real as rain. There seemed to be a somber feeling among the prison staff that the Weatherman was a dead duck. That his time was near. The sand in his hourglass was running out. Take the strange case of Dr. Yauch.

Dr. D. Yauch, as his nametag read, ran the prison hospital. He appeared to be about the same age as Dixon Bell, but he had the demeanor of an old fart. In school he had undoubtedly been the class nerd. His horn-rimmed glasses were probably surgically implanted on his face during puberty. Every month for two years Dixon Bell was sent to Dr. Yauch and ordered to undergo a complete physical. It was the doctor's job to see that the Weatherman was fit to be fried. Shortly after the federal court of appeals refused to hear his case Dixon Bell was led over to the hospital and into the good doctor's office for his monthly exam. As usual, they were left alone.

"Hey, Doc, may be less than six months now. Don't let it worry your little heart. I'll see that your bill gets paid."

Ignoring what the Weatherman had said, Dr. Yauch silently wrapped a blood-pressure cuff around his patient's right arm, then asked, "Do you have trouble sleeping at night?"

Dixon Bell rolled his eyes, snickered at the doctor's stupidity. He turned his head away, fed up with the whole charade, the sickening ritual of passing a monthly physical examination so that he could be strapped into a chair and electrocuted. The Weatherman made no attempt to hide his disdain.

"I asked you a question, mister!" The doctor's voice had suddenly changed. It was firm and harsh now, like a commanding officer demanding an answer.

Dixon Bell turned back to him, surprised by the sharp change in attitude. Through those nerdy glasses he could see real anger in the eyes of Dr. Yauch. It was then he realized that the doctor didn't enjoy these visits any more than he did. The son of a bitch was human after all. "Yes, I have trouble sleeping at night."

Dr. Yauch reached deep into his black bag of medicine. "I think what you need, Dixon, is a sleeping pill. Just one pill." He held up a milky gray pill the size of a lemon drop and lowered his voice to intense, almost conspiratorial tones. "With this pill I'll give you the same warning that I give to all of my patients. This sleeping pill is very strong. I guarantee it will knock you out for the night. In fact, this type of sleeping pill is so strong that if you were to take four of them at one time, they would kill you. You would quietly pass away in your sleep. Do you understand what I am saying?"

Dixon Bell gulped down his surprise. "Yes siree, I believe I do."

"Good. Now if this pill works for you tonight, I'll give you another pill next month."

Dixon Bell had now saved two pills. God bless the good doctor.

That was another thing about his stay in Stillwater. God was behind bars. There was a Bible in his cell. A sweet lady from prison ministry gave it to him during a visit. She'd had his name printed in it. Probably an old fan. Anyway, once in a while Dixon Bell, a man who thought he knew too much science to believe in God, would page through this Bible, not really sure what it was that he was looking for.

His fellow prisoners would come to see him. A new inmate would stop by to talk almost every day. And, boy, could they talk up a storm. He told them little; mostly he just sat and listened. The way he figured it, the entire inmate population was there because of a woman. They got into a fight over a woman. They stole for a woman. They raped a woman. They killed a woman. Seemed just about every story in Stillwater had a woman in it.

It was 10:00 P.M. Lockup time. The Weatherman could hear the schlocky music. The news was coming on.

Every winter the Electric Star disappeared from the night sky. Every spring it returned. Then every night the star would get brighter and every day the sun would get warmer. But Old Jesse was slowing down. Some nights he wasn't finishing his chores. This night he made no attempt to finish. He spent most of his shift watching the sparkling star.

They probably thought it was just his age slowing him down, and being as how they all loved the old man he'd be allowed to walk the halls of Stillwater until the day he died. But it wasn't an aging heart that was bothering him. It was a troubled heart.

He sometimes saw the Weatherman in passing. He recognized him right away from the trial. He remembered watching him on television. Often he wanted to stop and say hello. Even in person he seemed like such a nice man. Maybe ask him about the star. But he never did. For in his troubled heart Old Jesse at last knew why that star was up there. It was up there for him. It hung over the valley for granddaughter Shelly and all of those murdered women. It shone for the Weatherman.

Before he realized how long he had been standing at the window, the morning sun came peeking over the bluff and the Electric Star disappeared. Old Jesse finally pulled himself away and pushed his broom down to the staff bulletin board.

IN THE CASE OF MCF-STW INMATE 137389
A VOLUNTEER IS NEEDED TO HELP CARRY OUT
THE SENTENCE OF THE COURT. PAYS BONUS.
SEE WARDEN JOHNSON.

Old Jesse calmly removed the notice from the cork board and stuffed it into his shirt pocket. Then he pushed his broom down the hallway to the warden's office.

THE CONFEDERATE

From the bedroom window on the second floor of their South Hill home they could see the golden river, could smell the wind through the pines up from the water. On warm summer nights, as was this night, they could hear the gulls and the geese at play after the boats had docked for the evening. For Rick Beanblossom these sights and sounds were a hallucinogenic drug that sometimes made him forget that he had ever left Stillwater, forget that his face and his innocence were casualties of war.

For Andrea Labore this river town just outside the Cities was as close as she would ever come to reclaiming the way of life she had known on the Iron Range. She could appreciate the same sights and sounds as her husband, could savor with him the redolence of the river. Never had she felt so contented.

It was a hot summer night two years back when she asked Rick to again ask her to marry him. The trial was over. Rick had left the station for the writer's life. What he hadn't planned on was the isolation. The monotony. Too much freedom and not enough discipline. He had money and time, a dangerous combination. It happened one of those dog days of summer in the dog days of his career, a day when Andrea stopped by his home in the sky. Only an hour earlier he had watched her deliver the ten o'clock news. Now they were sitting on the balcony, sipping wine and watching the lights of the city reflected in Lake Calhoun.

"And what became of the ring?" Andrea wanted to know.

"What ring is that?"

"The ring maybe I should have accepted."

"It might have fallen into the river while I was sandbagging."

"How far out in the river might it have fallen?"

Rick laughed. "Damn near halfway across. Hell of a throw. Threw my elbow out of whack."

Andrea laughed at his ability to joke at something that must have been so painful. She took off her shoes and let her toes play in the wrought iron that bordered the balcony. "If you were to get married," she asked Rick, "and I'm not suggesting you do, where would you do it? Like, would there be a honeymoon?"

"Well, if I did get married, and I'm certainly not planning on it, I'd probably take the lucky woman to Hawaii. Take the plunge there."

"Why there?"

"Sentimental reasons." Rick swallowed a large mouthful of wine and remembered back. "On my way to Fort Sam Houston, after I left the burn unit in Japan, we stopped over in Hawaii. One day the Navy took us over to Kauai, one of the less touristy islands. There was this point out on Hanalei, lush and beautiful. A lot of inlets and little peninsulas. I mean, you could hike right into a waterfall. Anyway, I remember all of these wounded soldiers sitting along this beautiful beach, wishing we never had to leave, more afraid of the society we were going home to than of the war we had just come from. And I thought, What a special place. I'd like to come back here someday for something really special." He took another sip of wine. "So if I was going to get married, and I'm certainly not going to, that's where I'd take her."

Looking out on the water, Andrea Labore could see the blinking red warning light atop the IDS Tower and the ring of newsroom lights just below. "I always thought—I know this sounds silly and vain, but I always thought that my being on television would attract better men, make me more desirable to a better class of men. Isn't that stupid? I think we all believed that going in. We're like that CBS logo, only one open eye."

"And?"

"Assholes," Andrea told him. "One asshole after another. Tall, handsome assholes. Rich assholes. Doctor assholes. Lawyer assholes. Political assholes. It's been a real eye-opening experience."

"The Weatherman calls me the Masked Asshole."

"Yes, but, ironically, women don't. I think men are more threatened by you than women . . . not just the mask but the war-hero status, the journalistic skills."

"Flattery will only get you so far, Andrea." He stood and leaned over the rail, watching the lights dancing in the water.

"Hey," she said, "I know you too well to flatter you."

"How well?"

"Well enough to know that you're the man I want to marry." She smiled just a little, just enough to fire up her great brown eyes.

"Is this a proposal?" Rick said, too breathlessly to disguise his feelings.

"Well," she said, moving over to kiss him, "will you?"

"Will I what?"

"Will you ask me to marry you?"

"Okay, but if you say yes, you have to buy your own damn ring." And they melted into each other's arms.

That was two years ago. She was asleep, her face turned away from him. Rick stole out of the fourposter bed and slipped on a pair of gym shorts. Rick envied his wife. Fifteen minutes after her head hit the pillow Andrea was out like a rock. Not even a happy marriage brought him peaceful sleep. He looked out the open window, the trace of a valley breeze filtering through the screen. The wind felt good on the bare skin below his mask.

The June moon was at perigee, the closest it would ever come to the earth. Its reflection off the river flooded the St. Croix Valley with enough night light to read by. Perhaps somewhere out there tonight somebody was reading his novel. After the initial euphoria of being a published author wore off, Rick too often found himself yawning and shrugging his shoulders whenever an unpublished writer asked, "What's it feel like?" They say that inside every newsman is a novelist struggling to be born, but inside this novelist was a newsman who wouldn't die, wouldn't even go to sleep.

On another hill in the same town sat a brilliant man in an iron cage, convicted, perhaps unjustly, of having killed seven times. Despite more than two years of trying, Rick couldn't prove the Weatherman's innocence. As with the Wakefield story, he waited for the dream that would tie together all of the clues and provide for him the dramatic answers. But the dream never came.

The author picked up the Weatherman's photocopied diary and rested in an overstuffed antique chair beside the window. Moonlight fell across the pages, across the precise southern script learned by rote in another river town where during the sufferingly hot and humid summers a breeze off the water was as precious as a cool Yankee rain.

For instance this story I tell second hand because I wasn't born yet. I heard different versions of the tragedy while growing up, but over the years I've been able to piece together a pretty good picture of what all happened that day. I had been conceived and I was fixing to crawl into the world in about a month when the roof literally fell in on us and left me and Momma to fend for ourselves.

My folks liked to fight. It didn't take a whole lot to set them off. Just a Saturday afternoon taking the clan to the movies would pretty much do it. I had a brother and a sister, four and five years old, Momma was eight months pregnant with me, and Daddy he was pretty much fed up with the lot of us. We were supposed to go to the two o'clock matinee but the fighting and fussin' pushed our arrival at the Saenger Theatre back to the four o'clock showing. They argued about the price. Most movies were twenty cents, but this was a Disney movie and Disney movies were a quarter. Daddy complained that meant a dollar just to get in the damn door. Once inside the movie house they argued about where to sit. Brother Alex and Sister being little all wanted to sit up front and stare at the screen with their mouths gaping. My Daddy who never quite got around to growing up liked to sit right up front too. Well, Momma wouldn't have none of that ... bad for the eyes, can't see or hear a thing, and on and on. The fight ended as per usual. They went their separate ways. Daddy, Brother Alex and Sister took seats right up front, while Momma with me stuffed inside of her huffed and puffed all the way to the very last row against the back wall. The movie began. Don't ask me what movie, I was told but I don't recall, but it was a Disney movie.

It was unseasonably warm and blustery for early December. Hot winds were kicking up dust and debris. Christmas lighting already decorated Washington Street, that's the main street through downtown Vicksburg. A charity football game was scheduled for that night and most of the town would have been there. Football and beauty pageants, that's the South. Folks ran about town wrapping up their Saturday shopping because the stores closed at 6 P.M.

But that day the clocks never made it to 6 P.M. They froze at 5:35. Without a second of warning a tornado dropped out of thunderheads over the swamps of Louisiana, jumped the river like a Jack-in-the-box and tore into Vicksburg. It cut a diagonal line of death and destruction from the cotton compress on the Yazoo Canal to the National Military Park northeast of the city. And right in the middle of that fatal path was the Saenger Theatre packed with children and a smattering of parents.

When the twister had passed the only part of the theatre left intact was the little foyer and two rows of seats along the rear wall. Beyond that . . . the worst natural disaster in Vicksburg's history. The giant beams snapped like toothpicks bringing down the roof and the walls. The silver screen crumbled like a piece of typing paper. In seconds the sky went from day to night. Rain swept over the ruins in torrents. Can't be anything sadder than the wails of children in the dark crippled by something they didn't see and can't understand. Years later I would study the photographs. Truth be told, more people got out of that theatre alive than anybody who first looked at it could have imagined . . . but Daddy, Brother Alex and Sister weren't counted among the living. My momma was rushed to the hospital in shock. I was born premature that night.

The streets of Vicksburg looked like the aftermath of Grant's siege. But what took the Union general 47 days to accomplish took the tornado only 47 seconds. Christmas decorations hung helter skelter across mounds of rubble. Soldiers arrived and barricaded the intersections. 38 people were killed in that terrible storm that terrible day, too many for a small town. An especially high toll on children. Besides the Saenger Theatre the tornado also leveled the Happyland Nursery, killing young ones there.

After that, Momma took to drink. We moved in with Granddaddy Graham in the shotgun house above the tracks and that's where I was raised.

Momma told me before the tornado we lived in a big ole house off Halls Ferry Road near the Confederate lines. She'd even drive me by there at times and point it out. It was a big white house with pillars and it sat on a hill and it had a manicured lawn that rolled down to the road and the prettiest little garden filled with the most brilliant azaleas I ever saw. Of course, I knew early on we had never lived there, but I never questioned her. I think that's where Momma wanted to live.

Rick Beanblossom laid the Weatherman's diary on his lap. Reading by moonlight was a strain on his eyes. He felt a headache coming on. Andrea rolled over, sound asleep, her eyes closed, her breathing even. He watched her sleep and thought of how much he loved her. He knew her now, knew the qualities behind the perfect face. Understood her quiet intelligence, her thirst to know more about life. He admired the way she had grown as a journalist, as a human being, admired the way she had forced him to grow.

The man in the mask leaned an elbow on the window-sill and in the sweet stillness of a summer night stared out across the valley. He could see the old courthouse on the hill with a bronze soldier a hundred years old standing guard. He could see the bluffs of Wisconsin so green and lush not even the night could darken their allure. And where the St. Croix River left town and headed for its rendezvous with the Mississippi Rick could just barely make out the pitched roof of a guard tower between the pines. Tomorrow he would pay the Confederate prisoner there another visit. He couldn't help wondering if this visit would be his last. When the air turned cool, when the leaves dried up and fell to the ground, the Supreme

Court of the land would decide the fate of the Weatherman.

Each inmate was allowed eighteen hours of visitation per month. The hours were from 1:30 to 9:00 P.M. At two o'clock Rick Beanblossom signed in. He surrendered his driver's license and had his hand stamped. Within the prison walls the man in the mask had become a familiar sight. *"He's that writer married to Andrea Labore."* A guard ushered the most famous husband in Minnesota into the visitors' lounge. Compared with the county jail the room was a coffeehouse. There was a "no contact" area where booths with Plexiglas separated visitor from inmate, but it was used only for disciplinary reasons, for the inmates who couldn't keep their hands off their visitors. Most of the area resembled a comfortable depot lounge: vinyl chairs with wooden armrests, strung together in neat rows and watched over by a guard at a desk.

It was unusually busy for a weekday afternoon. The only empty row of chairs was in the back along the children's section, where the kids played while Mommy visited Daddy. On this afternoon no children were present. Rick studied the fairy-tale characters painted on the wall as he waited for Dixon Bell.

The guards held the door for him as the Weatherman entered. Two guards escorted Stillwater's only death row prisoner whenever he moved through the halls; at times it looked more like an honor guard than a security precaution.

Rick Beanblossom and Dixon Bell never shook hands. They were as awkward as they had been the first time they ever met. They kept their backs to the others in the room. The guards left them alone. News and weather took seats facing the wonderland over the play area. Fluffy white clouds were painted in a bright blue sky. The Queen was there, as was the White Rabbit. Humpty Dumpty sat on a wall. Alice enjoyed tea with the Mad Hatter.

"How is Andrea?" asked Dixon Bell.

"She's good. Puts a lot of work into the house. Hates

the long commute to the station. She sends her best to you."

The Weatherman's face almost turned into a smile. "Send her my best, too."

"Would you like for her to come and see you?"

"No. Tell her please don't." The silence was chilling. The Weatherman leaned forward. He nodded at the mural. "Humpty Dumpty looks like your Hubert Humphrey. What were those famous words of his, about human rights?"

"Dumpty's or Humphrey's?"

Dixon Bell laughed, relieving the tension. "Humphrey's."

" 'The time has arrived to get out of the shadow of states' rights and walk forthrightly into the bright sunshine of human rights.' "

Dixon Bell leaned back in his chair. "Ain't them pretty words."

"That was at the Democratic National Convention in Philadelphia in 1948," Rick said, educating the man on death row. "It was the first convention to be televised. After his speech the southern delegates walked off the convention floor in protest and stacked their party badges on a table in front of the TV cameras. After the cameras left, they picked up their badges and went back inside. No cameras were there to cover Humphrey's famous speech. Television had come to politics."

"I tuned into Sky High News the other night. Other than Andrea I hardly recognized the place, or the faces."

Rick agreed. "They got a new set. It looks like 'Sesame Street' to me. Ron Shea took that anchor job in Washington. The new anchor is named Stan Butts. They call him 'the butthole from Cleveland.' The new weather girl is from Salt Lake City."

The Weatherman shook his head in disgust. "Dumb blonde. Doesn't know a cool front from a storm front. What became of Jack Save-Me-Jesus Napoleon?"

"He's working for a television consulting firm in Des Moines. He's one of those TV doctors who run around the country trying to heal broken stations. Dave Cadieux went to work for a video production company in Los Angeles. Nobody ever hears from him.

"Charleen Barington?"

"Settled her lawsuit out of court. Lives in Dallas. Divorced. Works at a consulting firm for beauty pageants."

"Gayle the Ghoul?"

"Got married. She edits a magazine in Chicago. Her husband writes for a newspaper there."

"Chris Mack?"

"Took a PR job with Northwest Airlines."

"And Andy Mack dropped dead right in front of the weather wall."

"Yes."

"Television. What a business."

"Yeah, what a business."

After another uncomfortable interlude Dixon Bell announced, "I know what Andy said just before he died."

Rick looked up, startled. Impossible. How could he know? Rick and Andrea had told nobody about the puzzling last words muttered by the old weatherman as he lay dying on the studio floor.

Dixon Bell smiled, then broke into his favorite Andy Mack impersonation. "And in Rugby, North Dakota, today it was forty-eight degrees. And in Myrtle Creek, Oregon, it was fifty-five degrees. While down in Bogalusa, Louisiana, the temperature got all the way up to eighty-one degrees. Hard to believe."

Rick's heart dropped back into place. "That was Andy."

The Weatherman admired the clouds painted on the wall. "I see the National Weather Service finally got the Nexrad system up and running. It looks phenomenal. They say its radar would have spotted the Eden Prairie tornado."

The former television news producer got up from his chair and walked to the sky-blue wall. "Hell, you did that, and you didn't cost taxpayers three billion dollars." What had seemed impossible only a year ago now seemed inevitable to Rick: the state was going to execute this man who had saved so many lives that day. "There's a fingerprint expert from Scotland Yard speaking at a police chiefs' convention in Chicago next month. I told Stacy I might take copies of the transformer print there along with the AFIS information and get his opinion."

"What are you trying to tell me?"

"Just that we're still working on it."

Dixon Bell sighed. "I wonder where I'd be right now if that tornado had shown up on computers, and that fingerprint hadn't."

Rick Beanblossom took a deep breath. "Dixon, I want to have your diary published. At least let the local papers have it."

"No siree, absolutely not."

"You've never understood news, Weatherman. There are a hundred copies of your diary down at the county attorney's office. It's going to leak out anyway, page by page, and every page will be out of context. If the Supreme Court doesn't hear your case, the only thing that's going to save your ass is a PR campaign launched at the governor. In his heart Ellefson doesn't believe in the death penalty any more than I do."

The Weatherman nodded in agreement. "You're right. I've never understood news. What exactly does this 'off the record' mean?"

"It means that you never said it, and I never heard you say it. You know that."

"But I mean, to really maintain a trusting relationship with all those secret sources of yours, you have to be pretty true to this 'off the record' stuff—kind of like a priest, huh?"

"Yeah, kind of like a priest."

"Betray one source, you lose them all?"

"Probably, yes."

Dixon Bell glanced over his shoulder. The guard at the desk was on the phone, paying them no attention. The Weatherman lifted a piece of paper from his shirt pocket. It had been folded and tucked so many times it looked like a tiny present. He held it out to Rick. "Here, Kemo Sabay, this is for you."

Rick Beanblossom reached for the note but Dixon Bell jerked it away, the devil's grin breaking like lightning across his face. "But you see, it's off the record."

"What does that mean?" asked Rick.

"That means I never wrote it, and you never read it." That crazy look was descending over the Weatherman. "It's for your eyes only. Not to be opened until after my death—be that next month, or be it the next century. Is it a deal?"

"Only under one condition."

"No conditions."

"One condition," Rick demanded. "Could this note—or whatever it is—could it save your life?"

The Weatherman began laughing; his shallow, mocking laugh.

"C'mon, stay with me on this, Weatherman. The sun is setting on this story."

"No. The words on this piece of paper can't save my life."

The newsman with a thousand sources, and a thousand promises to keep, took another second to think about this odd request from this incongruous man. "Okay," he said. "It's a deal. Off the record."

"Forever?"

"Forever."

Dixon Bell handed over the note.

Rick Beanblossom rolled the small rectangle between his fingers. "Why are you giving this to me now?"

"Because I don't want to see you anymore."

"And why is that?"

"Let's just say I'm tired of looking at your ugly face."

Dixon Bell was back in his cell for the 3:30 lockup. Rick Beanblossom brought out the devil in him. At what point would the masked asshole read the note? Would it matter? Just before the bars slid closed, Carol Theguard handed him his daily bundle of mail. He sat on his bunk and listened as a thousand prison cells slammed closed and the body count began. The afternoon sun was streaming through the tall windows, causing a precipitate rise in the temperature. The giant fans in the day room only blew the hot air around. The Weatherman flipped through the mail, checking the postmarks. He always opened first the letters that came from the farthest away. Today there was a letter postmarked Honolulu, Hawaii. No return address showing. Without opening it he held it up to the light like a private detective. He was getting good at this. A prison game he'd invented: forecasting the contents of his mail.

The letter was handwritten in a beige envelope. It had the faint scent of island flowers. It was from a young woman. It was a friendly letter, but the stationery had a military feel to it. It was a very personal letter; she wanted something. He ran the envelope beneath his nose and could almost smell the ocean breeze. Then it hit him, stronger than any letter delivered in prison had ever hit him. This letter was from a girl he had known long ago. A girl he loved? A knot grew in his stomach—nothing to be afraid of, but the knot was there. Letters had always been his undoing. He slowly peeled open the resealed envelope and removed the sheet of paper. He unfolded it and read. The Weatherman was right on all counts.

Dear Dixon Bell

My name is Su St. Germain. I am a nurse at the Tripler Army Medical Center in Honolulu, Hawaii. Though I am now an American citizen, I am Vietnamese by birth. Like many Vietnamese Americans I came to the States in 1975 after the war was lost. I was a four-year-old orphan then. Upon arriving in Hawaii I was put up for adoption. I'm told I was very cute, and it was these cute looks I used to charm a naval officer and his wife into adopting me. I grew up a Navy brat. But I was very lucky. They were wonderful parents, retired now and living on Maui.

So why am I writing you? Those of us who were forced to flee our homeland have formed something of a refugee club here in Honolulu. Members of our club have told me a story about my escape from Vietnam that I only vaguely remember. I remember this nice man who found me in a crowded room and bought me a bowl of soup. I remember bombs falling on us and I was very scared. I remember the man chasing an airplane and trying to put me on it, but I didn't want to go. Then they pulled me out of his arms and into the airplane with all the crowded people and I couldn't stop crying. That is all I remember. But others in our club are much older than I am. Two of them were on that same airplane. They have told me the plane was overcrowded and everybody was afraid they were going to crash. The pilot was trying to take off so no more people would get on board. They were fighting to close the door when a big man came running down the runway chasing the plane with a little girl in his arms. The little girl was me. My friends believe this man was the weatherman at the Tan Son Nhut Air Base.

Over the years I have tried to find out who this weatherman was so that I can thank him. But all of my letters to the Air Force have come back with the same dismissive answer. "Sorry, your request is for CLASSIFIED information. Your request has been DENIED."

I have read in news magazines of your trial and your conviction. I am very sorry. One of the articles said that you were a meteorologist in the Air Force and you were stationed in Vietnam during the fall of Saigon.

Mr. Bell, were you the weatherman at the Tan Son Nhut Air Base on April 29, 1975? Did you find a lost little girl at the evacuation center and race to put her on a plane to America? If you did, I am that little girl. I would like very much please to hear from you.

I am married (yes, he too is in the Navy) and I have a little girl of my own now. We hope to have another child soon. It would mean a lot to me and my family if I could tell them more about how I came to America. If you can help me in any way please write me at the address below.

I'll be praying for you.

Sincerely
Su St. Germain

The former Air Force officer dropped the letter on his bunk, the bunk where he now had three sleeping pills safely tucked away. He grabbed the roll of toilet paper from the shelf and blew his nose. He swallowed the lump of pride in his throat. He looked at the bars on the door and felt swallowed up in shame. Little Tan Jan. Who'd have thought it? Dear God, what to tell her? He swiped at a tear. Dixon Bell read the letter again. When he was finished he read it one more time.

He left the rest of the day's mail unopened. He stepped over to his desk and picked up the Holy Bible. He knew enough to turn to the New Testament. Dixon Bell found himself paging through the Gospel According to Matthew. At chapter 16 he smiled. Seems even Jesus Christ

had taken a stab at weather forecasting. Christ said to the
Pharisees, "It will be stormy today, for the sky is red and
threatening." Matthew didn't say what happened after
that, so it was a safe bet that Christ blew it and it was
sunny all day. The Weatherman returned to the bunk with
the Bible. When he finished reading an hour later, he
marked his spot with the letter from Tan Jan.

THE WARRANT

On the day the Weatherman was scheduled to leave the Ramsey County jail for death row in Stillwater, the deputies lined up beside the sally port to shake his hand, joking he was the first prisoner in the jail's history who actually stuck his head right through a wall. He smiled a sad smile at the thought of that day. And he thought of other times. He thought back to the children who gave him a standing ovation for merely walking into their classroom. He remembered the night Sky High News won the ratings war and they drank champagne out of styrofoam cups like the one he now gripped in his hand. And, of course, of the afternoon he picked the tornado out of the sky over Eden Prairie and sounded the first warning.

He remembered the first time he laid eyes on Andrea Labore. She walked into the newsroom in a gold plaid pantsuit over a yellow blouse. The bright colors set off her big brown eyes and her shiny autumn hair. He was thunderstruck. Frozen by her beauty. Recognizing the Weatherman from television, she smiled at him from across the room. Then Chris Mack slapped him on the back. "Be careful, Dixon—she once killed a man who looked at her wrong."

He remembered his first night on Memphis TV. He was so awful, so tongue-tied he was sure he was going to be fired. Thank God it rained cats and dogs that night, just like he said it would. When he was honorably discharged from the Air Force after twenty years of service the pilots he had guided through the storm clouds threw a party for him in the control tower. Why no planes crashed that night is still a military mystery.

He remembered the Vietnamese people who thought he

was God because he could read the weather. He saw himself running down the runway chasing a transport plane with the only girl who ever loved him back begging not to be released from his arms. Then the newsreel of his life came to an end.

Weeks had passed since the letter from Tan Jan. Summer had rolled to an end. The first Monday of October had come and gone. The United States Supreme Court had returned to work. Now Dixon Bell sat on the edge of his bunk with a lethal combination of five sleeping pills in the palm of his left hand and a styrofoam cup filled with cold water in the fist of his right hand. Light from the new moon of the falling leaves slipped through the windows and the shadows of the iron bars spilled over him. In the dark those pills looked like the lemon drops he sucked on as a boy. He wished that somehow the glass of water was a glass of wine. The snoring and deep breathing of a hundred men locked behind bars filled the block. Once in a while a toilet flushed. The guard on the graveyard shift had just moved by his cell, counting bodies. They'd been locked up all day because of the Weatherman. But nobody complained. Nobody blamed him. He wore a badge of respect among the inmates, especially those in the Seg Unit. Death row. Now he was leaving them.

In the hours before lights out they yelled, "Fucking bastards!"

"You hang in there, Weatherman!"

"Our hearts will be out there with you!"

In his previous life as a TV weatherman these men were the scum of the earth whose crimes he saw at the top of the news show. Now they were the only family he had left.

That morning the cells were not opened and a lockup began. Several times a year this happened. The entire prison population would be put under lockup. These lockups were unannounced. Every inmate was confined to his cell for two or three days. Meals were delivered through the bars. Access to telephones was denied. To ensure that all television sets and radios were out of commission the main power was switched off and emergency lighting was used, giving the entire fortress the dim, unearthly glow of a submarine. Then the guard staff went cell to cell with flashlights and dogs, searching for contraband—weapons, drugs, cash. Breakfast was delivered to Dixon Bell's cell that morning, as was lunch. By dinner time the prison grapevine, which operated under full lockup, signaled something was amiss. No searches were being conducted. There was something happening in the outside world that they didn't want the inmates to know.

It killed the Weatherman to be denied his two hours of yard time. The leaves were showing their true colors. The air was crisp and clean. The barometer was on the rise. Birds were on the wing, heading south. In Minnesota the autumns are fleeting. He lived for one more day in the sun. But when the double-barred entrance to the Seg Unit clanged open after dinner, it didn't take a sixth sense for Dixon Bell to realize there would be no more days in the sun. They weren't coming to search the cells. They were coming for him.

He was white with fear. He worried about his pills. This was the first lockup since the good doctor had addressed his sleeping problem. He looked up. Warden Johnson was standing on the other side of the bars, as was the deputy commissioner of corrections. They were accompanied by the chief of security and four guards. The warden gave a nod of his head and Carol Theguard unlocked the cell door. Johnson stepped inside. The others waited in the day room.

The Weatherman stood and faced the warden the same way he had stood more than two years earlier and faced Judge Lutoslawski as the judge, in a sorrowful voice, sentenced him to death.

Warden Johnson was more straightforward. Phlegmatic. "Stacy Dvorchak called me from Washington this morning. She wanted me to be the one to tell you. The Supreme Court refused to hear your case. Governor Ellefson signed your death warrant at three o'clock this afternoon. The commissioner will set the date of your execution tomorrow morning. Then you'll be moved to the isolation cell in the house. Get your things together tonight and let us know what you want done with them. You will not be allowed to take anything with you."

"My Bible?"

"No, there's a Bible out there."

"But this one has my name in it."

That was six hours ago. He was all alone now. Just him, five sleeping pills, and glass of water. The Weatherman stared into the face of his blackened Sony and tried to picture himself warning viewers of an approaching storm. Stay off the ice. Get an early start in the morning. Bundle up the kids. Y'all enjoy the weekend, it's going to be a good one. For every day of every season a cliché that he could spit out without even thinking. Wherever his travels took him, he left with memories of the weather: the humidity of Mississippi, the heat of Vietnam, the soft green of Tennessee in the springtime, the blazing autumns of New England, and the winter sun rising on a blanket of pure white snow over pine-laden Minnesota. There was something about the weather he loved and hated in all of those places. And each place he departed left a vacancy in his heart, the ache to feel and breathe the weather there one more time. It was never people he missed, but a chilly breeze through the trees, the dazzling sun on his skin, a thunderstorm being born, or the refreshing cool smell of a dying drizzle. A life dictated by the weather.

Dixon Bell looked up from the television set at the Sky High News weather calendar posted on his cell wall. It was on this October date nearly three decades ago that he ran his heart out in a Homecoming football game and then the next night went to the dance alone, stood off to the side like the court jester as the school crowned a queen.

One night while on death row this Homecoming Queen had come to him for the last time, not the frumpy, dumpy woman who testified at the trial but the eighteen-year-old southern belle who so obsessed him in his youth. When he opened his eyes in a half-sleep he guessed it was one of those ungodly hours when dreamers dream and writers write. The windows in the day room outside his cell that ran three stories to the ceiling were tinted blue, and bright moonlight filtered through the bars. It was in this blue moonlight she appeared, floating before him like the goddess he'd made her out to be.

Lisa Beauregard was resplendent in a formal evening gown that had nuances of royal red. It was not a gown a girl would wear to the prom but something a bit more special, like the attire of a young woman attending her first military gala on the arm of an officer. Her brown eyes sparkled. Her silky hair flowed down over her shoulders. Pearls ringed her neck. Pearls dangled from her ears. Her gold-ringed fingers were clasped in front of her, a Mississippi Queen in the regalia of southern aristocracy.

He smiled up at her—a genuine smile, one from the heart. Lisa smiled back the same way. A smile that said, You were a special friend to me, Dixon Bell. Thank you for loving me. Thank you for reminding me that I was once pretty and popular and boys followed me through town and vied for my attention. It was the smile he saw so often in the halls of Vicksburg High School. The smile he dreamed of in Vietnam. And, yes too, it was a smile that said good-bye forever.

For then her smile turned ugly, the dream a nightmare. Slowly waking up, he remembered where it was he was sleeping. The saintly image of the first girl he truly loved began to vanish quite slowly in the blue moon glass, disappearing, disappearing, fading away until, as with the Cheshire Cat, only a malicious grin remained.

"Do you have any final words before the will of the people is carried out?"

"Yeah, fuckhead, I got some final words. Y'all want a confession? I did it. I killed them all! Not just eight of them. I'm responsible for every unsolved murder from New Orleans to Duluth. Hundreds of them. I fucked them, then I killed them. Some of them I killed first, then I fucked them. Let's do it, cuz y'all got the right man. I killed them all, ya fuckheads!"

Dixon Bell began to cry, tears streaming into his hands and over the sleeping pills, causing them to stick to his palm. He was not a meteorologist. He was not even the local-yokel weatherman. He was a convicted murderer sentenced to die in the electric chair. Through his tears he saw the Holy Bible on his desk, the Holy Bible where he had a letter stashed from a woman who wanted to know if he was the man who had saved her life, the Holy Bible in which his name had been printed. Oh, yes, Jesus Christ thought he too could read the weather, but in the end he failed miserably and they put him to death in the rain.

Dixon Bell wiped his runny nose with the sleeve of his shirt. He dried his eyes. He got up off his bunk and poured the cup of water into the toilet. He dropped the five pills into the water one at a time. Suicide required courage he did not have. He pushed the lever and watched euthanasia flush away. Then the Weatherman got down on his knees. He folded his hands over the toilet bowl. He bowed his head. And for the first time in his life he said a prayer.

THE RITUAL

And so continued the slow waltz with death. The state commissioner of corrections in consultation with Judge Lutoslawski set the date of the execution. At the stroke of midnight on the evening of October 31, Dixon Graham Bell was to be electrocuted, the first scheduled execution in Minnesota since 1906.

The third and final cell of the Weatherman's incarceration was six feet by eight feet, even smaller than his cell in the Segregation Unit, which was smaller than the triangular cell he had destroyed at the Ramsey County jail. The state was boxing him into a coffin one foot at a time. He was put on death watch and it was every bit the nightmare he feared. His stay in this brick sepulcher was not meant to prepare him, it was meant to break him, so that when the time came to take the long walk he would be spineless, nothing but flesh and jelly. Death would be as welcome as a warm spring after a long, cold winter.

The isolation cell had been whitewashed and left void of amenities. There were only a mattress over a shallow bunk, a pillow, and a heavy blanket. A seatless toilet and his Bible. Nothing else. No sink. Not even a window. They had done the cruelest thing that could be done to a meteorologist: they took away the sky.

Most states that exercise capital punishment have hundreds of men on death row. Minnesota had only one. Everything was new. The state tried to proceed as if the routine were common practice, but the guards were almost embarrassed by the ritual. The low-watt bulb in the condemned man's cell was never turned off. Days without sun. Nights without dark. Every move he made was monitored both electronically and physically. A guard sat outside the cell and watched him twenty-four hours a day. Even when he sat on the toilet a guard sat and watched. Hanging from the ceiling above the guard was a surveillance camera pointing inside the cell. Another guard sat in the Security Center and watched him from there.

If he needed toilet paper, he had to ask for it; the same with a toothbrush and toothpaste. When done, he returned them. He was given one sheet of typing paper and a fat pencil with a dull point. He had to return them as soon as he had finished his writing. He was allowed one newspaper or magazine at a time, to be returned immediately when he'd finished his reading. Other than the Bible, books were forbidden.

They dressed him in a blue jumpsuit that made him look like an auto mechanic. White socks and blue slippers. His meals were served on a paper plate, his coffee in a paper cup. The only utensil he was given was a plastic spoon that they would collect right after the meal. The cook considerately sliced the meat for him, but for the most part he took to eating with his fingers. After a week of this nonsense Dixon Bell lost his appetite. He stopped eating. He lived on bread and coffee. It was not a hunger strike; there was not enough time to starve to death. The Weatherman simply sickened of the ritual.

"You haven't been eating your meals."

"No siree, I haven't. What are you gonna do, arrest me?"

Seemed every time Warden Johnson turned around, Dixon Bell was messing up the ritual. The warden didn't enter the cell, just excused the guard and leaned against the bars. "I need to know what you'd like for your last meal, Dixon. I'll get you anything you want. That's the tradition."

"With all respect, Warden, I think you know what you can do with the last supper."

"Yes, I thought you might say that. Also, as a veteran you are to be awarded an American flag upon your death for the service you gave to your country. Who do you want the flag presented to?"

"Why don't you wrap the last supper in it."

Warden Johnson rarely lost his composure. "I'm trying to be as fair to you as circumstances and the law allows.

But I'll bend. I'll do my best to grant any last request you might have."

The Weatherman laughed, his evil laugh. "Can you get me a woman?"

"Is that what you want?"

Dixon Bell almost saved the taxpayers of Minnesota an electric bill because he about dropped dead when he heard that. Then he thought a minute. He thought real hard. No, it wasn't a woman he wanted. "I want to meet the man who's going to throw the switch. The executioner. I want to talk to him."

"Dixon, that's ridiculous. It's strictly against procedure."

"There ain't no procedure. I'm the first."

Warden Oliver J. Johnson stood there and thought about it. Finally he said, "I'll only promise you this . . . I'll talk to that person and see what that person thinks of the idea."

"Person" was a euphemism for "woman." They were going to have a woman throw the switch. Dixon Bell watched as the warden left the Death House. "Lousy bastards," he muttered.

It was not the horror of his final destination that bothered Dixon Bell as much as the waiting. He was forced out of monotony to watch television, the second-cruelest thing that could be done to him. On a chair outside his cell next to the guard sat a portable Sony. He was constantly reminded that it was a color TV, as if they still made black-and-whites. The guards turned it off and on for him and changed the channels whenever he asked. In other words, the guards spent all their time watching the Weatherman on their surveillance TV watching his TV set.

"Do you have any final words before the will of the people is carried out?"

"Yeah, asshole, I got some final words. You lock me in a tiny cage where I can't even walk back and forth and then you try to make up for it by giving me a fucking television set. 'And it's a color TV!' Fuck y'all to hell! I hope this execution is televised. Then I can show you Yankee faggots how a real man dies. He doesn't go out wimpering apologies or babbling to Lordy Jesus. No siree.

He goes out screaming at the top of his lungs, 'Fuck y'all to hell!' Live and in living color, 'Fuck y'all to hell!' "

The isolation cell was only thirty feet from the chair. The infamous long walk was really a very short walk. Dixon Bell was told he would not be allowed to see the death chamber until the end.

Once a day, usually late in the afternoon, they would test the chair. Suddenly and without warning there would be a loud clunk and all of the lights would dim. If this test was conducted to make the Weatherman shudder, it worked. It reminded him of those old Frankenstein movies he and his granddaddy had watched on late-night TV when he was a boy—sparks jumping all over the laboratory as the electricity shot into the monster's brain.

One day they came into the cell and measured him for his burial suit, the clothes in which he would be executed. They wouldn't tell him what he'd be wearing, but he suspected it wouldn't be from Pierre Cardin.

By watching the reports on television and gathering yesterday's weather data from the newspapers Dixon Bell was able to make his own forecasts. Though not nearly as accurate, he was still batting above .700. The autumn colors were at their peak now, and it pained him to be missing the closing act in Minnesota's theater of changing seasons. Whenever the door to the outside world was unbolted and opened, the Weatherman could smell the leaves. As for the colors, he had to settle for what he could see on his TV.

Stacy Dvorchak remained in Washington, where she filed another desperate appeal with the United States Supreme Court. She publicly vowed she would be camped on the front lawn of the home of the Chief Justice when it came time for her client to take the long walk. Dixon Bell was not hopeful. His only prayer seemed to be the international outcry aimed at Governor Ellefson's office. Here again he was not optimistic. The governor had signed the death penalty bill. He had signed his death warrant. Why would he now commute his sentence to life in prison, unless his conscience would not allow the Weatherman to be killed?

He was allowed only one visitor a day. For one hour. They could sit in the cell with him. Rick Beanblossom requested a visit nearly every day, but Dixon Bell shot him down. He could no longer face that mask. Yet ten days before the execution date he did grant a visitation request to a friend and foe of a different sort.

When the outside door swung open, Dixon Bell could smell the cigarette being extinguished in the grass. The hacking cough rattled through the Death House. The Marlboro Man to the bitter end. He appeared near death, wheezing up a storm. The guard was worried about him as he unlocked the cell door. Les Angelbeck took a seat on the bunk beside the Weatherman. He caught his breath. The guard held on to his cane outside.

"You look like hell," Dixon Bell told him. "I'll probably outlive you."

"No," said the captain, clearing his throat, "I'll see you to your grave, Dixon." He paused for the longest time, carefully measuring every breath, every word. "On the other hand, I met with Governor Ellefson yesterday. I believe the governor would consider commuting your sentence to life imprisonment if you were to confess to your crimes."

"Strange offer," Dixon Bell said with an ironic chuckle. "If you know for sure I'm guilty, you'll let me rot in prison for the rest of my life. But if you're not sure, then you'll kill me."

Les Angelbeck didn't argue the point. He glanced at the Sony on the chair outside the cell. "I see you got a TV set there."

The Weatherman glared at the rectangular monster on the chair. "It was television that ruined the South. Television did more damage below the Mason-Dixon line than Sherman's march to the sea."

"Yes, it's pretty much made ghouls of us all." The old police captain picked up the Bible. "Is this yours, Dixon?"

"Yes, it has my name in it. I've been reading it. Ain't that the damnedest thing? I'd always believed science and religion were incompatible. They're not, you know?"

"Yes, I know."

"Are you going to be there when . . . ?"

"No. Do you want me there?"

"No, please don't."

"Do you have any family left?"

"No, there's nobody. Thank God."

Les Angelbeck laid the Weatherman's Bible on the bunk and looked about the sparse cage of steel and concrete.

"Donny Redmond's son won a basketball scholarship to Florida State. Isn't that funny? Full circle."

"Seems a lot of people are returning to their roots these days."

"My daughter is trying to get me out there to California. She doesn't think I can survive another Minnesota winter. Quite frankly, neither do I."

When the conversation died, the dying policeman and the condemned weatherman sat in stony silence. No coughing or wheezing even. It was the longest anybody could remember seeing the Marlboro Man go without a cigarette in his mouth. Down home a friend was defined as someone you could sit in silence with and not be embarrassed by the silence. That was the feeling Dixon Bell enjoyed as they shared their last hour in the isolation cell—though how in hell he could end up friends with the one man who had done the most to see that he was convicted of multiple murders was beyond explanation.

"It was the fingerprint," Les Angelbeck finally said.

"It's not mine," answered Dixon Bell.

The veteran of World War II, the veteran of a thousand criminal investigations, fought his way to his feet. The guard unlocked the door and slid it aside. Les Angelbeck clutched his heart in agony and glanced up at the dull but omnipresent light in the concrete ceiling. "There is one loose end I'd like tied up, if you would, Dixon. For my own peace of mind. What became of the letters in your diary, the letters from that Lisa woman?"

"I really don't know, Captain. They were tucked into the diary in the weather center. I have no reason to hide them from you now. As far as the trial goes, those letters wouldn't have changed anything. I still believe somebody stole them to hurt me."

"Or to protect you?"

The guard handed him his cane as he stepped outside. The cell door was closed, the electronic bolt shot locked with a bang.

Dixon Bell stepped to the door and clutched the bars. "This ain't television, Captain. All of the answers won't be explained to you five minutes before the hour. This is a tragedy. You're going to have to think about this one for the rest of your life, however short that may be."

The old cop turned on his cane and shook his head. "My

heart may be failing me, Dixon, but it's still telling me I got the right man, and I sincerely believe the only fair penalty for that man is death. Good-bye, Weatherman."

With seven days to go before the date of the execution Warden Oliver Johnson paid another visit to the Death House. An elderly janitor followed behind. Again the warden excused the guard. Johnson stood outside the cell, the old man over his right shoulder. "Your former employer, Channel 7 . . . their suit to broadcast or tape the execution was rejected in federal district court. The judge called the idea 'ghoulish' and their argument 'asinine'— unusually harsh words from a federal bench. It's doubtful there will be an appeal."

Dixon Bell stuck his hands through the cell door and rested his wrists on the crossbar. He was tired and weak. He was dropping weight fast. "Shoot, I was planning to use that air time to give the ninety-day winter forecast." He looked at the janitor, then back at the warden. "Who's our friend?"

"Dixon, this is the man you wanted to meet, the man who has volunteered to throw the switch that will take your life. He agreed to see you. His name is Jesse."

Dixon Bell was shocked—poor choice of words, but that's the way he felt. Old Jesse, everybody called him. He'd been at the trial. The Weatherman stood frozen in place, staring through the bars at this pathetic old man, this janitor he sometimes saw push a broom through the Seg Unit only to stop in front of his cell and stare out the window at the sky as if he were searching for a star. He checked with the sober face of Warden Johnson just to make sure it wasn't a joke. "And you're going to let him do this?"

"I'm sorry. Nobody else came forward. It'll be kept secret."

Dixon Bell turned his hostile gaze back on Old Jesse. "Will you be paid for this mad act?"

"Yes, sir, I will."

"How much, may I ask?"

"Five hundred and sixty-five dollars."

"And what are you going to do with the money?"

The executioner was clearly uncomfortable with the

question. He turned to the warden for help, but none was forthcoming. "Well," he finally drawled, "I thought I might buy my great-grandson a new bicycle. Maybe one of those fancy Schwinns."

In an instant tears welled up in the eyes of Dixon Bell, but he didn't know if they would be forced down his face by grief or laughter. He swallowed hard and put a hold on the tears. Damned if a smile didn't cross his face. By God, he did not live in vain. They could nail him to their electric cross now. He knew the meaning of life. It was all for a Schwinn. "Don't screw it up," the Weatherman warned him. "There ain't no need to torture me."

"I'll do it right, Mr. Bell, just like the warden tells me."

"Thank you, Jesse. Thank you for seeing me."

"**S**o what did he say to you?"

"Who say what to me?"

"The Weatherman. C'mon, Jess, everybody knows you were in there."

"Didn't say nothin'. I just swept up a bit for him. Then he done thank me."

They were in the electric shop beside the Death House, Old Jesse and shop supervisor Dwayne Rossi. Old Jesse would be responsible for the actual death, but Rossi was in charge of the Death House equipment. The execution was less than a week away. Rossi held the death cap in his hand. "This whole headset works was shipped up here from Florida. I'll be damned if I know if it's put together right, but I'm supposed to inspect it."

"Looks right enough to me," Old Jesse told him. "Wouldn't for sure want that thing on my head."

"Oh, no, this ain't right. Looky here, someone already stitched in the sponge."

"Ain't that where it goes?"

"Yeah, but it's gotta be soaked in salt water. It can't be stitched in until the night of the execution." Rossi pulled on the sponge. A large chunk of it broke off in his hand. "Awful cheap-ass sponge for such an important job." He accidentally tore off another piece. "Aw, Christ!"

Old Jesse watched intently as the supervisor tried to

put the sponge back together with about as much success as all the king's men had with Humpty Dumpty.

Rossi tossed the sponge bits to the floor in frustration. "We'll have to get a new one, Jess. If I give you some money out of petty cash, can you pick up a new sponge tonight?"

"What kinda sponge?"

"I don't know . . . a sponge is a sponge. Just make sure it's big enough to fit over this wire mesh."

So on his way home that night Old Jesse stopped in at Woolworth's and bought a new sponge for the death cap. Nobody explained to him the difference between a natural ocean sponge and a man-made synthetic sponge. Nobody explained the flammable difference.

THE LETTERS

Andrea Labore came out of the bathroom, sat on the edge of the bed, and grabbed hold of the corner post. She slipped her hand under her bathrobe and pressed it firmly against her stomach. She breathed deep, still nauseous.

At the foot of the bed the portable television set was glowing. The schlocky music began to play and Sky High News came on the air. Andrea had left work early, drove home sick under dark and threatening skies. Sitting in the anchor chair next to Stan Butts was Katherine Thompson-Jones, or Katie Tom-Jon in the newsroom, where everybody had a nickname. She was young and beautiful and overeducated, a real brown-eyed beauty up from Missouri. She spoke with that perky twang in her voice that made her sound fresh and appealing. The photogs loved her. Now she was the fill-in anchor. For the most part Andrea ignored the bitch, gave her the cold shoulder.

"Hundreds of peaceful protesters, thousands of letters from around the world, and too many phone calls to monitor have not changed the mind of Minnesota Governor Per Ellefson. The word is still 'go' for this week's execution of convicted serial killer Dixon Graham Bell ... a former meteorologist in the Twin Cities."

Andrea sighed. With smoke and mirrors they were now pretending he had never been employed by Channel 7. Watching the news at home was like putting in another thirty minutes of work. She muted the sound.

Rick had left her a note and a flower on the pillow.

Andrea
Like I told you on the phone, this inmate at the Wisconsin state prison in Waupun is now claiming he

murdered the Indian girl at Birkmose Park in Hudson. He matches the description the jogger gave that day. This could be the big break. It couldn't have come too soon. I called Stacy in Washington. I'm driving over to Waupun tonight to see if he'll talk with me. Be back tomorrow. Hope you're feeling better. I love you.

Rick

Andrea folded the note in half and placed it on the night table along with the flower. Then she reached into her bathrobe pocket and pulled out another letter, a letter addressed to her at the newsroom. It was still unopened, but she knew who it was from. She ran her fingers over the state seal. She'd thought about ripping it into a hundred pieces unread and flushing it down the toilet along with her vomit. She thought about that again; then she opened the envelope and held the letter under the lamp light.

Dear Andrea

You won't talk with me on the phone, you haven't answered any of my letters, so let us make this letter the last letter I write you. I know how foolish it is at this point to write about my love and my hatred for you, but there are some things I want to say before we get on with our lives.

Your scorn for me is unjustified. Though you've always pretended they don't exist, I have two daughters. No man has more respect for women than a man with daughters of his own. You made the decision, Andrea. You had your precious choice. The truth is you valued your television career just as much as I valued my political career.

Your marriage is a scandal. Did you marry out of spite? To spite me? You didn't do him any favor. Do you know what everybody is saying? If it weren't for that mask, you wouldn't be good enough for him. You're the one who should hide your face.

If we had met at a different time you would now be Minnesota's first lady. That may not sound like much from beneath the bright lights of your anchor desk, but ten years from now you'll be just like ev-

ery other woman who took a seat in that chair—
forty, divorced, and unemployed. What shallow lives
you people lead.

Goodbye, Andrea.

                                                    Per

Andrea Labore wiped an angry tear from her eye. She
looked at her television set, where the young and effer-
vescent Katie Tom-Jon was giggling at something the
new weathergirl had said to her.

Who could have charted such a life? From the swimming pools on the Iron Range to the Olympic pool at the
University of Minnesota, she swam against the tide to
make something of herself. She didn't fail as a policewoman, she walked away. She'd faced a moment the average cop never has to face and she handled the situation
with decisive and deadly force. Then she entered the most
competitive business in America, where her police training came in handy and she rose to the top. Television was
a cruel business, where women are forced out the door by
the age of forty and men follow a decade later. A business
where they chase ratings and gossip with as much zeal as
they chase the news. Where they hand out awards like jel-
lybeans. An exciting but unforgiving business where every year another graduating class of bimbos and bozos
line up outside the door to get inside the door so that they
can get their faces on television. The mistakes Andrea
made along the way were as grandiose as her ambition.
But for now the coveted anchor chair was hers.

She had always attracted the wrong kind of men. And
always they grew tired of her. Rick was different. He
would always be there. In the end the man she chose to
marry made up for his face with his heart. Now mother-
hood was less than nine months away. Who could have
charted such a life?

In a corner of the bedroom was a bookcase Rick had
built for her. He was good with wood. It was something
he could do alone. When they moved into the house he
winced as she lined the shelves with the novels of Anne
Tyler and Alice McDermott and the narcissistic autobiog-
raphies of network news stars, co-authored by real writers. He said to her, "Who else but TV reporters would
have to have somebody else write their books for them?"

Andrea stepped over to the bookcase and pulled an obscure novel from the shelf, that hardcover book where
wives hide the letters their husbands must never see. She
sat with it on the bed and tucked the governor's lethal
venom between the pages. Then she flipped a few pages
and pulled out a different letter. A note really. Scribbled
on school paper.

My Dear Dixon
About the date I owe you ... isn't there some other
way I could repay you for the wonderful friend
you've been? I didn't mean for you to misunderstand
my feelings for you.

Andrea slipped the note back into the book and flipped
a few more pages. The next letter she retrieved was yellow and brittle. It was torn at the folds, as if it had been
opened and read a thousand times over the years. She
held the letter with the tips of her fingers barely touching
the frail paper.

My Dear Dixon
I read your letter and have thought about it ever
since. I wish you wouldn't refer to it as your "sad
story", because it is only "you" who has made it sad.
You have asked me out so many times and each time
I have tried to say no as sweetly as I can ...

Andrea read the entire missive. It sounded like a letter
she'd been forced to write in high school—sadly, the kind
of letter teenage boys force young women to write every
year. Girls grow up so much faster than boys. They just
don't understand that.

... Please take my advice and don't think I don't understand how you feel, but I'am sorry you don't
understand how I feel, that makes the answer NO!
                                        Love
                                        Lisa Beauregard

Andrea Labore was a television reporter, not a criminal
lawyer. She had to think fast that day in the weather center. Task force detectives would be there shortly. Some

protective instinct kicked in, the need to help this man who felt he loved her. She reasoned that without the letters all they had on the Weatherman was circumstantial evidence—enough to convict, maybe, but hardly enough for the death penalty. She was half-right.

Andrea glanced over at Rick's note on the night table. Her husband was trying to stop the execution every way he knew how. She could do no less. The purloined letter written by a southern belle so many years ago was carefully refolded once again and tucked neatly between the pages of a novel nobody would ever read. Andrea returned the book to the shelf, its place reserved in dust.

She gathered pen and paper. She had a letter of her own to write. She put the flower to her nose. Then, in the ever-present glow of the television screen, the queen of the evening news knelt beside her bed. She folded her hands together and bowed her head as she had done every night as a child growing up on the Iron Range. And for the first time in years Andrea Labore whispered a prayer—a prayer for the three men who loved her.

THE EXECUTION

TIME: 23:51
DATE: 10/31
TEMPERATURE: 39°
BAROMETER: 29.84
RAINFALL: .36
WIND: N 11

Minnesota Governor Per Ellefson turned away from the digital weather station on his desk, the electronic gift that had been presented to him by a TV weatherman from the Channel 7 newsroom—a weatherman now nine minutes away from execution by electrocution. The governor walked to the window. Rain was falling on the Capitol grounds. No lightning. No thunder. Nothing so dramatic. Just a steady, dispiriting drizzle. November would dawn cold and rainy.

The dim lights that were the city of St. Paul fused with the midnight weather, casting an unearthly aureole over the modest skyline. Trees were black and bare, the dying embers of autumn blown into soggy piles along the gutters. The statue of a proud and noble Viking stood guard at the Capitol steps, his back to his descendant. Per Ellefson pulled a letter from an envelope and leaned against the window. Raindrops streaked the glass.

My Dear Governor

I did not marry out of spite. As hard as it is for people to accept, I married for old fashioned reasons—love and respect. Now there's life inside of me again, from the seed of a man whose face is as physically ugly as your face is beautiful. This life I am going to let live. But this is not an answer to your letters. This is a plea for mercy.

I am asking you to spare the life of Dixon Bell. Unlike my husband, who is too often blinded by his righteousness and his wounds, I believe the Weatherman may indeed be guilty. The black hole of hatred in the soul of Dixon Bell may be so deep that he should never be allowed to walk among free people again. But such a gifted man has so much left to give us that it would be a crime to snuff out his knowledge of the heavens. Please commute his sentence to life in prison.

You once told me that being from Minnesota used to mean something. You've been governor of our state for five years. What do we stand for now?

For the love we once shared, and I did love you, I beg you to spare the life of the Weatherman.

Andrea

Per Ellefson turned his back on the dispiriting drizzle. He sat down at his desk beside the telephone. He put the letter to his nose and inhaled her perfume one last time.

The electronic weather station captured his eyes with its fluorescent digits.

"No matter how wrong you are, Governor, you'll always be right about the weather."

The time flashed 23:59. The temperature was 38°. The barometer continued falling. So did the rain.

"Carol, is it still raining?"

"Yes, it is."

"Do you know the temperature?"

"No, Dixon, but it's cold."

Dixon Bell bent over the sheet of typing paper on the concrete floor and scribbled his final thoughts with the fat pencil. Chills set in. Goose bumps ran up his arms. He tried to concentrate on the letter. The words he was putting to paper were so warm and inviting he wanted to crawl into the written page.

Carol Theguard choked back the tears. "You're going to have to finish up there, Dixon, they're coming for you."

Then the bolts shot open on the heavy steel doors to the Death House. Death squad arriving. The Weatherman hurriedly scribbled his last forecast.

He struggled to his feet, almost too weak to stand. Carol Theguard collected his paper and pencil through the bars. It was 10:30 P.M. The death squad arrived with a black briefcase and chains to prepare Dixon Bell for execution. His regular guards then stepped into the isolation cell one by one. They shook his hand and said their farewells, most of them choking on their words. "Good-bye, Weatherman." Their role in the ritual was thankfully over. Carol Theguard gave him a big hug, tears on her face.

"See that letter gets mailed, please."

"I will, Dixon." She turned him over to the death squad and ran from the house.

The death squad entered the isolation cell. They were large men, three of them, and though they were dressed in Stillwater guard uniforms Dixon Bell had never before seen their grim faces. They probably worked the towers. It was time to barber the prisoner for the chair.

They dragged in a stool and ordered him to sit, the way a man would talk to a dog. An apron was thrown around his neck. His unkempt white hair was removed with electric shears. Then they smeared his stubbled scalp with Gillette Foamy. They ripped open a pack of disposable razors and went about shaving his head. Just when he thought they had finished humiliating him, they held his face tight and shaved off his eyebrows.

One of these cold, hard men squeezed a white conducting gel into the palms of his hands and rubbed it into Dixon Bell's bald head, a gob of it, giving his scalp a thorough massage. The gel dried chalky white, leaving the Weatherman with a hideous, ghostly appearance. They brushed him off and swept out the cell.

"Take off all of your clothes and put on these clothes."

With so many bodies in the tiny cell it was hard to move. Dixon Bell stripped himself of the prison garb. He had dropped so much weight during his three weeks in isolation that his bones were beginning to show through the colorless cast of his skin. The Weatherman awkwardly crawled into his burial suit. Everything was black and white and one hundred percent cotton. White boxer shorts. White dress shirt. Black trousers. White socks. Black slippers.

When he was dressed he was ordered back onto the stool. Another squad member pulled a pair of scissors from the briefcase, stooped, and cut open the inside seam of his right trouser leg, cut it up to his knee. They shaved his right calf and rubbed in the conducting gel with the same care a trainer would give a horse.

Then the death squad removed the stool, stepped outside the cell, and waited. The door was left open. Dixon Bell sat on his bunk and stewed, naked and cold above the neck. He hugged his Bible like a child with a teddy bear. The Weatherman had refused to see the prison chaplain, saying he would deal with God in his own way.

At 11:30 P.M. Warden Johnson arrived and sat beside him on the bunk. "How are you holding up, Dixon?"

"All right. Did we get a good crowd?"

"Listen carefully. I want to explain what's going to happen now so you won't be alarmed by anything." And with that Warden Johnson talked Dixon Bell through the final steps that would lead to his death. When he was done explaining the procedure, they sat on the bunk like old roommates. They talked about football. The Cowboys were doing well. The Warden was a Packer fan. The Vikings were riding a three-game winning streak into Sunday's game. After a few minutes of sports trivia the Warden stood and nodded to the death squad.

Oliver J. Johnson stepped out of the cell. The death squad stepped in. "Stand up, please."

The Weatherman stood. They threw heavy chains around his waist. The way they went about their task it was obvious they had been practicing on each other. "Hold out your hands."

Dixon Bell did as he was told. "Y'all going to the show?"

They clamped on the four-point handcuff restraints and adjusted the torture pins.

"Not talking, huh? You guys are just pissed off because I got a better seat than you."

Two of them dropped to the floor and locked the manacles to his ankles.

They stood up and spun him completely around. Then they stepped back so that Warden Johnson could admire

their work. The warden nodded his head in approval.
Nothing left to do now but listen to the ticking of the
clock. Morbid wisecracks were coming to mind every
second, but Dixon Bell swallowed them. They stood in silence.

Then came a strange sound from outside. A wonderful
chanting sound, unmistakable in its passion. A thousand
voices. A choir of convicts. The Death House was sealed
tight, and Dixon Bell couldn't make out what they were
saying, but he knew it was a cry for justice, a cry for him.

11:45 P.M. Warden Johnson stepped back into the cell
and placed a hand on his shoulder—a humane little touch.
"It's time, Dixon."

The long walk.

The Weatherman took a deep breath. The wisecracks
were gone. He wasn't angry, nor was he frightened. He
just felt incredibly sad. It was the same type of sadness
he felt when he was a little boy and his momma told him
the story of how his daddy and his two siblings were
killed by the tornado. For the first time in weeks Dixon
Bell stepped out of the isolation cell. He looked the thirty
feet to the death chamber. The door was wide open. It had
been closed when he first arrived. Now it was a bright
light at the end of a short tunnel. A death squad guard
took hold of each arm. The other guard stood behind him.
Warden Johnson stepped to the front and led the way.
They passed by the small booth where the old janitor
would be sitting, probably paging through this year's
Schwinn catalog. Then, almost as soon as it began, the
long walk was over. The Weatherman stepped through the
armored steel door and into the death chamber.

Dr. Yauch was standing along the wall in his white
robe, his stethoscope dangling from his neck, his hands
shoved deep into his smock pockets. The good doctor
paid no attention to his star patient. Just stared coldly into
space. A prison hospital intern stood beside him, his eyes
wide with morbid curiosity.

Dixon Bell's first view of the death chamber was a real
eye opener. He had always pictured it dark and gloomy,
but it was a white room, brilliantly illuminated. Strangely
quiet. The big wooden chair looked as if it were crawling
with snakes; there were enough straps and buckles for a

football team. The glossy oak finish had been buffed to a shine. The death squad ushered him to his seat.

It wasn't until Dixon Bell took that special place reserved for him that he lifted his head to the witnesses, the two dozen ghouls who in the guise of justice or journalism had come to watch him fry. Track lighting hanging from the ceiling and directed at the chair made it difficult for him to see their faces, but it looked as if every seat was taken. Standing room only. Mostly men. A couple of women. Some notebooks were open. A few pencils fluttered back and forth. He didn't see anybody he really cared about.

The death squad worked methodically. The first of the broad leather straps went around his chest and pulled him back into the chair. The second and third straps tied his forearms to the wooden arms. Only when his arms were buckled tight were the special handcuffs removed.

More straps followed. Two straps went over his wrists. One went around his waist and pinched his stomach. Another went over his lap and caused his thighs to bulge. It was beginning to feel like a Houdini stunt. The ankle straps went on last. When they were secure the manacles were removed from his legs.

An electrician kneeled before him as if he were going to wash his feet. The electrician parted his right trouser leg and strapped a leather anklet to his calf. The anklet was lined with cold copper and tied so tight it cut off the blood to his foot. Maybe they were being sadistic, or maybe it was just their lack of experience, but every restraint was skintight. The electrician connected the polished electrodes to the anklet. Dixon Bell glanced down and saw the thick black cord snake away behind the chair. It looked just like the deadly water moccasins that whip through the Delta waters.

The ritual continued. They placed a microphone before him. The last press conference. Warden Johnson stepped up to him, very official. "Dixon Graham Bell, would you like to make a final statement before the will of the people of Minnesota is carried out?"

The Weatherman, bound like an animal, squinted at the strange faces melting into the lights. The most shameful feeling rained down on him. His mouth was parched, his tongue thick and leathery. "I'm thirsty," he mumbled. "Can I have a drink of water?"

"No. I'm sorry."

Dixon Bell tried to lubricate his mouth with saliva. He thought a second. "Dress warm," he said, "it's going to be a long, hard winter." He felt faint with sorrow and closed his eyes. He opened them. "Y'all take care now."

They took the microphone away.

The guards tilted his shaved head back at an uncomfortable angle. They shoved a mouthpiece between his teeth. "Bite down on this real hard." They fastened a fat leather chin strap around his jaw, so taut it was almost choking him. His head was now locked firmly into the wooden headrest. That's when the Weatherman spotted him.

He was standing in the back row, behind the chairs, his hands tucked into his jeans pockets under his sport coat. Maybe it was fate, perhaps it was the mask, but Rick Beanblossom's blue cotton face was the only face he could see. He locked onto the Marine's eyes and it all came together—a repeat of that moment in the elevator years ago, the day of the tornado, the day the Weatherman's world began to spin out of control. But this time the man in the mask wouldn't be riding up with him. This was the last thing Dixon Bell saw before they blinded him, the faceless face of Rick Beanblossom, his eyes filled with pity, rage, and just a touch of understanding. He had everything the Weatherman ever wanted. Everything but a face.

Then they evened that score.

The guards drew a black leather mask across his face and buckled it like a boot, fixed it so hard he was close to smothering. The mask was to keep his eyes from popping out of their sockets and to hide any violent facial contortion.

The new sponge Old Jesse purchased at Woolworth's had been soaked in salt water and stitched into the headset, the death cap that would fry his brain. It was lowered onto the Weatherman's bald head like a thorny crown. It felt cold and slimy. The saline solution dripped down around his ears and trickled down his back. Lastly, they plugged him in.

Never had Dixon Bell known such blackness. This was

as dark as dark gets. The leather mask across his face felt rough and cold and smelled of a new shoe. The rubber in his mouth tasted of his football days at Vicksburg High School. Lisa crossed his mind—not the frumpy woman at the trial but the southern belle he had given his heart to so many seasons past. It was safe to cry now. He thought he heard some people mumbling as the first tears rolled over his cheeks and ran like sweat from beneath the mask.

Dixon Bell sat in the electric chair and waited. And waited.

What the hell are they doing?

Then it got so quiet he could hear the tears streaming down his face. In the final seconds of October he accepted his pathetic fate. But, God, it was so damned unfair.

The Weatherman choked on a sob and thought of Andrea.

The clock struck midnight.

When Rick Beanblossom arrived at the prison on the night of the execution a crowd was gathered outside. Two crowds. On the east side of Stagecoach Trail, on the lawn beneath the prison wall, hundreds of somber and peaceful protesters held candles under their umbrellas. They were all represented—Amnesty International USA, the National Coalition to Abolish the Death Penalty, and the Ecumenical Religious Task Force on Criminal Justice—but most of the candle holders didn't belong to any organization.

"We live in Stillwater . . . and we don't think this is right . . . We just wanted to be here. That's all."

They sang chorus after chorus of "We Shall Overcome." They did a haunting rendition of "Amazing Grace." The temperature was slowly dropping and their warm breath became visible, rolling out before them as their mellifluous voices wafted over the walls and through the prison grounds.

The west side of Stagecoach Trail, across the street from the prison wall, was a different story. Death penalty cheerleaders outnumbered the candle holders almost two to one. Some waved angry torches that flickered and died in the cold, soaking rain. Some repeatedly flicked their Bic lighters. Others carried signs that read stuff like, ASK NOT FOR WHOM THE BELL TOLLS, IT TOLLS FOR BELL ... THANK GOD IT'S FRYDAY ... BUCKLE UP, BELL, IT'S THE LAW ... and DON'T MESS WITH MINNESOTA.

"Hey, this is a hometown crowd. We've been waiting for this in Minnesota for a long time. Just wanted to be here."

The sheriff's department formed a line between the two crowds. News photographers paraded back and forth, their klieg lights brightening the dark, rainy night. A hawker was peddling souvenir electric-chair pins. Cars, windshield wipers flapping, had to run a gauntlet of state troopers before being allowed to park. Satellite trucks and news vans lined the parking lot, thick black cables snaking over the sidewalks and onto the grass. It was just past 10:00 P.M. TV reporters were doing their live stand-ups.

"Stan, I've been to a few of these in Florida when I was working for a Tampa station, and this is a good turnout, even by Florida standards. As you can see behind me here . . ."

Rick Beanblossom stood above the media circus; stood on the steps of the main building and watched the rain falling over the dark valley. His valley. God's country. The wind and rain had stripped the trees of their natural beauty. Fallen leaves lay decaying in wet piles. Despite the news event of the year there was a strange and eerie stillness over this valley named holy cross. Rick closed his eyes.

The Wisconsin inmate at the state prison in Waupun told Rick Beanblossom a harrowing story, about how he had dressed to kill, then went out and brutally murdered an Indian girl that beautiful autumn morning in the park overlooking the town of Hudson. The problem was he had told a similar story once before. Just prior to the highly publicized execution of an Alabama man, he confessed to that killing in frightening detail. Alabama authorities thought he sounded pretty convincing, but it didn't stop the execution. Minnesota authorities simply shrugged their collective shoulders. Dixon Bell was never charged with the Hudson murder. Any confession to the killing was irrelevant.

Rick shivered, turned his back to the inclement

weather, and ducked in the front door. He brushed the raindrops from his sport coat and stepped up to the glass booth. "I'm here for the execution," he told the guard.

The big guard at the desk, whom Rick had never seen before, gave him that baffled stare he had grown accustomed to over the years. "What the hell is going on?" the guard demanded to know. "We were told you'd have a special escort. Top secret and all that shit. What are you doing waltzing in the front door?"

"My name is Rick Beanblossom. I'm a burn victim. I have a media pass to witness the execution."

The guard threw up his hands in embarrassment. "Oh God, I'm sorry, I thought you were the executioner. Yeah, I've heard of you. You wrote that book. Do you got your pass, Rick? I'm sorry about that. Bernie here will take you down to the cafeteria. That's where you'll wait until they walk you out to the house."

Rick had his hand stamped with invisible ink. He signed his name in the log book. Bernie the guard issued him a badge, which he clamped to his coat. He passed through the metal detector and was then escorted down to the cafeteria.

The ritual for the witnesses was almost as bizarre as the ritual for the condemned man. More than two thousand people had written letters to Warden Johnson asking if they could be witnesses at the execution. The warden chose twenty-four of them. They were confined to the cafeteria. The place reminded Rick of the cafeteria at his junior high school, huge, cold, and filled with echoes. Tables and chairs were bolted to the floor. A balcony for guards hung overhead. He recognized some family members of the victims from the sound bites he had seen on the news, but there were only two or three of them. Most of those gathered were news people or state officials. He nodded to the few faces he knew. Others stared at him, as befuddled as the guard at the front desk first was.

"He's that burned guy married to Andrea Labore."

"Is she going to be here tonight?"

The room had the stale atmosphere of a bad party. Soft voices and whispers were the unwritten rule. A full meal was being served, everything but a roasted pig with an apple stuffed in its mouth. Witnesses shuffled through the cafeteria line ordering their free food. Rick wasn't hungry. He grabbed a Pepsi and downed a pair of aspirin. He checked his watch. It was 10:30. Andrea would remain in the newsroom until it was over.

He sat at a table away from the others, an old habit that was hard to break. Redd Battlemore came and sat beside him. Redd was the old salt from the *Pioneer Press*. The crime beat was his life. "Never thought I'd live to see this in Minnesota," he said to Rick. "But then I never thought I'd see casino gambling here, either. Or a domed stadium. Or a snake like Per Ellefson in the governor's office. The Nordic Nixon. He'll let him fry, Rick. You mark my words. He'll let him fry."

The man without a face reflected a moment on all that was lost. "Not exactly the land we inherited, is it?"

"The wife and I, we've been looking at some property in Wisconsin, up by Hayward. Pretty country. Might build there when I retire. Of course the wife wants to retire to Florida, but I'll be damned if I'll live in a state that does this kind of thing. And you, Rick?"

"No, I'll never leave Minnesota."

More than an hour later, 11:40, uniformed guards along with the deputy commissioner of corrections arrived to usher them across the prison yard to the Death House.

It was still drizzling. Rick was wearing only his blue sport coat and faded jeans. The temperature kept falling. The wet cold cut to his bones. As they walked across the muddy, floodlit prison yard a strange feeling came over him, as if a thousand angry eyes were watching them pass. They were. Nasty shouts began to rain down from the dark windows.

"Write the truth for a change, you assholes!"

"You gonna throw that switch, Masked Man? Even in war it's against the law to kill a prisoner!"

"If they can kill him, they all can kill you too!"

It began as a single chant from a lone inmate in the north wing—a prisoner who had done his homework. In seconds there were several prisoners chanting. Then it seemed the entire prison population was at their bars chanting, a violent, passionate chorus that chased the group of witnesses as they solemnly paraded to the Death House. It was a spooky chant from inside the walls that mixed with the eerie version of "Amazing Grace" being done outside.

"Human rights! Human rights!"
"Human rights! Human rights!"

It was a proud, defiant chant that grew louder and louder, almost terroristic in nature, and it didn't reach its zenith until they were inside the Death House and the steel door was sealed and locked.

When they had taken the tour in the daytime the death chamber had looked stark and stuffy. Now in the hour before midnight in the cold rain it was bright and foreboding—blizzard white and ominous.

In the left corner of the room stood the American flag. In the right corner stood the flag of Minnesota with the state motto showing: *L'Etoile du Nord.* The Star of the North. Rick thought the Spark of the North would be more appropriate. Between the two flags, on the black rubber mat on the linoleum floor, sat the big, fat oaken chair. Hot white lights shone down on it like on an anchor chair in a television studio.

Thirty folding chairs were set up on three raised platforms, almost like in a showcase theater. There was nothing but a few feet of space to separate the witnesses from the electric chair. A sign on the back wall said NO SMOKING. A red phone hung on the wall next to the door. Fire extinguishers were lined up beside the entrance.

None of the witness seats were assigned. Everybody moved about in an awkward game of musical chairs. The seats up front were the last to be taken. Rick walked up the aisle between the chairs to the back wall and stood. The large round clock read 11:45.

They waited patiently; the minutes seemed like hours. It was the longest Rick could remember a group of reporters ever going without one of them cracking a morbid joke.

Then they heard him coming down the hall, the way Marley's ghost came for Scrooge. The haunting echo of the rattling chains passed unimpeded through the walls of the Death House. Warden Johnson stepped into the chamber. He was followed by the Weatherman. Audible gasps slipped out of those who had known Dixon Bell. His head and face were totally hairless and sickly white. His once sharp eyes were bloodshot and raw. His fat had melted away, leaving the big man starved in appearance. He was manacled at the ankles. His hands were clamped into that horrid pair of handcuffs which were locked to a chain around his waist. His chalky face showed more confusion than fear. The death squad guided him to the chair and sat him down beneath the spotlights.

The electric chair faced the witnesses dead on. Dixon Bell raised his head and squinted. Rick couldn't tell if he'd been spotted or not. He watched as they strapped the Weatherman into the chair the same way doctors had once strapped the charred Marine into a bed. The chair seemed to have three straps for every appendage.

When they were done dressing him for slaughter, an electrician wired his right leg. Then they placed a stand before him and pointed a microphone up at his mouth. It looked like a chrome erection.

Warden Johnson stepped forward. "Dixon Graham Bell, would you like to make a final statement before the will of the people of Minnesota is carried out?"

Rick wanted to cry as Dixon Bell asked for water. Then the Weatherman mumbled his final forecast and said good-bye.

They took the microphone away. The death squad pushed his head back and fastened a strap across his chin. His head was locked into place. He was almost choking. Then for a second, only a split second, Rick Beanblossom was sure he had caught the Weatherman's eye. He was begging him for help. But Rick had done all that he could. The winds were against them. He tried to convey that message as they buckled a piece of black leather across the sorry white face of Dixon Bell. Now only the top of his glossy scalp was showing.

The death squad lifted the death cap and fitted it over the shiny bald spot. It was a ghastly-looking helmet. The electrician stepped forward again. Another heavy-duty power line was plugged into the brass electrode protruding from the top of the crown. The electrician stepped behind the chair to a power box.

Now it was 11:57 and there was nothing left to do. Rick Beanblossom had never known such silence. Over and over again he swallowed his hurt. His anger was building. He folded his arms to squeeze away the chills.

11:58. Nobody was talking. Nobody stirred. Only the Weatherman fighting for air. They could hear the falling rain. Rick stared at the red telephone on the wall.

11:59. Rick thought he heard a man swear under his breath. A woman up front began sobbing.

The clock struck midnight. And Warden Johnson nodded to the electrician.

When Old Jesse arrived at the prison on the night of the execution, the crowd had just begun to gather. He'd been picked up in an unmarked state car by two plainclothes prison officials. He thought this was silly since he only lived four blocks from the prison and he enjoyed walking to work. But on this night this is how they wanted things done.

He was kept under wraps until 11:00 P.M. Then they escorted him to the Death House. Old Jesse sensed from the beginning how different things were. Nobody would talk to him—Old Jesse, the friendliest man in Stillwater. When an inmate was given the silent treatment, that inmate still had a friend in the night janitor. But now he felt as isolated as the Weatherman.

Just before they started for the Death House, the ritual got even sillier. They handed the old man a black hood and told him to drape it over his head.

"What's it for?"

"Just do it, Jess."

Old Jesse put the hood over his head. It was too big. The eyeholes fell down to his cheekbones. He looked ridiculous. He pushed the holes up to his eyes with his fingers and held them there as they took the long walk across the prison yard.

Even with the stupid hood over his head, even with the night sky black and rainy, Old Jesse knew the Electric Star was up there. He could feel its savage spark in his bones. Terrible memories came flooding back to him, memories of love and jealousy, and of another man whose life he had snuffed out more than three decades ago. He thought of his pretty mamma lying dead in the back of the bus. Of Eleanor Roosevelt coming to inspect the conditions. Of granddaughter Shelly pinning on that badge that said Edina Police, then slipping that prison-made billy club through her gunbelt.

"He's guilty. He's guilty. I was at the trial every day."

Old Jesse was mumbling a prayer as he walked into the Death House.

Warden Johnson was waiting for him.

The warden calmly explained the procedure one more time. Then he asked the executioner to step into the booth and wait patiently. At 11:30 P.M. Old Jesse took his place in the electric closet ten feet from the chair. He closed and secured the door, wiped a speck of dirt from the Plexiglas. He sat down behind the executioner's control panel. He pushed the hood's eyeholes back up to his eyes. Two amber lights were glowing, staring him in the face like cat's eyes. He examined the switches below the lights.

CIRCUIT BREAKER CONTROL
TRIP   CLOSE
PULL
LATCH
CANCEL
MADE IN USA

Over the next fifteen minutes Old Jesse relived his entire life, from the low country of South Carolina to the lake country of Minnesota. From the railroad tracks of St. Paul to the long halls of the state prison in Stillwater. From husband and father to convicted murderer. Inmate to executioner. It all passed before him, as if he himself were the one scheduled to die.

Like most men Old Jesse had loved his dear wife. And like many a man he had also loved his lover. When he found the woman with that other man he went into a rage, a rage that resulted in the poor man's death. Funny thing was, the man probably had more rights to the woman than Jesse: he wasn't married; Jesse was. It all happened so many years ago that both of the women had long since passed away of old age and broken hearts.

Out of the corner of his eye Old Jesse saw the passing parade. The Weatherman entered the death chamber. A winter chill overcame the janitor. He was sorry he had volunteered for this. What was God's plan that made him do such things?

Before heaven could provide him with an answer Warden Johnson stepped up to the window and raised two fingers. Two minutes. Old Jesse nodded his head and turned to the amber lights above the switches. He was shaking. Since he didn't expect to see the warden again until it was all over, he pushed the hood up to the top of his head so that he could see what he was doing.

The seconds ticked by. His heart was pounding so loud it killed the sound of raindrops on the roof. The ghosts of his past wouldn't leave him alone. He wanted to weep, but he couldn't decide in his mind who he'd be weeping for. For Momma? For granddaughter Shelly? My God, could he shed tears for the Weatherman?

Suddenly and without warning one amber light went off and the green light came on. Old Jesse nervously threw the green switch on the right-hand side. The power surge kicked in with a loud dull crunch that startled him. Then the other amber light went off and the red light came on. Old Jesse paused a second. He blurted out, "Forgive me, my sweet Lord."

And the executioner grabbed hold of the big red handle on the left-hand side and tripped the switch.

At first there was no unusual noise. Nothing unexpected. No buzzing or frying. No sparks flying along the wires. Just a dull clunk and the lights dimming. Other than that, execution by electrocution didn't sound any louder than a microwave oven. Until the screaming began.

As the first current passed instantly through his brain, the Weatherman bolted upright in the chair. His barrel chest heaved. He pulled at the straps until it looked as if they were going to snap. He appeared to be shivering.

They were less than thirty seconds into the electrocution when Rick Beanblossom's burn-victim instincts sensed something was wrong—something was terribly wrong. It started as a sizzling sound. Then blisters began popping on the exposed right leg. Next came the unmistakable sound of oral and nasal fluid gurgling. Rick took a step forward.

White sparks flew from the electrodes. Steam escaped the death cap. Still, nobody knew whether that was normal or not. The Weatherman's hands changed colors, flesh tones to ashen tones. A purplish saliva came drooling out the bottom of the black mask and ran down his neck and into the white shirt.

Rick Beanblossom kept moving slowly down the aisle between the folding chairs, inexorably drawn by the repugnant memory of burning flesh.

Forty-five seconds into the electrocution a small blue flame appeared under the death cap and did a jig across the forehead. There were gasps in the crowd.

Rick Beanblossom screamed—screamed almost as loud as he had that fiery day in Vietnam. "No!"

And just when it looked as if the little blue flame had heard the Marine's order and was ready to flicker out— the Weatherman's head burst into a fireball. Flames climbed to a foot above the death cap. Smoke and fire erupted from beneath his right leg, burned up his trousers to his lap.

Everybody in the chamber lost their wits. Sharp explosions sounded like bombs. Glass flew through the room. The lights above had popped. Now it was only the glow of the Weatherman's burning body lighting the death chamber. A human torch.

Folding chairs were knocked over as the witnesses fled to the back of the chamber. Rick Beanblossom kept screaming as he dropped to his knees before the flaming Weatherman.

Warden Johnson jumped over to the executioner's booth and slashed his finger across his throat. But to his horror Old Jesse didn't appear to be in there. He stepped up to the Plexiglas. The needle on the voltmeter was stuck at 2,000 volts. The automatic cycle had failed. The old man was curled over in his chair, his hoodless head buried against his clenched fists. The son of a bitch was praying.

Warden Johnson pounded on the glass. "Turn it off! Turn it off!"

But Old Jesse went right on begging for forgiveness.

"Override! Cut it, Jesse, cut it!"

The executioner bowed his tearful head even further and prayed the most beseeching prayer of his life.

The warden finally lost his composure. He was frantically trying to force open the door. "Override! Look at me, you stupid old man!"

Back in the death chamber from hell the Weatherman

did the physically impossible. Driven by a power far greater than his own, his big right arm, the arm convicted of killing seven women, ripped the leather straps from the chair. Hot rivets ricocheted off the walls. His right arm was free now and he was beating the flames on his head with his hand. His muffled groans could not be heard above the screams of the witnesses. His white shirt caught fire.

Reporters would later write how the fiery execution seemed to burn on for an hour, flames reaching for the ceiling in slow motion. But the killing lasted only minutes. Two minutes. The automatic cycle failed to cycle down and back up, but after 120 seconds of 2,000 volts the electricity did cut itself off. The flames engulfing the Weatherman began to flicker and die. Warden Johnson returned to the chamber area just in time to see Dixon Bell's last violent jerks before his body slumped in the chair. The stench and the sight nauseated him. He motioned to the death squad. "Extinguish him!" The warden placed his hand over his mouth and nose.

The death squad, coughing and choking, stepped toward the fiery chair with extinguishers and coated the Weatherman with a white cloudy foam.

Through it all Rick Beanblossom, down on his knees, had closed his watery eyes and covered his eardrums. Still he could smell the burned flesh. He could hear the shouting.

"He's still alive!"

Indeed, his chest was still heaving, as if the Weatherman were struggling for every last breath. The fleshy remains of his free right hand were twitching.

"He's dead—they're muscle spasms! Get away from him!"

"Don't touch him, you'll burn yourselves!"

"Get back! For God's sake, get back."

Rick finally opened his eyes. Dixon Bell's foam-covered body was slouched and quivering in the big oak chair. Flecks of ash fell like black snow from beneath the headset to his shoulders. The back of the electric chair was still smoking. The headset was charred, the wires melted. The black leather mask had fused with his facial skin. The fingers on his strapped left hand appeared broken where they had dug into the wood.

And through his tears Rick Beanblossom was sure he could see the tortured soul of the Weatherman as he left his smoldering body below and sailed up above the clouds, where the sun shines all the time and spirits dance where the wind doesn't blow.

"What's in it?" said the Queen.

"I haven't opened it yet," said the White Rabbit, "but it appears to be a letter, written by a prisoner to—to somebody."

—Lewis Carroll
Alice's Adventures in Wonderland

THE EPILOGUE

Dear Su St. Germain

I have received many letters since my ordeal began, but yours was the most touching of them all. So touching it breaks my heart that I cannot help you. I am not the man you are looking for. I'm very sorry.

I left Vietnam just before Christmas 1974. To the best of my knowledge I was not replaced due to the American withdrawal. Because of the sensitive nature of our work and our importance to the war machine our records were classified.

I would like to believe that it was a weatherman who sprinted you to freedom. There is no greater thrill in meteorology than sharing our knowledge of the heavens with children. I'm sure he'd be very proud of you. But, Su, the decisions made in war that take lives and make lives are made in split seconds. More often they come from the heart and the gut instead of the brain. Though that day at the air base is precious to you, to him it may have been just another crazy afternoon in an insane war. I think the best thank-you to that soldier is for you to live a good life.

Funny as it may seem, the longer I sit here in this house of death watching television the more sane I feel. It's the world outside that's going mad. Tonight that world is cold and rainy. My cell is freezing. In an hour they will shave my head. Then I'll take the long walk, down to the death chamber where they will strap me into their new electric chair. It is under these conditions that I put these last rambling thoughts to paper and send them off to a woman whose life was touched by a weatherman.

There is talk about a last-minute reprieve from the governor. A life behind bars. The political prisoner locked in his cell turning out one great essay after another. Then in my senior years millions of admirers finally win my release. I walk out the prison doors. The TV cameras surround me. I proclaim my innocence one last time. I live out the rest of my life sipping rum and Coke on the Gulf Coast while young people come to pay homage. Of course, it is only a dream. There will be no commuting my sentence to life in prison. This governor doesn't have the mettle for it. The state is going to kill me.

I always saw myself dying on a beautiful autumn day with the sun setting over the land of ten thousand lakes. Ten thousand leaves of ten thousand colors would be falling over me as they lay my body down. But this year the leaves fell before I did, and outside it is raining. I will die in the cold drizzle of November.

My other dream is of home. If I could walk out of this prison tomorrow free and innocent, I'd run home to Vicksburg. I'd run home in a minute. I'd take a job at the local TV station and I'd tell the folks how hot and humid it's going to get, or I'd warn them about thunderheads piling miles high in the Delta sky. I'd buy one of those antebellum mansions over the river and I'd fix it up real nice, turn it into a bed and breakfast where Yankees could discover for themselves they don't need shots to visit the South. And on those suffering hot and humid, lazy Mississippi days I'd sit out on the front porch, suck the sugar from the ice of my mint julep and watch the muddy river roll by. Friends and neighbors would stop up. We'd talk about nothing in particular, mostly the weather. More serious topics would be banned. Once in a while I'd politely correct their sweet ignorance.

"Do you miss it up there in Milwaukee, Dixon?"

"Minnesota. I lived in Minnesota. Yes, I miss it."

Will you do something for me, Su? Will you pray for me? Will you get down on your knees, close your eyes and talk to God about me? Tell him of the good I did. Ask him to forgive the bad. He never put a more tortured soul on this earth.

I have asked that my remains be cremated. Finish what the state began. I want them to take my ashes down to St. Paul and spread them over the Mississippi, that mean, unappeasing river. The river will take me home.

Falling temps tomorrow. Increasing winds. Snow flurries. Long winter ahead. Carol the guard is yelling at me. I hear doors opening. Death squad coming.

Live a good life, Little Girl.

Dixon Bell

Rick Beanblossom took the photocopy of the Weatherman's last letter and rolled the pages into a scroll. He held the letter in his scarred hands as if it had been found in a cave off the Dead Sea. So much love, so much hatred in such a gifted man.

The man without a face stood beneath a stone cross where St. Paul's Summit Avenue came to an abrupt end at a park on Mississippi River Boulevard. Winter was in the wind. A cold front was sweeping across the land. The setting sun was hidden behind a mountain of black and white clouds up from the end of the earth. Below him the mighty river went on its mean, unappeasing way, while over its steep banks of naked trees on the west side the skyscrapers of Minneapolis stood like icicles in the colorless twilight. A flashing white light caught his eye. It was the warning light atop the IDS Tower, where from the newsroom below, Dixon Bell had foretold of the coming storm.

The outcry over the botched electrocution was deafening. Up and down the state editorial pages raged with indignation. TV news hired sketch artists to re-create the fiery last minutes in the Death House. Out of a sense of honor and principle Warden Oliver J. Johnson submitted his resignation to the governor. Democrats wanted the governor's resignation too. Others called for a special session of the legislature to abolish the death penalty. Instead, Per Ellefson issued a moratorium on executions, even though no one else in Minnesota had been sentenced to death.

A preliminary investigation into the execution of Dixon Graham Bell has uncovered two human errors and a mechanical failure. The failure of maintenance personnel to line the headset with an appropriate sponge. The mechanical failure of the automatic electrical cycle. And the failure of the volunteer executioner to override the electrical cycle. Despite these failures the prisoner died during the first application of current. All breathing and muscular activity was involuntary, a motion undertaken by the prisoner's nervous system after his death. However, all executions are suspended pending the results of an independent investigation.

Arthur Svenson
Spokesman for Per Ellefson
Office of the Governor of the
State of Minnesota

But Rick Beanblossom believed in his heart the malfunction was at the beginning of the process, when the state said it would kill killers to show that killing people is wrong.

In a ghostly tree above him sat a bird's nest, but the birds were gone. Barges were pushing downstream before the river froze. Behind him Summit Avenue ran east like a decorated ribbon through the charmed neighborhoods of old St. Paul, while out before him Minneapolis and its snowy-white suburbs were pushing farther and farther west, the Los Angelization of a dying prairie. The memorial cross towering over him was dedicated to the men who sacrificed their lives in World War II. "Greater love hath no man than this," read the inscription. But the veteran of Vietnam wondered if the war was really how they would be remembered, or would they more likely go down in history as the generation that brought the world television?

"What have you done for me lately?"

"That's my line. How goes the writing life?"

"My publisher wants a book about the case, incorporating his diary. I meet with the editors tomorrow."

"Who'd want to read a book about a TV weatherman?"

"I think a lot of people would, if it's done right."

"And in this book you would of course argue his innocence?"

"Not necessarily."

"There was a woman strangled in a parking ramp in Des Moines last night ... during a thunderstorm. ... A coincidence, I'm sure."

"I saw that on the wire. I'll check it out. I could use your help on the book."

"I'm afraid I can't do that. Winter is coming on. I'm leaving the state. Retiring for good this time, to where it's sunny and warm."

"My God, I don't know what to say. I wouldn't have had a career without you."

"No, you would have had a career, it just wouldn't have been as colorful. You're on your own now. Good-bye, Masked Man."

And here may well end the story of the Weatherman, but for a note he had slipped to Rick Beanblossom in the Stillwater prison the last time they talked.

Those news instincts of yours were no match for a woman's intuition. Or the gut feeling of an old cop. You see, Andrea was right about me all along, as was Angelbeck. But you? When you pulled that cotton mask over your face you also pulled the wool over your eyes. I believe that the monster that lay inside of me for so many years lies inside of you. *It* lies in all men. Your obsessive love for Andrea was no different than mine. When she at first said no to you, you chose to take your own life. I chose to take the lives of others. Nothing but boiling temperatures await me. I will roast in hell for what I've done. If I remember right, you have sources there. Check with them once in a while, just to see how I'm doing.

Perhaps in the end each of them had found what they were looking for; maybe they were only looking for one another. Rick Beanblossom found a pretty face. Andrea Labore found a good man. Les Angelbeck found his last case. Dixon Bell found death.

The November sun sank into the prairie. Barometric pressure began falling, ever so slightly. The black and white clouds were melting together the way a pure stream melts into a polluted river. An arctic wind set him to shivering. The man in the mask checked his watch. If he left now, he could get home in time to watch his wife read the six o'clock news. He'd catch the forecast, grab a bite to eat, then go to bed. Rick needed the rest. He would be a father soon. He had another book to write. Tomorrow he would board a plane for New York. He stuffed Dixon Bell's last letter into his coat pocket and took a long last look at the polar sky over the Sky High newsroom. Life in Minnesota would go on, but the *quality* had slipped away with the autumn wind, as if the Weatherman had taken it with him.

The temperature dropped below the freezing point. Snow flurries circled the black leather nose of his blue cotton face. The north wind chilled him to the bone. Rick Beanblossom took a deep breath.

Yes, it would be a good day to fly.

If the weather holds.

THE
ACKNOWLEDGMENTS

To research *The Weatherman* I took a job in the news-room at WCCO-TV in Minneapolis. I worked there for three years. Special thanks are owed to the people at WCCO who took the time to teach me television news, especially John Lindsay, Trish Van Pilsum, Julie Kramer, Peter Molenda, Bill Enderson, Dale Dobesh, Pat Kessler, Darcy Pohland, Bill Kruskop, and Sandra Lindquist.

To my friends Paul Moore, at WCCO, and Judy Nelsen, formerly at KARE-TV, for their critiques along the way.

To my friends in Vicksburg, Mississippi, Gordon Cotton, curator of the Old Court House Museum, and Cliff and Bettye Whitney, resident owners of the Corners Bed & Breakfast Mansion.

To Frank W. Wood, commissioner of the Minnesota Department of Corrections, Retired Commissioner Orville B. Pung, and Warden Robert A. Erickson for their tour of and information on the Stillwater Correctional Facility.

To Deputy Rick Horst for his tour of and information on the Ramsey County Adult Detention Center.

To Amnesty International USA for their wealth of material on capital punishment.

And to Dr. Ronald J. Glasser, former Major, United States Army Medical Corps, now in private practice in Minneapolis. Author of *365 Days*.

I began writing *The Weatherman* in the summer of 1988. It was completed in February of 1993. A special thank-you to author and historian Albert Eisele, Viking Penguin editor Al Silverman, and Washington, D.C., attorney Robert B. Barnett, who made publication possible.

S.T.

FEAR IS ONLY THE BEGINNING